going NOWHERE

ALI MARIE

Copyright © 2023 by Ali Marie

All rights reserved.

No part of this book may be reproduced in any form or by any electronic or mechanical means, including information storage and retrieval systems, without written permission from the author, except for the use of brief quotations in a book review.

Cover Designer: Anna Friesz

Photographer: Wander Aguiar

Editor: Jenni Gauntt

Formatter: Jenni Gauntt

Dedication

Thank you to the random pickup truck at the front of my neighborhood at five in the morning as I headed out to a horse show one Saturday morning. Wrote the first few chapters through voice notes on the hour and half drive. My heart, reeling to tell Maren's story.

Thank you to the Outer Banks for being so beautiful and serene when I visited. To small towns for always being an inspiration for the setting behind the characters.

PROLOGUE
Maren

My phone vibrates with a text from Trayton. Rushing me to hurry up before we get caught. Not to mention it is two in the morning, and I am doing my best to creep through the house without the dog hearing me or stepping on any creaking floorboards.

Luckily, I stored my luggage in the back of my car after dinner last night in order to not complicate my escape. My parents were busy cleaning the kitchen and thought I was outside cleaning my car. Lord knows good ol' Ruby could use it. Looking at her now makes me wish she was going with me. Too many memories inside and out with that gal, though it would not be right to take the car my parents gifted me on my sixteenth birthday now that I am leaving.

With luggage in tow, I hastily pace up the street, where I see Trayton's truck tail lights. He jumps out without saying a word and loads my luggage in the back under his truck bed cover. We both sit quietly as he drives us out of town. I don't even turn to look back because I already feel my heart has been ripped and gutted out of my body. I dare not picture the look of disappointment on my parents' faces when they find my letter along with my cell sitting right next to the envelope. Let alone my brother, Dawson.

A tear slips down my cheek as I imagine the shock to someone else dear to my aching heart. It is all too late now. The damage is done and is being handled by the three of us leaving.

We were a month away from having the world at our feet in college. Myself heading north to Dartmouth, and Trayton heading to UT on a football scholarship. Both of us escaping our small town for something more.

One night ruined all of our plans as, a month later, I received the news I was pregnant, post squatting over a Walgreens toilet to pee on five different sticks. Only for the cleaning lady to find me crying on the floor once proof of the truth hit me. Proof that all my grand plans, all my parents' grand plans were ruined. Being that Trayton can be a typical douchebag, I was unsure how he would take the news, but it went surprisingly well. He genuinely seemed excited, which, for the life of me, I still do not understand why.

While my mind runs a mile a second, I feel Trayton's hand take mine. "We are going to be okay, dollface. I promise you. I have the best solution."

"You have not even told me what the solution is, Tray. Let alone where we are going."

"Tennessee. We are going to see my sister." My eyes go wide, as I stare at the *Leaving Nags Head* sign, mumbling "Okay" as I settle in for the long drive. I have nothing left to say with my feelings of us going nowhere, my life now going nowhere, but I have the inkling Tray believes we are going somewhere.

Trayton's family is very well off as they own the majority of the rental properties along the Outer Banks. Not to mention the star quarterback who got a full ride to UT. The town's big star, just like his father back in the hay days. The judgment that will be passed on him will be much heavier than what I will receive. Staying behind meant my dad would want to murder him and toss his body off the boat in the middle of the ocean for the sharks. My brother will assist in the murder, while my mother lectures me on my appearance and saving face.

She loves hard but disciplines even harder.

Trayton's parents, I believe, would make him own up to getting me pregnant, probably make him marry me because, again, we need to save face in this town. Then his mom would make my life a living hell. She is the most pretentious person I have ever known in our sea town. She comes across as all Christian and sweet, but I have heard the crazy stories about her from Trayton as well as seeing an incident firsthand a year ago at a party.

The fact that I am carrying a spawn that is related to his family sends chills through my entire body.

Several stops and naps later, we arrive at his sister's home in Nashville. Luckily, Darcy is not the evil version of her mother. She was, of course, always the homecoming and prom queen in high school, graduating with my brother two years ago. I never considered her just a pretty face, and damned to anyone that ever did.

Darcy has always been smart, calculated, and collected. Everyone enjoyed her company, and no one had lived up to the standards she set when she went off to college.

Until Jimmy Connley.

I was at the wedding with the rest of town when she married Jim Connley and was just as surprised as the rest of the town when Darcy decided to become a wife and mom after college. Pulling all the strings behind her husband. She thrives off being behind the scenes of her husband's cases, running the school's PTA, and hosting fundraisers. Again, lucky her for snagging a rich man who compliments her and the Adair family.

Jim is the upcoming lawyer in a family of lawyers that serve the talent in and around Nashville. Two kids in and a lap of luxury. Nothing less for the Adair Princess. As we pull into the long driveway, I see a mansion of a house peeking through the expanding Whiteoaks. They seem to be living life up out here, as expected. I just hope Tray has a plan that does not include staying here.

Slowly sliding out of the truck, Trayton takes my hand as we walk up the steps to the large white French doors. Before he even knocks, the doors are swung open with a shocked Darcy and Jim.

"Little brother, you have a lot of explaining to do."

Tossing him a withering scowl, I whisper to him, "Did you seriously not give her the heads up?" Tray shoots me a look to be quiet, only for me to glare back, pushing my nails into crescent moons on my palms to gain composure.

"Y'all come on in and get settled so we can chat. Dinner will be in about an hour," Jim states. We take seats on the couch across from the loveseat Darcy and Jim share.

"Now, little brother, I need you to tell me why you are here and what your plans are."

Trayton's mouth opens and closes like a fish gasping for air. Realizing he is not going to speak, I decide to. I blurt out I'm pregnant and then talk us back through how we ended up at their house. Darcy does not even seem phased, or she has extraordinary power over her emotions as I wind through the details.

"I figured as much. Mother and Father are not happy this happened, Trayton, and the fact you didn't stay to discuss this situation with them has them both throwing glass bowls." She turns to look at me. "And you, missy, I had such high hopes for you. Always knew you were too good for my brother, and now you got yourself knocked up and stuck to him."

I forgot how blunt Darcy is, taking my emotions back a bit as she continues on. "Right now, our parents are pleading the fifth on you having Trayton's baby, with the whole town in speculation of where the two of you went. Which leaves me to believe your parents and brother know nothing, correct?" There is no other answer to give past my shakiness and avoidance of looking at her. She sighs, "What's done is done, so now we move forward. You both can stay here for as long as you need, but we expect for you both to help out and attend school. Whether it's community or online. Got it?"

We both nod our heads in understanding.

My head races on how I need a job, now school, and baby planning. I royally fucked up.

Fuck me!

I feel Tray nudge me forward as Jim leads us to a spare guest room on the second floor at the end of the hall with its own bathroom.

I need time to wrap my head around all of this.

We both start to unpack, knowing we are here for the long haul.

"You okay, dollface?" he suddenly pipes up.

"As good as I can be, you?"

"Yah, I think we will be alright. Come here and give me a hug." I do and pray we truly will be alright. I don't acknowledge the shadow of guilt that casts over his eyes before pulling me into his arms.

CHAPTER 1
Maren

FOURTEEN YEARS OLD

Becoming a teenager is harsh. Becoming a teenage girl is relentless and cruel. I literally spend most of my day controlling my emotions, feeling overly stressed, fighting heated feelings about my brother's best friend, and dodging an overbearing mother. To top it off, I'm entering high school as a measly freshman.

Our town is small, so it's not that I am dealing with an overwhelming number of people I don't know or a giant school to navigate, but having to be on the bottom of the totem poll all over again. Not that I am not in all AP classes already, but now it all counts. My journalism pathway is defined to the tiniest of details to ensure I am accepted to Dartmouth. Summer internships are accepted between now and senior year to gain real-world experience in the field.

Right now, I am working through the next item on my "Succeed" to-do list. *Item 252: Get published in the local paper.* My first submission will be on the Fisherman traditions in this town. Has this been written before? *Absolutely.* But it's been twenty years, and not with my spin. My goal is to hone in on the personalities, the slang, the history that has created this town from the sea to the ground. *SLAM!* I jump, hearing the back door into the kitchen.

"Hey, Mar," I hear in unison from a group of boys. My brother, Dawson, and his friends strutting in from rowing practice. "What'cha working on?" I feel his breath on the back of my neck, his lips tickling my ear being so close. Calmly, taking a deep breath to inhale his scent, I school myself before answering. "Well, this is the first article I'm writing to see if I can get published in the local paper."

Pulling out the chair next to me, he takes a seat. "Can I read it?"

"It's only my sixth draft, Ford. I'm still working through it." His bottom lip pouts out just enough to make him even cuter before I am graced with his big amber puppy eyes. "Ugh, I hate when you do that... Here, read," I murmur, passing my pages over to him, because, yes, I do my best writing with pen and paper before I type my works out on the computer. Something so vintage and calming about actually writing on paper. Documenting with a pen that cannot be erased with one button or hardware crash. Unless lit on fire, these papers will remain intact after I'm gone.

There is a sense of pride I feel when I think that even after I am gone, my work could still mean something to someone. Could change the course of a plan or someone's action against humanity. *Big ambitions, I know.* But through all the shit I have bared witness to in my short life, I feel in my soul this is my destiny. No one has ever told me otherwise. Have only been encouraged to pursue this dream and persevere in my need to make a change throughout the world.

Putting my focus back on Ford, his face is stoic. He beats me every family game night due to his lack of emotions and facial expressions. Another part about him that not only infuriates me but also I respect about him. He can flip the switch on what little emotions he does share, and you'd be none the wiser if he hates you or loves you. If he is plotting your death or planning the best day ever. I notice, though.

When Ford is angry or hurt, his amber eyes darken to near mocha brown, to the point you no longer see his pupil clearly. If he is genuinely happy, his eyes remind me of the most golden field of sunflowers on a sunny day. Thinking or indifferent, they are a calming swirl of golds and browns. Just like they are now. Turning to the last page, he nods his head.

"Come on, man, let's go!" Dawson shouts, walking out the door.

"Give me a few minutes," he shouts back. Another thing I adore about Ford; he makes time for me. Pulling me from my thoughts, he says, "This is amazing, Maren. There is no way they won't publish this."

"You think so?"

"I know so." Giving me his confident grin, I'm reminded yet again how fast he makes my heart beat. "I better go before they leave my ass," he grumbles, laughing and standing up.

"Where are you headed now?"

"Down to Tuckers for a study group and dinner."

"Well, have fun," I say, disappointed he won't be with me for dinner. Now, dreading being alone with my parents at the table.

"Of course, see you around, cupcake." He bends down, kissing me on top of my head before I watch him run out of the house. This exchange felt different, but couldn't have, *right?* I need to focus on my future and not my never-going-to-happen chance with Ford Merrick.

SIXTEEN YEARS OLD

My house has always been *the house* everyone comes to, since as long as Dawson has been in middle school and my friends only followed suit. There is always extra food and chairs pulled up to the kitchen table. Days where we start with a small group hanging at the pool would be a full-fledged crowd by evening.

My mom loves playing host, loves being surrounded by all the kids, and even their parents come and hang out with her and my dad. Today is no different. A larger graduation party will be down at the beach this weekend, but tonight is to celebrate Dawson and Ford graduating. Dawson was named Valedictorian, and Ford named Salutatorian. Both headed to Harvard in the fall to pursue their tech dreams.

For me, I will be heading into my junior year without Dawson and Ford being around. Dawson and I have our moments of wanting to kill each other, but we are also very close. I know I can always count on him. Ford, who basically lives with us now, has grown to be more of a constant, partner in crime, secret keeper, and dream catch over the past couple of years. More so now than when we were younger.

Now, here I am, watching both guys and their friends, trying to wrap my head around how different this place is going to be in two months. I must be in my thoughts for a good few minutes because I snap out of it when I hear, "Mar, watch out!" from my friend Jessica. I turn just in time to fall backward into the pool, no thanks to Dawson himself. I swim up to the surface, pissed.

"You looked like you needed cooling off, Mar," he chuckles.

"You're dead and owe me a new phone." I scowl as I pull it out of the soaked back pocket of my jean shorts.

"Shit, Maren. Never have your phone near the pool."

"*Shit*, Dawson. Don't push people into the pool unless you know for sure."

"Here, give it to me. I'll bag it in rice."

"Thanks," I mutter, still angry at Dawson for being a moron. Here I thought I was going to miss him.

"You good, cupcake?"

"Yeah. Let me guess, your idea?"

"Nope, not this time. All him. Scouts honor," he swears, shooting up the symbol to me.

Rolling my eyes, I give him a dismissive wave. "Whatever, you were never in Scouts." Turning to swim over to the ladder to step out, I feel an arm wrap around my waist.

"Don't go yet." Turning in his arms to face him, we are nose to nose. Ford's gaze doesn't let up, but my eyes are looking side to side in a speedy manner while my heart rate beats rapidly. He tucks several wet strands behind my left ear, then leans in close, whispering, "You are already so wet. You should just stay here with me." My eyebrows shoot up as my green eyes go wide.

"Ford Merrick, are you flirting with me?" I question, only to squeeze my thighs together under the water. He gives me a Cheshire grin that melts all my logic away on why he and I will never be.

His palms cover both sides of my face, and I lick my lips. "I leave soon for college."

"Yep, I know." I look away, hiding my turmoil of emotions when answering.

"Couldn't have gotten here without you."

"I seriously doubt that. You just needed time to adjust and adapt. I always knew you would make the best decision for your future."

"It's not my future I am concerned about." I gasp. He leans in with his head in a slight tilt.

"Cannonball!" is all I hear before I am pushed under the water.

Once I break the surface, Ford is gone.

Damnit, Dawson.

Sigh. I get it, though. Dawson trumps me. He is Ford's best friend, soon-to-be college roommate, and then they have plans to be business partners. I'm just an emotional shoulder to lean on when life is being a major bitch. To both, I am just the sister who is growing up and needs protection from all boys. For them to continue to boss around and make decisions for me.

Hopefully, with them states away in the fall, I can find my own path that includes boys, some fun, and maybe a little bit of trouble. I need to get over Ford and keep pushing down my journalism path.

EIGHTEEN YEARS OLD

"Mar, can you believe we graduate tomorrow?" my best friend Allison asks while we take our usual table at the pier.

"Honestly, no. It seems surreal. Not going to lie either, pretty bummed we won't be together."

"Agreed. But you are my excuse for weekend trips. I'm just over at Brown." Three more of our friends join us, and we all order the usual seafood platters.

For me, I am taking my time hanging out, eating, and enjoying these moments of peace. Not because our time is lessening together but because Ford and Dawson have been home for two weeks already. We act normal around everyone, but there is a new awkwardness if we find ourselves alone together.

Ford seems tense and quiet, but now he makes a point to be close to me, where our skin is touching, sending shivers throughout my body. Close enough, I can hear him breathe softly, like he is right by my ear. Then, when I try to approach him or talk about it, he stalks off. Then he will be the same ol' Ford once we are around my family and friends again.

It also has not stopped him and Dawson from threatening my current boyfriend, Trayton. He and I have been on and off for the last year. We were best friends at first but seemed to find a certain comfort with one another.

We both have big dreams of leaving this town, share ideals and humor, plus Trayton is hot. Like any stereotypical star quarterback on the football team, *hot*. Hence Paul Walker in *Varsity Blues*. The making out is great; the two times we have had sex have been good, nothing earth-quaking, though. It was more of me not wanting to head to college as a virgin, and he was happy to oblige.

We have no plans to continue a relationship outside of being friends once we leave in the fall, but I know we will stay in touch. The two of us will be back here like everyone else during the holidays and school breaks. Along with that, he made me *pinky* promise I would come to a few of his games. Because yeah, how many freshman quarterbacks get to walk on the field as first years?

Trayton Adair for the University of Tennessee, that's who.

Nonetheless, I am proud of him and love him as a friend. This does not stop Dawson and Ford from constantly giving Tray hell when he is around. So now, it just becomes a pissing contest I refuse to be part of when it starts.

Mom thinks it's great I have two older brothers to keep boys in line and me out of trouble. Even with the guys miles away, someone was keeping tabs on me. Endearing at first, but then just pissed me off. To the point I would stop answering my phone when Ford called or even yet really wanting to push my boundaries to see what Ford would actually do with his threats. Twice, he showed up unexpectedly.

Honestly, I would not be surprised if there were several more times, but he didn't show his face.

The first time was New Year's Eve of my Junior year. There was a huge party at Allison's, along with underage drinking. Her parents were there, and we all turned our keys in to be locked up as everyone would be crashing at her place.

Some *spy* recorded me dancing on the outside bar by the pool. I got seething texts from Ford about needing to behave, quit drinking, and not be stupid. That pushed me to strip down to my bra and panties in twenty-degree weather, and adding in the ocean breeze, it was cold. Then I threw back multiple shots, which then led me to fall into the pool. Luckily heated, but once rescued, I was freezing my ass off.

Ford and Dawson were at the house the next afternoon when I returned. Not even able to argue, though, because they did the same shit when they were in high school. But it always came back to the fact that I needed to be more careful since I was a female and their sister. I called bullshit and stomped away. Not communicating with them for weeks.

The second time was spring break this year. We somehow convinced our parents to allow us to partake in Panama City Spring break. My argument was I needed to have more worldly experiences and see places to be able to write. Senior year was my last year of fun before adulting in college. To top it all off, they let Dawson, Ford, and a few other boys go to Cancun for their senior trip, where the drinking age is sixteen.

There were twenty-two of us teenagers and six parents. Three beach houses were booked to accommodate all of us, with a set of parents in each.

We were a bunch of seniors ready to party it up like the old MTV days. The days were spent tanning on the beach and swimming. The nights were spent clubbing, post pre-gaming at the house. Until the night we met several gentlemen who were adamant about getting us over to a western bar. Eighteen to get in, twenty-one to drink. *No problem there, right?* Probably one of the more stupid-er things my girlfriends and I had done was follow hot older men from one place to another.

By that time, it was midnight, and we were sober but looking to have a grand time on our night out. Jessica and Alison were all about checking a few types of men off their "fun" list. Feeling we had strength in numbers, we went along for the ride. Tray and his buddies met up with us in their golf cart with their fake IDs. An hour in, what I thought were virgin daiquiris were not. Jessica was making out in the corner with one guy, and Alison and I soon found ourselves on the bar with other dancers, dancing in our tight, cleavage-showing, raunched clubbing dresses and heels. Then by the time we left, I was sweaty, dehydrated, and exhausted. Bed was calling my name.

I woke up the next morning to a Ford in my face. He threw me over his shoulder, carried me out of the house, down to the ocean, and threw me in.

"You done acting out?" Ford shouts at me as I wade out of the water.

"You bastard!"

"Original," he scoffs, rolling his eyes. I charge him, trying to knock him over. Only to be captured in his arms against his body. Unable to move an inch.

"You need to calm down."

"Fuck.YOU. Ford. Do not tell me to calm down." He holds me tighter, kissing the top of my head. Taking a deep breath, I seethe, "I hate you. Why are you even here?"

"Good to know your feelings," he sighs. "I'm here to make sure you are alright. You weren't answering my calls or texts. Trayton said he left you at the bar last night and hadn't heard from you. You know, your boyfriend is a real piece of work." Rolling my eyes, he continues. "Tray posted on his social media about how hot his girlfriend was and having the time of his life in PCB." I see red. Not quite sure at the moment to whom more of my anger is targeted at. Trayton for being a dumbass, or Ford for being here like I need protecting.

"I need you to release me... NOW!" I growl out. He does, and I push off of him.

"I've been sleeping. Like a normal fucking person would do after a night out. Yes, I had been drinking. Yes, Tray left me there, but only because they were going to Hooters, and the girls and I wanted to stay till closing. Trayton and the boys are staying at the yellow house down there."

"Why would he not make sure you got back okay? Or even check on you?"

"Who knows, and who cares. I'm not his responsibility, nor yours, Ford. Let me just have fun. I promise you I will not end up dead in a gutter somewhere. But you have got to back.the.fuck.off."

"What if you are my responsibility?" My eyes widen, as I look up at his perfect chiseled face of softened features.

"Don't go there, Ford. You are off living college life, and I am heading out in the fall, with you and Dawson looking to head to

California once you graduate. Please do not ever say things like that. Things you don't mean or intend to act on." I look away, making my way back up to the house.

"Maren... Maren, look at me." I stop and slowly turn around, hearing his gutted voice.

"Please know that I will always come back to you. I just want you safe." It's taking all of my lack of energy not to let the tears fall in front of him. This is what he does. He says shit like he wants me, wants to be with me, but I can't tell if he is just taking on the role of a controlling brother like Dawson. Or if he means to say more because he loves me just as much as I love him. Have always loved him. I stand there, locking eyes with him.

"I'm fine, Ford. Just go. I'll see you in a few weeks."

Now, here we are on graduation day. The day I can officially say "Kiss my ass" to and look ahead to my future of travels and writing.

CHAPTER 2
COMING HOME
Maren

SIX YEARS LATER

A few months ago, I finally found the courage to call my mom after a *Jesus take the wheel* moment on the side of I-40. The sun was out, and then, within minutes, the sky went dark with a downpour of rain. Traffic slammed on the brakes, sending my ragged-out jeep fishtailing and then sailing into the cement barrier on the passenger side. Some burly man was at my side in a heartbeat, calling 911 and looking me over. Luckily, nothing seemed broken, just bruised from the seatbelt with adrenaline still pumping through me. I knew instantly my jeep was demolished. Fluids were pouring out from the undercarriage and a shattered windshield. Not to mention, the entire body of the passenger side crunched in from the cement barrier.

That's where I lost it.

In the pouring rain on the side of I-40, my knees curled up to my body, shaking and sobbing. Begging and praying for a change. For a way to not just survive but to thrive. Pleading to his mercy to guide me back home where I belonged. Where Lexi and I both needed to be. The burly man even bent down to pray with me. Grasping my hands in his, he murmured, "You know, miss, sometimes it is when we hit the lowest of lows that we find the strength to rise to our best selves." I told him I hoped so because any lower, I would be swimming with the river of lost souls. He chuckled and then ran to his car to grab an umbrella to shield us as we waited. He was constantly texting on his phone, which made me feel even more guilty that I was keeping him from somewhere or someone. I had refused his offer to sit in his luxury sedan with my drenched self, so he waited with me until the ambulance got there. Followed by Jim.

As I was looking over from the back of the ambulance, I noticed the man and Jim talking with shifty glances my way. Once cleared, I realized the man was already gone before I could get any of his information to properly thank him. Getting in the car with Jim, I asked, "Did you, by any chance, get that man's name and number? I would really like to thank him somehow."

He hesitates. "No, I didn't. Nice fellow, but he was just being a good Samaritan. Not the kind of guy who wants extra attention for doing a good deed."

"Makes sense, I guess," I say, staring out of the window and watching my jeep being towed away. *Great! Now I have to go car shopping. Plus, I had gotten a killer deal on my Jeep. I really loved Reba.*

That evening, I called my mom. Something or someone was tugging at my heart. Telling me I could not prologue the inevitable any longer. We needed to find our way back home. To say she was shocked to hear my voice was an understatement, and a great deal of tears were shed through forgiveness and regrets. I let her know she had a granddaughter named Alexis, but I call her Lexi for short.

What I don't let her know is how hard it has been being a single mom, finishing school, and joining the workforce world. Honestly, if it weren't for Darcy, I would have given up a long time ago. Let's just say my motherly instincts are not great, but we survive. Lexi has become more like my sidekick than a typical five-year-old child. I basically have a five-year-old going on thirteen most days. Her instincts are spot on, sharp as a tack, and vibrant as a rainbow after a storm. I also didn't tell Mom that a week after we arrived, Trayton left me to attend UT several hours away and never looked back. Tray's only seen his daughter three times in the last four years. I kept it to myself that I was naive in thinking we were both giving up our dreams for a new one together. I left out details of my pregnancy and complications. No details offered about hardships and self-doubt.

Up until Lexi was three, I lived with Darcy and her family. She and I had become best friends, especially after Trayton left the picture. Their parents are still denying Lexi's existence. Darcy's kids have been wonderful in helping out with Lexi and keeping her amused while I studied. Darcy would babysit when I went to work, though she would never take a dime from me. So when I finally moved out, I stuffed half of my savings in a drawer that I knew she would find later with a note saying thank you.

For the last two years, my girl and I have been living in a decent apartment near my assistant job outside the heart of Nashville. Being that Jim knows everyone in town, he was able to score me the assistant job at another firm's office. Though not my dream job, it puts food on the table and pays the bills for now. I had refused Jim's offer multiple times by putting me with his sister, who is over at the Nashville Gazette, as a temp so I could at least be around writers and the vibe, as he put it. Due to wanting to keep family and work separate, especially when I was still living in their house, he finally caved and found this one for me with an old college buddy of his.

I filled my mom in with all the good in my life and let her know how much I missed home. I eventually choked out, "I want to come home."

She sobbed even harder and said, "Of course, my sweet girl. We all want you back home. How soon can you get here?" It was hard to let her know I needed some time to tie some loose ends up in Nashville before I could leave. I promised to send her photos and call daily, though, until I left. That seemed to ease her down from driving all the way here to snatch us up. Since I had Alexis, I have realized more than ever the importance of the bond between a mother and daughter. My heart and soul yearn for that bond to be replenished with my own.

Now, here Lexi and I are, driving away from the only town in my "new to me" Acadia—still can't get over the deal I got—and the only family she has ever known, as we head back to the only family I want to fall back into.

Ford

I WALKED UP from the first floor, where we made it into a home office space, to see Dawson leaning against the counter on his phone, looking in shock. He holds his finger up at me, making sure I don't leave. Grabbing water from the fridge, I take a seat at the bar area in the kitchen and wait. I watch his facial expressions, ever-changing with one-word responses. He hangs up and turns directly toward me with disbelief written all over his face. A look that has him questioning his own sanity for a minute.

"So that was Mom with some news." I sit, waiting for him to continue. "Our presence has been requested for family dinner tonight."

"Okay. I am always down for a home-cooked meal, but don't we typically do that on Sundays?" Checking off the days of the week in my head, I note that it is only Wednesday.

"Yes, we do. But there is a special guest coming tonight. Actually, two." Dawson's face twists up.

"Just spit it out, man. I hate riddles."

"Don't flip out, but Maren is coming home. Along with her daughter, Alexis." I try my hardest to push my poker face forward. Dawson has always thought my feelings toward her and the whole situation was brotherly. Never knowing that I had been in love with her for years. Biding my time until I was back from college and stable and had the time to devote to her. Becoming the man she believed I always could be. Wanting to be worthy and all deserving of her. I also thought her having space to live her life a bit while I was away would be a good thing.

Never in a million years did I expect two years of me being gone, she would run off pregnant with that bastard of a tool. What hurt worse was that she did not even say goodbye to me. Other than the quick snip-it from the letter she left her parents, apologizing to everyone, and to tell Dawson and me she loved us. *That was all.* Then, she just disappeared.

"Man, what are you thinking? You seem deep in thought all of a sudden."

"Just thinking about how much she has probably grown up and changed. How much time has passed. Uh, you sure I need to be there?"

"Positive. Why would you not?" he asks, looking at me like I just asked the dumbest question ever. "Mom did threaten we were to be nice this evening and not bombard her with questions and emotions. She wants to make it an easy transition for the both of them."

"Why now?" I ask unknowingly aloud. Dawson doesn't even flinch at the question. Probably because he is wondering the same damn thing.

"Apparently, Mom has known for weeks now but didn't want us to do anything rash. She wanted us to have the element of surprise. She thinks if we have less time to think about it, the less angry we will be. Remember, her boys always need to be on their best behavior."

I chuckle and shake my head. There could not be anything more true than that last statement from Dawson. "Not a problem. Well, let me go take a shower, and will be ready to go."

In the shower, I try to control my emotions of rage, excitement, of being pissed off but elated. My heart was broken by a person who I cannot even hold responsible because she never knew my true feelings. Sure, I made *jokes* and said shit like telling her I would always come back to her. Teasing her with lingering touches. Telling her how she needed to be treated and threatening the boys that hung around her. She didn't need to fear her brother and I leaving her when we were gone for months with college. That we would always protect her and be a phone call away.

Did this girl really never recognize my feelings for her? *Maybe she never thought of me other than another brother.* Did she not recognize the fact she brought out the softer side of me? How I always made a point to sit next to her at events and at home, find a way to touch her, to talk to her. I have known this girl since I was eight years old when my family moved to this town.

Dawson and I became instant friends when we ran into each other at the theater to watch the newest *Marvel* movie. He approached me with a fist bump because he liked my *Doctor Strange* costume. He was decked out in all *Captain America*, with Maren being all shy by his side in a *Black Widow* hoodie with matching sweatpants on, and a ponytail. We quickly bonded over our odd obsession with *Marvel*. We were constantly over at each other's houses playing *Marvel* games, which led to us realizing all the other cool things we had in common and that our brains functioned on the same wavelength, which came to inventing and thinking of future possibilities. Just two Big Bang-like nerds here. We found ourselves in all the same gifted classes and clubs.

Time went by, and I found myself typically over at their house more and helping Maren with math homework or projects. Not because she ever needed my help but I just felt the urge to be near her. So, I would come up with shortcuts in math to show her or some elaborate idea for a project but was too big of a concept to complete herself.

I strived to find what she and I had in common. She was a *Marvel* fan, but not huge like her brother and I, but she did attend every premier with us and re-viewings. I had an obsession with space; she loved Pluto from *Disney*, and I had much respect for Pluto, the now non-planet.

We both enjoyed searching for shooting stars at night and watching solar eclipses. Her favorite candy used to be a Hershey bar, which then became mine and now is the only chocolate bar I will eat. I found that Maren was easy to talk to and just be with, with no expectations. With other friends and even Dawson sometimes, it was always planning the next million-dollar idea or flaws in a hypothesis. With her, we talked about everything. From books she was reading, to favorite school subjects, to her letting me read all her essays and writings because she needed critical reviews on her work.

Since I can remember a little Maren, she was addicted to reading magazine articles and writing her own. Obsessed with news and what was going on around the world. She wanted to become a world-renowned journalist. Be a cause of change and effect with her words.

Maren looked at the world as a pearl that needed to be shined and delicately cared for. At that time, she believed there were no "bad" people, just bad situations that people found themselves in. Thought everyone could be saved. When she grew up and realized that some people were just "bad," she changed her tune on not everyone can be saved but would pray for them instead.

She always had me laughing with her running list of those she felt could be saved versus those she would just pray for. It consisted of world leaders, convicted felons from the news to Oscar down the street, who constantly taunted her with his pet spider. I mean, a legit tarantula that he would sometimes bring to school. He would place that thing on her books, her bookbag, the lunch table, or set it on Maren's front porch and ring the doorbell, all while recording her freaking out and posting on social media.

Dawson and I had even threatened to kick his ass more than once to no avail. Though unfortunate for Oscar, there was a "tragic" bike accident on the way home from school one day where he fell over, and the creature's plastic home hit the pavement and shattered. Fingers were crossed that the thing died on impact, but it crawled out. Before Oscar could get himself up to catch it, the spider was gone. Took off so fast and went into the bushes. Never to be seen again. Of course, I told Maren the creature was dead because she would have been beside herself, thinking it was lurking in the shadows to get her. Oscar never messed with her again, even when he purchased another one several months later.

Over time and at such young ages, she became my confidant. Looking back now, it seems rash and unexplainable. What nine or ten-year-old needs a person to lean on? Let alone one that is two years younger. That is what she became, though.

Especially after we found out my mom had cancer, and it was found too late with a deep-cutting diagnosis. When I thought I was too cool to cry in front of Dawson, it was her shoulder I cried on with no judgment. Because men who cry were just boys, and I no longer thought of myself as a boy at ten. I was invincible like the rest of the kids my age, coming into our own. Maren had a way that had me caving to my emotions. To deal with them head-on.

When my mom passed away when I was shy of eleven, Maren and her family were there for me. My dad took her loss harder than I could have imagined. Started drinking and barely held on to his job before he passed by his own hands when I was fourteen. Time and Maren were the only things that healed my guilt of not being enough to keep him here. To keep him sober. During that time, though, I would spend most nights in their guest room, and many of those, Maren would crawl into my bed just to hold me while I fought my emotions. My mom was gone, and my dad was wallowing in his own pain to even take care of me.

At fourteen and the loss of my last parent, with no known relatives, the Harts took me in with open arms. All my anger, teenage rebellion, and destructive ways. Never passed judgment, just loved me and tried to guide me down righteous paths. All easier said than done as I felt I just had so much anger in me to let loose.

My grades were failing, all ambition lost. When Dawson wasn't around, and I wasn't out trying to pick a fight, I would spend time with Maren without a second thought. She was my stability. The reason I somehow got my shit together and was able to go off to college with Dawson. To stick to our plans for college life, getting out of this town for a while, inventing something incredible, and to become rich and famous together. We had a brotherhood pact.

I didn't want to let down my best friend, who had taken me in when I was abandoned. I owed him so much for keeping me sane and helping me get back on track. I owed the Harts everything for taking in my troubled ass. Providing me a home and all the love. Never once did they make me feel like an outsider. Only as part of the family. Mrs. Hart became Madre, Mr. Hart became Dad, and I already looked at Dawson as a brother. It was Maren who, by then, I wanted to be more than just an added family member.

I watched her grow up from a scrawny six-year-old girl to a beautiful lady edging into adulthood. When she left, I constantly toed the line between tearing the world down to find her and stopping to think maybe she just needed time and would come back on her own. But time turned into years. Dawson and I were coming into our own with the App research and creation.

Before I knew it, we had been swept up into the Silicon Valley lifestyle, parties, lots of drinking, and women. Learning that I could control how much money I could make and how to pleasure a woman and teach her how to pleasure me. But that's just what it was. Just pleasure behind the wall of no emotion, no connection.

Three years in with all the benders, becoming a complete asshole to everyone I knew, even Dawson, it was time for a change. Maybe what pushed me over the edge was waking up with a broken nose from Dawson due to the fight we had the night before and him calling me out on all my bullshit. No one had done that since Maren. The girl that haunted my dreams when I was not so obliterated to think.

Hell, she still does.

The girl I wished was the body against me in bed, the mouth my cock slid in and out of. Wishing she was the whiskey I drowned myself in nightly to stay warm and forget about the stress of owning and building a business, all the legal shit, and the emotional toll of being alone in a crowded room. To forget her just for a little while.

The last time I saw Maren was when Dawson and I came home for her high school graduation that summer. We were all so proud of her being valedictorian and all she had accomplished. She had the whole world waiting for Maren Hart, and we all knew she was going places and would fulfill her dream of being a journalist, traveling the deep edges of the world. I wanted a front and center seat to all of it.

She looked exquisite that night. Her long brown hair twisted up off her neck that I wanted to kiss and lick so badly, while she donned a short shimmery green dress that made her piercing green eyes sparkle even more when the lights beamed on her. Legs for days even though she walked around barefoot everywhere because she hated heels. Hated shoes, period, for that matter.

The night of the graduation party, I remember running into her boyfriend, Trayton. I threatened him to leave her alone—that he was not good enough for her. Only to counter back with, he would ruin her forever. That, not only for me, but no one would also ever want her again. That got him a broken, bloody nose, more if Dawson had not pulled me off of him to get his own swing in.

In hindsight, we probably pushed him too far. Also in hindsight, I should have made more of a point to get Maren away from him that evening and forever.

Shit!

I'm not sure how I am going to react tonight or where my

feelings still lie. All this dredging up the past has my mind whirling like a black hole. All I know is my heart is guarded because of *her*. I have dated a few women, fucked many, but they were all vacant eyes staring back at me. None of them had the all-consuming effect on me like she had all those years ago.

CHAPTER 3
HOME BASE
Maren

I PULL into my parent's driveway with a sense of calm mixed with panic. Six years have passed since I have been home. Time passed in the blink of an eye without being a stranger to my body or my heart. I left here a terrified eighteen-year-old, driving down the path of destruction, going nowhere.

Now, here I am, returning as a panic-stricken twenty-something who feels she can still cause a path of destruction. This time it isn't just about me, but also Alexis. She deserves to be surrounded by a family who will love her and support her. To give her the solitude and stability that I have lacked all these years.

"Mommy, are we here?"

"Yes, we are. You ready to meet your Glam-ma and Papa?" Lexi nods her head in excitement while unbuckling herself.

Before I can get out of the car myself, she is already out, waiting impatiently for me on the sidewalk with her stuffed panda bear, Mr. Pickles, in hand. My self-assertive, independent little twin. I honestly could not thank the stars enough for blessing her with my looks instead of Tray's. Not that I would love her any less, but it makes all of it much easier not having to see a mini him looking back at me on a daily basis. Alexis was born with a ton of hair, and instead of it falling out like I thought it would, her hair continues to grow. With the length being down past her shoulders in tight curls now with a shade lighter than mine. Her piercing green babydoll eyes win everyone over in a heartbeat.

Our hands fold into each other as we make our way up the few steps onto the front porch. Taking a deep breath, I knock.

The door swings open with my mom on the other side, completely stunned.

"Hi, Mom."

"Oh my, Maren, come here!" she squeals, tugging me into a tight hug, though my other arm is still linked to Alexis.

"Mom, I would like you to officially meet your granddaughter, Alexis."

"Baby girl, come give Glam-ma a hug." Without hesitation, Alexis releases my hand then runs into my mom's arms. "We are going to be best friends, aren't we?" I hear her whisper in Lexi's ear. Lexi gives her an enthusiastic nod and goes in for another hug. My mom soon pulls us both into the house. "Frank, our special guests have arrived!"

"Oh, Mom, you did not go all out, did you?"

"Of course not, my dear. Just family for tonight. Dawson and Ford will be here shortly." Hearing the name Ford stops me in my tracks.

God, what must he think of me?

I truly hope he never thought I abandoned him or never cared. I was always in love with him, but he was older, and in college by the time I felt I could do anything about my feelings. Even with all the girlfriends I had, Ford was the one person I was the closest to and could depend on.

He and my brother would come home on holidays and the summers, which I looked forward to the most. I thought one time he was actually going to kiss me in the pool, but then Dawson showed up, so Ford dunked me completely underwater. Our relationship was day and night.

When it was just us, I felt I had all of him and who I knew he was. Place anyone else in the picture; I was treated like the annoying little sister and always picked on. Especially if Dawson was around, they would team up on me. They were my two greatest protectors but also played the roles of a nemesis.

Who knows if there ever could have been something between us if I didn't get pregnant or stayed. I can only imagine that now he is married, if not at least seeing someone. Many times, I wanted to call or text him. To let him know I was fine, to properly say goodbye, but could never get the nerve. I never dared ask my mother either in the last couple of months we chatted. Mom only told me that Dawson and Ford created some formulas for a custom dating app that they sold for a pretty penny while they were in California.

Now, the guys are back home, helping with the family business of boat storage and fishing. Along with dabbling in projects as investors here and there. She brags about how they really made a name for themselves over in Silicon Valley and are doing well.

"Sunshine, you are finally home."

"Hey, Dad." I grin, giving him a hug back.

"I have really missed you, kiddo."

"Me too, Dad. Me too."

"Now, who do we have here?" he asks, looking at Alexis, who is standing next to my mom now.

"It's me, Papa. Don't you recognize me from Facetime?" she murmurs as she studies him with her gaze.

Chuckling, he scrunches his nose. "I think you're a little taller in person, sweet pea. Can I have a hug?" Just like with my mom, no hesitation, she runs straight to him for a bear hug.

"I see that, Dad." Lexi giggles as he sneaks a piece of candy in her hand. He chuckles, and she whispers something in his ear. "Great, they are co-conspirators already." Looking back, my mom is grinning from ear to ear.

"I am so happy you are both finally home where you both belong," she says, pulling me in for another hug.

"Let's not ruin both of our makeups before dinner, Mom." We both know there is a lot to say and discuss, but right now, we're both elated to be under the same roof again. Right then, I hear the door open and looking back into the living room, I gasp. Dawson and Ford. *Ford.*

"Did we miss the family reunion already?" Dawson spits out.

"No, we just got here a bit ago," I choke out, slowly walking toward him, pleading for forgiveness with my eyes.

"Come here, sis. Things haven't been the same without you around to bother," he mutters, pulling me into his muscular arms and then messing my hair up.

"I missed you so much, and I am so sorry, Dawson. I didn't know what to do."

"Well, I'll have my two cents to say at another time. Right now, I am happy you are home. Now, where is my niece?"

"She is in there with Mom and Dad." I throw my thumb over my shoulder, pointing to the kitchen while goosebumps take over my body from a glare on the other side of the room.

Once Dawson walks away, I find the courage to say hi to Ford. He just continues to stare at me with his hands tucked in his front pockets. Even with the death glare I am receiving, he looks sexy as hell. My eyes slowly graze down his body, admiring how much more filled out in muscle he is now from years ago. How his dirty blond hair is longer than the crew cut he used to rock back in the day. That his amber eyes seem to be darker and sadder than I remember.

"Ford, please talk to me. It broke me to leave without saying goodbye to you. Please know that." I step closer to him to close the distance between us. His mouth opens but then closes. "I heard you and Dawson are doing well in business." He nods. I step closer. "I heard you finally sold that old Dodge and bought a brand-new truck." He nods, and I step in closer to where I am toe-to-toe with him. His body vibrates in agitation, being this close to me.

"You look good, Mar. Welcome home," he says without a shift in his stoic look.

"He speaks." I act in shock, hoping to get at least a smirk from him.

Nothing.

"Can I please have a hug? I have really missed and needed you." If I were not paying close attention, I would have missed the second his eyes lightened a bit and his expression softened. Ford slowly wraps his arms around me, making me feel I am truly home. He kisses the top of my head and strokes my back with his palm the way he used to. His leather brandy scent surrounds and comforts me all at once.

This is what my heaven is, but I know this is not my forever. This man will never accept what I did and who I am now. Mom hollers for us to join them for dinner, causing us to pull apart quickly. The loss of his warmth weighs me in desolation. Walking in the kitchen detours my mood when I see my brother with my daughter in his arms, dancing around the table.

"She sure is a mini you, Maren," Dawson says.

"Attitude and everything." I laugh. We settle down for dinner, taking our usual places around the table. The exception is the extra chair with a booster seat for Alexis that is wedged next to Mom's side. My dad and Dawson claimed their places at the ends of the table, leaving Ford next to me. How it has always been.

Mom gives me a subtle wink across from the table, leaving me wondering if it was due to her having Alexis and not to worry or the fact that she made sure Ford and I sat next to each other. I look over at him, locking eyes, so I smile. With a small smirk back, he digs into his food, never making eye contact with me for the rest of dinner. Though, I did feel his eyes burning a hole through my soul several times.

Ford

"Fuck me. No, seriously fuck me to whoever is in charge up there," I groan out in frustration in the bathroom to myself.

Right after dinner was over, I excused myself so I could separate myself from Maren. Not even two hours in and she is so far under my skin and thoughts, making me an utter mess. I knew hugging her was a bad idea, but when have I ever been able to tell that girl, no?

Never. Not fucking ever.

My body took over my mind when I kissed her head, wafting in her vanilla jasmine scent. Sadly, the scent I have in a bar of soap that I used to smell when I missed her. My hands running down her back like it was the most natural thing for me to do. Thankfully, I was saved by the bell when Madre called us for dinner because my cock was getting harder every second she clung to my body.

I am positive dinner was delicious as always, but it was too hard to concentrate with Maren right next to me and her mini twin staring me down from across the table. Alexis's hair is curlier than Maren's in a lighter shade. She looks like a true baby doll with her piercing large green eyes that mirror her mother's.

She is adorable and sharp as a tack. I won't deny it gives me some relief that Alexis looks more like Maren than Trayton.

Which brings me to think, where is that prick? The whole town knows he has been at UT playing football for four of the years, then was drafted. Surely, he did not leave these girls alone. Darcy would never budge on information about Maren. She made it sound like she was unsure of Maren's location anytime she came home to visit, or Dawson and I would call just to see if she was yet willing to share what she knew. I even thought about showing up at Darcy's house to plead, but always talked myself out of it. Maren didn't want to be found.

There was no social media linked to her, no phone to track. Could not find her name in any registry for loans, housing, or even work. At some point, I started to believe Darcy that she had no clue where Maren was hiding.

Leaning against the sink, I dwell on the scenario a little more before I make haste out the door to find Maren and ask a few questions.

CHAPTER 4
PAST IS THE PAST
Maren

After dinner was over, Mom stated we would have dessert later on, post everyone's stomach settling. Meaning, she was going to drag this evening on with all of us under the same roof for as long as possible.

Some things never change.

While she and my dad cleaned up, that gave me the opportunity to take Alexis on a tour of the house. She would be staying in my old room while I resided down the hall in one of the guest rooms. For me, this was a short-term plan. I need to find a job, hopefully here in town or remote, and then a place to live. I am thankful my parents' house is large enough to accommodate the two of us without feeling crowded, but we have been on our own for at least the last two years.

Eventually, we will need to have our own space and independence back.

Summer is just about over here in the Outer Banks, reminding me I need to make plans to enroll Alexis in school within the week.

God, I hope she fits in.

I'm leaning up against my old doorway, watching her unpack her dolls and toys. Rearranging my room to fit her style. Being precise about where she puts each object. I also notice Mom has my closet full of new clothes for her. She feels she has to make up for lost time, and I feel all the guilt in the world for making her feel that way. So it won't be me who says a word to her about spoiling Alexis. Lexi deserves the world for having to deal with the parents she was given.

Trayton's parents still refuse to believe she exists, so not sure how they are even going to handle finding out we are back home. Darcy promised not to tell them. We both know it will only take a few days for word to get to them about our arrival in this small town. Let alone, I am unsure when—or if—Trayton will come home to visit them. Last I heard, he was waiting to be drafted to an NFL team.

I smell his leather brandy scent before I hear the creak in the top step. "Hey, Ford. Need something?"

"Nah, just come to check on if you two need anything." He seems more relaxed than earlier but still has a nervousness to him.

"We are good. Lexi is just settling in, in my old room."

"Where are you going to be staying?"

"The blue room down the hall... Oh wait, is that okay? I forgot that it is your room."

"No, it's totally cool. We live ten minutes up the road now. We also only do sleepovers for Christmas now, so I can take up another room for when the time comes. Don't sweat it. Besides, I think I moved most of my stuff out, but let me know if you need me to grab some things."

"Will do. Gosh, I hope I am not here in December. It seems like a lifetime away."

With a pensive, confused look, he asks, "You're leaving again?"

"No, not leaving town, but hopefully Lexi and I will be settled in our own place by then. It has just been me and her for so long; this seems like a step back, moving home. I mean, I know it needs to happen for the time being, but I can't live with my parents forever. Though I am sure they wouldn't complain."

Ford chuckles. "No, they would not."

I can feel his stare prickle my skin as the silence grows awkward. "Just ask, Ford. I won't lie to you."

Ford's giant statue leans up against the door frame, gnawing his bottom lip between his teeth, thinking before he speaks. "You and him still together?"

"No," I spit out, knowing that is not the only question running through his mind.

"Have you been dating?" he asks, causing my eyes to glance at him with a *what the hell* look.

"No, not at all. No time."

"Is he in the picture? Meaning helping out with Alexis?"

"Nope, and I could care less if he ever is." Ford lets out a "*Huh.*" Right then, Mom comes up the stairs to see us chatting but wanting to check on Lexi.

"Why don't you two go outside and talk? I will help Alexis finish unpacking."

"Are you sure, Mom?"

"Yes, now go before I put both of you to work." His and my eyes meet with the look of knowing what that meant, so we race down the stairs out the front door. I take a seat on the swing while he sits in the closest rocker.

Laughing, I shake my head. "Remember that time she made us move all that junk from the garage to the attic because Dawson told her we were bored."

"I could have killed him that day," he states, laughing. My heart squeezes together at the sight of his beautiful smile. The smile that used to make me come unraveled when he would come home from college.

Then I notice the awkward silence that fills the air. Even the birds stop chirping as the smile slips away, and his face turns stern. "Maren...you care to elaborate on what the hell happened during all this time?"

"Ummm, I can to an extent... But you can't tell anyone, not even Dawson. I'm not ready for my parents to know the full truth." His jaw tenses and fists clench. Not sure I am even ready for him to know the truth, but I could never lie to him or skirt around the inevitable.

I proceed to tell Ford how, after a week of living at Trayton's sister's house, Trayton left. Only leaving a note that he needed to live out his dream and parents' expectations. His parents were supportive of this and that he would sign over all rights to Alexis if I wanted him to. He never meant to be a family or take it this far, but he wanted to try and do the right thing. His sister, Darcy, did not want me to make any rash decisions before I even had Alexis, as if she wanted to see if Trayton would come around after she was born.

Tears stream down my face when I tell him Trayton has only seen his daughter a handful of times over the five years. She is almost six and has no clue who he is to her. The times he has come around, he was distant. Alexis decided for herself that she did not care to be around him at all, regardless of who she thought he was.

On her fourth birthday, I mailed him the paperwork to sign, and he did. No call, no discussion, just mailed them back signed. Trayton is no longer the legal father of Alexis. Ford comes to sit next to me, wiping my tears away with his thumb.

"I could kill that son of a bitch," he murmurs.

"I know, but it is for the best. I will tell Alexis the truth when she is older, but I promise, on my own life, she will never feel an ounce of love missing from her life."

Bringing me in to kiss my forehead, he whispers against my skin, "You are not alone with this, Mar. Between your family, you, and me, she will be the most loved little girl in the world. I promise you that."

"Thank you. That means everything. You were always the best protector."

"Yah, about that." He pauses and looks pensive again. Right then, the screen door swings open, making me quickly separate from Ford's hold.

"Mommy," Alexis squeals as her face and hands are covered in melting chocolate ice cream dripping from her cone, barreling toward us.

"Oh wow, you are a mess, child."

"Who are you calling a mess?" she quirks back. Sending my eyes in a roll because I know where this is headed.

I laugh and go to pick her up. "I am not saying you are a mess. I am telling you, you are covered in a mess." Her mouth goes in the shape of a ring, now understanding what I mean. I see Ford chuckling in the swing at the site before him.

Mom soon comes to the rescue with wipes, helping to get her cleaned up. Once she is, plus a new shirt, Lexi takes my spot on the swing next to Ford. His eyes go wide, and all I can do is grin. I take a seat in the rocker, waiting for the show to start.

Alexis is sitting on the swing with her thinking cap on, while her hands are placed on top of her leg, drumming her fingers. Ford looks like he is holding his breath, possibly thinking if he does, she will forget he is there. He definitely gives me the vibe of not being around a lot of kids. Then, unexpectedly, Lexi places her small hand on top of his thigh and pats it.

"Can we talk?" she asks Ford in her adorable voice.

Looking at me, then back at her, he apprehensively mutters, "Sure." I know rapid fire is coming.

"What's your name?"

"Ford."

"Favorite color?"

"Um...green."

"Favorite second color?"

"Uhhh, gray."

"Favorite number?"

"Eight."

"Favorite Disney movie?"

Panic rises on his face. "Disney movie?" he reiterates, and she nods.

"Going with Hercules." Lexi makes a face like Ford has lost his mind.

"Do you like my mommy?" I have no idea where this is going.

"I do," he says without hesitating.

"Do you think my mommy is pretty?"

"Yes."

"How are you related to me?"

"I am a very close friend of the family."

"Okay," she says quickly, then slides off the swing.

"That's it?" Ford asks.

"For now. You got six out of eight right. You did good."

"I didn't know I could give right or wrong answers." He truly looks stunned while I hold in my laughter with my hand over my mouth.

"Of course, silly. It was a quiz. I am going back inside now to see Uncle Dawson."

"Okay, sweetie," I say as she walks in the house. I turn to look at Ford.

"What the hell was that about?"

Trying to get through my laughing, I choke out, "She only does that to people she likes but needs to figure out. She is constantly reading people, so beware."

"Shit, she is like you a hundred times over. That's scary, Maren. She is too little to act like that."

"She is a wickedly sharp five-year-old. Lexi is like Dawson and me combined. It is very scary at times. Spell a word once, she has it memorized. Photographic memory like Dawson too."

"You are doing a great job with her, Mar. I see she has your habit of biting her bottom lip when she is thinking, and your sense of humor."

"Just wait, she is just getting warmed up." We both laugh, and it feels so good to be doing this again with him. To be home and feel an ounce of normal, just for a small moment.

"Oh, before she interrupted, did you want to say something?" I ask, remembering our previous conversation.

"Yes, I think we..." The screen door opens again, and out walks Dawson.

"I am ready to go, how 'bout you, man?" Dawson asks Ford.

"Um, yah. Sounds good."

"Cool. Mom packed us dessert to go."

"She is the best." Ford looks back at me. "Well, we can talk later since I am being summoned home."

I smile through the sadness that seeps in with him leaving. Dawson gives me a hug and tells me he will see me later this week. Expecting Ford to pull me into another hug, I receive a punch to the arm instead. He laughs as he moves quickly away from my aim. Much less intimate than our previous encounters today, but I also know Dawson was not around. Dawson always joked about us getting together and that he would kick Ford's ass if it ever happened.

Sometimes I thought he was jealous of how close Ford and I were growing up, but Dawson is the extrovert in this group and was always on the go. Those two men in my life might be identical on the genius scale, but they could not be further apart in personalities. After I wave them goodbye, I head in to face the music of my parents' wrath.

CHAPTER 5
MOVING FORWARD
Maren

"Maren, come sit." My dad pats the couch cushion next to him. My mom has Lexi entertained enough with *Sofia The First* on TV, then joining us by sitting in the chair across from us. Awkward silence between the three of us fills the room. I refuse to be the one to speak first, afraid of the word vomit that will explode out of my mouth of too much information that they may or not be wanting to hear. Several points of my life that I am not fully ready to indulge them in.

Finally, my dad clears his throat to speak. "We are so happy you are home. Alexis being here is just a blessing, and we want you to know that you both can stay here for as long as you need. Okay?"

"Thank you," I say without making eye contact, twirling the whale tail ring Ford gave me for my sixteenth birthday that I never take off.

My dad continues, as I continue to avoid eye contact. "We need to move forward. All of us. What happened is in the past without any way of changing it. Maybe we failed you somehow that led you down the path you took," my dad says, shaking his head as wetness fills his eyes.

"No, Dad. If anything, it would be the complete opposite. I feared the disappointment in your eyes and Mom's. I feared the destruction it would cause this family by throwing my life away." *The dam has been unleashed.* "I am so sorry to the both of you for what I did and for being gone for so long. I never thought it would take me this long to get back home. But please know, you two never failed me once, it was me failing you."

Pulling me into his arms, my dad rocks me. "Oh, baby girl. Nothing you could ever do would be failing us. You are finally home, and that is all that matters."

Nodding my head against my dad's chest, Mom moves over to the couch with us and rubs her hand up and down my back for comfort. "My sweet angel, you have grown up too fast for this mom's heart, but know we love you so much. We also love that adorable little girl you brought home." Mom winks at me, causing me to smirk. "Let us just make a commitment from here on out that whatever is going on, we handle together, okay? We want nothing but happiness for you both."

"I promise, Mom." Sitting back up from my dad's arms, I glance back and forth between them both, seeing nothing but love in their eyes.

"Now, can we discuss the father of this child? Do I need to hire a hitman, murder him with my own bare hands, or just break a leg?"

I look wide-eyed between my parents to find some comical relief, but there is none. "Um, none. Trayton is not really involved in her life. I don't expect him to be either. I wouldn't worry about him right now. The only ones in his family that love Lexi like family is his sister Darcy, her husband, and their kids. So please be kind when they do come around for the holidays. I would have been in a world of hurt without Darcy's support through all of this." Shrugging my shoulders at their shocked looks, I continue, "Trayton's parents have never cared to know her, and Trayton made his decision to walk away from her to choose fame."

"Please tell me you did not carry on a relationship with him for all those years. He has been in more headlines than I can count with women, parties, and football."

"No, Mom, we were not. We ended long before his claim to fame." Refusing to let her know he left a week after we arrived in Nashville. Shattering all my hopes for a normal future of a family. I was young, dumb, and blind, but they do not need to know any of that. It will really throw them over the edge, right when I believe we are moving forward.

They will never forgive me if they know that as soon as I left, Trayton left me for good, yet, I still refused to come home, let alone call home. They will never understand the shame and disappointment I put my own self through. That I unfortunately put my sweet baby Lexi through before she was even born.

My dad speaks up, pulling me from my thoughts, "Well, if I ever see him around town, no promises I won't throw a punch in his direction. His parents have never mentioned anything in regard to the situation all these years. They talk to us as they always have. As though none of this ever happened, so what you said makes sense. This family is happy to protect both you and her from them however we need to. Time is of the essence before they know you both are back in town."

The silence covers us, as what will the almighty realty moguls, the Adairs, do when they come face to face with the two people that can tarnish their son's reputation and their name.

I made an inner decision to speak up this time. "I was able to finish my degree in English. Not that I will be a traveling journalist anytime soon in my life, but I do have work experience with being an assistant for a big firm in Nashville. I was thinking of entering the student-teacher program to complete the prerequisites needed prior to taking the exam I need to acquire my teaching certificate. I know this is not my dream of becoming a world-renowned journalist, but I accepted that notion a while ago. Alexis is my first priority, and for the both of us to eventually have our own place to live and a life she will be happy in." My parents nod in approval. "I will get a job to cover our expenses while we live here, along with my savings to help out. Lexi will be enrolled in kindergarten this year, so she will be out of your hair during the day but may need help in the evenings for whatever job I can pick up." I see Mom look at my dad, then back to me.

"My angel, let me tell you how this is going to go." I feel my blood pulsing through my veins because though my mom is a charmer, she is a stickler for her way of handling situations. Which is part of the reason I left in such a hurry all those years ago.

My mind is boggling with not knowing what words are about to fly out of her mouth. Bracing myself for what is to come, as I know in my heart that this conversation is edging too tranquil for even her. "Your dad and I fully support your student-teaching and teacher path. I am sure Mrs.Elrod, the principal of the high school, will be more than happy to assist with the request. But under no circumstances will you be taking an evening job. You will be home with your daughter and us. Dinner as a family, unless you have plans with friends or a date. We do not want you missing out on time with Lexi, plus you need time to study." She just threw me over in left field, as my jaw slacks open with wide eyes. "Close your mouth, Maren, you aren't catching flies. I know this might be a shock to you, but we want to support the two of you during this transition. Okay?"

Twiddling with the ring on my right hand again, I fight to suppress the tears swimming in my eyes so I can respond. But they drop down my cheeks unbidden, and all I can do is throw myself into my mom's arms. She knows my answer, and I can breathe a little easier than I have in the last several years.

My parents have nothing to prove to me, but they are protecting me and Lexi from the fears and struggles I have had dealt with being away from home. Being on my own with a baby, then a toddler, and now a child, who acts too grown for her age. My dad joins us in the hug.

Lexi must sense the emotions in the room enough to pull her gaze from her show. Noticing us, she runs over and joins in. "Are you okay, Mommy?" she murmurs, patting my cheek with her little hand.

I go to grab it in mine and give it a little squeeze. "Yes, my sweet girl, I am okay. We are going to be okay." My words cause all of us to collapse into another large hug with Alexis in the middle of it all.

"We are home, sweet girl, we are home."

Ford

LISTENING to Dawson's incessant chatter about Maren's choices all the way home for the entirety of the eight minutes it took to get here could have been easily the death of me in that very moment.

The moment we arrived, I quickly walked into the house, telling him I had a headache, and took the stairs two at a time to head up to my room. Now, I am laying in bed, staring at my ceiling of glowing constellations thinking about her. As much as I wanted to walk in that house tonight, keep my distance but be polite, all that thought process flew out the damn window like pig shit when she stood in the same room as me.

I can hear Dawson now ranting to his girlfriend, Izzy, downstairs. She must have pulled up as soon as we pulled in. Me, being too distracted to notice if so.

Madre didn't want to overwhelm Maren and Alexis tonight, so she requested that Izzy skip this one dinner. Luckily, Izzy is pretty chill. She had no clue who either one of us were when we all met. Dawson and she hit it off immediately on one of our nights out in the city back in the spring.

When she found out Dawson was a millionaire, it was her who wanted to walk away. She confessed she was a simple small town girl from Georgia, who wanted no part dealing with a high roller. I still laugh when she calls him that, even more so with his billionaire status.

Once he convinced her to visit him in Nags Heads, meet his parents and friends, she realized he was none of the sorts. We can dress up in our thousands of dollars Armani suits to talk shop with the best of them, but we both know where we belong. Here in this coastal town and who we were raised to be. Basically, me being raised by his parents, though my mom did her best until she couldn't.

I hear Dawson beam about Alexis, telling Izzy how adorable she is and how he hates that he missed the first five, almost six years of her life. How pissed he is at Maren for leaving. To be honest, I am not sure if he will ever forgive her. Tolerate Maren yes, but earning Dawson's forgiveness is no small feat. Another reason why I have kept my feelings for Maren under wraps for so long. Dawson has threatened every boy that has ever looked his sister's way, with me right there with him.

He even had his drunken moments confessing how jealous he was of how close she and I were growing up. I am not sure how he will ever take the news that I have loved his sister for years.

Now there is a mini Maren, *shit!* Maybe I just need to lock this down and move on. *Fuck!* Because I did a spectacular job of moving on while she was gone. Occasional dates here and there aside, no one interested me to be serious with. Though, I slept with a few to cure the urge.

Unexpectedly, I realized it was not the sex I was craving, but the closeness and touch from the one person I had never been intimate with but craved throughout my entire being. The one that was always next to me, her arm linked in mine, sitting on my lap, or just next to me through the good and bad. This evening only proved my thoughts honest when I held her in my arms.

I find myself torn between my best friend and the girl I have loved most of my life. I need to approach this with one before the other. Do I ask permission from Dawson first? If he says no, do I respect his wishes and never try with Maren? *Would I be able to walk away from her?* Or do I talk to Maren first to check her feelings on all of this? To see if there could ever be an *us* before I blow a hole in the boat for no reason? She just came home today. I know I need to give her time to reaccumulate to being back along with Lexi.

Huh, that little girl is something.

Not sure what was going through that little mind of hers during our chat, or her million question quiz I was being judged on without knowing. Just like Maren. Finding tricky ways to figure someone out, to get in their head a little more. Just like Maren, I am sure there is a method to the madness that lies within.

Mar was always the one that could get me to share and open up about anything. To be myself in a world that expected me to be something else. In a town that for years I was known as the ill-tempered fucked up orphan that was going to end up in jail with blood on my hands if I didn't get my shit together. To stop losing my head over the little things, bashing people's faces in, and not drive like I was on a race track.

CHAPTER 6
NEW BEGINNINGS
Maren

Mom and I head inland this morning to register Alexis for school and meet with the high school principal for student-teaching. School starts right after Labor Day, so I want to make sure we have plenty of time to prepare. We decided to stop first at Nags Head Cafe for breakfast. A staple in our weekend ritual Mom and I used to have. I knew coming into town would be a big step for me. This town knows no boundaries along with sharing everyone's secrets. I realize now I was not fully prepared for the gawking mouths and wide-eye stares. All I can do is smile and wave as we sit down in our usual booth.

"That cannot be my favorite little Maren?" I hear a squeal heading in our direction.

"It is, Haddy. How are you?" I ask.

"I am well, dear. Even better now to see your smiling face. Now who do we have here?" Haddy questions as she bends to her knees to be on level with Lexi.

"This is my daughter, Alexis. Lexi, baby can you say hi to Mrs. Haddy?"

"Hi, Mrs. Haddy," Lexi says with a smile, putting her little hand to shake.

Haddy takes her hand and swoons. "I am so happy you are back, Maren, and this is an extra little treat seeing your mini twin." Mom and I laugh because of the truth. Again, thankful that the only rumors spread were that I ran off with Trayton to God knows where, but as soon as he showed up at UT, no one was the wiser. It just became the question of where did Maren go and why? My mom was kind to fill me on the rumor wheel early this morning over coffee. Haddy takes our orders and shouts out to everyone to turn around and eat. To mind their own business. Good ol' Haddy calling people out on their shit. Some things never change.

Lexi is coloring next to me quietly. I am avoiding eye contact with all glances in our direction.

"So, new day. New topic," my mom pipes up, and this is how she has always started our conversations when she wants to know the latest scoop, except this time I know nothing. "You and Ford seemed to be talking quite a bit before they left?"

"Yah, we were just catching up. I really missed him."

"He missed you, you know. I think he took you leaving harder than anyone. He tried to hide it, but for a while, he would not even come to the house."

"Really?" I ask, stunned. "Why would he avoid being at the house? That's his home too."

"Oh my sweet angel, have you always been this blind?" she asks, making me choke on my drink.

"Obviously, Mom," I mutter, tilting my head to Lexi, like duh. "What am I missing?"

"Ford avoided the house because you were not there. He has always had strong feelings for you." I give her a look like she has lost her marbles. "I am not sure why he has never acted on them and how blind everyone has been to the two of you. Especially last evening. I saw that hug between the two of you, the pain and love in his eyes."

"Mom, you can't be for real right now?"

"Oh, honey, but I am. You know I love that boy like my own son, so I am telling you this to protect both of you. Don't lead him on, Maren. He's been through enough loss and hardship in his life. You leaving shook him. Luckily, being away at college was a good distraction then there was California that I think was a whole other level of distraction," she murmurs, making dramatic motions with her hands and eyes. "By the time the two finally came home, he seemed to be mentally over you, if you know what I mean. But there were walls built around him like a fortress. So, if he is what you want, then I fully support the two of you, but do not go breaking the man's heart again."

"I...I...I don't even know what to say. Besides, I literally showed up on your front porch yesterday." She rolls her eyes at me in annoyance. "Of course I have always had feelings for Ford. I was the annoying younger sister that tried to be everywhere they were. He and Dawson were always jerks to me too. Then when it was just us, I could see all his heart and potential. I cried for days when they left for college. It was mostly tears for him, fear of him not coming back. Fear of him returning with a girlfriend."

"I know, honey." She clasps her hand on top of mine in comfort.

"We are all grown up now. Plus, I have a kid. He doesn't want that. Besides, he has to be seeing someone."

She shakes her no. "No, he is not seeing anyone, nor has he seen anyone serious. I'm telling you, he built a fortress around his heart. I hear stories of his relations with other women, but never anything serious. And don't go making decisions for him about Lexi. You don't know what you don't know. So now is not the time to let your naive crazy self show."

Now I glare back at her, before I feel a pull on all my senses to glance at the front door. Ford has just strutted in, in all his sexy manly-ness. Relaxed fitting jeans with a gray Henley, hair disheveled. Like who looks that damn good and single. There was never a doubt in my mind that Ford was the whole package. When I was younger, I hoped for a chance with him, but now I am not sure what is in store for us. He doesn't even notice me, so I turn my attention back to my mom, who apparently was still talking through my Ford zone out.

"You deserve to be happy, Maren," she finishes.

"Got it, Mom."

As Haddy delivers our food, I shift my eyes to look in Ford's direction only to find his eyes are locked on me. I conjure up a smile, welcoming him to come over if he wants. He says something to the waitress at the bar area and then heads over with his coffee.

"Hello, beautiful ladies." He leans in to kiss Mom on the cheek, telling her good morning, then slides into the booth next to me. His brandy and leather scent wafts over me with a hint of cinnamon this morning.

"Good Morning, Ford, your ears must have been burning this morning," Mom states, leaving me turning red.

Sending me a wink, he says, "Can't imagine why I am the topic of conversation this early in the day."

"You have no idea, Ford," she laughs. I shake my head in full embarrassment now.

"Good morning, Ford." Lexi looks up long enough from her pancake stack to acknowledge him.

"Good morning, mini bar."

Her face twists as she stares back at him dumbfounded. "Mini bar?"

"Yes, that is my nickname for you, because you are sweet like my favorite chocolate bar and a mini version of your mother."

"I guess that makes sense." Lexi shrugs and turns back to her pancakes. She is still debating on how to attack them. It won't be me asking to cut them because I know the tantrum that it will lead to. I see Ford watching her with concern and looks at me.

Before I can warn him, his speaks, "Hey mini bar, want me to cut those up for you?"

Mom and I hold our breath as I warned her on the phone before we arrived home, and she got a little show of Miss Independence this morning when it was time to get dressed. I brace myself, as Lexi stares back at him. She then shrugs her shoulders and says, "Sure." We exchange looks, neither one of us is going to say a word about what just happened right now. Ford cuts them up for her, passes the plate back to her, and lifts the syrup, asking if she wants some. "Yes, please." I am just in shock at how well these two are getting along, and Lexi lets him help her. She rarely lets me help with anything. It is either show her once, and she has it, or she is so determined to figure it out herself.

Once we are finished eating, Mom excuses herself to the restroom with Lexi. Leaving Ford and I alone at the table. Haddy refills his coffee, and then we just stare into each other's eyes. I look away to shield my blushing face. My mom has me thinking something is possible with Ford. The other voice in my head says too much time has passed.

"Did you have a good night back home?" I can tell he is trying to create small talk.

"Um, yes, I did. We did. Your bed is really comfy. Reminds me, I have a bone to pick with Mom about why your mattress is so much better than my old one." He laughs.

"Well I am glad you are enjoying the bed. I bought the same mattress for my bed now."

My eyes light up. "Oh really? Maybe I should come test that one out too." Words fly out of my mouth before I could stop them. I don't miss the slight grunt he makes before clearing his throat.

"You are welcome anytime, Mar." He smirks, making my heart melt and cheeks blush. This man is too good looking for his damn good. It would help if he were an asshole, but he is far from one. I let out an awkward giggle, pulling his direction to my mouth. His stare makes me lick my lips, then bite my lower lip, with hooded eyelids looking back at him. He clears his throat and moves a bit in the booth. He seems uncomfortable.

Laying cash on the table, I gather my belongings to get moving along. "We best be going. Busy morning ahead." Ford slips out of the booth so I can escape. "Good seeing you again, Ford." Before I have two steps away from the table, he pulls my hand back. The electrical current is fast and sizzling, causing me to shudder under my breath.

"Maren, wait." He must have felt it too because his hand moves like he was shocked. I turn to look at him directly. "Dawson and I are flying out this afternoon for a few meetings in New York. So we will be gone or I would want to do this sooner. But, can I take you to lunch next Monday?" *Did the "Ford" just ask me on a date?* My green eyes go wide, and he can sense I am not sure what to say. "Only if you can get away. Thought we could catch up with no distractions."

"Oh, you are leaving?" Pain shoots through my heart at the thought of him being gone so soon after I just came home, but I will it not to show, biting my bottom lap in frustration. "Um, I can go, Ford. Just tell me the time and place."

"I will pick you up at eleven. Hand me your phone." I do as he says, looking at him oddly. After a few clicks, he hands me my phone back and his dings. "There. Now we have each other's new numbers." All I can do is nod and smile as the familiar pain of Ford leaving strikes me once again. I am not sure I am elated that scenarios of him leaving still pain me this much after all the time passed.

"Okay, let me catch up with those two that snuck out," I spit out, turning to leave in a rush. My mom grins like she knows, causing me to grin like Lexi in a candy store.

"Come on you two, let's go get Lexi registered for school." We both follow as she leads the way.

CHAPTER 7
NEW YORK
Maren

Yesterday was a busy day, but Lexi is now registered for kindergarten with an old friend of mine, Harper, as her teacher. I'll be honest, it was nice to catch up with her and tell me that she forgave me a long time ago for just disappearing.

Hindsight, I wish I would have told a few of my girlfriends or wrote their numbers down on paper to message later on. Even so, I ignored quite a few emails from friends reaching out. Alison and Harper had both threatened to track me down, pull me out of hiding, then murder me themselves. I even ignored my own brother and Ford.

Needless to say, Lexi thinks Harper, or as she calls her Mrs. Kips, is the best teacher ever and even received a special tour of the school and classroom for being a new student.

Afterwards, I went to meet with Principal Elrod, who was my Honors English teacher the last three years of high school. She was more than happy to approve my student-teaching through the University I used for my English degree and paired me with one of the older teachers I knew some friends had, Mrs. Lambert. Fingers crossed that this all goes swimmingly, and I can line up a job for the following school year. My plan is to at least be a substitute for the spring semester.

All in all, two days in, I feel that life is coming together back home. For me, that also means shit is going to hit the fan at some point. Until then, I am just going to keep spinning toward the future.

Mom has "hired" me to be her side chef for next weekend for the church's baked good fundraiser on Sunday down at the docks. This fundraiser is to raise money for the Cleats family, whose little boy has been diagnosed with an inoperative brain tumor at this time and will be starting radiation next month. Pakston is only four with several years of tests, hospital visits, and possible surgeries ahead of him. One thing this community does is rally behind those in need.

With that, Mom has us running errands all today, picking up and gathering supplies for the hellacious baking week ahead. Lexi has been a trooper all morning with being dragged everywhere and meeting new people. Another instance where we two differ. She loves being in a crowd, surrounded by busy-ness, people and life, where I am most relaxed and happy in the comfort of my home, in pjs, having tea with a book or Netflix.

Now being lunchtime, we stop at the Shipyard for lunch. Upon entering, I am taken back with nostalgia. Three of my summers were spent here waitressing. The booth in the back where my friends and I would hang out after school and on the weekends, sipping our shakes and eating cheesy bacon covered fries. How easy life was then, to only complain about the little meniscal everything days that drove us crazy. A new generation of teens now seem to run the joint.

Sitting down in the booth that overlooks the harbor, I feel the most at peace here. Overlooking the landscape of familiarity. The landscape that consists of what my dad and his father before him built and owns. Speaking of, I see my dad walking in, in his work overalls with his boating yard shirt underneath. Being the jolly kind man I have always known him to be, as he stops to talk to Ed, The Shipyard owner, several cooks and waiters before he even gets to our table. He takes a seat next to Mom, with Lexi and I on the other side.

Kissing my mom on her forehead, he asks, "How are my favorite three girls today?" She gleams over, and I laugh to myself as nothing has changed between those two. A love I have always craved to have. A relationship of support and love I can now only dream of.

"We are good. Almost finished with collecting all the items. Lexi has been perfect all morning." My mom beams about our morning. Lexi smiles, and I can tell she is loving her new family and life. To be doted on, which she deserves. My dad engages Lexi in conversation about her morning along with a few games of tic-tac-toe after we place our orders.

"So, have you heard from Ford?" my mom asks. I was wondering when she was going to.

"No. Have you heard from Dawson?" I question back.

She just laughs. "No, I will hear from him when they get back in town and have no food, and they are starving," she says with an eye roll.

Shrugging my shoulders, I mutter, "I don't expect to hear from him. He owes me nothing. Besides, I am sure he is busy with all those meetings he spoke of." Looking over at Mom, she only raises her eyebrows at me.

"That's probably it." I only know that look and that exact saying, always means something. Something she will never tell but will find ways to push me to figure it out on my own. If one person in my life loves a riddle, it would be my mother.

Letting out a sigh, I look back to the boats floating nearby. Again, falling back into the trance of what was. How Dawson, Ford, and I used to run barefoot up and down those docks. Help the fishermen load and unload their supplies and catches when we were out of school. How we used to help Dad hose the docks down at night so we could get him home to dinner on time, to avoid Mom's fussiness.

How many times did Ford and I just sit out over there on the jetties in the early morning watching the fishermen head out for the day? Listening to the waves crash on the rocks, taking in the sunrises, laughing as the dolphins frolicked behind the boats waiting for an easy breakfast. Just the two of us in our own world. I hear a shrill, pulling me out of my memories.

"Now I heard from Haddy you were in town but did not believe her. How could your mom keep you coming home a secret?" I know that voice anywhere, so I lock eyes with my mom, before turning my attention to Mrs. Lezlie.

I slide out of the booth to stand up and give her a hug. "Hi, Mamaw. How are you?"

"Oh my dear, much better now that I have seen you. Do you care if I join you and catch up?"

"Of course not, Mamaw." Lexi goes over and sits between my mom and dad as Mamaw takes a seat next to me. I am waiting for her to notice Lexi and ask all her need to know questions. Mamaw, also known as Mrs. Lezlie, and my granny were two peas in a pod in this town that always knew the latest gossip. You wanted to know something; you went to them. Since my granny passed away in the fall of my senior year, Mrs. Lezlie found herself being the fill-in grandmother to all of us in need. Also, allowing her to get all the town scoop.

She smiles at Lexi and looks back at me. "Now, this must be Alexis." I nod and Lexi puts her hand out to shake Mrs. Lezlie's.

I let those two talk in circles until the mention of Ford's name brings me back to the conversation. "I am sorry, what did you say?"

"I was just asking your mom if she saw the pictures from last night's charity gala in New York."

"What's the big deal about that?" I ask.

"Because your brother and Ford were there. Just like they are there every year. And as always, both making the best dressed list and looking the most divine. I don't ever care for that one girl on Ford's arm, but Izzy looked stunning in her red Gucci gown." My mind is now swirling that Ford was at a gala and had a girl on his arm. I have yet to meet this Izzy chick who has my brother smitten.

Mamaw whips her phone out of her purse to share the pictures with my parents. My mom admits she has been sidetracked and had not checked her latest *Google* alerts on them. *Google-Alerts, what the hell?* Pulling my own phone out, I search for Ford Merrick and Dawson Hart. I am blown away by the amount of articles and pictures that populate my screen of those two. Sitting on top is from last night's gala.

Per the caption, Ford is dressed in a navy blue Armani suit, with a golden yellow tie and gold stitched handkerchief tucked in his jacket pocket for an accent.

On his arm, was a stunning, wavy-haired blonde named Grace. She wore a shimmering cream-colored dress with a slit up to her hip. Low back, but somehow the lack of material still pushed her boobs basically out of her dress. My face contorts when I continue reading, also learning from the caption that she is the New York Governor's daughter. This is no random escort to a party, he knows her. By their body language, they know each other very well.

I feel my mom's gaze on me, so I straighten my spine and throw my shoulders back as my poker face falls into place. Shooting her a smile, I show her that I am fine. She nods, and luckily I'm saved by food being delivered to the table.

My appetite has depleted, but I know better than not to eat this amazing shrimp platter in front of me without causing alarm. I indulge myself, and thankfully, Lexi is all about some shrimp. She decides to eat most of mine over her chicken fingers. Luckily, the rest of lunch and day go without another mention on Ford.

It is not until hours later that I am lying on the bed in my room, scrolling through all the articles and pictures of Mister Ford Merrick. I never let myself look him up in fear of what I might learn, let alone had no contacts back home to know what was happening. I had warned Darcy early on to never update me on *home* life unless it was an emergency.

Now I am trying to figure out when he became a rich, billionaire bachelor. When did he become a sexy, rich bachelor that the news and sleazy tabloids want to report on him and Dawson. I'm startled out of my head when I hear, "Mommy?"

"Yes, sweetie. What do you need?"

"I just wanted to check on you and bring you a cookie." I sit up to be greeted with her babydoll eyes and charming self, holding out a cookie on a plate with a small glass of pineapple juice.

"What is all this for?"

"You just seemed down after that Mamaw lady brought up Ford being at some event last night. I know this always cheered you up back home." Geez, this kid never misses a beat. Taking the plate and drink from her, I place them on the nightstand and pull her into my lap on the bed.

"Have I told you how much I love and adore you lately?"

She giggles, "Yes, just an hour ago you did."

I laugh out loud. "You are very intuitive, but I am fine. I promise. Did you have a good day?"

"It was a great day, Mommy. Glam-ma is going to let me help cook dinner tonight. She said it was on your favorite meals."

"Oh really? I bet it will taste wonderful."

"Don't you want to know what it is?"

"Nope. I prefer it to be a surprise."

"Okay. I'll come get you when it is dinner time," she squeaks, as she slides down my lap and skips out of my room.

I need to quit obsessing over this woman and Ford. He is not mine and never will be. First and foremost, I need to cancel the plans he has for Monday. As much as my curiosity wants to control my decisions right now, it needs to not play a role in my life. I learned six years ago; curiosity gets me knocked up to being a runaway to who the hell knows what direction my life is going in right now. *Deep breaths, girl.*

> Hey. Something came up, and I won't be able to have lunch on Monday. Hope your trip is going well.

Almost immediately my phone dings back.

FORD

Everything ok?

> Yep, just busy with settling in and Lexi.

FORD

Maren.

Maren, come on. Something is up. I can't get away right now, or I would call you.

> Dude. All is good. Have a good evening, Ford.

With that, I leave my phone on the bed to head downstairs. Me being alone with my thoughts and phone are not a great combination right now. I know Lexi helping my mom make dinner will be a nice distraction.

Ford

"Hey, D. You talk to Madre today?" I ask Dawson from across the dinner table. Another night of meetings with another group of college kids that believe they have the next best app needing investors.

"No. Why? Something up?" he asks, taking a sip of his scotch as the brunette next to him continues to flirt with him, with her hand on his thigh.

He acts oblivious, but I know he is just waiting for Izzy to walk through those doors and raise hell. Izzy is running late from a previous dinner she had with a few of her college friends, and Dawson prefers she handles these types. Says it's bad for business if he must be the bad guy. Plus, both of our lack of trust in women, based on history, we choose to ignore rather than speak or act upon most gestures.

"Nah. Just curious how Lexi and Mar are settling in. Are we back in time for dinner tomorrow?" Now Maren is back, she is all I can think of. Along with that adorable daughter of hers.

"Mom sent me a picture of Lexi earlier with Dad on the dock. Seems things are okay." He pauses, taking another sip. "Man, I am ready to head out whenever you want tomorrow. And yes about dinner. Izzy is coming to meet Maren and Lexi also."

"Nice. That will be good for them." The waiter brings me

another bourbon just as Izzy walks in. Dawson and her lock eyes from across the room, telling me it is show time. I honestly think these two get off with screwing with people.

"Hey, baby." Izzy struts over to Dawson, placing a kiss on his lips. The brunette looks shocked and removes her hand quickly. Izzy motions to her to scoot over so she can squeeze in between the two of them.

My phone vibrates in my pocket, pulling me away from the conversation Izzy is having with the girl next to her. It is from Maren, and she just canceled our lunch date for Monday. That does not seem like her at all.

> Everything ok?

MAREN

Yep, just busy settling in and Lexi.

She just yep-ed me. She only does that when she is avoiding an honest answer. She rarely has ever told me "yep," but I've seen her say it plenty to other people over the years.

> Maren.

> Maren, come on. Something is up. I can't get a way right now, or I would call you.

MAREN

Dude. All is good. Have a good evening, Ford.

"Ford....Ford, you okay?" Izzy snapping her fingers in front of my face pulls me out of my shock of just being called Dude from the love of my life and that she just blew me off. Izzy looks concerned, and Dawson looks confused. We are literally in the middle of a pitch, and I just zoned out.

"Yeah, I am fine." Downing my drink then pushing back from the table, I get to my feet. "Please continue, but excuse me for a few moments." With that, I walk through the lobby to find a sliver of quiet and call Maren.

Fuck, no answer. Calling Madre would be crazy, right? It's not like we are together. Fucckkk!

Running my palm over my face in frustration, I dial another number. "Hector, hey! I want the jet ready to leave the runway by seven in the morning. Got it?... Thank you. See you in the morning."

If she won't answer my calls or texts, then she will have to answer me in person. Heading back to the table, I push everything else aside so we can finish this damn dinner meeting. Best I drown her memory in bourbon again so I can concentrate. At least for tonight anyways.

CHAPTER 8
SUNDAY BEST
Maren

I SHOULD HAVE KNOWN my mom would drag us to church today. She is ready to show off Lexi and get her involved in the community. In contrast, I am happy to remain non-existent for the time being. Not including the fact that I am exhausted from staying up all night, trying to figure out why in the hell Ford called me back to back. Then I reverted to obsessing over him and Miss Grace Kay Quinnby, the Governor's daughter.

Yes. I did enough stalking to know her full name, the names of her best friends, and where she loves to shop per her *Instagram*. Her date of birth and that she graduated with her master's in business four years ago from Princeton. Also, her white mini poodle is named Gucci like the designer. She has won many pageants, a role model in society, and New York's sweetheart. *Seriously, not even going to compete with that.*

"Come on, Maren, we need to go!" my mom hollers from downstairs. Good thing my mom went shopping and bought Lexi and me brand new church clothes.

Jesus, I think you and I and her need to have a few words today about shopping now!

Throwing on my new olive green ruffled hem dress with butterfly sleeves and slipping on my black ballet flats, I head down the stairs. I am greeted by my little girl donning one of the many

Matilda Jane dresses my mom has purchased from an old friend of mine up the street. Decked out with a matching headband and shoes. Lexi smiles at me with the cheesiest of grins, and my mood disappears while feeding off her happiness.

"Rumor has it the Adair's are still in the Virgin Islands, so no fretting over them today," Mom states as we walk out, making the air easier to breathe, knowing I do not have to face them for another day.

My Ford distraction caused me to forget that walking into church this morning was going to be like a high school reunion.

Take me now...please! I say in my head with my eyes closed and head tilted back. By the time we get Lexi checked in to Sunday school, my week is booked up with lunches and drink dates along with my contact list growing in my phone. I take a seat next to my dad in the pew as he hands me my old bible. A book I have not picked up since I left home. A book that belongs to a greater being that I am sure I have cursed, cried to, and prayed to on more occasions I care to remember. The choir starts to sing as the last few people trickle in before the service starts, then we bow our heads in prayer.

Service has started, and I am in my own head praying and being thankful for what I do have. Convincing myself that I am going to be alright. That Lexi and I will be fine now that we are back home. Better plans lie ahead for us.

With my eyes closed, taking in the sermon, I feel a tug on my hair. Convinced that it's someone's little brat, I refuse to acknowledge it. Then it happens two more times. *Deep breath, Mar.* That is when I smell him as if he is surrounding me. The hair on my neck rises, I feel the brush of my hair to the side.

"Good Morning, Maren." His voice sends tingles through my body causing goosebumps to populate over my skin as he whispers in my ear. "Can't ignore me now, can you?" I breathe in, holding my breath. I must be imagining Ford being here.

Looking up to the church ceiling, I mutter, "This is not what I prayed for this morning," in a low whisper. Feeling like God is chuckling down at me. The choir begins to sing *Amazing Grace* as we all stand. Ford slides into the pew next to me. Shaking my dad's hand, he then leans over my dad and I to kiss my mom on the cheek. That's when I notice Dawson and his girlfriend on the other side of Mom.

When in God's name did they get here?"

My eyes go into a sidelong glance in Ford's direction, in his gray slacks and form fitting, muscle hugging button-up white collared shirt, only to catch him staring at me while singing just as loud as the other churchgoers. *This is not awkward at all.* I decide to look everywhere in the church at anyone but in Ford's direction.

Near the end of the service, the pager the Sunday school teacher gave me goes off. I excuse myself quietly from my family to head through the double doors. Only with Ford, hot on my heels. Doing my best to ignore him, I head to the classroom where we dropped off Lexi. She is sitting in the corner by herself crying, knees bent up to her chest. I rush to her side before the teacher can get a word in. Pulling her into my arms to hold her, I see Ford getting the recap, and he looks angry while I watch his attention go from us to a little boy on the far side of the room.

"Lexi baby, what's wrong?"

"Just some stupid boy being mean." My face contorts, trying to hold back my mixed emotions of laughter and anger.

"We are in church, so let's not say stupid. Can you tell me what this boy said or did that made you so upset?"

"I told him who my daddy was, and he called me a liar." I honestly cannot say I am ready to have this conversation or can imagine who she thinks her actual dad is.

"Lexi...who do you think your daddy is?"

"It is Trayton Adair. Aunt Darcy's brother."

"Wow. you really do not miss a thing, do you?" Alexis nods her head, and all I can do is grab her up and kiss the top of her head.

"You want to talk about this more when we get home?" She

nods her head again, then lays her head on my shoulder, and we walk out. I leave Ford in there scolding the little boy to tears. *Good, that little shit deserves it for questioning my baby girl. Now making me have a conversation with a five year old I was not planning on having for a while.* We walk out to my parent's car to wait since church just released.

Ford comes over, now with his sleeves rolled up, placing his right hand through my hair, while he places his other palm on Lexi's back. "You both okay?" Ford has always been protective of me, but this feels like a whole other level.

"Yeah, we will be."

Lexi lifts her head off my shoulder. "Ford, will you hold me?" We look at each other with complex faces, but he doesn't hesitate. Holding his arms out, I pass her off to him. Lexi wraps her arms around his neck, and he kisses her forehead as she snuggles into him. The vision in front of me is making my stomach churn with emotions.

God, she deserves a father that wants her, that loves her, that will chase the monsters under her bed away, and threaten bullies with an inch of their lives for her.

"Is Alexis okay? What happened?" my mom asks as she rushes over.

"Just some jerk kid calling her a liar about her daddy because he famous in this town and now a NFL player." My parents both give me a concerned look, knowing this might turn into a big-deal conversation today and planning on how we need to handle this situation moving forward.

"Let's head over to Grit's Grill first for brunch and give us time to think." My dad is a stickler for tradition regardless of if the sky is falling or ground collapsing beneath him. I won't lie though, it's these moments I am thankful for it the most. It grounds my feet for stability, which is a huge aspect I was missing the most of the past several years. Not as much financially, but mental and emotional stability. To know if I falter, there are arms to catch me. To know that Lexi has family and people surrounding her that will catch her as well.

She may never have the love of her biological father's family, but she has this group of people surrounding us. To me, that is more than enough.

"I want to stay with Ford," Lexi pipes up as everyone begins to head to their cars and head to brunch.

"Well sweetie your car seat is in Glam-ma's car. Besides, you will see him in just a few minutes," I say back to her. With her head shaking *no* before I can finish my sentence and clinging tighter to Ford, I sense she is about to throw down.

"Mar, we can come get my truck later. I will just ride with you all."

"Seriously, Ford. You don't have to cave to her every demand." I am starting to get annoyed. He can tell with the side-eye he glares back at me. I am trying to move past the thought of having a chance with Ford, but now my daughter won't let him go. He isn't helping either with her odd attachment to him. Letting out a sigh, I give in. "Sure. Let's load up."

Ford

MAREN IS PISSED AT ME. Maybe I overstepped today by accompanying her to Lexi's classroom, addressing the issue with the teacher and then threatening that little shit until he cried.

That can't be it, though.

She has been weird with me since her text last night. The shock of her tense body when I showed up at church this morning said enough. I knew she was having an overwhelming moment, watching her twirl the whale tail ring on her finger, over and over again, while biting down on her lower lip.

Sitting across from her now at the table, I cannot keep my eyes off her. Still reeling that she is back home, here in front of me. No other woman compares to her beauty and heart. No other woman makes my mind stop all logical thinking. I never had the need with anyone else to be possessive, to make mine solely. *Only her.* I walk around with a constant hard-on just being in the same room with her body and sensual scent.

Lexi is sitting right next to me. She has not let me leave her side since earlier at the church. Dawson is sitting on the other side of her, trying to distract her with coloring and games on his phone. Izzy is sitting next to Maren, grilling her with a million questions of what it was like growing up with the two of us and what she has been up to the last several years. I can tell in Izzy's mind, she needs Maren to be her best friend.

To Maren, Izzy will not be fully accepted until Dawson marries her. Maren has always kept her tight circle of friends small to avoid drama and let downs. Just how I have always known her to be. Polite to everyone she meets, will help a stranger, but you do not know Maren to her fullest in all her quirky-ness until she says so.

"Oh, Izzy, you looked gorgeous in that dress of yours at the gala," Madre pipes in to help Maren out.

"What about me, mom?" Dawson questions back.

She smiles. "You both made a stunning couple. And might I add, Ford, you looked devilishly handsome."

"Tech world's hottest bachelor right there!" Izzy shouts across the table and laughs. I catch Maren's eyes drift down, and her whole body locks up. "Maren, did you see the pictures? Maybe you can join us next time, now that you are home." Izzy nudges Maren in the shoulder when asking.

Maren looks up and locks eyes with me. "I doubt it. Not really my scene. Besides, I would just be the lone wolf with you and Dawson and Ford and his date." *Fucking Bingo!* She saw those damn pictures. A relentless growl releases from under my breath, causing the table to turn and look at me. I clear my throat and excuse myself.

Luckily, Lexi doesn't say a word, so I head outside for some fresh air, trying to wrap my head around Maren being jealous of Grace. If she only knew that Grace secretly swings for her own team but pretends in the public eye for her father. You would think this day in age everyone would be past all the hiding and shame, but some situations are harder than others, I guess. Running my hand through my hair, I realize I need to make a move sooner than later. I just hope Dawson can get over it.

I hear the door chime when someone opens it. "Ford...um, food was just delivered to the table."

"Maren, wait. Can we talk?"

"Sure, if you can make it quick." There is no making this conversation quick as I close the space between us. I subtly tuck her hair behind her ear, running the tips of fingers down the side of her face. She closes her eyes, then slightly leans into my touch.

"Maren, I have missed you so much. So much about you that I have missed, I'm not sure where to begin... You are just exquisitely beautiful."

"Ford," she whispers softly. Before I really overstep, I pull her into my arms and hold her. I feel her hesitation, but she caves to wrap her arms around my waist. I could stand here for eternity with her in my arms. My palm naturally begins to guide itself up and down her back as I feel her relax more against my body. It is not until a throat clearing pulls us out of our state, to notice Madre standing there. She just smiles and tells us to head in and eat before everyone gets suspicious. Trailing behind Maren, I whisper loud enough that she can hear me, "Mar, Grace is no one but a friend."

As if she threw a knife in my heart, she murmurs, "Ford, it's fine. You are a grown man who can date whoever you want. You don't owe me an explanation."

With that, we take our seats at the table and act as if those peaceful five minutes in each other's arms meant nothing.

Maren

By the time we got home from brunch, Lexi and I were both ready for a nap. We agreed to talk about her dad when we woke up. Waking up an hour before dinner was not planned, but I believe we both needed sleep and cuddles. Laying in Lexi's bed, I see her staring at the ceiling.

"What'cha thinking?" I ask.

"I'm not sure." She pauses to bite her lower lip. "Why did that kid think I was a liar, Mommy?"

"Because he does not know you or our situation. Yes, your daddy is Trayton Adair, but we as humans have choices throughout life. Unfortunately, he chose his dreams over being a father. I know that hurts now and always will, but also know it is for the best." I have never been one to sugarcoat things with her. Possibly because of my bruised ego and broken heart, but I always want her to have a clear picture on life.

"The boy mentioned him being a star football player. What about your dreams?" she asks, putting her small hand in mine.

"I've had many dreams, but the moment I held you in my arms, I knew there was nothing else I wanted more than to be your mommy."

"That's good. I couldn't live without you. You're my favorite person."

"Oh, sweet girl, you are my favorite person too." Pulling her into my lap, I cup her cheeks. "Do you have any questions about Trayton or about anything?"

"No, not right now. I know I am good without him. I remember him always having a mad face when he looked at me. We can find me a better daddy. A daddy, like Ford, maybe?" Her eyes brighten up in excitement as the words leave her little mouth. All I can do is pull her closer in to rock her.

"We shall see, sweet girl, we shall see."

Then I think of Ford. How protective he was of both of us today. He held me in his arms at the diner, but his hold felt tighter than I remembered. His tone was more intense than I recall. Why did he feel the need to tell me about Grace? I remember his heightened emotions from when I would help him calm down after a fight or him letting the anger get the best of him. He would just hold me until his breathing stabilized while the anger and hurt slipped away.

Now he holds me as if he can't let me go. Like I may disappear on him again. I can't imagine losing my parents at such a young age like he did. My selfishness never let me see what pain my leaving could do. At least not until Mom mentioned it earlier this week. Ford has lost a lot, so I need to reassure him I am not leaving and that he will always have my friendship.

CHAPTER 9
BAR SCENE
Maren

ALMOST A WHOLE OTHER week has come and gone in a blur with no word from Ford since Sunday. He skipped out on dinner that night also. Dawson covered for him saying he was tired and jet lagged, tired. Just wish I knew what his real damn problem was because his mixed signals are giving me whiplash. Those fleeting moments in his arms, I thought he was going to say something of importance, even had the crazy thought he might even kiss me, but then no, he ghosts me for days.

Just fuck, say what you mean and mean what you say!

Why is that thought process so hard for others? I only said what I said to him because he has never given me a reason to be jealous or angry with him being with someone else. I have never *been* his. My heart has been his for as long as I can remember, but he will never know that.

Now, it's Tuesday evening with me heading into town to meet some girlfriends for drinks at the local bar, Lucky Twelve. It apparently is a ritual for them and my first time attending. My parents have offered to watch Lexi for the night and stated Izzy and Dawson might come over for a movie night.

Wearing my favorite hip hugger jeans with my soft gray tee with a low back and boots, I head out to the bar. Once I enter, I am greeted with outlandish screams and shouts of my name. I think they are still stunned that I'm back home. It legit has turned into a sorority party in a blink of an eye as more ladies have joined our table. For hours, we sat in this back booth catching up. Some of those girls surprised me by coming back to this town, others I expected to never leave. Excusing myself to catch a breather, I head to the bar and sit on one of the stools.

"Another Jack and coke please!" I shout over the noise, sliding my glass over to the edge of the bar. Right then, I feel the presence of a stranger.

"You new in town?" he asks.

Grabbing my drink from the bartender, I take a sip then turn to him. "Define new?" I am quickly impressed with how easy on the eyes this guy is. Has a young Ewan McGregor vibe going on in jeans and a Matchbox -20 shirt. "Nice shirt by the way." I smirk, turning back to face forward. I hear him chuckle next to me, causing my lips to curl up over my glass.

"Well let's see, I have lived here for three years and have not seen you around."

"Well, that is because I left six years ago and just got back to town."

He startles me. "Oh shit, you're Jim Hart's daughter, aren't you? Maren, right?" This causes me to throw my drink back and ask for another.

"That's me. Lost and now I have been found. YAY!" I cheer, slightly bringing my hands up in the air like pom poms.

"Didn't mean to offend, just you have been the talk of this town for a few days now." The urge to down my new drink is tempting, but I only drink half.

"Ha, good to know." Putting my hand out to him, I murmur, "Well you have officially met me, Maren Hart."

His grip is firm as he shakes my hand. "I'm Duncan. Nephew to Jerry Heed."

"Yah, I know your uncle. Used to help him out in the summers. Good Man."

"He is, but not getting much younger and never had kids,

so I left my California life to come out here and help him out for a while. Have to say it has been a welcomed lifestyle change."

"Shit, California. Yah, you are far from home, fisherman. Please enlighten me on what you did before coming here?"

"I worked in PR for some of Hollywood's finest. Always putting out fires, trying to keep them from creating them to begin with all on lack of sleep, parties, and drugs."

"Wow, the shit you know and have seen. I would love to pick your brain one day of how the other half lives."

Laughing, he says, "How the other half live? Trust me, sweetheart, they would be jealous if they could see us here."

"Mar, there you are?"

"Oh hi, Anna, do you know Duncan?"

"I have seen him around a few times. Are you coming back to hang with us?"

"Yep. Let me just grab another one." I motion to the bartender who looks annoyed with me already.

"Before you leave, Maren, can I get your number?"

"Sure." I toss him my phone because I know damn well my fingers will not find the right numbers with this tipsy feeling. Once I get my phone back and drink in hand, I head back to the sorority sister table. "See you later, Duncan."

"I hope so!" he shouts back.

For the next thirty minutes, I am filled in on all things Duncan. The married women drool over him, only a few of the single women have been able to bed him. According to this group, I have a good chance of bedding that fine ass. All knowing damn well everyone in this bar can hear all conversations from this loud ass table of women.

All of a sudden Ford's name is brought up. Now, I feel my buzz fading. My first thought is that they want to discuss the hottest bachelor in town, but no. I soon realize everyone is staring at the front of the bar, where Dawson and Ford take seats. I quickly turn around, but feel the gaze burn into my bare back.

"Ladies, calm down. It's just Ford and Dawson," I say to them with angst.

"Easy for you to say, Mar. One is your actual brother, and you basically grew up with Ford, so technically, he is family too," Harper spits out, followed by, "Again, tell me how the two of you slept under the same roof and you never tried to get with him?"

"Harper, shut up," I grumble, finishing off my drink, annoyed. "I am going to sit with my other friend."

Slowly getting up, I head back to my stool next to Duncan. After planting my ass, I raise my glass to the bartender. This time he looks over to Dawson and Ford before back at me. I slam the glass down on the counter, demanding my next one. "Just give her another one, Sal. I'll make sure she gets home okay." Then Ford turns to flash me a sexy smirk that causes me to melt a little.

"Already coming back for more conversation?" Duncan asks.

"Have you not paid attention to what I am dealing with over there? It is like an entire girls' weekend crammed into a few hours." He laughs, placing his hand on my upper thigh. The heat rises in my body. I honestly can't tell if it's from Duncan's touch, or Ford trying to set me on fire with the glare I am avoiding.

Sal so kindly brings me a drink with a look at Duncan. "Bring her a water, too, Sal."

"Aren't you being chivalrous?" I joke.

"I feel like that is what you deserve. Someone that will take care of you."

"Oh, do you now? Well, good observation. I'm guessing you want that someone to be you?" We lock eyes when I turn to face him.

"If you want me, I would like to be. To be that someone for you."

"You talking one night or for a while?" I may be drunk, but this man is sweet talking me out of my panties, and I need to get some wits about me. I could be the next Virgin Mary with my abstinence.

"I will take whatever you are willing to offer."

"Hmph, I might need some more whiskey before we continue down that road."

"As you wish. Sal, another round please." Duncan spins my stool so I am facing him, and my knees are locked between his long, bent legs. "Tell me, you drowning in a broken heart, sorrow, or just looking for a good time?" *Well that's the loaded question, isn't it?*

"No, not really. Good time, I guess. I haven't been with a guy in six years since one knocked me up and left. That guy was a douche canoe anyway. And the guy I grew up with and loving wants nothing to do with me. So no, no broken heart here. Just haven't been out as an adult in ages." I quickly come to the realization I blurted out more than I should have. "Hmmm, yeah, I probably just said way too much. Sorry."

He gives me an inane look, but says, "Okay, I'll go with that story." We begin to chat some more about his life here versus California. He really is nice to look at with his rugged look and hilarious. Some time goes by accompanied by more drinks, before there are two shadows looming over us. My eyes are already rolling before my brother speaks.

"Maren, you ready to head home?"

"Nope, I am not. Besides, I thought you were at the house tonight." Still refusing to look in their direction, I swirl the drink in my glass.

"No. Was kicked out for girl time."

I conjure up a laugh. "Sucks for you." I lift my cup to my lips, taking another swig of my drink.

"Alright, Mar, that's enough. Let's go," Dawson growls out.

Looking over at Duncan, I giggle. "Did you hear another voice? I see him looking back at the two giant men behind me.

"Are they both your brothers?"

"No!"

"Yes!" Ford and I exclaim at the same time.

Dawson shakes Duncan's hand. "Nice to see you again,

Duncan. I am her actual brother. And Ford is just a close family friend."

I slowly turn around in my seat to look at them only to make eye contact with Duncan on my way back to staring at the bar. Like a lightbulb went off in his head, he gasps. "Him?"

"Him, who?" I ask back.

"Shit," he murmurs then stands up, throwing cash on the bar. "I'll see around Maren. Good meeting you." I see him say something to Ford, then pats his shoulder all manly like before walking off with Dawson.

What the hell just happened?

I literally was ditched by a guy, and now Ford is sitting on his barstool. "Drink this water, Maren." I open my mouth to argue, but he stops me. "Maren, drink the damn water, then I am taking you out of here."

Just to piss him off, I chug my water quickly, only to wash it down with the remainder of my Jack and Coke. Without warning he picks me up, slinging me over his shoulder. Though my view is of Ford's incredible ass in jeans, blood is rushing quickly to my head, warning me a hangover is going to happen but not before I need to vomit. The brisk sea air hits my face as soon as we are outside, and Ford gently puts me down, swaying next to his truck.

"Is Dawson not coming?"

"No, he can't stand your ass right now. So, he is going to get Izzy. He trusts me to get you home." Pulling open his door, he lifts me into the seat and buckles me in. "Let me be clear, Maren. It has been a long while since I've been in a fight, but I will break my spell if I see another guy lay his hands on you." Letting out a sigh of defeat, I close my eyes. No energy to argue.

Ugh, damnit!

Barely a week and I'm causing a scene.

To be fair, I never really had a chance to cause a scene in my formative years.

Ford

MAREN IS LIT. I know better than to take her home like this, so I head over to the local Bed and Breakfast to get her a room. Knowing this will only lead to rumors to be had tomorrow, but let them.

The thing no one knows is, I am more than happy to have my name twisted up with Maren's. Gossip this past week has already been centered around Maren coming home, leaving her open for all scrutiny along with the town playing close attention to her and Alexis. This tells me it will only be a matter of time before the Adair family catches wind of their granddaughter in town. I look over to find Maren passed out against the window, taking gentle breaths through her slightly open mouth. I run in to get us checked in, requesting a cottage in the back with an ocean view.

Though the sky is dark with only stars twinkling, I can hear the waves lap against the shore with the white caps touching the night sky. Carrying Maren in from the truck to the bed, my body heats up as she rolls in closer to me. These cottages only have king size beds, leaving me lying next to her. I'm trying to give her a bit to see if she wakes up on her own, so I can give her some aspirin and water. Also, wanting to make her aware of where she is, so she does not panic in the morning when she wakes up.

Flipping on the TV with low volume, I begin to flip through, finding the Discovery Channel. My lucky night, a special on Pluto not being a planet. *This should be good and hold my interest for a bit.* I open up my Hershey bar I grabbed from earlier and relax.

An hour later, barely keeping my own eyes open, I hear Maren groan out. "Oh my god, I'm going to be sick." Knowing she has no idea where she is, I quickly jump out of bed, pick her up, and rush her to the bathroom. Placing her gently next to the toilet, I grab the hair-tie off her wrist to throw her hair up in.

Several minutes later, she looks close to passing out post-vomiting for several minutes. She murmurs, "Shower." I am slowly finding humor that Maren is so displaced, she has yet to acknowledge me, let alone where she is. Moving behind her, I turn the shower on, set the temperature, then turn around to find her stripping down.

This is no sexy striptease, as she is pretty wobbly and stuck in her shirt. I slowly walk over to her, helping peel her clothes off her body. *Fuck, she is stunning with her curves, perky breasts, and peach ass.* She almost slips when stepping into the shower. I pull her back out, demanding her to sit on the toilet.

"Stay, do not move." Walking into the next room, I grab an extra towel and washcloth. I'm half surprised she listened when I walk back in, seeing her still sitting there with her eyes half closed. Pulling my shirt off, then slipping out of my jeans, I hear a gasp. Her eyes pop open wide and lock on my body the whole time as I undress. "Come on, let's get you cleaned up." Leaving my boxers on, I carry her back into the shower. She doesn't even say a word, just uses my body as a leaning post while I wash her down.

Maren moans as my hands run up her thighs, her slick trimmed slit staring at me in the face. Tempting me to touch, to taste. A deep groan releases out of me when I stand back up away from temptation. Taking advantage of Maren when she is tanked is not ideal.

"Ford," she whispers from her red stained lips, placing her hand on my bare chest. Her touch scorches my skin with desire.

"Maren," I whisper back, tucking in a few loose strands from her messy bun I made.

"Ford, will you ever want me?" Her voice cracks as this question catches me off guard. People do say honesty is spoken in inebriated states. Maybe I can at least take advantage of this moment, to see how she truly feels about me.

"Why do you ask, Maren?" I counter back.

She closes her eyes and lets up a long, sad sigh. "Because, I have always wanted you. I never had the chance to tell you how much I loved you before my life went to shit."

Bingo! I have a chance.

But I'm startled, seeing tears are now streaming down her face. "Mar, you do not know how long I have wanted to hear those words from that satiable mouth of yours. My gorgeous Mar, words will only inadequately describe the need and want I have for you. But I refuse to take advantage of you in this state. Let's have this conversation tomorrow when we both feel better…okay?"

Maren nods her head yes as I carry her out of the shower. Sitting her on the edge of the bed, I dry her off and dress her back into her underwear and my undershirt. Handing her a bottle of water and Tylenol that I picked up from the kiosk at check-in, I walk back into the bathroom to dry myself off, then pull on my jeans.

By the time I walk back into the bedroom, Maren is passed out on the bed. I slowly slide the covers out from under to cover her up. I crawl up the other side of the bed next to her. Not long after I lie down, she snuggles close up to me, making my mind race in a million directions. Maren Hart just told me she has always wanted me. Maren Hart loves or loved me.

Fuck. What do I do with this information? Will she forget all about this night when she wakes up in the morning?

Morning comes too soon with the ringing of my phone. "Hello," I answer groggily.

"Man, you with Maren?"

"Yah, did your mom not tell you I checked her into a cottage last night?"

"No, she did. Just wasn't sure you were still with her. Her car is in the harbor parking lot. Can you bring her to meet me for breakfast, and then she can drive her car home? "

"Uh, sure. Everything okay?'

"Yep. Just want to have a few words with my sister."

"Okay, see you at the cafe in forty."

I roll back over to see Maren still peacefully sleeping. Not knowing how the rest of the day is going to go, I slide my arm over her, pulling her body closer to mine. I just need a few stolen minutes breathing in her scent and letting myself enjoy her body close to mine.

CHAPTER 10
WAKE UP
Maren

I WAKE up with a sense of unsureness. Slowly opening my eyes to the outside world, I am quick to discover that my room is not where I ended up last night. Then I feel a tug on my body, pulling me closer to another. With my eyes wide, my gaze slowly rolls up the legs covered in jeans to an adonis of a body to find Ford's eyes meeting mine. "Um...good morning," is all I can spit out.

With a glint of amusement in his eyes, he murmurs, "Good morning, Mar. Sleep good? How's your head?"

"Ummmm, I believe so and surprisingly fine." Now that I think about it, I slightly remember Ford handing me some pill last night and drinking water. "Thanks to you I guess," I say with a smirk.

He sits up slowly, with me still locked in his embrace. "Oh, so you remember last night?"

"It's sorta scattered at the moment. WHY? What did I say or do?" In this moment, the clarity of me in Ford's t-shirt, curled up in bed with him could only mean one thing, right? *I slept with Ford last night! Oh shit! And fuck, I don't even remeber it? How drunk was I?*

Sitting straight up and jumping out of bed, Ford catches me as the dizziness pushes me back down to the edge of the bed. Now he towers over me, but soon bends down face to face. "Relax,

Mar. We didn't do anything. Well, I did have to help you in the shower after you vomited your soul away, but that was it." His hands rest on top of my thighs as I try to digest that he saw me naked.

Oh for the love of Heavens. Ford saw me naked and washed me but did nothing else. Am I pissed he didn't make a move, or relieved that we didn't sleep together in my drunken stupor?

With my emotions firing throughout my brain, I place my head in my hands for a minute.

"Maren, you okay? Look at me?"

"I don't think I can, Ford. I am so embarrassed right now. Can you just leave so I can get myself together?"

"No can do. Your brother wants to meet you for breakfast and then you can drive your car back home."

"What on earth does he want this morning? Is it about last night?"

"Not real sure. Just playing delivery boy today."

"Huh. Speaking of last night, why are we here?" Ford's smirk turns into his serious scowl.

"Well, I knew you would not want Lexi to see you in this state, nor cause a fuss in the house. I would have brought you back to my place, but felt best you and Dawson not cross paths in the state and moods you two were in last night. This...this was the next best option," he says, looking around. "I was actually hoping to have a relaxing morning with you out on the front porch, but your brother has summoned."

Sigh. "Thank you, Ford. You always do your best looking out for me. Let me know how much I owe you for the room, and I guess I need to get ready." We both stand up together, mere inches from each other. His fingertips glide down my cheek, then he pushes some hair behind my ear. I can feel it in my bones he is about to say something to shift my world, but I am not capable of hearing any of it this morning with a headache trying to push its way through. "I probably should go get ready and brush my teeth."

Ford steps back for me to pass. "There is toothpaste and a toothbrush on the counter for you and your clothes are folded up on the shelf over there."

"You are the best, Ford Merrick," I spout, heading to get ready.

We pull into the parking lot across from the diner, where my car is parked. I jump out of Ford's truck to toss my shirt and shoes in, as I left his giant shirt on and just tied it at the back. I really did not want to be seen wearing the exact same clothes from last night. I also grabbed my spare pair of flip flops from my trunk. Ford is still sitting in his truck, so I walk over to his window that he has rolled down. "Are you not coming in?"

"Nah, I'm sure he wants to talk to you himself," Ford says, nodding toward the diner.

"Um, you know he is going to tell you word for motion later on, so you might as well witness this in person." He lets out a low laugh, knowing what I just said is true. "Besides, the least I can do is buy you breakfast after last night."

"I would have preferred breakfast by the beach, but I guess this will do." Ford turns off his truck and climbs out, now standing toe to toe with me. "Do you remember anything else from last night?" I quickly look down at my feet, because how can I tell him that on the ride over, the whole night came swooshing back into my mind. Like a wave of nausea taking over as I witnessed myself confessing my feelings for him, to him.

"Um, a little bit. I remember crying in the shower, so my apologies if that was totally awkward." He grabs my chin to make me look at him directly, though my eyes want to wander elsewhere under his intense stare.

"Nothing you do will ever be awkward. Nothing you do will make me think less of you."

"Ford, you have always been too good to me. I don't deserve to have you in my life."

While still holding my chin in one hand, he glides his fingers down my cheek slowly, slowly thumbing the corner of my lower lip. "Maren, I need to be honest and tell you something. Something I should have told you a long time ago." All I can do is hold my breath, my eyes glued to his with my heart beating like a drum in my chest.

Ring! Ring!

"Fuck!" Ford shouts, making me jump from the moment I thought we were having. "Hey."

"Hey yourself. You know I can see the two of you from the window, right." I can hear my brother's voice through Ford's phone, so I turn to look and wave at him. "What the hell are you two doing?" he asks.

While Ford stares at me, he answers back, "Nothing man, just talking. We are walking over now." He hangs up on my brother, pushing the phone in his pocket, jaw ticking, then placing his hand on the small of my back as we quickly pace over to the diner. Once in, we slide into the booth across from Dawson. He stares at both of us with angry intent.

I look over to Ford, who still has his jaw still ticking and all tense, then back over to my brother with a glare. "Can I help you, Dawson? Or did you drag me out of bed for shits and giggles this morning?"

"You weren't even in your bed, Maren. So don't give me that shit."

"Schmantics!" I love my brother, but lord can he make my blood boil like no other. "Dawson, you summoned me here," I spout as the waitress comes by to take our orders. Dawson and Ford seem to order half the menu, while I just order a simple scramble bowl and black coffee.

Once she leaves, Dawson finally decides to speak. "I am ready to give you my two cents." All I can do is gawk at him. Ford carefully places his hand on my thigh and squeezes, letting me know he has my back and to stay strong. Reminding me to breathe as I brace myself for my brother's wrath. "Maren, I love you but hell. That was some fucked up shit you did. Honestly, I am past the how's and why. Thankfully, you and Lexi are back home now, but you need to know I'm not sure I can forgive and forget like Mom and Dad have. I had to pick up the pieces while you were gone. Ford and I both had to guide them through the loss of you. Put our own lives on hold, wondering when Hart's prized daughter would return. And then you come home, acting like you never left and being a bitch to my girlfriend, soon to be fiancé."

Ford moves quickly out of the corner of my eye, but I see Dawson raise his hand in the air to him. "Shut up, Ford. You are not coming to her aide this time. So damn over the two of you, always ganging up on me. That is one thing I have not missed while you were gone."

Fuck me and my life. Is this really happening right now, in the middle of the diner? Dawson seems to think he is controlling his hushed harsh voice, but from the looks of those around us, he is not.

In the lowest whisper I can muster, I spit, "Fuck you, Dawson, and the magic carpet you rode in on. I have not come back acting like all is fine in the world. But I can act like everything is okay in front of my daughter. I can try to help her and myself settle into this new life for us. I can try and appease Mom and Dad right now, for all the wrong I have done to them. No one asked you or Ford to pick up any slack for me." I grit my teeth, wishing I could just scream and yell at him, but I don't want to cause an even bigger scene. "But thank you for being there for OUR parents and for each other. Don't think for a minute I have had it easy over the last several years, because I've been through hell. Still there to be quite honest. As for Izzy, I have been nothing but nice and myself. Excuse me for not rolling out the red carpet for our introductions. Or concealing my resting bitch face to be fake. She was literally thrown at me after you all showed up out of nowhere for church, then dealing with a kid bullying my daughter over who her biological father is, on top of a slew of other emotions."

Grabbing my keys and phone off the table, ready to leave, I stand from my seat. "You wanna stay pissed off at me over the last six years, by all means, be my fucking guest. I'm pretty pissed off at myself too. But don't come at me like you are so damn high and mighty with all your money, snotty girlfriend, and fancy house." Looking over at Ford, I shoot him a glare. "You have anything to say?" His eyes widen, and he opens his mouth like he is about to speak. "Fuck off, both of you!"

I storm out of the diner, running across the street, then jump in my car. I see Ford run out of the diner toward me, but I take off. I am over everyone and their adverse emotions today.

Ford

AFTER MAREN DROVE OFF, I was tempted to hop in my truck and chase after her, fear rolling through me as if she was going to leave again. I also know, at this moment, I need to be the guy my best friend needs, so I walk back in and sit across from Dawson. Food is already sitting on the table, and I have the waitress box up Maren's to take to her after. "Well, that couldn't have gone any better. Don't you think?" I say, looking at a bewildered Dawson.

"Shut the hell up, man. Thanks for the backing."

"That was not my battle, man. That's some shit you two need to work out on your own and probably not in public next time."

"Yah, don't I know it. I picked this spot for neutral ground, so it wouldn't turn out like that. Shit! She sat down with that princess bitch face, and I lost it. Her attitude, no help at all."

I start laughing. "D, you know good and well your sister is far from acting like a spoiled princess. She may look like one and deserve to be treated like one, but we know she is far from being one."

"You always have her damn back," Dawson states, as he shoves a fork full of pancakes in his mouth.

"No, I do not. I've had your back plenty over the years. But geez, man, cut her some slack. While we have been living it up and gallivanting around the world, she has been a single mom trying to make a life for themselves. It could not have been easy to come back home after being gone."

"It's her own damn fault, Ford. She made that choice."

"Agree. That she did. But she is home now, trying to make things right. So let her find her footing and try. And when has Mar ever been over the top with any girl you brought home? I thought she treated Izzy pretty fair compared to most."

He sighs, dropping his fork on the plate. "Izzy is different. I'm getting ready to propose and make her part of the family. Izzy thinks Maren hates her."

"Again, Maren just got back into town. She does not know Izzy. Izzy didn't grow up with us to know Maren and how she works. Let alone, you are just springing this news on everyone you are getting ready to propose. Why haven't you mentioned a word to me?"

"I don't know, man. Having Lexi around makes me want to have babies. And I love Izzy. I just feel that it's time for the next step. It has been three years, and we are both older, wiser, stable."

"Well, congrats, man. I'm happy for you. You just need to tell Izzy how Maren works and give Maren some time. She will come around."

"Sure. Enough drama for today. We have that conference at two today. Any plans until then?"

"I'm going to drop this food off at the house, then head home to finish those analytical files. Don't forget, Dad wants us down at the dock by five tonight to help with the unloading. Those boys are coming in from a week out at sea. Plus, we need to start prepping for the possible impending hurricane"

"Okay. We can head over after the meeting. I'm going to head out and check in on the Meyers account." We both throw some money on the table and walk out. Going separate directions. Being in the destructive path of a hurricane is the furthest from my mind right now. Dawson needing to chill over Maren right now, and me needing Maren not to be pissed at me also. Hell, it's only nine-thirty in the morning.

CHAPTER 11
SCRAMBLED
Maren

Thankfully, I walked into a quiet house with no one to witness my tear-stained cheeks and wind-tousled hair. Mom had called me on my way home, stating she was taking Lexi down to the docks to help Dad out this morning, so I have the house to myself for the time being.

I strip out of Ford's t-shirt, only to find myself holding it to my nose, breathing in his leather brandy scent. Then, just as quickly, finding myself angry with him for the whiplash of emotions and being part of the ambush this morning. I throw his shirt down on the floor with the rest of my clothes, then jump into the scalding hot shower.

The hot water burning my skin is exactly what I need this morning. Letting the water pour over me, my mind reverts back to this morning with my brother. *What an asshat.* I'll admit I was a bitch, but he started it. The only thing I may apologize for is calling his girlfriend snobby. I know Izzy isn't, as I actually really like her, and they seem really happy together. Let alone, he mentioned soon-to-be fiancé, so she must be worth keeping around. *Fine, I will apologize for the comment against her, but nothing else.*

Now, what about Ford? He has been in my bubble since I got home. Which is not unusual based on how close we were growing up, but this is different. Not that we are not adults now, and Dawson is not being a jokester, but neither is Ford. Other than the punch in the arm on the first day and a few jokes here and there, he has been different. There is an intensity about him I can't seem to read. Not to mention the extra closeness because if he looks at me with those darkening amber eyes and tempting lips one more time, while standing a mere inch away from me, it will be me losing myself completely.

In those last few times, I could have sworn he was going to kiss me. Just like in the pool all those years ago. *Surely not, though, right?* He is Ford and I am Maren. He is my brother's best friend. He is practically family. Most people in this town call him my brother. Women in this town and I am sure many others want a piece of Ford.

Ford is apparently a billionaire, where I am a single, jobless mother living at home with her parents. *Yeah, there is no way he wants anything to do with me. Regardless of what my mother has mentioned either.* He just missed me because we were best friends too many moons ago. Now maybe it is just lust or wanting to sate some part of sleeping with a mom. *Who the hell knows at this point! Ugh.* My mind is literally all over the place. I need to go take a nap.

Once out of the shower with my bright red skin, I throw on my sweatpants and of course Ford's shirt. No one is here to bear witness to what I came home in, let alone it belonging to Ford. After towel drying my hair, I make two braids, set my alarm, and curl up in bed. My eyelids are growing heavier, while my body and mind slip into a deep sleep.

Ford

ONCE I LEFT THE DINER, I called Madre to see if Maren was out with them on the docks or at home. I had her breakfast and wanted to make sure she ate something after last night. She let me know Maren was going home and would be coming out later in the evening to help with the rest of us. I pulled into their driveway, taking a deep breath as to how to approach her after the shit show at the diner.

Grabbing the bag of food and her coffee, I walk up and into the house, pausing to hear her or something. *Nothing.* Making my way up the stairs, I can still feel the steam rolling out of the bathroom so she must have taken a shower and is now in her room. *Do I barge in accidentally or knock?* By the time I get to her door, I take a quick listen but hear nothing.

With a lite knock while opening the door, I whisper, "Maren." Once all the way in, I see her curled up in her bed. *God, she is beautiful. Like a sleeping angel.* I snap a quick picture before heading over next to her only to notice she is still in my shirt with PINK written across her sweatpants, dragging my attention to her ass. I take another picture just to have it for later. *Not a creeper or a stalker at all.* Placing her items on the nightstand, I try to coax her out of sleep. It takes a few tries and me tickling her feet before she shoots up in fear.

"You are so dead!" is shouted at me.

Her words only cause me to chuckle hard. "I would like to see you try, Mar. Really."

Rubbing her eyes and yawning, she grumbles, "What are you doing here? Wait, I'm not currently talking to you, remember?"

"No, I don't remember you saying you were not talking to me. You just seemed mad and not talking to your brother." She lets out a pissed-off moan, making my dick twitch. It was already alert when it caught her vanilla jasmine scent and then saw her lying there. "Hey, I brought your breakfast, you need to eat."

"Look at you being my knight in armor," she snorts with an eye roll.

"I do what I can. Now sit up and eat, before I force-feed you."

"You wouldn't," she grits through her teeth as she sits up.

"Try me. I dare you." My mind is pleading that she does. Maren gives me a sideways glance as she reaches for her carton of food. A look that tells me she is thinking about daring me but unsure if she should. She licks her lips staring at her food, then comes back at me with hooded eyes. I can feel the heat radiating off her body as I inch closer to her on the bed. My body aching to have her closer, to touch her skin. A slight giggle slips from her lips, and I lose all control.

A grunt releases from me as I throw her food carton back on the table, straddling her with my body, while locking her wrists in my hand above her head against her headboard.

What the hell has come over me?

It's like a possessive monster has taken over my need for her. My lust and longing for her. Knowing my face is stern looking down at her, all she does is smile back up at me. A tease that ignites my insides as if it's a parched forest of brittle trees. "Maren," I groan. Her eyes stay locked on mine as her tongue parts her lips to slick them up for me. I dive in, kissing her like I'll die without her air. Her mouth opens for our tongues to tangle together. My hand loosens around her wrists, guiding it slowly down her arm, gently down her neck and back until I reach her ass. I clench her peach-ness in my hand, and it's perfect.

She is perfect.

Maren's arms wind around my neck, and her hand tugs at my hair tightly. Wanting more, us both needing more. I'm quickly losing touch with reality. That the girl I have been in love with all this time is underneath me. Giving the impression she wants *this*, as much as I do. Regardless, dream or reality, my mouth and tongue are determined to taste every single millimeter of her. Sliding my tongue down her neck, I suck her skin just below her ear. My hand slowly glides up her bare stomach under my t-shirt she is still wearing until I feel her naked breast under my palm. An elated moan slips out of her when I gently tug and pinch her nipple with my fingers, grinding my hard cock against her center.

"Ford," she whispers. Before she can say another word, unable to allow her to ruin this moment between us, I lean back in, devouring her mouth. Silencing her words to breathless moans, her hands grip my shirt in her fists.

"Hello, Maren? We're home." Maren pulls back, then pushes me away quickly, jumping out of bed.

"Mom and Lexi are home. Um...I..I.. I can't even think right now. What just happened? Wait, don't answer that."

"Maren, calm down. We do need to talk at some point. But I can tell you, that was..."

"Hey, Mommy!" Lexi runs in to give Maren a giant hug, giving me a second to adjust my hard self, before assessing the fact that I am in her mom's room, standing next to her. "Hi, Uncle Ford. What are you two doing?"

I bend down to give her a hug. "Just talking about the game plan for this evening and all the things we are going to teach you when the boats come in. You up to the task?"

"I'm ready, Captain!" she shouts out and salutes me, making me chuckle.

"Oh, there you are, Lexi. I didn't know where you went off to." Mom steps in the room now, assessing the situation. "Lexi, come help me pack up lunch and snacks for later. We will leave you two to it." As she backs out of the room, she sends us a wink. I know Madre knows my feelings for Maren.

We talked years ago, not long after Maren took off. I was having a hard time coping, losing myself in bourbon. Having meaningless rough demanding sex. The only things I felt I could control was how much I could drink and women in the bedroom. I had already lost my mom, then my dad, followed by Maren disappearing. Everything else in my life was going wonderfully, but when Maren left, it's like she shattered my heart and took my soul.

Once the door closes, I look over to Maren, who looks five shades whiter than her usual tan self. I stand directly in front of her and reach out to gently cup her cheek, my thumb grazing the corner of her mouth. "Maren, you okay? Blink twice if you are?" Before I know it, she slams her fist into my chest. Not that her tiny fist did much to me, but I see how quickly she regrets her decision, holding her hand close to her now. "What was that for?" I ask, pulling her hand up to my mouth and kissing each knuckle one by one softly.

Her eyes close with a soft moan, but then open quickly as she yanks her hand away. "Ford, we can't?"

"What do you mean we can't? You mean right now or ever? Because we just did and could do it again." She looks worried, scared almost.

Maren begins to turn the ring on her finger as if not knowing what to say. "I...I don't know, Ford. This is just a lot, and I can't afford to be broken into pieces again. Plus, I have Lexi to think about. I'm not even sure what just happened or what you are expecting out of me."

I need to control my emotions because they are boiling up into hurt and anger right now. The last person I want to let them loose on is her.

"Maren, the only thing I expect is you just being you." Feeling defeated that she regrets every second of our sudden moment together, I mutter, "I need to head home and prep for a call. See you at the docks later. And when you are ready to have a conversation about what happened, let me know." I bend down to kiss her on the forehead, then walk out of the room and out of the house.

CHAPTER 12
DOCK TIME
Maren

After Ford left and I calmed my body down enough to function like a human, I flew downstairs to see my mom and Lexi. All the while they were packing up, I picked the snacks to shovel in my face. I was famished. The breakfast Ford brought over never landed on my table but the floor instead during that *moment*. Mom slapped my hand a few times because I kept stealing out of the containers she was packing.

"Lexi baby, why don't you head upstairs to get washed up and clothes changed. Ones that you don't care to mess up."

"Okay Glam-ma," she squeals as she skips away.

Mom looks over at me, raising a brow. "So, did we interrupt something?"

I plop onto the bar stool, leaning over so my face is against the marble. I mumble out, "Are we really about to have this conversation?"

"Yes, I believe we are." I can tell she is smirking just by the tone of her voice.

Sitting up on my elbows, I look back over to her. "He kissed me. Like swoon-worthy kissed me." She shrieks, and I have to tell her to keep it down before Lexi comes running down here being nosy.

"I don't know, Mom. I completely freaked out on him. He

could do so much better than me. I'm not even sure if he wants a relationship with me or just thinks I might be easy." She gives me a harsh look. "I know, that's harsh to say, and I'm not easy nor do I think Ford is like that. But Mom, it's only been a couple of weeks since I've been home, and I feel like I have turned his whole life upside already. He comes to my need even when I don't ask. Same for Lexi. He shows up unexpectedly, like constantly. I don't want him to feel obligated to be any more than he has all my life if he doesn't want to. He is some fancy, sexy bachelor APP billionaire now. I'm just a poor, single mom. Not that I have changed much beside my mini me, but I'm sure he has. It's been six years and even then, him and Dawson were gone at college most of the time." I pound my head back on the marble countertop.

"Oh, my sweet girl," she whispers as she runs her fingers through my hair for support. "The only advice I am going to give is this. Trust your heart and your instincts. Don't make decisions for Ford. He is his own person who is capable of making decisions without your help. I promise all will turn out the way it should be and that it will make everyone happy."

"Sure," I scoff as I sit up and lean into her. "I missed you so much. I missed this."

"Me too, baby girl, me too." She gives me a hug, then continues packing. "Want to tell me if I am embarking on World War three bringing you and Dawson together today?"

"Ha, he cried to you, didn't he?" I say, laughing.

She chuckles back, "I wouldn't say he was crying but pretty upset about how it went down."

"Well, he was being really rude and set me off. He thinks I had it so easy while being gone and so easy now. I hate how I left and why I left, but I can't change any of that. Nor can take away the pain I caused everyone. Saying sorry is not enough, I know that. But he thinks he has me all figured out as an awful person and untrustworthy. Hell, maybe I am."

"No, and I had my own words for Dawson because Ford told

me what happened first." I roll my eyes on Ford being as much of a momma's boy as Dawson. "You know Dawson, he is a hard one to crack and thinks everything is black and white. Where you see all the gray in between along with all the colors surrounding an issue. The two of you are just going to have to work it out. I told Ford to stay out of it, unless physical harm was going to occur." She laughs like that is not a possibility. I on the other hand have wanted to slap or strangle my brother on numerous occasions. We both turn as we hear Alexis running down the stairs. "Well, we can finish chatting later. Go get ready, and we will head out and have lunch with Dad. Your new dock boots are in the mud room, so grab those on your way out."

"Thanks. Give me ten." Sliding out of the stool, I smile at Lexi, noticing a large bruise on her forearm. "Alexis, what on earth did you do, sweetie?" Bending down to her level, I examine the deep purple and black coloring that is at least three inches wide if not as long.

Mom comes running over to inspect as well. "I never saw her fall, and she hasn't cried about anything."

Slightly pressing on it, I ask, "Does this hurt?" Lexi shakes her head no. She has a smile on her face, so I decide to let it go. "Alright, well just be careful out on the boats and docks. Let me know if it starts bothering you, okay?"

"Okay, Mommy, but I'm fine, really. Oh, can we call Aunt Darcy?" Darcy and I have been texting back and forth since we arrived home but have not had a moment to converse. I let Lexi take my phone and facetime.

Darcy and Jim pop up on the screen, wide smiles on their faces. "Hello, babydoll! What are you up to?"

"About to go help at the docks. Ooooo Auntie, I know the secret of who my daddy is." I see Darcy's eyes go wide through the phone. My palm running down my face in exasperation, I wonder where in the hell this comes from. We talked about him a few nights ago, but I thought it was a done deal.

Peeking my head over Lexi's, I roll my eyes. "Oh you know.

Just some little boy calling our little one a liar because who she said her daddy was. Because said little girl knows everything." Darcy and Jim laugh, knowing all too well how quickly Lexi picks up on things she hears, sees, and feels.

"Wow, well despite how that conversation went, we miss you both so much. The kids are going to be bummed they missed your call. We shipped them down to the islands with my parents for the remainder of summer. They will be back by the end of the week."

"That seems like a great way to end the summer. I forgot school starts next week for them. Lexi gets to wait until after Labor Day," I speak.

"Are y'all prepared for the hurricane? Do you need to come here?"

Lexi speaks up. "We are good, Auntie. Mommy says we have a plan. The fisherman said it won't hit us. We will just get a lot of rain and some wind. Dawson and Ford will help us to stay safe and will be staying with us for a few days once it comes."

"What do you mean they are staying with us? I quickly ask. News to me."

"Mommy, did you already forget? Silly mommy. Ford said once the thing moves closer to shore, they will come over, and we can all camp out cause the power is going to go out."

"Got it," I say, trying to hide my anxiety of all of us being in the same house together, and my thoughts flood my mind with scenarios.

Darcy knowing all too well how things work here, she giggles. "So how is your Uncle Dawson and Ford?" Darcy asks Lexi.

"Great. Uncle Dawson is funny and his girlfriend knows all the princesses so she is fun to hang out with. Uncle Ford is always around when not traveling, helping out Mommy or Glam-ma and Papa. I've taught him all the princesses too!"

"Oh, so Uncle Ford is always around, huh?" she asks, giving a wink. I roll my eyes. "That sounds amazing, babydoll. We are so happy you are settling in." I let Lexi go on about her life here and let them know Mr. Pickles is doing well, too. She even brings him up to the camera. Everyone blows kisses to each other through the phone, with Darcy stating she will text me later when she has a date of her parents' return.

After hanging up the phone, I kiss Lexi on the head before I excuse myself to get ready.

It's about six thirty in the evening, and I can't remember the last time I pushed my body through such labor-intensive work. Come to think of it, it was probably my last summer here. Though I make a point to run every day, my muscles are puny compared to what they once were.

All the tourists are back from their fishing trips, so we helped them unload their catches. Helped those that wanted to clean and gut their catch so they could cook them later. My dad makes the experience a whole thing about learning the process and being able to cook and eat what you fished. I'm surprised I was still able to slice through the fish so cleanly. Maybe my dad is right, it's like learning to ride a bike. You never really forget the "how to." Though I am pretty certain if you were to put me on a bike right now, I would topple over.

Ford hasn't said much to me, though, I feel the stares and glares. He and Dawson have Alexis helping with cleaning and rinsing down the boats as we unload them and refuel for the next day's adventures. Dad is thinking we may be able to get another day or two in before the Gail winds become impossible to ignore and no longer safe to be out on the water. Taking a quick break, I watch the guys teach Lexi knot tying. I am sure someone will soon be tied up. It is just a matter of who and when at this point.

By the time we finished with the fishing charters, the commercial fisherman, or as I used to call a few of them,

Crabmen, began pushing inward to the docks. Typically, their arrival times would be spread out through the day or even days, but we have a hurricane heading in our direction, spinning out in the Atlantic.

Hurricane Ophelia is ripping the seas with her category four outburst and is predicted to get even stronger before landfall. All we can do is hope she deviates from her current path over the next several days. Best case, she doesn't slam the east coast at all and spins the other direction. Worst case, she slams right into the upper North Carolina Coast, with us receiving a heavy blow by her. Therefore, the crews set out last week for a long haul to return with as much as they could. Knowing they would only be able to fish or crab within the Inlets or canals for a while.

I see a familiar boat pull in first. The *MaryAnn*. I pull two dollies down the dock so we can stack the containers and roll them up for the trucks to deliver to the warehouses to be sorted. The crew shouts at friends and family, even a few welcoming me home. My dad and the guys talk shop with the Captain over the catches and how the seas are looking. Along with any predictions, because if you live in a small sea town with fishermen, they are the best weatherman to have.

Sometime later, after all was unloaded, the boat was scrubbed down and rinsed with all sails and knacks tied and put away. The Captain moved the boat over to his spot to tie down. The rest of the crew headed up to the pier to meet loved ones and home. Many stopped by to give me a hug or high hive to officially welcome me back home. It seems my return has even traveled through the seas.

The *Sinna-Star* pulls in next. I remember this being Ned's boat, but I also know his nephew was not out with them because he was at the bar the other night.

"Coming, I'm coming." I hear shouting up by the restaurant entrance. As if I spoke him in to existence, I turn to see Duncan running down the planks toward us. "Well if you are not a beautiful sight to see right now, Maren." I giggle because I bet this man can talk and smolder his way into anyone's panties.

"Hey, Duncan. How's it going?"

"Much better now I get a view with you in it."

"Ha," I manage to get out. "To the man that left me at the bar last night with my brother and friend."

"Woah there. Now, I knew you were safe in their hands, and I was not about to compete with Mister Merrick over there or get on either one of their bad sides. Rumor has it, they know people."

"They know people?" I blurt out, then start laughing. "They are not part of the fishermen mafia, Duncan. Oh, I just met you and feel like I need to keep you around for humor."

"You can request my presence anytime, Maren. You have my number."

"As do you. I do appreciate a little bit of chivalry from a man. So, keep that in mind, Duncan."

He steps up to me then places a gentle kiss on my cheek. "I did tell Merrick that if he didn't claim you soon, I would." I step back in shock, mouth agape, staring at him. "Wait for me after this unloading, and we will chat some more." This guy can make a pig's cheeks rosy. I nod back at him, still in shock, as he runs off to jump on the boat.

"By all the shrimp, is that the Maren Hart I see?" I turn my attention to Ned wheeling his way down the dock.

"Hi, Ned," I murmur, bending down to give him a hug and kiss his cheek.

"Rumor had it you were back. Just hadn't seen you yet."

"You didn't miss much, I promise. I try to stay hidden as much as possible."

"Now, I don't believe that. You had Duncan all beside himself last night when he came over to check on me. Could not stop talking about how pretty you were and how he enjoyed your laugh."

"Don't be talking trash about me, old man!" Duncan yells from the boat.

Ned cracks up laughing and shouts back, "Don't worry! I'll talk you up sweet, so she takes a chance on you."

"You two need to hush. I'm just back in town, not looking for any romance."

"Unless it's that Ford over there glaring this way." I turn to find Ford wrapping a rope up and around his forearm as Dawson pulls out the knots. I glare back to see if he notices. I realize he does when he yanks on the rope hard enough, about pulling Dawson overboard.

"What the hell, man?" Dawson yelps out. Lexi laughs at the two of them, then Ford hangs the rope up on a hook to begin his march over.

"I will see you later, Maren. I need to go supervise these ruffians."

"Okay, bye, Ned." Great, now I'm left here alone for whatever wrath is coming my way.

Ford

I'VE SPENT the last several hours watching Maren in those damn short ass shorts and tight tank top, being hot as hell as she guts fish, stacks containers, deals with blood, and talks shit with deckhands like it's just a regular day for her. To top it off, every man around is ogling at her like she is a piece of meat. Even a few of the women caught a few glances. Then fucking Duncan shows up and starts flirting with her, making her laugh and smile. I think she might have even blushed in his presence.

All while, I'm over here trying not rip my arm off with this rope every time the waves crash into us, and Dawson holds on to the other end in the boat for dear life. *Now why in the hell are those two staring at me?* I need to go talk to her before I go insane.

"Oh shit, sorry, D. You good?" Dawson flicks me the bird as I almost just pulled him overboard. "Taking a break!" I shout over my shoulder as I head to Maren and Ned. *Perfect, Ned is leaving.* Even with the smell of the sea, guts of glory and fish, I can only smell her once I'm close enough. To me, that is way better than the fresh air right now.

"Hey, can you take a break to talk?" Her eyes are intense when she looks up at me under the light post.

"Sure, I just need to bring these last two dollies up there. Want to grab that one?" She nods her head behind her. I walk and grab the handle and follow her lead. Once loaded into the truck, we walk over to the outdoor sink to wash our hands and arms. I soon pull her around the corner where no one can see us from the docks and the windows on the restaurant are too high.

Placing my hands on her hips, I pull her closer to my body. "Have you thought about this morning and if you want to talk?" I get a nod that I barely notice because it's fairly dark where we are standing. She loops her fingers into my belt loops, tugging me a little closer.

"We should definitely talk. Put everything on the table to see if we land on the same book."

"We are in the same book, Maren, I think I am just several chapters ahead of you."

"Well that might just be the problem then, don't you think? We need to do some research and review then," she states as her right hand glides up my abs to my chest. Stopping right above my heart. My body feels as though tremors have taken over on the inside, and my cock is at full stance. I lean in to kiss her as I thrust my hips toward her. Switching places, so now her back is against the wall, she lets out a soft gasp as I hike her leg up over my hip to grind against her. "What happened to talking?" she asks breathily.

"We can talk later, right now, I just have the urge to feel you against me. Even if it's only for a few minutes. Kiss me, Maren. I'm begging you to."

With that, she laces her fingers through my hair, pulling my mouth down to hers. Our tongues entwine like fire and ice as an explosion goes off between us. There is no way she is not reciprocating the same tingles as I am right now.

"You are playing with fire right now, Ford," she whispers in my ear. Before I can even respond, I hear Dawson calling my name and getting closer. I quickly pull away, leaving Maren breathless and steadying herself against the building as I lean against the porch railing several feet from her.

"Dude, did you not hear me hollering for you?"

"No man, sorry." Dawson eyes Maren, and then his eyes shoot back to me. "What are you two doing over here?"

She speaks up first, "Just taking a break and talking. He helped me get the last of the containers loaded for the boat."

He nods his head like what other reason would the two of us have to be hidden away over here. "Okay. Well, the last boat just came in, and Maren, I think Mom wants you to take Alexis home to wash up and bed. She passed out in Dad's office."

"On it," she says as if she is about to walk away and follow Dawson. I'm about to reach for her hand to pull her back, but Dawson turns back around.

"Are you seriously going to go on a date with Duncan?" he asks Maren.

She freezes in her footsteps. "Um, I don't know, Dawson. He seems nice enough, but I'm not really looking for romance right now. Why does it matter?"

"Just need to know if Ford and I need to threaten him now or later." *What the fuck?* I think to myself. *What gave him that impression?*

"Jesus, you two," she snaps and walks angrily off. Dawson just shrugs his shoulders at me like nothing new. Dawson is going to keep me on Mar's hit list if he doesn't knock this shit out. I've already decided I will not approach him until I have a better idea of what Maren and I are or could be.

Maren

I DROVE Mom's car home to get Lexi to bed. Of course, Ford offered, but I knew they needed him to finish. Luckily, Lexi woke up as I carried her into the house and upstairs.

"Hey, sleepy head, we need to get you washed up because you smell like a fish."

"That's so gross," she groaned.

"Want to take a shower or bath?"

"Um, bath. I don't have the energy to stand up."

"Okay, you want some help?"

"Yes, please."

"Alright, go get in and I'll be there in a few minutes. Let me at least get out of these clothes covered in fish guts. Remember, not too much water."

"Okay, Mommy."

As she enters the bathroom in her room, leaving the door open like she is supposed to, I rush into my room, stripping off my clothes and bag them in the trash. There will be no getting that smell or blood stains out. I throw my hair up in a messy bun, lotion myself up to smell decent until I can take a shower myself, and throw my sweatpants with a t-shirt back on. All under five minutes. Still got the mom rush going strong.

Jogging back to Lexis' room, I pull the shower curtain back as

I approach, ready to tickle her when I spot a large purple bruise on her lower back. "Lexi baby, did you fall against the boat or something?"

"No, Mommy. Uncle Dawson and Uncle Ford were very careful with me, and I never fell once." Alarm bells are ringing in my head that something is off. Am I really rushing to the emergency room over a couple of bruises, though? I can call the doctor in the morning to get her in for an appointment. We need to do that anyway to establish care for her and transfer records over from Nashville.

"Okay, sweetie, I believe you. Just be careful, okay?"

"Yes, Mommy." I help her finish scrubbing up with lots of bubbles, wash her hair under the faucet, and rinse off. While the water is draining, I have her stand up and slowly turn in her spot so I can do a look over her body. No other marks or bruising other than the two I have already found and the gash on her knee from falling off her bike a few days ago. Wrapping her in a towel to pull her out of the tub, I let her dry off and put her PJs on.

"Let's go get you in bed, and I'll blow dry your hair there." She happily follows, sitting cross legged on her bed in front of me as I begin to brush and try her long beautiful hair. All the while, she tells me all the things she learned today along with how much fun she had with yawns in between.

Twenty minutes later, she is tucked in, sleeping away as I hold her tight in my arms.

CHAPTER 13
LIKE A HURRICANE
Maren

With the impending hurricane, businesses are starting to shut down for the remainder of the week, allowing those to prepare and hunker down. She has grown from a Cat 3 to a very large Cat 4 in the past several days. Our fishermen are still convinced we won't get hit head on but will still be in the path of havoc as she moves closer to landfall.

Even the doctor's office is only taking high-need cases and follow ups. That it would be next week before Dr. Carlton could see Lexi, pending power is back on and lack of disastrous flooding. In the meantime, they told me to monitor her, and if I felt the bruising became an emergency to take her inland to the hospital. The nurse chalked it up to her being a young kid and playing hard. I didn't disagree with her but wanted to be on the optimistic side of this, so I would just monitor her until we could get in next week.

Though it may only be three weeks since being back home, it feels like months have gone by. We are settled, and my parents make no fuss about dwelling on the past. Only that we are here now and what the future holds. School is only a couple of weeks away at this point, so Mom already has us booked to go school shopping next week at the Bay area mall that is a ferry over. I've gone ahead and ordered several clothes and school supplies for myself online for student teaching and a few clothes for Lexi that I know she will like. I have my savings keeping me afloat right now, while my parents refuse to let me help with bills. I randomly show up with groceries and have managed to cook a few meals.

At first, Mom would protest, but now, we have a schedule of who cooks when, and all ingredients must be turned in on Mondays before grocery Tuesday. Yep, we are back to structure. Which Lexi enjoys and strives for in all parts of her life, just as my mom does.

Ford shows up at the house or wherever I am every chance he gets. I joke that he has a tracker on me. He has yet to admit or deny it. I am just greeted with a sly smile when I mention it. There have been no more intimate moments recently, which probably is for the best at this point.

When he isn't stalking me, he is traveling to New York and California a day or two at a time. When he finds me in public, he always greets me with a kiss on the cheek, and if Lexi is around, he props her on his shoulders while hanging out during our errands. Even has popped up at two more girl outings with Dawson and hung out at the bar. I limit myself to three drinks now and then, only water. *Lesson learned!*

If we are at the house, we have stolen moments of our gazes locking or light touching on the arm or leg as we pass each other by. Even in the few moments of quiet we have gained just to talk; they are short lived. He is always up for hanging out with Lexi in whatever she is doing. I love catching them curled up on the couch together, watching *Sofia the First* or princess movies. Ford now seems to have all knowledge of princesses and the story plots.

I try not to get myself revved up about those two being so close. Ford has always been a staple of my life. At the end of the day, he is part of this family; my parents are his parents at this point in every sense. They wanted to adopt Ford when he was a teenager, but he denied them as he felt he would be betraying his mom. So, as far as legality's go, my parents were and are legal guardians for him.

Now, it's Saturday, and despite the looming Hurricane Ophelia, we are preparing for the bake sale; for little Pakston must still go on. Rain or shine, the community will make the best of it tomorrow. Another reason why I love this small town and its hosts.

The remainder of the week has been spent preparing businesses and elderly homes for the incoming storm. No one wants to leave until we know for sure where Ophelia might hit. Still, per our town's fishermen, the census says we will be on the outskirts as she slams in below us, closer to Wilmington. Ford and Dawson live right off the beach, so once their house was boarded up, they came over to help us, as we are just a few blocks back from them. Not much was said between the two of us, but there was also not any alone time to speak either.

On the bright side, the Adair's decided to stay on the islands to wait out the hurricane. They hired a company to handle all the logistics of preparing their house and rental properties for the storm.

Around four in the evening, I am spent from baking cookies, brownies, and candies all day. Exhaustion feels in my mind and body, knowing tomorrow is round two. Lexi even got in the action of decorating with sprinkles. She is also covered in flour from head to toe.

"Hey, angel, can you take these over to Dawson and Ford?" I look over to see a giant bag filled to the rim with a variety of cookies, a red velvet cake, and a homemade pizza casserole and taco casserole.

"Mom, why are these going to the guys? We did not just bake all day for them, did we?"

"Oh no, honey, but I always make extra for them to have, along with a few casseroles. You know neither one of them cook."

"Why don't you just make them go to the fundraiser and spend their money?"

She laughs. "You really have been gone way too long, angel. The boys always match and double the raised amount. Also, they would buy the table out and not share with anyone if they do not have their personal stash."

Nodding my head as I understand now, I murmur, "Sure, Mom, I will run this over."

"Perfect, I already texted you the address. I will get Lexi cleaned up before dinner. So don't worry about her."

"Okay." Turning to hug Lexi goodbye, she shoves another cookie into her mouth. All I do is laugh and whisper "good luck" to mom. Grabbing the bag and casseroles, I head out.

Once I looked at the address, I knew exactly where their house was. To say I'm shocked that they bought out the McIntyre's wrap around porch beach house is in understatement. It is a weird setup of three floors. Wide as it is tall that includes eight bedrooms throughout the whole house, and a pool in front with an ocean view.

From what I remember, the house was a subtle blue, covered with wide open windows throughout the front. This makes me more curious as to why they decided on this one and curious as to why the McIntyre's moved. They have lived here all their lives; kids went to school with the guys and the year after. There were always parties here and bonfires nearby. Parents welcomed all of us over anytime to hang out, and someone was always grilling. Even after their own kids went off to college, it was still the hangout spot. I am sure mostly due to being such a huge football booster sponsor.

I pull into the circular drive on the backside of the house. Well, it still looks just the same on the outside. Walking up the steps, I take in the big swing on the porch that overlooks the garden. It's a serene place to relax as you can still hear the crashing waves. I knock a few times and get no answer. I see Ford's truck in the open garage, so I knock again. Nothing.

Twisting the knob, I find the house is unlocked. Which is not uncommon for this town. "Hello!" I holler out, stepping into the house. Closing the door behind me, I notice the whole main level is now an office area and gym. I remember the kitchen is on the second floor, so I head up that way to put the food on the counter. I easily become nosy and start on my own personal house tour.

Is it really wrong when I am related to one of the guys who lives here?

The second floor has the kitchen and living room area, as well as a large table for dining. Three bedrooms are also on this floor as I go room to room. It seems all of them have beds and items for guests, but I notice one is larger than the other and has a large blown-up size picture of Dawson and Izzy hanging up.

Once I make my way around the second floor, I slowly walk up the set of steps to the third floor. The view up here is amazing. There is a large entertainment area with a television and pool table, along with being wired up to speakers. A huge bar area sets off to the side of the entertainment area. All this with a view that looks to the water.

Two doors off to my left and one to my right, I begin to make my rounds. One on the right is just another extra bedroom with a shared bathroom into another guest bedroom. All fully furnished and ready for guests. Walking back over to the left, I swear I hear water running. Opening one door, I notice I am in a very large room where it looks as if the walls have been taken out, being replaced with decorative columns for support. Leaving the room to be the particular length of the house that has large bay windows down the back wall.

Looking around, I realize this is Ford's room. The giveaway is the one corner dedicated to the solar system and all things space. His quirk has always been his obsession over it. Many nights growing up, he would set up a telescope for us to watch the changes of the moon, planet appearances, and my favorite, watching for shooting stars out on a blanket on my parents' roof.

This half seems to be his entertainment area with a TV and couch to chill. Whereas the other half looks to be his actual bedroom, with his giant bed with its nautical theme. Running my fingers down the dresser, I notice the picture board I gave him when he went off to college is hanging above it. Still housing all the same pictures with only a few new ones. I take notice the rushing of water is becoming louder as I step further in the room. I eye the door that leads to the bathroom. He must be in there. Is he alone? I never noticed any other cars earlier, but that means nothing in a small town where people walk and bike everywhere.

Shit, I really need to get out of here.

My conscience is starting to weigh on me. Just as my nervous self goes to turn around, I slam my knee into the dresser, causing me to go down. A yelp releases from me. *Fuck a duck, that hurt!* I hear the water turn off and try to scramble to my feet. Slowly but surely, I make it to the door right when I hear the bathroom door open. There is no running down these wooden stairs so I try to take them as quickly and quietly as I can.

"Hello? Dawson? Izzy?" Ford must think someone is home. Halfway down the stairs, I slip on the damn steps in my flip flops and limp, falling to my ass. I am going to leave here bruised and broken at this rate. Trying to pull myself up, my knee gives out. It is then when I see Ford at the top of the stairs with just a towel wrapped around his waist. A vision of etched stone abs, hard pecs, and a ripple of muscles down his arms from his shoulders. I am in a state of shock to acknowledge him saying my name and heading toward me.

Before I know it, Ford is carrying me bridal style back to his room. Laying me gently on his bed, he carefully removes my flip flops and puts a pillow under my swelling knee. My mouth is still slacked open, unable to speak.

"I am going to put clothes on, and when I come back, we will talk," he states sternly. I nod my head in return, realizing I need to snap out of this daze. A few minutes pass before Ford graces me with his presence. Luckily with clothes on so I can concentrate. His relaxed gray tee and gym shorts leave nothing to the imagination.

"I am so sorry, Ford. I was not trying to snoop. Was just

curious about the changes that have been made in the house. Some are pretty extreme." He nods with a smirk.

"What are you doing here to begin with? Dawson is at Izzy's tonight."

"Yeah, um, Mom sent me to deliver desserts and casseroles to you guys. They are downstairs on the counter." Silence lingers between us as he studies my face. "Well, again, sorry to intrude. I will get out of your hair now."

Once I go to stand, my leg feels like it wants to give out on me again. "No," Ford says, grabbing my wrist and pulling me back on the bed. Our eyes lock, my breath hitches, and the heat burning into my skin from his touch makes me feel faint. Breaking our stare, he pulls my legs back into the bed, propping the pillow once again under my knee. His touch is like fire to my body. "What did you do?"

"Um, well, when I was *not* snooping, I got nervous, didn't pay attention to my surroundings, causing me slam my knee on the side of your dresser."

"So that is what I heard."

"Must have been. I tried to sneak out and down the stairs before you caught me, but it is hard to be stealthy when you can barely walk, plus in flip flops. I slipped on the edge of the stairs and went down. Hence, how you found me." I shrug, while he begins to laugh. "It is not funny, but my total karma for snooping. I know."

"You know I would have given you a tour. All you had to do was ask." He grins at me again, and I just want to die in embarrassment right now.

"I know, but it did not seem like anyone was home, until I reached your room and heard the shower on."

"Were you *not* going to snoop in there too?" I cover my hands with my face. He pulls them back down. "At least let me look at your beautiful face when I embarrass you." Now I am heated and flushed, gawking at him. Ford Merrick just called me beautiful, again. "Stop looking at me like that, Mar. You know you are."

"Whether I do or not is not the case. You do, and that means everything." I try to sit up a bit to be more face to face with him. His palm gently caresses my cheek, causing my face to lean into his hand more. Since I've come back, the attraction has elevated. I am unable to truly deny the feelings I had so many years ago when I'm with him.

"I was not supposed to see you until tomorrow for the fundraiser and then family dinner," he says, almost in a whisper. His lips are inches from mine.

"I'm sorry, did I ruin your plans?" I say back softly, inhaling his Irish spring soap that he must still use, that I have always loved on him.

"I was going to steal you away after dinner so we could finally have that much needed conversation about the book."

"Oh yeah, the book," I state back with a nod, trying to get my nerves under control.

"But now you are in my house, lying in my bed looking like a tasty dessert. My mind short-circuited as soon as it caught you on the stairs."

I place my hand on his upper thigh. "So does that mean your body is winning the war so no conversation?" I ask, looking down at his prevalent erection in his shorts.

"Maren," he whispers. I hum back as if I agree to anything he is about to do or ask. Avoiding the looming conversation of what the future holds for us, for me and Alexis. I don't fit in his world. Let alone, being in his arms was the last place on my mind when I returned.

I came back to give Alexis a home with family and to have the chance to focus on me a little, to make more of myself where I can be proud of the person I am. Be someone my daughter admires for more than just being her mom but to show her we never give up on our dreams.

Ford

FUCKING GIRL OF MY DREAMS, Maren Hart, is in my bed. My primal beast wants to take over and completely dominate her body with mine. My heart is racing while my mind loses all sense at the very sight of her. My dick is hard as stone, and she has taken notice. The fact that she has not freaked out with me being this close to her right now is promising. The fact that she seems to be teasing me is only heightening the arousal within. I whisper her name as if asking for permission. When she hums back, I am done.

My lips crash onto hers; her hand grips the nape of my neck while my hands wind themselves in her hair. Her tongue swirls around mine, pleading for more. Maren pulls me down on top of her on the bed with a slight moan that escapes between her plump lips in between kissing. I feel as though I am having an out-of-body experience with her in my arms right now. My right arm lowers itself down her front, finding its way under her shirt to her breasts, then reaching behind her back to unhook her bra. She notices and moves, sending me in a panic that the moment is over. Instead, she pulls her shirt up over her head, tossing both shirt and bra onto the floor. Licking her lips when her eyes lock on mine.

Taking her lead, I slip out of my shirt and then look in

admiration at this body before me. Her breasts are plump and perky. I instinctively put my mouth on one of them and suck. She moans louder, throwing her head back, fisting my hair. I feel her hand glide down my stomach and into my shorts. She strokes my shaft, causing me to lose all control. Standing up, I shuffle out of my shorts, leaving my boxer briefs on, and pull hers off, only leaving her in hot pink laced panties.

"Take me, now," I mutter under my breath. Climbing back on top of her, her legs fall open to my width. Maren's green eyes shimmer with lust and need. "You are perfect, Maren. I want to explore and devour every inch of you." Then I suck her nipple into my mouth as she finds my shaft again and begins to stroke me off, pushing a groan out of me. Her other hand brings me back to her sweet mouth. She tastes like the sweetest chocolate. Knowing she was stealing scoops of icing and batter today from baking.

Pulling her hand out of my shorts, I flip us over to where I am on my back with her straddling my erection. She slowly starts to grind against me, grabbing her breasts in her own palms and squeezing. She locks eyes on me again as one of her hands slides slowly down her stomach into the seam of her lace. I follow to get a show of her fingers circling her clit, while she grinds against me. I bite my bottom lip to hold back from coming right at the spot.

Fuck. She is an angel sent from the heavens just for me.

I can tell she is getting close, but I want to be inside her when comes. To feel her contracting walls. For my cock to give her all the pleasure. To know I am the one that pleases her. I quickly sit up, pushing her gently to the bed as I strip from my boxers. Kissing her breasts and down her stomach, I lave her with my tongue until I reach her soaked lace. Slowly, I pull them down to her ankles and off of her, taking in the sight of her body. Her sex, so pink and wet for me, with the perfect thin airstrip of hair showing me where to land.

I look up at her face to make sure she is okay with what I have planned. She looks slightly nervous.

"Maren, tell me no, and I will stop." She looks to be having a debate with herself. I move back up her body and kiss her gently on the lips. "Beautiful, what's wrong?"

"Nothing, it's just...um...shit." I let her lay there for a moment, my cock's tip dripping in pre-cum over her body. "Maren, whatever it is, just say it. You can trust me."

"I know I can. Just not great timing. Ford, let's just say it has been a long time since I have had sex."

"How long are we talking, Mar?" I mentally slap myself for asking. Why the fuck does it matter, but I can't deny that it has me intrigued because it excites me. She has not been sleeping around all this time.

"Not to ruin the mood or anything, but not since the night I got pregnant with Alexis." I hone my emotions in, trying hard to keep my mouth from slacking open. *Fuck me! She hasn't had sex in six fucking years?*

Deadpanning her, I say, "Maren, I am not going to strip you of your newly found innocence on a whim in my bedroom." I catch a tear roll out of the side of her eye. "I don't mean it like that, I just want the act to be special, wait no, it would be special regardless, but...fuck!" I roar in frustration. "I can't say what I am trying to mean."

Her hand reaches for my face. "It's fine, Ford. Don't worry about it, seriously." She lifts herself up on her elbows to move herself from under me.

The beast within pins her down beneath me. "I'm not letting you leave without pleasing you first. Without you knowing how much I crave and want you. So, when I do finally put my cock inside your cunt, you won't dare question my feelings or thoughts for you. Understood?" Maren's green eyes widen at my demand, but she nods her head in understanding. "Good girl. Now lay back and let me have my way with you."

I start by playing with her nipples between my fingers until they pebble and perk up at my touch. She is already withering beneath me, and this is just the beginning. My hand glides down her stomach, over a long scar that looks like it's from surgery. I bend down to kiss every millimeter of it; she tenses for a few seconds, then relaxes. My hand glides over her center. She is soaking wet when I press one finger into her core. Pulling out, I slowly replace one with two fingers to stretch her tightness. Maren's back arches off the bed with her eyes alight. Pumping my fingers in her a few times, I take them to suck them in my mouth.

Fuck, she tastes of the sweetest thick cotton candy that melts in your mouth. I want more. I need more.

Jumping off the bed and pulling her ass to the edge of it, I bend her knees and station her feet on the fringe, spreading her wide for me. My fingers move in tight circles over her nub; my tongue licks slowly up her slit, savoring her cream. Then I am all in, licking, lapping, biting every part of cunt that I can get. Pushing her to her edge, then pulling away when I sense her climax closing in.

"Ford," she moans out, gripping the bedspread with white knuckles.

"Do you know how long I have waited to hear my name roll off your tongue in ecstasy?" I see her shake her no. She is breathless and squirming. Using my left hand, I pin her lower half down to keep her from moving, using my thumb to create circles around her nub again. Then with my right hand, I plunge two fingers back into her core, alternating between them and my tongue. Watching her unravel by me, and me alone. Her moans are making my dick weep into its own release.

It's at this moment, I decide no one else will make her feel such pleasure. No one else will make her come or know love and desire like I can. Maren will only experience all this through and with me alone. With her thighs trembling and toes curling, I murmur, "Come for me beautiful. Let go."

She moans loudly, then I feel her core clench around my fingers as she comes undone. Cleaning her up with my tongue, she is breathless, coming down from her high. "What the hell was that?" I hear her whisper under her breath.

Crawling over her, I purr, "That was bliss being served." Then

I lean in, taking her mouth to mine. Letting her taste herself on my tongue releases another moan from her mouth. Stepping back, I take her in with glowing cheeks, hair a mess, and flushed body. *Perfection.* "I'm going to clean up, and then maybe we can order dinner and have that conversation? Do you need to be home for Lexi?"

She makes me laugh as she stands up, taking my comforter with her to cover up as she grabs her clothes that were thrown across my floor. "Um, no. I can text Mom. I'm sure it will be fine with her."

"Great." I reach out and grab her, pulling her body back to mine. "You don't need to be shy around me. I already know the placement of all freckles and scars on your body."

"Hmmmm, I doubt that, along with the stomach pouch."

Tightening my hand around her hair, just enough to pull her head back so she had to look up at me, I mutter, "You, Maren, are perfection, My perfection. You created a beautiful child from this insatiable body of yours. You have been the siren to my dreams since I was fourteen. If you have new freckles and marks, I'll find them and memorize those too." Her breath hitches as if just figuring out how serious I have been this whole time. Kissing the tip of her nose, I say, "Get dressed, I'll order us some dinner while you talk to your mom."

Heading to the bathroom, I look in the mirror and am greeted with the biggest grin stretching across my face like the Joker's.

I just tongue fucked Maren Hart in my bedroom, in my house. A teenage boy's wet dream, a man's deepest desire.

Plus, she is still here willing to talk. I need to hurry out before she disappears on me.

CHAPTER 14
MISTAKE
Maren

My body is still trembling, emotions on live wire as I try to put my clothes on. Did I really just do *that* with Ford? My brother's best friend and roommate, my childhood best friend, secret crush, practically my brother?

Making my way carefully downstairs, I hone in on the liquor cabinet. I pour myself a shot of vodka and throw back. *Deep breaths, girl, or you won't make it out of here sober.*

"Maren?"

"Down here!" I shout up to Ford, and in the blink of an eye, he is in front of me.

"You good? I didn't drive you to drink, did I?" He causes me to laugh with his sad puppy face.

"No, just calming my nerves."

"Good idea. Pour me one please." I do and slide it over, taking another one for myself. "Hibachi good?"

"Only if you order from Fuji."

"Like there is any other place to order from. What do you take me for, a chooch?"

A giggle slips out of me, I have no other response for him. He jumps on the phone to order, and I walk over to the living room to text Mom. Based on all the emojis she sends back, it seems she has no problem with me not returning any time soon. "Don't forget extra egg rolls!" I yell out to Ford in the kitchen.

"I'm not a schmuck, Maren!" he shouts back as he gets off the phone.

"What are you from New Jersey now? What's with the chooch business?"

Sitting down next to me, he leans in and says, "Izzy makes Dawson and I watch Jersey Shore when she stays over."

"Makes you?"

"She bribes us with food. We can't pass up a good meal."

"Of course. The only way to a man's heart...food." He dives into tickling me all over. "Aggh, stop, I can't breathe," I try to yelp out between the laughs.

Finally, he relents, pulling back from me. "Speaking of a man's heart. Can we talk about mine?"

"I'd rather your heart be up for discussion than mine, so by all means." Looking him dead in the eyes, I brace myself for what words are about to escape his lustful mouth. All of a sudden, I hear Adele's *Hello* blare through the house. "What just started playing music?"

"It's the doorbell. Dawson thought it would be funny. Um, it's definitely not the food," he mutters, looking at his watch. The same watch that was his dad's, the one he has never taken off. "Let me check the camera on my phone to see who it is and if we can ignore them."

He walks over to the counter to grab his phone, and right then, we hear the door open, and a woman's voice beams from downstairs, "Honey, I'm home," followed by laughing. My guard is up as I already know this person is not Izzy.

As soon as I see the blonde hair come into view, my gut tells me it's *the* Grace. Ford's face drops when he sees my face turn into stone. Like I'm not even there, I watch her strut over to Ford and pull him into a kiss. My eyes go wide as I watch the scene unfold before me. He doesn't recoil as quickly as I expect him to, but once he does, he says hi to her and turns to me for introductions.

The flash of jealousy streaking through her blue eyes is not lost on me. I stand up to shake her hand, as she pulls me into a hug. "Oh, I have heard so much about you, Maren. So happy to finally meet you. You are every bit of beauty Ford and Dawson have said. Ford, baby, please tell me she is coming to the event next month? Would love a girl's day with your childhood friend."

Ford gleams as if he just got an extra Hershey bar from the vending machine. "That's a great idea. I'll give Maren the dates to check her schedule. Um, we just ordered dinner, but I am sure there is plenty if you are staying, or we can all go out."

"Perfect. Dinner in sounds good. Oh, baby, can you please grab my bag? I plan on staying a night or two, then I was going to steal you back to New York until the hurricane blew over."

"Yeah, let me go grab it. But Dawson and I decided to stay here through the storm. We won't be getting hit directly, but we need to stay." He glances over in my direction when he says it.

"Oh, well do you want me to stay longer?"

"Trust me, Grace, you won't no part the chaos the storm brings. You will be safer back home."

She looks at me and then back at him. "Very well then."

"Excuse me, I am going to head to the bathroom real quick." I hurriedly head to the guest bathroom upstairs. Once the door is closed behind me, I collapse against the frame. *So much for me thinking there was a small chance.* Not that we have done a lot of talking, but she hasn't been mentioned since he came back from New York and made it sound like they weren't together. Now she comes strolling in kissing him and calling him baby.

What in the actual fuck! Decision made; I'm leaving. Looking in the mirror one more time, making sure I look just as good to fuck as her, I walk out and back downstairs. Ford catches me halfway down them. "You, okay?" All I can do is deadpan him. "Mar, Grace and I aren't together. We are close friends." My face un-changes. "No one really knows, but Grace is a lesbian. I will say she used to be bi-sexual, but then, years ago, she decided she only wanted to be with women and has ever since. She has confessed no interest in me at all nor I to her."

"Really?" I ask back harshly. I may be in line for the next Virgin Mary, but I can sniff a tricky bitch when she comes around.

He gives me a reassuring nod. "Please stay. I know you were about to make some excuse to leave."

"What happens when I do leave, Ford? You two going to have a sleepover and gossip all night in the same bed?... You know what, I don't care. I'll stay for dinner only because I'm hungry and really craving Fuji, but then I'm leaving you two to it." Before I let him speak, I slam into his shoulder to pass him and head into the kitchen.

Just in time, the doorbell rings again with food to shovel in my mouth to help keep it shut. Grace and I smile at each other, neither one looking to answer the door, so Ford heads down to grab the food. While waiting, I pour myself and miss pageant queen a shot and then another followed by another. "You are a stealth one, Maren. I need some food before I can chase after you."

Ford stares at me in disbelief. "Planning on getting drunk again, Mar?"

"Nope. Just plan on hovering along the lines of confessions, but sober enough to drive home." His head whips in my direction, giving me the satisfaction of catching his attention. Now he knows I remember confessing my love for him. He also knows I've had just enough to let my playful bitch come out to play.

Him and Dawson have seen one too many underaged drinking nights with me to know which way the drinking scales go. With me balancing at the center, it is anyone's guess of what's to happen. Sort of like the angel and devil sitting on my shoulders. He shakes his head at me, and I smirk back. We all head over to the table to set everything out as Ford grabs plates, since now there are three of us. Ford takes a seat at the end of the table, with Grace and I on either side of him.

I decided not to speak much during dinner. Letting Grace tell me all about her and Ford's relationship from when they met, dated, *so you know they slept together*, to when she fell in love with a model in Milan that broke her heart to now being back in New York, figuring out her next steps. That she loves working behind her father's political campaign and help drive decisions for the better.

Really, she might just be the next Mother Teresa, but I really don't want to stick around to find out. Ford is very complaintive of her through the meal and tries to find common ground for the two of us.

By the time we are done eating, I am over the whole dynamic. I help clean up dinner, then make the announcement I am heading home. Making up a lie that Mom had texted me, stating Lexi was asking for me, and it was getting late. I won't lie and deny that I saw the disappointment on Ford's face, but a gleam of excitement was on Grace's.

Ford excuses himself from Grace's absence to walk me out. Coming behind me down the stairs and out the front door, he asks, "Mar, you sure you're okay?"

"I swear, Ford, I would be a millionaire by now if I charged you for as many times you ask me that daily."

"Sorry, but I can just tell when something is off with you."

Almost to my car, I whip around. "Can you, Ford?" *Damn, I'm a bitch right now*, I think to myself as I glare and look at him sideways. As if I am questioning him if he knows me at all, even though I know damn well that he still does. His amber eyes darken, and I know I hurt him. "Sorry. I didn't mean for that to slip out. I'm just tired and need to get back to Lexi."

"You sure I can't drive you home?"

"No, I'm good. But thanks. I'll just see you tomorrow at the fundraiser." I refuse to ask what his plans were with the woman that now is standing on the front porch, looking down at our interaction. Ford leans down to kiss me softly on my lips, then opens my car door for me to get in.

"Oh wait, Maren, Can we chat for a second?"

"Um, sure," I say.

Grace practically skips over to us. "You can go, Ford, this is girl talk."

He gives me a look of distress, and I roll my eyes. "It's fine," I say.

With a kiss on the top of my head this time, he says goodbye and heads up on to the porch. Grace moves in closer to me and in almost a whisper, she says, "Maren, I know we could be best friends for Ford's sake, but we won't be."

"Excuse me?" I jolt, taken back by her statement.

"See, I could always sense Ford loved and missed you greatly. Way more than a brother to a sister. When we met, I was able to break down a few of his walls, but he always felt guilty for some reason, and I started feeling more like a therapist than a girlfriend. Don't get me wrong, the sex was always incredible, but I needed him to miss and want me. So, I left this time. Went off to Paris and Milan for several months. Sure, I had a good time with several others, and I admit the story about Kimmy was true, but Ford never begged me to come back. When I did return, he seemed uncomfortable around me. He confessed that he could love me if things were different for him. That I made him feel stuff again, but we could be nothing more. That's when I decided to tell him I was fine being friends because I only had a thing for women now. The relationship between us would strictly be platonic."

I dig my fingernails into my clenched fist, trying to fight the impulse to punch her. Looking up on the porch where the porch lights have now turned on due to the growing darkness, I realize Ford can barely see us, let alone my facial expressions. Nor can he hear us. Playing dumb with the sneaky bitch, I sigh, "Grace, what's your point?"

"My point, Maren, is that we are both gunning for the same

guy. That you coming back only put a dent in my plans, but know I will prevail. He will be mine again."

Looking her dead in the eyes and gritting my teeth, I force out, "Take him. I don't *fucking* care, Grace. He is all yours."

Without another word, I slide into my car, slam the door, and drive off. Not shedding a tear until making it to the stop sign a street over. Only pulling my emotions together once I drive up my street toward home. Knowing I don't need this drama in my life. Knowing I will not put my heart on the line or my own health at risk again to fight to be heard and loved. I won't risk my own daughter's well-being for a chance of a sliver of happiness.

I'll put my big girl panties on so Ford and I can remain friends and endure Grace or whomever if I need to. My trench in the sand has been dug, and only a force of nature can fill the depth of the hole.

Spying my mom at the kitchen bar when I stroll through the front door around nine at night, she sits there with two wine glasses, patting the stool next to her for me to join. I watch her take a sip of wine before she speaks. "Lexi is sound asleep in bed. She had a great evening but was exhausted."

I nod, taking my seat. "How did you know I could use a glass? Intuition?" I ask, looking at her questionably.

"Well, some of that. Plus, Ford called. Said you sped off tonight."

"Oh, really?! Please enlighten me on what else was said, Mother."

"You know I prefer you to hide your crazy in public, but I think I'd like to hear your version first before I go and cast my actual feelings about it."

Angrily laughing, I say bitterly, "Nope. I'm not spilling the tea until you tell me what good Ole Faithful said."

This makes her laugh loudly this time. "Gah, it's been ages since I heard that name."

"You know it's fitting. He ran to you and ratted me on me every chance he could. Not like he wasn't out there getting into fights or dabbling in drugs, but Lord forbid Maren snuck out to a party or was at the beach with Kelsey and Collin instead of Alison. I used to think you hired him to trail me. He always seemed to be in the know of where I was and who I was with. Even when he was off at college."

Now I'm fuming over all the times he got me in trouble or an extra lecture from my mom. There were also plenty of times he never told her but would show up and carry me out of places. He never failed to somehow sweet talk his way out of me being pissed off and to forgive him or stated he just wanted to hang with me for a while because he was going through shit.

UGH! The nerve of that man.

"I promise you, angel, I never hired him. I don't think he did any of it to benefit me but to benefit you. Keeping you out of trouble was his own goal. He's always been protective of you. You know that better than anyone. His faithfulness lies with you, not me."

Nodding my head, I sigh. That man is infuriating. The fact that he still runs to Mom before me about me is enough to make me drive over there, slap him hard across the face, tie him up, and threaten to throw him off the docks. Not that I actually would, but I would love to put some actual fear into that man. Throwing my wine back, then refilling my glass, I say, "Spill it, Mom."

"Fine. He explained to me that Grace showed up this evening. That he felt was all fine until you sped off. When he asked Grace what happened between the two of you during your "girl" talk, she started crying. Said you seemed threatened by her and that you stated you would never be friends with her."

My jaw drops. "We aren't catching flies tonight, my dear." My mouth slams shut as she takes another swig of wine and continues. "Ford felt awful about the situation and wanted to reassure you Grace is just a friend." She pauses, looking solemnly at me. "It's just not like you to go and be so hurtful to someone."

"Hmmmm, wow." Refilling my glass again, I slightly chuckle

to myself. Mom refills her glass, too, waiting for me to speak. I just look at her. "Mom, Grace is a conniving bitch."

She sips her wine gracefully. "Go on."

I start at the beginning of the evening, leaving out that Ford gave me an orgasm with his tongue. I lead her to believe we had a brief makeout session but agreed we needed to talk before things went further between us. By the time I finished retelling the events of the evening and ending with what Grace told me, Mom had filled her wine glass two more times and pulled out a mini charcuterie board we found ourselves snacking on.

"That conniving little bitch," she lets out in a gasp.

"You cannot say anything, Mom. Ford needs to figure her out on his own. I'm not getting involved."

"I won't say anything to him, but angel, you are already involved."

Sighing, I pop a green olive in my mouth. "I know," I say feeling defeated. "But I'm not integrating myself further into that mess."

She hugs me tightly, then stands up. "Well, let's sleep on it. Tomorrow is going to be a long day. Let's get some rest. Love you, angel," she murmurs, patting my back.

"Love you, Mom." Turning in for the night, I grab the board and take it to my room with a water. After washing my face and changing into my pajamas, I crawl into bed with my book and phone. Checking my phone, I see a text from Ford from an hour ago.

FORD

> Make it home, okay?

> Yep.

FORD

> Seriously, Maren?

> Night!

My phone starts ringing, and I hit ignore.

FORD
> Answer.

> No. Going to sleep.

FORD
> Please, Mar. We should talk!

> Nothing to talk about. Turning my phone off - night!

Pulling my pillow over my face, I scream into it. *Deep breaths, girl!* Then I calmly sit back up to finish my board of cheeses, turkey, and olives while I dive into a re-read of my favorite novel, *Persuasion*, until drifting asleep.

CHAPTER 15
SUNDAY FUNDAY
Maren

My family and I arrived at the church for the seven in the morning setup just like everyone else in this town. The church sermon will take place outside at ten over by the front entrance of the church. Even with Ophelia knocking at the bay's door miles away, her dark clouds and winds are starting to creep in. Making the sky an eerie swirl of purples, blues, and grays. Hopefully, the rain holds off for at least another day, so we can make this a successful fundraiser for the Cleats family. Looking around the area, I spot Harper and her husband that she met in college over at North Carolina State. I wave them over so they can set their booth up next to ours.

Hugging, she lets out a giggle. "I just can't get over that you are here. I missed you so much and had so many life moments without you." Her tone then turns serious. "It was really hard, Mar."

"I know, but I'm here now. We promised once to always be best friends, and I intend to keep that promise this time around. I can't apologize enough, though. You know that right?" She nods. "It was hard not reaching out to anyone back home, especially you and Alison. Between you both and Ford, you were my confidants." Laughing, I mutter, "Of course more so you, because you always knew of my crush for Ford." She laughs with me.

"By the way, how is all that going? I heard he whisked you away to the B&B the other night, and rumor has it, you were at his house last night."

Shaking in my head, I grimace. "Don't get me started on that whole situation. Grace is in town."

Her mouth quickly forms an "O" shape. "I never cared for her much. Ford brought her to town a few times so we would bump into them at the bar or down at the docks. You can definitely tell the girl was not comfortable being in this town and out of her hoity-toity world."

"Well, she also isn't a full devout lesbian either as she proclaims to Ford. Sure, she takes part in extracurricular activities with just about anyone, but she totally has it in for Ford."

"Shut-up. NO!" I fill her in quickly about last night before Lexi comes over with chocolate icing all over her face. Harper is left speechless, staring at me dumbfoundly. "Don't say anything, Harp. He needs to deal with her without me getting involved."

"My lips are sealed. Let me go help Josh with the set-up so you can help with Lexi. We'll talk later."

Turning to pick up Lexi, I giggle. "My child, what have you gotten into?"

She taps her finger on her chin, thinking of what she wants to say, then sighs. "Mamaw had homemade chocolate donuts. She gave me three."

"I'm guessing you ate all three?" She nods her head yes, while I grab the wipes out of my bag and hand her two of them. Lexi takes them and vigorously cleans her face.

"All better?"

"Yes, baby girl. Much much better!" I baby-talk, kissing her cheek then putting her back down. "Can you help Glam-ma organize the table? I know you will be amazing at it."

She beams with excitement. "Yes! I'm on it, Mommy," she squeals and skips off to the boxes to help Glam-ma. I head over to the coffee cart to grab Mom, Dad, and myself a caffeine boost because we all are going to need some to make it through this.

Waiting in line, I look around in awe of all the people that have shown up to take part in this event for the Cleats, knowing many more will be here for church and after to shop.

"Morning, beautiful." I hear as I feel a presence behind me. The air is now filled with a sensual juniper and vanilla scent.

Slowly, I turn around, unsure who I am going to face but knowing it won't be Ford. My lips tip up in the corners. "Good morning, Duncan. You and Ned partaking in today's festivities?"

"We are. We are raffling off a few deep-sea fishing charters for next spring and summer. Also, I heard your mom makes the best chocolate truffle cookies on the island."

"Probably the best in any state you will find," I say with a smirk. He gives me a wink that melts my insides just a little. "That is nice of him to donate to the cause. I know it takes away from the profit." He nods, then shrugs his shoulders with indifference.

"So, you know you owe me a date because you blew me off the other night."

My eyes go wide. "Oh, shit. I'm so sorry, Duncan. I needed to get Lexi home and was sidetracked. Please don't take it personally."

"I won't as long as you let me take you out tomorrow night?"

"Um, you know we have an impending hurricane that we are due for the whiplash at some point tomorrow."

He chuckles. "You got me. I was hoping to get you alone and then have you trapped with me somewhere for hours." He steps closer inside my personal bubble, our bodies are just barely touching. He runs his hand up my arm.

"As nice as that sounds, I will need to take a rain check. See that little girl over there, skipping around with her curls bouncing while she laughs?" He nods and smiles. "That's mine, and we have plans to bring in the hurricane since it will be her first one. I need to be home with her."

He turns me back to him with his hand on my arm again. "I'll be honest. It bewilders me that you have a child, but I promise to respect you and her. Why don't we plan for something later in the week then?"

"Okay. I'll think about it."

"You are killing me, Maren Hart."

"Can you promise me it won't be a date but just friends hanging out in a public area? Two people getting to know one another?"

He taps his toe and ticks his jaw for a few seconds. "I can do that." Putting his hand out to shake on the deal, we do. Sending both of us laughing.

"Alright, let me grab these coffees and get back to my family."

"Until later, Miss Maren Hart," he says as he strolls away, whistling. Once I grab the coffees and head back to our table, I notice Dawson, Izzy, and Ford have arrived. Ford looks like hell with messy hair and shadows under his eyes. Not his usual put together self. I guess Grace got her way last night. *Where is she anyways?*

"Mommy, look who's here! Uncle Dawson, Uncle Ford, and Princess Izzy," she squeaks as she points to each one in excitement.

"I see. And Princess Izzy?" I ask, smiling.

"Um, yeah. Since I'm not really part of the family but we both love princesses, we decided to address each other that way. I hope that's okay?"

Laughing, I say, "It is completely fine, Izzy. I think it's adorable, and I love that she has taken to you so well. I'm not all into the whole Prince Charming saving the Princess ideal, so I'm glad you can share that together."

"Since when?" Ford asks.

"Since when, what?" His words catch me off guard. I didn't even know he was listening.

"You used to love fairytales and pretending to be a princess."

"I grew up, Ford. I realized the only one that can save me is myself, and we don't always get the love we desire." With that, I turn away and go over to Mom and Dad to hand them their coffee, leaving them to help set up Izzy's table on the other side of ours. Her family donated several items from their boutique on the mainland. I found out they sell homemade soaps and candles, along with custom apparel.

"Alright, I think we are all set up, and everything is out. You all ready to head over for the sermon?"

"Sure, Mom. Come on, Lexi." She comes up and holds my hand along with my mom's on the other side of her. Once we get to the large white tent, we take ours seats a few rows from the stage. Before I can etch my thoughts out loud, Ford sits next to me. *God, you need to stop with the games in your house. It's not funny.*

"Maren, we need to discuss last night."

"No, Ford, we don't. If you think I was so awful to her, then by all means leave me alone for good. I'm not getting caught up in ex-girlfriend drama."

"For your information, I sent her to a hotel last night and told her she needed to head back home."

Huffing, I reply, "Oh, Well I hope she got what she wanted before she left." Not saying any more than that, I turn my attention back to the front. Not wanting to look at him anymore. Maybe I am being petty, but to hell with them. I don't have the mindset or emotional capability of dealing with this type of shit drama. Let alone from the one person I have never wanted anything from but to be loved.

"You are making it really hard not to curse right now."

Deadpanning him and through gritted teeth, I spit, "Then move."

I get a quick glance of his fists clenching. "Maren, you need to stop acting so childish."

"Excuse me? I'm trying to prepare myself for the sermon of God, but you want to recap your ex-girlfriend dropping by for a surprise visit. Time and a place, Ford." Swirling my finger in the air, I raise my brows. "This isn't it."

He visibly gulps, shaking his head back and forth trying to refocus himself. The choir comes out and starts to sing *Mighty to*

Save allowing me a moment to take a deep breath. Looking over at Lexi between my parents, my smile returns. She is as happy as a little cherub on Valentine's Day.

Soon, I feel a hand settling on my thigh. Slowly turning my head back to Ford, I'm stopped halfway by his mouth up to my ear. "Maren." He says my name like a warning on his lips, sending a shudder down my spine. "I've already had a taste of you. We are nowhere near done yet. I will devour you until you surrender your trust and faith to me."

My breath hitches, but I keep my eyes forward as our Preacher steps out to the podium to speak. My core is burning, my panties are wet, and I'm not sure how I am supposed to conduct myself after *that*.

All the while, he is next to me singing the last verse of the song, like he didn't just sexually arouse me in church of all places. I only let my eyes move to catch a glance of him with his bible open on his lap, soaking in the words of the sermon. Me, on the other hand, I have no idea what is being said, being preached to us for the love of God. *Literally*. Before I realize how much time has passed, service is over, and we are released to start the fundraiser.

"Mommy," Lexi snags my attention, "can Uncle Ford join us while we walk around?"

Once again, before I can find an excuse to dismiss the idea, he has her propped up on his shoulders. "Come on, mini bar, where do you want to start?" She points in the direction of the toy table. For a few minutes, I feel like the third wheel, but after a bit, we all fall into laughing and enjoying the moment. She needs this more than my want to ignore Ford. I gave Alexis ten dollars this morning and told her to spend it wisely, so she is definitely looking at all her options before making an impulse buy. Which also causes us to circle back to previous booths to rule out items.

Finally, she decides on a giant, ombre pink dream catcher that Ford covers the reminder six dollars she was short on. I can't blame her; the dreamcatcher is gorgeous, threaded together with large white and cream feathers hanging from the circle. She makes me promise that I will hang it above her bed when we got home.

Once settled, I let her run over to our booth to show off her purchase, leaving Ford and I alone. "Here, let me pay you back."

Placing his hand on mine, he says, "No, Mar, you owe me nothing."

I let out a frustrated sigh. "Ford, what are we doing? What is all this?"

"Do you seriously not know, Maren? It is what I have been trying to tell and show you for weeks now. But every time I get close to saying what I need to say, someone shows up or something happens."

"Just say what you need to, Ford, because your nonverbal thoughts are giving me emotional heartburn. And I will not be between some billionaire and a governor's beauty queen daughter."

I can feel his mood shift from anxious to annoyed. "Listen carefully to me, Maren. Because this is the last damn time I will have this conversation with you about her. Grace and I are not together. She is not who I want. You are. Her and I are strictly friends... Don't you get it yet?"

I look up into his saddened amber eyes, cocking my eyebrow, because honestly, for once, I am not sure what he is trying to say. Because there is no way those were are the words I need to hear—want to hear—are what he wants to say. We are literally standing in the middle of this event with people walking all around us. Ford brings his hands up, cupping my face with his palms, tilting it so I look directly up at him.

"I love you, Maren Hart. I'm done hiding behind my worries and fears about it. You wrecked me when you left, and when you returned, all my suppressed feelings and emotions came flooding back. There has never been anyone else for me other than you. I will give you whatever space you need to think this over, but please don't make me wait long. I have waited six years for you to come back home. All it takes is one look, one touch, one smile, for you to bring me to my knees. I am only yours, Maren. I swear. As well as who-ever you need me to be for that precious little girl of yours. I love her too."

Fire sparks inside me as Ford presses his lips to mine. Pushing his tongue through my lips, I hold my hands on his forearms while he continues to hold my face in his hands. My mind spirals until the sounds of claps and laughter pull me back to reality. I take in the site of people standing around, looking genuinely happy for us. For whatever they believe this to be because I still am trying to process his words.

"What in the actual fuck is going on here?"

"Oh, no," I whisper as I turn to see a fuming red Dawson on my left.

"Take it easy, D. I will explain everything, I promise," Ford says.

Dawson swings, landing his fist right into Ford's jaw. "I don't want you to explain a fucking thing, Ford. I just want you to get your fucking hands off my sister. She is off limits, Ford; you fucking know this."

"Yeah, man, I do. Shit!" he hisses, rubbing his jaw. "I can't fight my heart anymore. It has only always been her. Before she even left, it was her. While she was gone, it was her. It's still her after all this time." I'm just standing in shock, watching Ford stand up to his best friend, my own brother, for me.

"Dawson, honey, let's go talk over there. I think I can help you with this." My mom sweetly tries to coax him from the scene.

"Wait," he pauses, his face turning red with anger, "you knew about this? About these two?"

"I didn't know per-say, but I'm not surprised. Not many of us are after watching those two grow up together."

"He is her brother, Mom. He is family. My best friend. He can't have her, Mom."

"Oh come on, Dawson, he is not blood related, so don't make it sound scandalous. Second, yes, he is family, like my other son, and I honestly could not be happier for the two of them if they decided to finally be together. He is still your best friend and has respected your wishes for a very long time. You are all grown adults now, so it's time to make some changes in expectations. Plus, you should be happy it's Ford and not you know who, or some other guy you don't know."

"Damn, she already got knocked up by Trayton, so I guess she can't do much worse." That vindictive son of a bitch. I hear the gasps in the crowd. The suspected rumor was deemed true. Now I really am going to have to answer to the Adair's when they come home to this mess.

My mom's face is frozen in horror. "Dawson, you need to calm down or leave. Do not make me ask you again." Izzy looks at each of us in disbelief as if she's not sure what to say or do with Dawson. He stomps off with Izzy chasing after him.

Right then, blondie rushes up to Ford. "Oh my God, Ford! Are you alright?"

"Not now, Grace." I watch him do a double-take, then look back at me. "Why are you still here?" he directs toward her.

"Because you don't leave friends behind in their time of need." I see him glare at her, but then soften as she runs her thumb along his bruising jaw line. Rolling my eyes, I turn around to walk away.

My mom stops me first, and in a low whisper, she says, "Maren, why don't you take Lexi home before you both get bombarded by the town with questions. You're dad and I can do damage control from here. Take my car."

"I can take you both home," Ford states.

I look over to him with Grace standing by his side. "I think I just want to get home and have some quiet time and space."

"Maren." All I can do is throw my hand up to stop him from saying more. Then I rush to Harper, who has Lexi on her hip. Thankfully, Lexi seems oblivious to the scene that unfolded.

I whisper, "Thank you," to Harper and hug her, letting her know I'll call her later. And trying my damn-dest to get to the car before the dam breaks.

Ford

BEING spontaneous may not always be favorable in certain situations. I pissed off my best friend, became the talk of the town, and I'm not any closer to knowing what my relationship status is with Maren.

The air around us has turned cooler with the winds picking up and clouds growing darker. I need to let Dawson cool down before I speak to him. Hopefully that happens before this evening when we are all supposed to head to family dinner and then camp out there the next few days while we wait out the storm. Now add in Grace still fucking in town and showing up when shit hit the fan. We are headed to the hotel, so she grabs her bags.

As much as I need her to leave town or hunker down in the hotel, in my own conscience, I cannot do that to her. Grace is my best friend, other than Dawson. Yes, she is also my ex, but Grace was the first person who had me feeling emotions more than just a void. To enjoy sex instead of just a hard pounding into the next ass I found for release. She is four years of familiarity and a change for the better back then. Besides the roads have already been closed to travel in or out of the island until further notice.

Grace has been quiet on the ride to the hotel. "You going to say anything or continue to ignore me?" I ask. She sighs, continuing to remain silent. "Alrighty then. Let's go get your stuff. I can feel the rain moving in." She opens the door, and I follow into the lobby, up to the tenth floor to her room. I step in the suite behind her, watching her stalk off into the bedroom. Sighing, I lean down, placing my head in my hands on the kitchen counter. I smell the bourbon, before looking up.

"Here, take this." Grabbing the glass from Grace and nodding my head to thank her, I down the drink, letting the burn seep into my throat. She refills my glass and then one for her. "Ford, can we talk?"

"That would be great, Grace. You have only been giving me the silent treatment since we left the square. For whatever fuck reason you have." Grace steps closer to me, so we are toe to toe. It's only now I take her in, standing in the black and pink silk robe I gifted her years ago from a business trip in Singapore.

"Ford," she whispers, placing her hand on my arm. We lock eyes. "The truth is, I'm in love with you. Hearing you confess yourself to Maren today wrecked me."

"Gra-"

"Ssshh, let me finish. We had something back in the day, and I know you felt it too. Then I wanted more from you, but you shut me out. So, I left, and while I did fall in love with Kimmy, I realized I loved you more. We belong together. My family loves you; the tabloids and people love us together, I love us together."

She looks back up at me, placing her soft hand on my face. Like an old habit, I lean into it. Her lips crash onto mine, her tongue fighting for dominance against mine. Then I pull away, backing off with my hands up. "No, Grace. We can't, I love Maren."

"But you love me too, I know it." Her comment catches me off guard for a moment.

"I do love you, Grace, but not in the way that I love her. Not in the way that consumes my heart."

Tears begin to stream down her face. "Then go, Ford."

"Grace, I am not leaving you behind in the midst of a hurricane."

Wiping her tears away as quickly as they fell, she puts on a placating fake smile. "I'm fine, I will be fine, Ford. Just go. I just cannot be around you right now."

"I am so sorry, Grace. Please text me when you get somewhere safe." She nods. Kissing the top of her head, I walk out of the suite feeling overly anxious. The feeling of needing to get to Maren.

The rain was only a mist when I left Grace's hotel, but now, it's a heavy downpour as I head home after grabbing my own bag from the house. The weather is putting me in a worse mood as my thoughts battle the rain pounding the windshield for my attention.

As far as Maren goes, all I can say is she knows now. There is no more hiding, nor do I want to. I'm ready to move ahead with being with Maren and Lexi. I have my mom's diamond wedding ring in a safe. I remember Maren used to admire the ring, as it was an oval cut with lattice work around the diamond that was then laced with diamonds on the outside like a halo. I know Dawson has talked about him and Izzy building their own house once he pops the question, and he would just sell me his half of the house.

Maren and I could live there, or she can pick any house she wants; it would be hers. So many things I need to get in order. I wonder if she cared if I took early retirement to help with Lexi so she can pursue her actual journalism dream. I'll be and do whatever her wish is. I know she needs time to let all of this from today sink in, but she loves me too. I feel it within every nerve of my body.

On the flip side of all that, though, I saw the look of disappointment in me when Grace showed up at the fundraiser. When Grace's hand touched my face. I felt defeated by not being able to grasp the situation with everyone involved. Hurt by the last look Maren shot me before leaving. Knowing this is one more issue I am going to have to talk through with her. Now, Grace has admitted her feelings outright, and that is something I can't ignore either. I need to be honest with Maren and hopefully prove to her she is who I choose.

CHAPTER 16
HINDSIGHT
Maren

Once we get home, I take Lexi upstairs to bathe. I realized earlier she had chocolate in her hair and was a sticky mess from cotton candy. "You had all the sugar today, didn't you?" I ask her.

"Not all the sugar. We didn't stop by the Scotts' or Thistles' tables for fudge."

"We did not," I say, laughing. Allowing her to strip down, I get the water warm for her. I turn around to assist her in the tub, and once in, I freeze dead in my tracks as my eyes gaze over her body. *What in the hell is going on?* Several purple and black bruises cover her back, with a few more down her arms. I go to the front of her and in horror find more bruises down her legs. No longer just the two I have been keeping an eye on. She was in jeans in a light jacket all day due to the winds.

"Lexi, baby. I'm going to ask you a few questions. I need you to answer honestly."

"Okay."

"Does anywhere on your body hurt?"

"No, Mommy."

"Has someone laid a hand or anything on you? Like to hurt you?"

"No. People only give me hugs and kisses. Oh, and high fives."

"Did you fall or hit something today?"

"I fell off the slide this morning on the playground with Papa and then jumped off the swing but landed on my knees. That's it."

"Did you notice any of these bruises on your body this morning?" She takes a look at her body and behind her.

"Mmmm, some I do. I was thinking they were just beauty marks or something. They don't hurt when I touch them."

"Oh, okay. Well, let's do this, I'm going to wash you down real quick, and then we are going to head to the hospital to get checked out."

"Not the hospital."

"I know, baby girl, but something isn't right with all this bruising." I begin to lather up her princess sponge and gently rub onto her skin. Being extra careful around the bruising, though, she never flinches or reacts when I touch them. I run her hair under the faucet to rinse. Once out, I let her towel dry herself, put some pajamas on, and throw her curls up into a messy bun like mine. It is two in the afternoon, so I'm hoping the emergency room isn't crowded.

Somehow my calm instincts kick in, and I am able to safely get us to the hospital as the storm rolls in over us with a heavy feeling. I carry her inside as she is half asleep, but I know fear is what is keeping her awake. Heading over to the registration desk, I hear my name being called. Looking around, I spot an old friend, Angelica, Dawson's high school sweetheart, walking down the hallway.

"I could always spot you a mile away and in a crowd." She hugs me, and I try to pass off a smile. "Hey, this must be little Lexi I keep hearing about. I hated to miss girls' night but was on call."

"Um, it was fun, but no worries. It's apparently a Tuesday ritual," I mutter, trying to hold my RBF together as this is not the time to chit chat for me.

"Hey, Renee, I am going to take Miss Hart back with her daughter to room 102. Can you send someone back there for registration?" Before the girl can even object, Angelica is leading us back down the hallway and through the double doors. This is where I learn she is in the final stages of her residency and has already been offered a job here at the Outer Banks Hospital. She chose pediatrics, luckily for me, and has already won Lexi over by the time we get to the room.

"Let's put this gown on her while you explain what is going on." Angelica is nothing but calm and pleasant this whole time, while I am slowly losing control of my nerves.

Nodding my head, I walk over to Alexis on the bed and explain to her what's going on first. I learned a long time ago, we walk through all the steps in a process together. Then I turn to Angelica and explain that she is suddenly covered in bruises. Letting her know about the two I have found over the last week, but then this afternoon found several more.

As soon as I pull her pj pants down, Angelica gasps. Then with a horrified expression, she cringes. "So sorry, so not professional of me. I am putting in blood work orders right now. We will start there." She clicks away on her tablet.

As I take Lexi's shirt off to slip the gown on, Angelica comes over to do vitals. She talks to Lexi the whole time, explaining what she is doing with her stethoscope and little light. She checks her mouth, only to notice there are some very tender spots way up in her gums that seem to bleed by just a slight push. Angelica then looks over her head to toe, examining the bruises.

A nurse walks in to draw blood. She is kind and gentle, and thanks to my stars, Lexi has no problem with needles. She lets the nurse do what she needs to do to pull her blood into several tubes. Before she walks out, Angelica tells her STAT.

My phone rings, and I pull it out, seeing it's my mom. I hit ignore because Angelica is going over a few things with me and tests she wants to run. But she needs to run it by Dr. Hunt on call. "Just take a seat and try to relax. This is the frustrating part when we have to run several tests to rule out things and more tests to diagnose. I'll be back as soon as I can," she states before walking out. Lexi is laying on the bed, so I grab a warm blanket from the cabinet to place over her. She is so tired and will be asleep here soon. Kissing her on the head and taking a seat in the chair next to her, I call my mom.

"Maren, is everything okay? Why are you not home?" Looking down at the time on my phone, I realize it's almost five, and the event ended an hour ago. She raves on.

"I um.." I'm so close to breaking down I can't stand myself. I do a quick look at Lexi to see she is asleep already, so I step outside of her room. "Mom, can you come up here and sit with me at the hospital? I brought Lexi in." I hear the gasps and shocks of her voice. "She is covered in bruises like someone took a baseball bat to her body. Did you see anything on her yesterday?"

"No. She was adamant about taking a shower the last few days, so I let her and sat outside the bathroom door in case she needed me. By the time she came out her pajamas were already on. Oh, Maren, how could we have missed this? That girl is so independent and dresses herself 99% of the time before I can even assist. Let me grab some things, and your dad will drive me up there. Do you need anything?"

"No, I'm fine, and she has her stuffed Mr. Pickles with her and seems content."

"Okay, angel, I'm coming. Just hang tight." I hang up before she hears me cry. I slide down the door into a ball, wondering how and why I could have missed this. She would have never noticed the ones on her back, but surely, she would have mentioned them if they were anywhere else before today. But then again, she thought they were beauty marks and nothing of concern. They are deep purple, almost black in some areas. How did I miss this? *What have I been so wrapped up in that I was not catching her getting worse?* Boy drama, hurricane, working the docks, Ford drama, you name it! *Shit! I really have no motherly instincts.*

It feels like hours before anyone comes by, but when I check the time on my phone, it has only been forty minutes. I am so tired; my body aches, brain foggy, and I just want to know that my little girl is going to be okay.

Another nurse shows up to take some more vitals and ask more questions. Lexi barely stirs while she hooks her to a blood pressure cuff, pulse ox, and takes her temperature. Speaking in a whisper, she asks, "Have you noticed any changes in her routine recently?"

"Not that I can recall. We just moved here, so our whole routine has changed. I can't pinpoint anything distinctly." *What an awful mother I am.*

"Has she been more tired? Going to bed earlier or taking extra naps?"

"Yes and no. I feel like we have been non-stop since coming here. I took her naps or falling asleep on the couch as being exhausted from so much change and busy schedule."

"I see," she says, glancing back at Lexi. "Has there ever been an incident where she had a cut or scrape that kept bleeding?"

"Ummm..." My mind ticks through all the log files I have in my head. "Oh, yes. A several weeks ago actually. She was doing a craft and got a paper cut. It took hours for it to finally stop bleeding. I had called her pediatrician in the second hour the cut had soaked through three more Band-Aids. He said keep an eye on it and bring her in first thing in the morning. By that time, it had finally stopped, and she seemed fine. So, we didn't go in."

"Okay. Medical history since she is a new patient here." I pull out my phone and to the App of where her medical chart is logged. I pass my phone off to the nurse.

"As you can see, you can request everything from Nashville Regional. She was born at 32 weeks and stayed in the NICU for almost four months before she was healthy enough to come home with me."

She looks up from reading through the chart on my phone. "Cause of premature birth?"

I bite the inside of my cheek hard until I taste blood before I answer. "I was severely underweight. Dehydrated with high blood pressure. When I went in for my check up, they found her heart rate was low, and she had barely grown in the last month. It was decided to perform a c-section to remove her from my body so she would have a better chance at life...

Oh my God, did I do this to her? Is all this because of me?

"No, ma'am." This is the first time I have seen this nurse's face show an ounce of compassion. It took driving me to tears and a confession, but we got there. Now she is kneeling in front of me, wrapping her hands around my own. "Sometimes we don't have answers when asked why. God doesn't like to give up his reasons, and science cannot always tell us either. I will tell you, we will get to the bottom of the cause and help find solutions."

"Thank you," I cry out as my mom walks in the room. Her face is one of pure terror as I get up and hug her. "We don't know anything yet. Just having to relive some past details to bring them up to speed on her medical history."

"Miss Hart, I will get out of your hair, but before I go, do you know her blood type? It is part of the lab work we are running, but if you know, we can go ahead and see what is available as a precaution."

"She is B negative." Her eyes go wide.

"Please tell me you or someone in your family is B negative?

"No, I am A positive. Mom?"

She tries to think. "I don't think so, sweetie, your brother and I are both AB, and you are A positive like your dad. I think Ford is O positive based off some paperwork we had to file a while back. I would have to call around and ask."

"Is there a father in the picture?"

"Shit, I didn't even think about him. Um, I have no idea what blood type he is, but I can call his sister and ask. But he is not in our lives at all."

"Okay, thank you, Mrs. and Miss Hart. Dr. Hunt and Dr. Leets will be in shortly."

I was left in a room with a sick, sleeping little girl and a mom who will be demanding answers soon enough.

CHAPTER 17
NOT HIM
Maren

"Make the call, Maren. You know you need to," my mom says as she runs her fingers through Lexi's curls while she sleeps. I just keep staring at my phone wondering, *what if he is her only hope? Would he show up? Is he still selfish enough to let her die? Oh God, could she die?*

Taking a breath, I call Darcy. "Hey, what's going on?"

"Darcy, please tell me your blood type is B negative."

"Mmmm, mine is not, but I do believe Trayton's is. I remember looking over some of his medical releases he brought over one day, and it was listed and how rare it is. Why? What is happening?"

"I'm at the hospital with Alexis. She is B negative." It never occurred to me how rare it was until now, being faced with possible blood transfusions. "Darcy, I have no idea what is going on. Bruises started popping up on her about a week ago, but they were random but really bad looking. She didn't complain that they hurt, but then today, they are everywhere. We are waiting for answers. But the nurse told me it would be best if she had any relatives that were B negative because it's so hard to find."

"Jesus Maren. I am going to head that way first thing in the morning. I know my parents are AB and O positive, but I think it's my mom's side of the family where B negative runs from some science project from years ago I did research on. Let me reach out to T and tell him what's going on."

"Do you think he will help? He signed over all rights to her. He technically has no responsibility to her."

"He is an asshole but not a monster, Maren. Let me talk to him, and I'll call you back here shortly."

"Okay thanks, Darcy." We hang up, and Mom is giving me the death stare.

"Start talking, Maren Leigh."

Shit, she just dropped both names on me.

"Let's go out in the hall."

Once in the hallway where we can see the window to Lexi, my bottom lip quivers knowing it's time to tell the truth about what happened all those years ago.

"Mom, I don't even know where to start. I was hoping you would never have to know how everything came to be." I flutter my eyelashes, trying with all my might to hold back the impending flow of tears. "A week after we arrived at Darcy's house, I woke up early in the morning to throw up. Just like every morning. I had the worst morning sickness with her, and it woke me up early every morning and put me to bed late at night. On this particular morning, as I made my way back to bed, I found a note on the pillow. Trayton told me he could not disappoint his parents or give up his dream of playing pro ball. That he never meant to lead me as if he loved me, though, he did care enough for me to be honest at this point. The night, he talked me into finally sleeping with him for the second time, which was graduation night, and he purposely didn't use a condom.

"Apparently, Ford and Dawson pissed him off earlier in the night, and Ford even gave Trayton a broken nose. It was more like a pity fuck than anything else, honestly. He looked awful, and I felt bad. He didn't go in detail of what words were shared amongst them, but I'm sure it was the typical bullshit the guys always said to anyone I tried to date. Anyways, yeah, he purposely tried to screw me over and he couldn't believe I actually got pregnant from the one time that night. Thinking he pulled out in time. His guilty conscience was weighing on him, and after some heartfelt talks with his family, he left. Told me he would sign over all rights to her if I wanted him to, and I would never have to worry about his parents getting involved."

"That sorry, sick son-of-a-bastard." My eyes go wide because Mom is not one to curse in public.

I nod in acknowledgement and continue, "Darcy seemed just as shocked as I was the morning she found me distraught in bed. Not that I loved him, but I felt so betrayed. Humiliated. My heart hardened that day. Other than Darcy, I had no faith or trust in anyone." Mom looks as if she is about to speak up. "Don't, Mom. I quickly went to a dark place in my head. I stayed that way until I delivered Alexis. I had to deliver her at thirty-two weeks because my body was going to kill her. My body was not viable to keep her alive due to my constant dehydration and high blood pressure, and I was barely eating. I also went through a cutting phase up under my arms where the scars are less visible."

She reaches for me and holds me tightly against her chest. "My sweet angel, what hell you must have been in."

The tears finally break free, and I start sobbing. "I was, Mom. Once they put her in my arms for those few seconds, everything came to fruition. I realized who I needed to become for her. Lexi spent the next twenty-four weeks in NICU before I could bring her home. During that time, she was bagged several times due to her lungs being weak, and she couldn't breathe. IV fluids for weeks, and I could not even hold her again until she was six weeks old and fairly stable. She had finally gained some weight, and her lungs were growing stronger by the day. There were some other setbacks such as jaundice, and some random rash she got at nine weeks that lasted for two more weeks.

"We were past the point of trying to breastfeed, but she struggled with the bottle once they removed her PICC line for food. So they had to add one back in, but only use it when she completely refused the bottle of formula. I think this is why she never took to a paci either. She doesn't like to have random objects in her mouth. We finally found a nipple top she tolerated a week before she came home. As far as my own body, I ended up having postpartum hemorrhaging due to having placenta previa post the c-section. My body was so weak and tired, my blood pressure would constantly drop then shoot up. My heart was working overtime and that was the scariest. It was days before I could move myself in the bed."

"Why did Darcy not call us? Maren Leigh, what if you died? You were all alone. What was your plan?"

"I didn't have one, Mom." I shake my head. "The day we did the ultrasound, they sent me over for an emergency c-section because they needed to extract her. I made Darcy swear she would not call anyone. Only if it was actual death was she to call you and Dad to let you know and see if you would want Alexis or for Darcy to have kept her. Mom, I was constantly in a state of depression, being stupid, tired, and just not in the right headspace about anything. We ended up all being fine. It's a fifty/fifty shot on if I can get pregnant again, let alone carry to term."

Sighing, my shoulders slump, feeling defeated. "There's that now, but up till now, we have all been okay. Once she came home with me, I got my shit together, worked my ass to finish college, and got a waitressing job in the evenings to support us until I got the assistant job. Darcy and Jim were wonderful, and I owe them both so much. It was not until Lexi turned four that I sent the papers to Trayton to relinquish custody. There was no fight or discussion. He just signed them and sent them back the next day. He had seen Lexi a handful of times by then, but he was always cold to her. Never cared to try, and she never cared either, always keeping her own distance from him. I felt it was best to cut all ties with him than have to deal with him in the future if or when he grew a conscience again or a heart.

"His parents have never seen her or cared to ask Darcy about her. They believe she doesn't exist or not Trayton's at all. I changed my last name to White to keep from being found, as I knew Dawson or Ford would use their IT skills to try and find me. Darcy kept them at bay by stating she didn't know where I was. That I would just call and check in every once in a while. Used prepaid phones and paid cash as much as I could. Anything I could to stay under the radar. I had to prove to myself I could be the person you raised. To make something of myself. To support my daughter and me. I did not want to come back unless I was someone you could be proud of again and had my shit together. I'm so sorry, Mom." I fall into her arms, and we both cry with each other.

Hours have passed of us just sitting in the hospital room with Lexi. Waiting for answers. Nurses have come and gone to draw more blood, take pictures of the bruises, perform an EKG, and just to check if we needed anything. Mom caught Dad up on everything, and fortunately, he isn't telling the guys about us even being up here so I don't have to deal with their drama right now. He is going to take them out for a few beers to get Dawson and Ford back on the same page and distract them for a while longer. Hopefully at least until we get some answers. We are supposed to be starting our hurricane camping tonight. Something Lexi was super excited about. Though, I doubt home is where we will end up any time soon.

I even showed Mom the horrifying pictures of my pregnancy. Darcy was adamant about me logging that time for Lexi and having pictures. I think they will just become her nightmares. Like when Bella in *Twilight* was pregnant, and her baby was sucking the life out of her. Maybe not to the point of Hollywood dramatization, but pretty damn close. For seven months, you could barely tell I was pregnant. By the time they cut her out, it looked like maybe I was housing a deflated soccer ball in my belly.

Now, I have to say I am much healthier with a little curve, and my muscle tone is back mostly everywhere but my lower stomach. It took me a long time to love my body again and gain my own physical and mental health back. Something I no longer take lightly, or willing to lose again.

Knock, Knock.

Dr. Leeds—Angelica—walks in with whom I am presuming is Dr. Hunt. An older man around his fifties, I'm guessing, but very handsome with his overpowering tall, built frame topped off with glasses and thinning brown hair. We all shake hands and introduce ourselves. Lexi had just woken up before they entered, so Mom is sitting with her on the hospital bed.

Dr. Hunt passes me a few papers. "Miss. Hart, what I just handed you goes into detail on what we are about to discuss. Please ask all the questions you need to, alright?" I just nod my head, waiting for the ball to drop. "We ran multiple panels of bloodwork on her. Several came back showing she is severely anemic. We want to start on a blood transfusion as soon as possible. I understand she is B negative, correct?"

"Yes. Her aunt is contacting her biological father to see if he will help."

"Okay, great. As soon as you get an answer, please let us know. In the meantime, we do have one bag coming in from UNC. They just so happened to have a liter, and luckily, it's the closest. Delivery will be in a few hours, but Alexis will need more. The next thing is, we need to start treating her for Thrombocytopenia. She will need to have platelet transfusions." Mom and I look at him in shock, though, we have no idea what he just said. "I know, it is a complex word. But basically, it means her platelet level is low. For example, normal range hangs around 150,000 platelets per microliter. Alexis's platelet count is sitting right now at around 19,000 and dropping based on the results from the samples we've taken twice, hours apart. Right now, I suspect the anemia and thrombocytopenia are indirectly connected. We need to run further tests.

"First, we need to take her back for a bone marrow biopsy. This will be making a very tiny incision to grab a very small piece of her bone marrow. It may cause the area to be a little sore for a bit, but her body will not miss the sample at all. The biopsy should give us answers behind the anemia, plus rule out any cancer-causing issues taking place behind the scenes." He pauses, looking at all of us in the room with him. "Any questions so far?"

"Um...so many questions I have, but I think I just need to process the information you shared for a moment...um... Oh wait, so it seems we have a couple of diagnoses, a kinda treatment plan, but what does this mean short term and long term for Alexis?"

"No, I understand. I gave you quite a bit of information to digest, and I will leave it to Dr. Leeds to help break down my doctor's brain verbiage. I know I speak too technical at times. But short term, we will keep her here until we notice a positive change with the blood transfusions and platelet transfusions. We will be putting her on medication, possibly two based on how her body responds. Both medications push the bone marrow to produce more platelets on its own, which is what we want. Also some steroids just as a precaution. Short-term, I would say at least a week and probably another. Based on what we find with the biopsy, and I will order a CT scan also, those will give us a path for longterm.

"I'll be honest, I have seen this diagnosis be a fluke, post treatment. Never returning with no underlying cause. With that, I have had to relay news for underlying causes with long term prognosis not all ending well. I ask that you all keep a level head over the next several days until we know more. No thinking of the worst or even the best outcome right now. Just be positive, and let us do our jobs as doctors and nurses, as you do your jobs as mother and grandmother. I will leave you in Dr. Leeds' care, and she will report to me of any changes and will be working on her case. I promise as soon as I have information, so will you."

He reaches out to shake my hand. "Thank you, Dr. Hunt. I really appreciate everything you are doing." He turns to leave, and

I take a look at Lexi whose piercing green eyes are watering with tears of the unknown.

"Can I show you something?" Angelica asks. She walks me over to Lexi. "Alexis, I am going to lift up your shirt to show Mommy something, okay?"

"Okay," she says in a low voice while holding my mom's hand.

"You see how in this area when you look closer, it's almost as if she has little purple and red pin pricks everywhere?"

Looking closer at Lexi's lower back, I nod my head. "I do. And I see now how it differs from the bruise up here."

"Right. This is a sign of little blood vessels leaking and rising to the top of her skin. Whereas the bruising is occurring because the blood in her body is rising to her skin, and there is no protection from the platelets with even the slightest of touch. She has both up and down her legs also, which is the most common place. You can tell she is starting to get them on her arms; they are just not as prominent yet as others."

"Angelica, I am just lost for words right now. I know we need to wait on answers, but what are the do's and don'ts with this? How much freedom can she have or is she expected to sit in this bed for hours on end, doing nothing? Can we take her outside, can she have visitors, bring outside food, picnics? Can we touch her, hold her?" Pushing back the tears, I take a deep breath before I scare Lexi even more.

"First we are all going to take a deep breath. 1, 2, 3, breathe in, hold...now release. Any better?" We all shake out heads no, which she lets out a giggle. "Well at least it distracted you for 2.5 seconds." She gives me a heart-felt smile. "As for do's and don'ts. Yes, you can hold her, just be aware she is going to bruise easily and fairly quickly. We all need to be extra careful around her head because a slight bump or knock could cause a brain bleed. Remember, she is lacking the platelets for clotting and protection. Yes, you can bring her stuff from the outside world, yes, she can visitors, but only two at a time. Visiting hours are from eight in the morning until eight at night.

"As long as there are no issues, Maren, you are more than welcome to sleep in her room. There is a fold out sofa. But, right now, I am going to take Alexis to the third level for her CT scan. Then, from there, we are going to move her to the Pediatric floor which is level two. Get her all situated in a new room. I will say this will be the time if you need to run home and grab anything or even go take a breather and grab something to eat. We will get her fed once we have her in her room and before we start the medications."

"Can I just stay with her?" I ask almost pleading.

"It really was more of telling you what you need to do nicely than requesting. But I get it, Maren, I do. Here is my cell phone number; I have yours in her chart. Text or call if you need to check in every five minutes, but I promise you, she is in the best place and in the best care right now. I will text you her room number as soon as we get her settled."

I'm a shaking mess of nerves now, twirling my ring around on my finger. "Thank you, Angelica. Um, can we get a time frame?"

"I'd say give us at least an hour and a half. Just to have wiggle room for the CT scan and room assignment."

"Um...okay." I go and sit down next to Lexi. "Okay, baby girl, Glam-ma and I have to step out for a bit, but sweet Miss Angelica, I mean Dr. Leeds here, is going to look after you. She is going to take you to a really cool room with a big machine to take pictures of the inside of your body. It's going to be really neat because you don't have to get undressed or anything. Mr. Pickles will be with you the whole time too. Just squeeze him really tightly if you get scared."

She throws her arms around me. "Mommy, I don't like this," she whines out.

"I don't either, baby, but we need to get you feeling better so we can get you home and start school and all the other fun adventures we have planned. I promise you; I will not leave your side unless the doctor asks me to because it's important. I just need you to be a really tough girl right now for the next couple of hours, alright?" She nods and holds Mr. Pickles close to her in a death grip. "I love you, Lexi. Dr. Leeds has my phone number if you need anything at all okay?"

"Okay, Mommy, I love you. Please hurry back."

"We will, I promise."

Mom leans down to hug her. "We will bring you back a special treat too, my sweet babydoll."

"I love you, Glam-ma."

Mom and I rush out of the room and the double doors of the hospital before we completely lose it.

We make it back to mom's car, but neither one of us wants to go anywhere. "I need to call Darcy and see if she talked to Trayton or not."

"Alright, let me call Dad and update him. Then let's run up the road and grab some dinner. We need to keep a level head about us right now for that little girl and re-fuel." I nod and walk off to a grass area, leaving her to call my dad in the car.

"Hey Maren, I literally just got off the phone with T, after it took me an hour to track him down. I won't lie, it took some persuasion, but he said he would come and donate whatever she needed. He has a few days he can take off, so we are going to fly there tomorrow morning together."

Her words have me crying so hard. "Thank you, Darcy. I don't know what you said to him, but thank you."

"You are family, Maren, and I love that little girl like my own. So, any updates?"

"Yes, we did. They are actually taking her back now for a CT scan of her body and then settling her into the pediatric unit. She is severely anemic and has thrombo...oh, shit, what's that damn word? Um, I think thrombocytopenia is it. Meaning her platelet count is low, hence why she is covered in bruises and tiny dots because her blood is leaking in places throughout her body."

"Jesus!" Darcy shouts. "Do we need to come tonight?" I can hear her typing, meaning she is googling everything she needs to know.

"Um, no. They found a bag of blood at UNC that is being delivered tonight and starting medications. They are getting her scheduled for a bone marrow biopsy but unsure when that will be yet. But hoping that gives us some answers as to why."

"Are you doing okay?"

"No, not really. Mom is here with me, and I told her everything from the beginning. I would say just keep Trayton out of her sight; she is liable to spin her wrath on him." A scene plays in my head, which makes me giggle.

Darcy starts laughing also. "You were picturing your mom losing her shit on Trayton, weren't you?"

"HA, I totally was."

"Nope, I can totally see it happening. I may have to pop some popcorn for the show, because honestly, someone needs to. You let him off too easily, and well, I'm stuck with him."

"I will just cross that bridge when we get there. Just text me your flight details, and I will let you know what room she is in once I find out. I'm going to try and get something to eat with Mom while we wait."

"Okay. take care of yourself. We'll see you soon, bye."

"Bye."

I walk back over to the car where Mom is leaning up against the passenger side door. "He is going to donate whatever she needs. Darcy and him are flying in tomorrow. She will text the details once she has everything booked."

"Wow. I'm impressed, but good. I am happy he can help her this way. Let's head to the diner up the road and grab some food."

"Alright, I can drive us."

CHAPTER 18
Ford

I DIDN'T SEE Dawson again until I showed up at the house for family dinner. He was already there having a beer with Dad when I walked in. Dad gets up to give me a hug and hands me one as Dawson proceeds to glare at me in disgust.

"Alright, boys, I'm going to say my two cents. We are going to talk to this through, and then we are going to move on because we have more important pressing matters to deal with than egos."

"Like what?" I quickly ask. "Wait, where is Madre and the girls?"

"They are out running errands, so it's just us men for right now." I noticed he answered my question quickly with his eyebrows synched. I sense Dawson feels the same when he cocks his eyebrow at him. Clapping his hands, he looks between us. "Let us get down to business." I cross over the kitchen and take the bar stool across from Dawson at the table. "Now, sons, we are going to move past this tonight, do you both hear me?"

"Yes, sir," Dawson and I say in unison. Dad might be the town's best friend, but us kids learned early on not to cross him. Especially not to fight with each other in his presence.

"Dawson, have you been so blind during Maren's teenage years that you never once thought Ford and Maren had a thing for one another?" He looks wide eyed at Dad.

"I mean, hell, I don't know. I always knew they were closer than Maren and I were, but we had a pact. Maren was off limits to Ford. He was always getting into fights and partying back then. But I knew she was the one thing that could calm his ass down too."

Dad looks at me then back to Dawson. "Do you think Ford is the same boy from back then, or has he grown up into a successful man who you call your best friend? Your brother? Even your business partner?"

"He has always been my best friend, Dad. He's my brother, regardless of who he is. But no, he is not the same Ford as all those years ago. Today just caught me off guard. Not just the public display for everyone to witness, but the damn fact that I had no fucking clue." They both turn to look at me for answers.

To Dawson, he feels betrayed. Not only because I want to be with Maren, but because I've never spoken a word to him about how I felt for her. *Here we go.*

"I know, and I promise it was not intentional to keep you in the dark. My head has been a fucking mess since Maren returned. Then she has her mini princess that you are in love with and just as protective of. Her leaving caused all that angst and turmoil in me, pushing me to channel it elsewhere. From the moment I saw her when she returned, I felt myself slowly being put back together, and because of that, it also messed me up so hard. Because how could I still feel so strongly toward someone that has been gone for six years? Who left without saying goodbye? I tried to keep my distance, but she is like a vortex that keeps pulling me in."

Pausing to take a deep breath, I pin D with a look. "Dawson, man, I contemplated telling you, but then I thought maybe I needed to pursue her first, to see if she even felt the same before I rocked the boat with you. Fuck, man! I couldn't take the going back and forth with her anymore. I lost it today. Seems like every guy in this town is talking about her, and Duncan keeps pursuing her. Then Grace showed up last night when Maren was over dropping food off, and it turned into a whole other level of hell. The night she got shit-faced at the bar and I took her to the B&B, she confessed her love for me. I've just been too chicken shit to confront her on it. And every time I do try, someone or some event happens, interrupting us." I give Dawson a moment to let what I said sink in. "I promise you, D, I was never out to hurt you or take advantage of Maren. It has just always been fucking her."

Shaking his head, the minutes tick by before he looks back up at me. "Fine, if the two of you and Lexi are happy then I'm good. Honestly, I cannot think of anyone I would rather have with the two of them. But I swear to God, Ford, you fuck this up somehow or hurt either one of them, or don't protect them as you should, you are dead to me."

"You can have my life if anything happens to either of them. I promise, D. I want nothing more than both of your blessings to marry Maren and adopt Alexis."

"Whoa, whoa, fucking whoa there, spaceman. Let me get used to you dating my sister before you marry her. Plus, I think Izzy would cut my balls off if you married Maren before I even proposed!"

Both Dad and I laughed. "Fair enough, brother, fair enough. But please do speed the process up. I have big plans, and I know you do, too, so let's get on the same page."

We pull each other into a tight hug, slamming our palms on each other's backs like men do. "Dad, when will the girls get back?" D asks. Right then, his phone rang, and he left the room, leaving Dawson and I to look back at one another knowing something else is up.

In the interim, I grabbed us another beer and let Dawson ask his burning questions about Maren and I. I answered as honestly as I could without embarrassing her since she had no knowledge of that conversation happening. Along the lines of when I knew I loved her. How I was able to watch her with Trayton all that time. Confessing that I had eyes and ears all over this place, keeping tabs on her while we were off at college. To say he was dumbstruck was an understatement. Hopefully, though, that only proves to him the lengths I will go to keep her safe.

Dad eventually walks back into the kitchen. His face is flushed, eyes watering up with tears as he looks between the two of us. "We need to head to the hospital, but first, let me fill you in on what's going on."

We run into the hospital in panic. I swear I could not drive us here fast enough between the traffic and weather. Just an hour ago, all seemed right in the world, now I'm pacing the waiting room, waiting for Maren and Madre to return from grabbing dinner. Dawson is ransacking the vending machine in stress as Dad just sits solemnly in the chair with his stoic face. We checked on Lexi when we arrived, but she had just finished with her CT scan and was waiting to be settled in her room.

We rushed out of the house as soon as Dad told us what was going on with Lexi, so Izzy is grabbing their clothes and toiletries to bring with her. I was in too much of a rush to get here. To have Maren in my arms, to tell her everything will be okay, and to give Lexi a hug and joke around with her, so I can see that babydoll smile of hers.

My skin suddenly prickles as my body senses her before turning around and laying my eyes on her. She runs into Dad's arms. "Oh, Daddy, this is so awful." She cries in his arms while he comforts her and pulls Madre into his arms as well. I hear a *ping* of a phone, and Maren steps from out of their hug to check her phone. Looking up at all of us, she says, "She is settled, we can go see her. Just two at a time, though. Um, it is already seven and visitation stops at eight. Mom, you want to take Dad there, and then Dawson and Ford can go? Or whomever. I'm fine waiting so you all can see her tonight."

I'm in awe of the woman before me. She is cracking but not faltering. She is bending, but I know she will not break. I take a step toward her and another. Our hands slowly reach for the other on instinct. She turns to look at me, then Dawson, who gives her a nod saying that he and I are good. He is good with us being together.

"Dad and I will go up there now, and then I will switch out with Mom when Izzy gets here," Dawson states.

"That works, I wanted to run to the gift shop anyways before I head up. I promised our girl a surprise." A slight giggle releases from Maren, causing my heart to drop. A sound of a sweet promise that she is okay under the hell she is going through.

Everyone heads to their destination as I sit down next to Maren in the waiting room. She is twirling her ring nervously, staring at the floor. "Maren, look at me please."

Slowly twisting her head to meet my gaze, my palm reaches for her cheek to caress it softly. "I won't make a promise that all of this will turn out fine, but I am going to promise you that I will do everything in my power for the best outcome. To ensure she has the best caretaker team of nurses and doctors, the best treatment, the best room, everything. Whatever she needs she will have, alright?"

With no argument, she nods against my hand, then collapses against my body for me to hold her. I do. With my arms wrapped around her, I glide my fingertips up and down her back to relax her. "What do you need?" I ask.

"Just to hold me and not let go," she whispers against my neck. We sit in silence in this position for the next twenty minutes. Madre shows up with a giant stuffed elephant and a bouquet of balloons. A Hershey bar for me, and a Milky Way for Maren to snack on.

Right then, Dawson comes over to switch places with Madre. "That kid is one hell of an ass kicker. Told me if all the princesses can overcome all the bad things that happen to them, she can too." He shakes his head in disbelief, making all of us laugh. "She has this, Maren," he says, pulling her into a hug.

"Thank you, Dawson," she says back to him. Right then, Izzy runs through the sliding doors, straight to Maren to hug her. They stand there for a few long seconds before breaking apart with Maren whispering, "Thank you." to Izzy.

"I'm going to head up, Maren, and grab your dad and say good night to Lexi. I will leave some time for Ford to go up with you to visit her."

"Okay, thank you, Mom." Maren turns to me, and we all take a seat while Izzy speaks prayer into us, the room, the whole hospital, and for Lexi. Not long after the parents show up, they leave with Dawson and Izzy. Knowing we will all be back here tomorrow.

CHAPTER 19
ELEPHANT IN THE ROOM
Maren

Ford and I arrive in Lexi's room to spot her stuffed between Mr. Pickles and the giant elephant Mom bought her, reading a book. "Hey, baby girl!"

"Mommy!" she squeals back. I rush over to hold her in my arms before she pulls all the wires off of her or out of the machines. "Uncle Ford!" she shouts in my ear. I move out of the way so he can hug her. "Come sit on the bed with me." She pats her little hand on the bed where she wants him to sit.

"How are you feeling, mini bar?"

"Okay, I guess. These medicines make me feel extra sleepy. So can we chat until I fall asleep?"

Ford smiles from ear to ear. "Of course. Anything you want, mini bar."

"Great," she says, pulling Mr. Pickles into her lap. Then she taps her chin with her finger, thinking while looking at Ford. I decide to pull up a chair because I know where this is going.

"Uncle Ford, question time." His face almost goes white, making me laugh out loud, having to clasp my hand over my own mouth to stifle the sound.

"Favorite color?"

"Green."

"Favorite second color?"

"I'm going with pink this time." Lexi aims a big grin at Ford.

"Favorite Number?"

"Still eight."

"Favorite *Disney* Movie?"

"Does *Spiderman* count as a *Disney* Movie?"

"Ewwww, that's worse than *Hercules*." She screws up her nose, sticking her tongue out at him.

"Do you like Mommy?"

"Very much."

"So she's still pretty?"

"She is beautiful, and so are you." He nods, booping her nose with his finger.

"Um, I already know you are not related to me so my new question is... Dog or Cat?"

"Dog for sure."

"Okay," Lexi says with a shrug.

As if flabbergasted by the abrupt ending of her questions, he shoots me a look that screams he's confused. "Okay? That's it? How did I do?" he asks in a concerned voice. It's like she knows how to twist his buttons, and I am here for it all day.

"Mmmmmm, seven out of eight."

"What did I get wrong? It was the *Disney* movie wasn't it?"

"I can't say. Try again next time." At this point, I am rolling with laughter on the floor, because with the way she is acting and twisting up Ford, you could not imagine we are in a hospital room with our world covered in gray clouds and gloom.

He looks at me wide-eyed. "She is just as bad as you, if not worse."

"Look, man, you're going to have to toughen up if you want to hang with us cool people." This makes Lexi giggle.

"Yah, I'm the cool kid." Ford goes to tackle her, but quickly remembers how fragile she is, so just pulls her into a hug and kisses the top of her head. "Can you stay Uncle Ford? Mommy can sleep with me, and you can sleep on the sofa bed. It pulls out. Dr. Angelica said it would be okay if you agreed."

Now I am in shock. "Oh, she is Dr. Angelica now. So, you are over here just planning your evening like you have nothing better to do?" I ask her, laughing.

"It seemed like a good idea." Shrugging her shoulders, she lays back down in her bed.

Looking at Ford, I nibble my bottom lip. "Seriously, don't feel obligated. I know you have work to do, and I'm sure you have plans."

"No, Dawson had our meetings postponed until the end of the week. There is nothing that can't wait right now."

Right then my phone *pings*. Checking it quickly, I see it's Darcy.

> **DARCY**
> Hey. I'm being bougie and flying on my brother's fancy private jet tomorrow. It was either this or have to fly commercial to Norfolk and drive down. We will land about seven in the morning, so ETA would be around eight.

> Sounds good. Just text when almost here. Room 216. Safe travels.

Crap! Based on everybody's tone this evening, I'm not sure Mom even told Dad that Trayton is coming into town. And if she did, she told him not to say a word to anyone else. *Now what?*

"Who's that?" Ford asks.

"Oh just... Just Mom checking in again." I'm honestly too exhausted to try to rock this boat right now. And if he spends the night tonight, I'm going to have to devise a plan to make sure he's not here when Trayton and Darcy show up. Hell, I need to make sure *nobody's* here when Trayton arrives.

"Really, Ford, those beds are not comfortable. So..."

He holds his hand up to stop me from talking. "I'm staying, Mar. Mini bar asked me to, and I want to fulfill her wish. And also, if it wasn't going to be in here, then it was going be me in the waiting room tonight. I am not leaving the two of you alone." He comes and gives me a hug, kissing me on the forehead. Right then, Angelica and two nurses walk in the room.

"Oh good, you're here. I just want to go over a few things before I head out for the night. Of course, Dr. Hunt is on call, and I will be back first thing in the morning."

"Um, okay."

"Hi, Ford, how are you doing?" she asks almost with a flirtatious smile. He shakes her hand like a professional, saying he's doing well.

"So, I have heard," she murmurs, sending Lexi a wink. The two thinking I don't see their little exchange "Now, Maren, I wanted to introduce you to Sarah who is our typical day nurse on the floor. Alexis met her earlier, but shift changes are about to happen in about five minutes so she will be switching out with Josie here." I shake their hands, and they move behind me to check on Lexi and trade off vitals and notes.

"The bag of blood is here, but Dr. Hunt decided to start it in the morning since we went ahead and started the medication tonight. We just do not want to overload her body this late in the day and make her feel worse than she may already feel. We should have the CT scan results back in the morning, and Sarah will get the bone marrow biopsy on the schedule for either tomorrow afternoon or the following day. We are just moving some appointments around on Dr. Hunt's schedule. Any questions?" I shake my head no as my brain has no fire power left to think. "Alright. We will stick to our game plan. Everyone can get settled in tonight, and we will hit the ground running first thing in the morning." She looks between Ford and I and smiles. "You know, I always knew the two of you would somehow end up together."

All I can do is let out a chuckle because I'm not even sure if we are together. The last twenty-four hours have become a complete blur. I honestly don't know up from down at the moment, and I'm hoping to fall fast asleep as soon as my head hits the pillow next to Lexi.

"Well, again, you have the button on Lexi's bed if you need anything right away. Josie will be in and out tonight just to double check vitals and her temperature."

"Thank you, Angelica, for getting her in so quick today and being on top of everything. I seriously appreciate it!"

"Of course, Maren! I hate that we are meeting under these circumstances, but I'm more than happy to help with her care." We hug, she says bye to Lexi and Ford and walks out. Sarah and Josie soon follow, with Josie letting me know she will bring us some blankets and pillows shortly.

As soon as the door closes, it opens again with another person in scrubs. "Hi, Miss Hart, I'm in for registration, and I just need to get some information from you as things have been moving pretty fast today."

"Of course." We go through all the typical questions of address, phone number, and emergency contacts. I hand over my driver's license and insurance card for her to scan. "By the way, we just have insurance until the end of this month so I will be calling them tomorrow to see what it will take to extend it through another six months, at least, as it was through my previous employer."

"Oh, okay. And just let one of the nurses know if you need to talk to somebody in financial services."

"Will do. Thank you."

"If you can just sign on that box when I tell you to. The first one will be to grant the team of caretakers to treat Alexis Jane Hart." I sign. "This next one is giving us consent for us to access all her medical records from Nashville regional." I sign again. "This one is just going over our hospital and HIPPA policy, and I will provide a copy to you as well." And again, I sign.

"The next one is giving the billing department consent to bill your insurance and stating that you will be responsible for anything that falls outside of payment or to your deductible." Not going to lie this one has me wanting to throw up on the spot. I can only imagine what the bill is like just for today. But I sign anyway and will worry about the rest of it when I need to.

"Okay, and this last one is your consent to give her blood transfusions, and the second half of this is for the platelet transfusions." I feel like I just signed my life away. "Alright, thank you, Miss Hart, that is all I need. Try and have a good night." I smile, and she leaves. Turning back to Lexi and Ford, I find them playing a game of cards.

"Where did you get those?"

"Nurse Sara brought them for me."

"Well that was very nice of her. What'cha playing?"

"Goldfish."

"Who's winning?"

"I am!" Lexi gleems.

"Really, Ford. You are going to let her beat you at goldfish?"

"She is ruthless!" I just laugh at them, deciding to capture this moment with a quick picture on my phone. They continue to play as I head into the bathroom to brush my teeth and wash my face before changing into sweats and a T-shirt. Once I come out, I see Lexi snuggled up in bed with Mr. Pickles and her elephant, barely keeping her eyes open. She's been doing a great job about not getting twisted up in her IV, which I'm thankful for.

"Hey, I'm gonna head down to grab some snacks and drinks. Do you want anything particular?"

"Um, I still have the Milky Way Mom gave me. Maybe just a Dr. Pepper so I have it for morning. I already have a water bottle on me."

"Just call me if you think of anything else," he mutters quietly, kissing me softly on the cheek before leaving.

Sarah comes in, bringing us blankets and pillows. I go about making up the sofa bed for Ford and putting an extra blanket along with one Izzy brought me on Lexi's bed. I lean over to check on her and realize she's already sound asleep. Turning all the lights off but the bathroom for Ford, I go ahead and crawl into bed and cuddle up with Lexi. Hoping sleep takes over for at least a few hours.

Ford

I TRIED my hardest not to listen in on Maren's conversation with the registration person. Not like I wasn't going to handle this anyways, but it only solidified that I need to handle this for her. She doesn't need to stress about medical bills when all she should worry about is making sure Lexi receives all the best treatment she needs. Walking out into the hallway, I find one of the nurses and have them direct me to the financial office.

"You probably have about five minutes before they close for the night. There is only ever one person here for the hours of five to nine."

"Thank you. I appreciate your help." I toss her a wave and walk into the office.

"How can I help you, sir?" the registrar asks, looking up suddenly, then grazing her eyes over me and smiling.

"I'm here to make sure all of Alexis Hart's medical bills are covered."

I can tell she is already flustered just by my presence, which means I can probably bend her to my will to make this happen without any issues.

"Let me get her pulled up in the system." The lady types away as I take a gander in the small office of paper charts and filing cabinets everywhere. "Okay, it looks like she was just admitted today so nothing has been filed yet. We are still waiting on charges to be entered." Pulling out my black card, I slide it over across the desk to her, making her eyes go wide.

"I need you to add this card to her account. Whatever you need to do, make sure all bills get paid through this card. There is not to be a bill sent to the house. Actually, send all bills to this address." I write my address on a piece of paper and hand that to her. "I will be handling all the financial needs for her. I am her mom's fiancé." A little fib has never hurt anyone for a generous gesture.

"Oh! That is very so very generous of you. Lucky lady."

"Not trying to be generous. Just looking out for the people I care most about."

"Well, you are just a handsome delight, and whoever those two people are, are very lucky in my opinion."

"It's me. I'm the lucky one, but thank you."

I let her type all the information into the system, and after a few minutes, she hands my card back to me and throws my address in the shredder. "All set," she chirps, turning the screen in my direction. "Here is where I updated the address and billing phone number so any and all bills will go directly to you. And this is where I input your credit card information on our secure site."

"Thank you! Please feel free to reach me by cell if there's any issue."

Walking out, my shoulders feel lighter since I feel like I got one thing done on my list. Now I just need to figure out how to get her and Lexi on my insurance plan or at least cover their insurance plan for a little while longer. I guess I can worry about that one tomorrow as it's getting late. I grab Maren a Dr. Pepper and myself a Sprite along with some Doritos and another Hershey bar before heading upstairs. I don't think I've ever been in the hospital when it's been severely quiet. My mom passed away in our home under hospice care, and well, my dad passed in that exact same house, so I never had to really deal with a hospital setting like this before. Thinking back to the days when my mom was still here, I send up a silent prayer to her to help look over Lexi and Maren during this time.

Once I walk through the door, I see Maren cuddled up already with Lexi in bed. Walking over, I pull the covers back over her arms and kiss the top of her head, then place her items on the food tray next to the bed. After one more kiss, I head into the bathroom to relieve myself and wash up before padding over to the sofa bed that I see has already been made up for me. I lay down to realize I may not be able to move tomorrow with how stiff this rock hard bed feels. With my head still racing, I pull up my stocks app to review, check emails, check current events, and scroll through mindless stupid reels on social media.

Before I know it, it's midnight with no sleep in sight. I try to quietly munch on my Doritos. Out of nowhere, a pillow smacks me in the face. Looking in the direction of Lexi's bed, I see the shadowed outline of Maren sitting up.

"Come here," I whisper.

She slowly slides out of bed and onto the sofa bed with me with her blanket, leaning her head on my shoulder. "Can't sleep?" she asks.

"Not really."

"Yeah, I think I got all the sleep I'm going to get tonight. Thanks to your chip crunching. I honestly think the whole hospital can hear you crunch and munch."

I flip her under me and start tickling her, but to quiet her, I smother her mouth with my own. She finally wiggles free from underneath me.

"Are you going to be nice now?"

"Maybe," she says huskily, biting her lower lip.

"Be nice and quiet and I won't tickle you. Because it will be you who wakes up the entire hospital."

"Ugh! You are such a brat!" she admonishes, punching me in the arm.

Moving in to kiss her on the forehead, I murmur, "But I'm your brat, so it's fine." Though I want to devour her lips, I know we need to talk about today amongst other topics. Right now, I'm here to be whomever she needs me to be, and let the chess pieces fall in line.

"Whatever." She rolls her eyes, then nudges me over so she can lay her head back on my shoulder. I turn on some action movie with the volume low and subtitles on. I am going to have to remember my iPad and headphones for tomorrow.

Within thirty minutes, Maren is softly snoring next to me in my ear. I lay down on the bed as her body moves to stretch across mine. Finally, I'm able to feel my body relax for the first time in a long while. Willing me into a deep sleep of my own.

CHAPTER 20
A STORM IS COMING
Maren

I WAKE to see Darcy's text that they have arrived at the hospital. Trying my hardest not to go into panic mode while sneaking out of Ford's arms, I hold my breath to stop my labored breathing. The moment I'm free, I rush to the bathroom. After brushing my teeth, I throw my hair back up in a bun and head out of the hospital room. I whisper a silent prayer that Lexi and Ford stay fast asleep as it's only six in the morning.

On the way down the elevator, I text my mom to let her know Darcy and Trayton have arrived. Then I find myself taking deep breaths to calm my nerves down. Though, I'm not sure anything could calm me down outside of a tranquilizer when having to come face-to-face with Tray after all this time, then having to beg him to do what's right by his daughter in a DNA sense only.

As soon as I exit the elevator, I see him and Darcy sitting in the chairs in the waiting room area, chatting. I stop at the receptionist and ask them to page Dr. Leeds to meet us here, so she can take him back to do the needed test. Twisting the ring around my finger, once again, I summon my feet to move. Approaching them cautiously, I mumble out, "Good morning, Darcy," stepping in for a hug. Then I shyly wave to Tray.

"Is that really the welcome you're going to give me, Maren?" I look at him with my eyebrows raised. *What the fuck was he expecting?* For me to roll out the red carpet and jump into his arms? Damn, he has some nerve and more confidence in him than ever before. Almost dangerous.

"Um... Hi, Tray. I appreciate it more than you know by coming here to do this for Alexis."

"I'm not the enemy, Mar. Can I at least get a hug?" My eyes quickly shift to Darcy, and all I get is a shoulder shrug. I step toward Tray for a quick hug, but he soon pulls me tight to his body arms in a bear hug. I can tell he's only gained more muscle as his solid body presses to mine. Letting my arms fall to my side in hopes he will let me go, he does the opposite, whispering in my ear. "You look more beautiful than the last day I saw you."

I step back, choosing not to play into his games. His old games of pulling me back into him with the little charm he possesses.

Luckily Angelica shows up just in time. Staring down at her tablet, she asks, "Is this our donor?" We stay quiet until she looks up. I watch her eyes go wide as she puts two into together who Lexi's actual father is. "Wow, none other than Trayton Adair. Mr. Football, setting the bar high in all his glory and now playing for the Giants," she excitedly states.

He puts his hand out with no recollection of who is standing before him. "Angelica. Angelica Leeds" she squeaks out, shaking his hand, completely fan-girling. I roll my eyes.

"This is Angelica Leeds, head cheerleader, graduated with me," Darcy states. A light smirk reaches across his face, which leads me to believe he does in some aspect remember her. The aspect that either involves a bed, a bathroom stall, or if she was lucky enough, the back of his truck bed at some point.

"Good to see you again, Angel," he practically purrs, causing her to blush.

"You too, Tray. Congrats on all your success." He nods but offers nothing more.

As if suddenly remembering why we are all here, Angelica says, "Now, if y'all would like to follow me, we're going to go back to one of the patient rooms to go over what's going on with Alexis. I need to get Trayton's medical history, and then if you agree to everything, we will get started on testing. Based on the test results, we hopefully will start the transfusion process."

"Alright, sounds like a plan," Tray says as he swaggers behind her.

I pull Darcy's arm back so we walk slowly together. "When do I get to see my niece?" she asks.

"I guess as soon as you want. I know she will be ecstatic to see you. I left her with Ford sleeping in the room so I definitely can tell you they are not awake yet and probably won't be before eight. Which visiting hours start at 8:30 so we can probably grab her some breakfast and then take it up to her and surprise her." It's then I look up at Darcy, whose mouth is gaped open, eyes wide. Shaking my head, I tack on, "A lot has transpired in the last twenty-four hours. More than I can even get my head wrapped around. But right now, all I can say is he is here, and Lexi is everyone's number one priority."

"Alrighty then. Sounds good. What about Tray seeing her though?"

"Well being that she knows he's her father, I'm not sure it's much of a secret to tiptoe around. I just need to give Ford the heads up because he is liable to kill him."

Laughing, she bumps her shoulder with mine. "Well, glad I came just for the drama! Hopefully there's some popcorn in the cafeteria I can get my hands on."

"Har har, Darcy. You were always the one to make jokes at my distress."

"It's my job as your sister-in-law." I just give her a look that says damn. Well, she knows she's not legally, but she just likes to prove a point. "By the way have you checked the weather?" I shake my head no. "You might want to. She took a last minute turn to the slight right, becoming a Cat 4. She is going to land right next to us. Not sure what's worse. Being a direct hit or the wrath of being on the outskirts to get the brunt."

"Shit, I forgot about that stupid storm."

Angelica turns around. "Darcy is right. The hospital is already preparing for the worst, moving patients. Called in staff that is available to come help. My plan is to get Alexis's biopsy in before noon today since all other non-life threatening surgeries have been postponed."

"Take a deep breath, Maren." Listening to my name roll off his tongue, I realize it's Tray who is in front of me with his hand on my shoulder. He winks then walks away. His actions send a shiver down my spine in agitation.

"Oh, before I forget, and so you're not shocked the hell out because I sure as hell was. Tray has like four bodyguards." My eyebrow rises in question. "Geez, Maren, if you would pay attention to the news or keep up with baby daddy, you'd know damn well he's a hot commodity."

"I don't doubt it for a second. But are four bodyguards necessary?"

"According to him and his asshole PR manager, Mike, it is. Mike insisted though. So, Tray insisted they sleep in and get some rest, and they could head to the hospital when they were ready this morning in order not to make a show of things. I'm not going to lie to you, Maren. He was pretty anxious about seeing you. And he's pretty damn anxious about what's going on with Alexis. He wants to do right by her, and he hopes you let him."

"The past is the past, Darcy. He shouldn't be anxious about seeing me. If anything, he should be anxious about seeing Lexi. She is the most judgmental child I've ever met in my life. I am over what has happened between us, and I'm finally in a spot in my life where Lexi and I can move forward as long as she's healthy. I'm not going to keep him from doing what's right by her by any means." Feeling frustrated with this conversation, I grit my teeth as my anxiety skyrockets with the feeling of there being more to unravel here.

"I know that. And I think he knows that, but he also knows how hard it was for you to accept that you need his help."

"Well, when the father of your child leaves you abruptly, then signs away all rights, it's hard to comprehend it, regardless of what the ask is."

She sighs in understanding. We finally make it to the exam room and all walk in. Trayton sits on the paper cloth bed. Darcy and I take our seats across the room. Angelica pulls out her tablet and starts going down the line of questioning. My phone buzzes in my hand, looking down, I see it's a text from Ford, asking me where I went.

> I had to come downstairs to do something.

FORD
> At 6 in the morning?

> Yes. I tried not to wake you.

FORD
> I awoke as soon as I felt the warmth of you disappear.
>
> You coming back up?

> Not at the moment. But do you wanna meet me in the cafeteria because there's something I need to discuss with you?

FORD
> Sure. Give me 10.

> Ok.

"Sorry to interrupt, but do I need to be in here through this whole process? There's something I need to go do and a phone call I need to make," I ask Angelica, trying to slip out.

"No, you're good, Maren. I can touch base with you later when I come to check up on Lexi."

"Okay, great—thanks." Turning back around, I look at Tray. "Tray, I'm not sure if you've made up your mind or not, but if Dr. Leeds and Dr. Hunt give the go ahead, I hope you will do right by Lexi. She is an amazing, intelligent, sweet, and funny little girl. She is worth my own life and then some."

His poker face sets in and tells me, "I understand." I smile gently before turning then walking out of the exam room to face the love of my life and let him in on what's going on.

I beat Ford to the cafeteria, grabbing us two coffees and two bagels with cream cheese, then take a seat at one of the few empty tables left. The hospital has a buzz about it this morning. I'm sure it's more so with the impending hurricane and emergencies than anything else.

Sipping on my coffee, I feel him approach as my back is turned to the entrance. He places his hands on my shoulders, giving them a tight squeeze, then kissing me on the top of my head. "Lexi is still passed out asleep. I told the nurse not to bother her until after eight because I think they kept her up most of the night," he tells me, then takes the seat next to me.

"Thank you. She will appreciate the extra sleep."

Ford looks at me cautiously. "What has your mind going so early this morning?"

Pulling my lips into a straight line, I debate what to say before speaking. "There's no way to really tiptoe around the subject, Ford. And I know you have been paying attention that Lexi needs a platelet transfusion, and we've established that none of us are a match. So, I had to make a phone call to Darcy." I pause for him to process.

"Darcy's a match? he asks, with a cocked eyebrow.

"No. Darcy is not the match, it's Trayton." His face goes

slack, and then his jaw pulses with anger. "Ford, Trayton is here right now, going through the questionnaire and getting tested to verify that he is a match. Before you say anything, I don't care if it was the damn devil that was a match for my little girl. I would still want him to donate. She is a rare type, and if he is her chance, then I am not going to fight against this." His jaw still ticking. "Can you please say something? I didn't want to keep this from you, and I am so sorry for not letting you know last night when I knew he was coming, but I didn't want you to take it out on Alexis or me—" His hand goes up in the air in front of my face.

"Do you honestly think I would take this out on Lexi? Or you? What the hell does that even mean, Mar? You and that little girl mean the fucking world to me. And I'm not the kid you used to console because I lose my shit."

"I know, Ford." He looks at me sternly, basically questioning the words that flew out of my mouth. "Or maybe I don't know, Ford, it's been six years since I've seen you. Add a few more of when you truly relied of me for comfort." He knows damn well that before he went off to college, his emotions were in check, and he was keeping a strange distance. Even when I could feel him crashing. "I'm just freaked out right now, and my emotions are all over the place, and I just, Jesus, Ford, I don't even fucking know anything right now."

Taking a deep breath to cool my nerves, I look directly at him, hoping he can the sincerity in my eyes. "I just wanted to let you know he's here, and that he's in the hospital. I'm praying all goes well, and he makes the official agreement to do what we need him to do. Which means, as much as I know you hate him, I can't handle the extra testosterone and egos right now."

Taking my hand in his large one, he murmurs, "I understand, Maren. But you need to not keep secrets from me. We've had this conversation. No more fucking secrets."

Looking down at our hands entwined together, I blow out a harsh breath. "I know. And I panicked. They got here way earlier this morning than I expected them to. I thought I had time this morning with you and Lexi to explain what was going on."

"Does he know about us?"

How the heck does he expect me to answer that. I don't even know what we are. Everything happened so fast yesterday, I don't know what's up or down at the moment. At my prolonged silence, I see hurt flash through his eyes. "I can tell you that Darcy senses there's something with us. And she, along with everyone else in this damn town, knows that I've always been in love with you. She also knows you've been hanging around a lot, and Lexi talks about you every damn chance she gets. Whether or not she's told Tray anything, I have no idea. But does it even really matter? He has no stake in this game other than saving his biological daughter's life at this point." I see him relax a little but not enough to ease my own tension.

We sit in silence for another few minutes, picking out Lexi's breakfast. Luckily, the noise in the cafeteria keeps our own silence from being completely awkward. Out of nowhere, I hear a loud breath of air being let out, feeling it across my neck. As if completely defeated, Ford leans his head against mine. "Dammit, Maren! I love you So *fucking* much. Along with that little girl of yours. I can't be angry, or the slightest upset with you ever. I will do my best to keep my hatred for him under wraps while he's here, but I swear, the second he starts shit with me, gloves are off."

Shaking my head to hide the smirk on my lips, I mutter, "If he instigates a problem then by all means. Have at it. Just keep Lexi out of it." I can't bring myself to tell him I love him. I'm not in the mindset to give him reassurance about us right now. I also internally can't deny the heat between my legs when he talks in his gravelly voice, or how he being close sets my whole body on fire. How he expresses his love for me makes me want to jump in his arms and stay there always.

My buzzing phone on the table pulls me out of my thoughts. Darcy texts me that they are heading to the cafeteria for some food. All questions and blood work have been completed, and all that's left now is to wait.

I can tell Ford read the same message I did. "You good staying or do you want to head back up to Lexi's room?"

"Might as well get this shit over with." He cracks his neck side-to-side, like he's getting ready to enter a boxing ring. I text Darcy back, letting her know that Ford and I are already in here, and we would wait on them.

About four minutes go by before I see two massive bodyguards enter in jeans and Henley's with earpieces, followed by Darcy and Trayton, himself, then followed by two more twins of the first two. *What in the actual hell?* The attention alone those massive men draw is alarming, then throw Trayton Adair in the middle of them. What is he thinking?

"You got to fucking be kidding me," Ford murmurs.

It's not even eight in the morning, and I have already reached my overtired delusional state. I'm convinced of it. All I can do is let out a white laugh because it literally looks like a fucking shit show is about to go down.

The posse moves closer to us, and as I take in another view, realizing one of the guys looks familiar, but I can't seem to pinpoint who or where. Once they reach the table, all the guards seem to spread out throughout the cafeteria with everyone staring at us.

"Sorry, Maren. They insisted," Trayton says sheepishly.

"Whatever. I just feel like they cause more attention, but that's between you and your people." My annoyance is making a show. I watch his eyes shift over to Ford. *Panic* flashes in his eyes, knowing something is about to be said.

Ford, trying to be a bigger man, stands up and puts his hand out to shake Tray's. Trayton slowly puts his hand in his, bellowing out a laugh. "Bro, you still following me around like a sad puppy dog?" I look quickly at Darcy, my eyebrows raised.

Ford lets out a harsh chuckle, drawing my attention back. "No, man. No following, just want to make sure she is safe.

We're together now. Soon to be married, and a happy family of three."

Darcy's and my eyes widen in shock. *Jesus! Now it's a fucking pissing contest.*

"Huh," Tray says, letting go of Ford's hand. "Well, I should say congrats is an order then." He shoots me a sly smile, giving me a wink.

Needing to change the subject before this becomes an all out brawl, I speak up. "How long did she say it would take for the test results?"

"About an hour," Darcy says.

"Okay."

Darcy pulls Tray with her, the guards already on the move. "Come on, brother, let's go get some breakfast before they deplete all the blood and platelets out of you."

He follows Darcy, thank fuck, and I turn to stare at Ford. "Well, that went well."

"Don't be a smart ass, Maren."

"When were you going to tell me we're getting married?"

"You know it's not a matter of if but a matter of when."

Flabbergasted, I sputter, "Oh—okay. Just let me know when to show up then." Rolling my eyes but smirking, I have to admit Ford has balls for what he just said. But this is nice. It's been a long time since we have had playful banter.

"Maren, I'm going to need you to be a really good girl if you want me to keep playing nice with that boy," he says with a husky growl in his tone, and I can feel my panties getting wet.

I feel the urge to egg him on, locking onto the energy to do so. A feeling of

distraction to the hell storm we are all embarking on. I stand up, ready to head back to Lexi's room but before walking away, I turn to Ford and say, "Yes, sir," in my huskiest voice, biting the side of my bottom lip. His eyes gleam with excitement and lust. And I love that I just left him there speechless. Now, sexual banter with Ford is an all-new ball game. *Batter up!*

Heading back up the elevator, I text Darcy, letting her know that when they're done with breakfast, which floor and room we were on so she could come visit. That I wanted to wait to bring in Trey until after the results. The less unnecessary drama I need in my life and hers is for the best. If the blood work comes back and for some reason Trey is unable to be a donor, there's no reason he needs to walk into her hospital room at the end of the day. After all, he has no rights to her.

CHAPTER 21
RAINFALL
Maren

By 9:30, Darcy, Ford, my mom, and myself are all hanging out in Lexi's room. Angelica is letting us break the rules. Stating it's because she knows us, but I have a feeling she has a crush on Trayton. Mom brought her favorite breakfast of blueberry pancakes and links sausage, homemade of course. Thankfully, her and Darcy have been getting along. I know Mom isn't Darcy's biggest fan right now, being that Darcy lied to everyone about my whereabouts, but I also know she's grateful for all the help she gave me and Lexi during the time I was gone. Even Ford found himself being kind to Darcy, though I'm not sure he will ever forgive her for lying over and over again. I'm just thankful he's unaware of the hidden circumstances.

We hear a knock on the door, and both Dr. Hunt and Dr. Leeds walk in. "Do we have a verdict?" I ask because they have a chance to write down Lexi's vitals.

"We do. The donor is a match and has agreed to move forward with the process."

I lose myself in full blown tears in my mom's arms. Then I jump up and go hug Lexi. "You're going to be okay, baby girl."

"Mommy—why are you crying then?"

"Happy tears, baby girl, happy tears. One step closer to making you feel better. I'll let the doctors explain to you."

Dr. Hunt gives a nod to Angelica to go ahead. "Alright, Lexi, we have a busy day ahead. First and foremost, we have you scheduled for a quick biopsy at eleven. Meaning the nurse is going to give you some medicine to make you very sleepy. Then Dr. Hunt here, who you met yesterday, is going to take a very tiny piece of your bone marrow which is located right here," she murmurs, showing Lexi by pointing to her own back.

Lexi's green eyes widen in fear. Looking back and forth between the two of us, pure panic sets in her face. "You're okay, baby girl," I promise her as she falls into a meltdown. I don't blame her. What almost six year old has any control over their emotions at this point; let alone, she has been a trooper through all the previous testing and having to stay here in the hospital. The wailing increases, and Ford walks over to sit on the other side of her. She folds into his arms while he rubs her back, whispering to her. Her breathing calms down right when the door flies open.

We all look toward the door to see an exasperated Trayton and his guards. "Is she okay?"

"You can't be in here, Tray, not right now," I sternly say. "How are you even up here?" I grit out in annoyance. We are already breaking the hospital rules with more than two people visiting, and now he has been stalking around the floor waiting for his opportunity? Staring at him, I notice his eyes are locked on Lexi in Ford's arms, and I catch a glitch of darkness skate across them. "Darcy, can you get him out of here please?" I can feel the anger rolling off my mom behind me, and Ford is clenching his jaw. With a deep sigh, she walks over to him to make a quiet exit.

"Wait," Lexi speaks up, her little cheeks red and blotchy, tears still streaming down. "Are you here to help me?" she asks in sniffles. He nods, then looks at me.

Fuck my life in this moment. I'm so not mentally prepared for this right now. I take her little hand into mine. "Lexi, yes, Trayton is here to help you feel better. See, you have a rare blood type and that comes from him. Therefore, he is going to donate some of his blood and platelets so hopefully you start to feel better while the doctors find the root of why you are sick."

She blinks then turns back to Tray. "Is it going to hurt you?" *Gah, this child!*

He walks closer to her bed. "No, I'm pretty darn tough. It hurts me way more to see you not feeling well." Awkward silence fills the air.

"Alright, now that *that* has been cleared up," Dr. Leeds says, "any questions for me? Alexis, anything for Dr. Hunt or myself?" She shakes her head, her little curls bouncing, then puts her head back against Ford's chest.

"How long will the procedure take?" I ask.

Dr. Hunt speaks up, "About forty-five minutes from the time we get her prepped and rolled out of the procedure room. I recommend taking a breather during this time."

All of us nod our heads. This room is becoming stuffy and enclosed. A breather is a welcome reprieve.

Clasping her hands, Angelica takes the lead., "Alright. I will give you all another few minutes to visit, and then we will ask you to step out as we get her prepped and taken to the procedure room." With that, she and Dr. Hunt walk out. All glaring in the direction of Trayton. He makes me feel unhinged with this newfound care he has for Alexis. Darcy must sense my aura because she grabs Trayton by the arm, leading him out of the room, closing the door behind them.

"I swear, Maren, I have never wanted to slap a person across the face as in that moment," my mom mutters, breaking the silence. I shake in my head in disbelief of the events occurring right now.

"Just stay away from him, Mom, and I'll make sure he does the same."

Angelica pops her head back in. "Just kidding, you guys, we are going to take her now. We just checked the weather, and Ophelia is approaching fairly fast. Dr. Hunt wants to get this biopsy completed so we can start her transfusions and work on a diagnosis."

Shit, I'm not ready. I pull Lexi into my arms. "I love you, and we will all be here when you get out, okay?" She sniffles, breaking my heart as she is trying to stay strong.

Ford kisses the top of her head and tells her he will watch whichever princess movie she wants after the procedure. Mom then comes in, pulling Lexi into a tight bear hug, trying to keep her emotions in check. We walk out of her room as the nurses talk sweetly to her and prep her. We walk into the elevator in silence. Everyone's emotions are on the tipping edge. Ford puts his arm around my shoulders. At this point, he is probably what is holding me up from dropping to my knees in a meltdown.

We exit the elevator in the waiting room, and I am happy to see my dad, Dawson, and Izzy here. We give each other hugs and update them on the latest with Lexi. Then Dad catches us up on what is going on back home, how the docks are holding up, and expectations of damage. Hurricane Ophelia is now on her way, edging off the coast of Stumpy Point, barreling toward us. Our only hope is she loses steam being half on land and crossing over Roanoke Island. The rain hasn't stopped for hours here, and the wind is only picking up speed. The meteorologists are baffled by her as she keeps altering course.

My phone rings, and looking down, I see Harper calling. "Excuse me," I say to everyone. "Hey Harp."

"Girl, what the hell is going on? Do you need anything?"

"Not right now, but thanks. I guess let's start with what you have heard."

"Only that Lexi is in the hospital needing a blood transfusion, and rumor has it, Trayton Adair is back in town."

"That pretty much sums it up. He is here to donate since he is her match. Of all things he could have given her, it had to be one of the rarest blood types." I try to smirk to show a hint of humor in my voice, but I don't think either of us are convinced.

Harper curses. "How is she holding up?"

"She is a damn trooper. Taking it as it comes, with minor meltdowns. Hell, she is doing better than I am, right now." I continue filling in Harper on the details.

"Well, we are hunkering down or I would be up there with you."

"I know, and I appreciate that. Just stay safe, and I'll keep you updated. You do the same, okay?"

"I will, bye." As I stare down at my phone on what to do next, I hear voices coming from the corridor.

Walking around the corner, I spot Darcy aggravatedly talking to one of the bodyguards. The one I can't seem to place on why he looks familiar. Inching closer I hear, "She can't know, Jones. It will set off a whole other level of catastrophe."

"I'm his lead guard, Darcy, I can't just leave. Let alone the little fact that we are in the middle of a hurricane." I let the sound of his voice sink into my thoughts. A calm but stern demeanor. Safe but bruting.

Hmmmmm...

Staying hidden behind a giant piece of stone artwork, I notice Trayton approaching from the other end. "Darcy, quit harassing my guards."

"Damn it, Trayton, you know damn well that if Maren puts two and two together, your head will roll. All of ours will."

"Will she really be that pissed off that I had someone looking after her?" My breath hitches in my throat, and I gasp. "Fuck," I hear roll out of Trayton.

Poking my head out, I see all three looking at me. Then it hits me. This guy, Jones, is the man who helped me the day of my car wreck. My mind flips through images of someone following me, always just being there. *It's this fucking guy! And he is one of Trayton's men? What the actual fuck?* I hear them yelling my name, but I dash to the elevator with Trayton hot on my heels. *Fuck*, he slips in right before it closes and pushes the STOP button. "Why would you push the stop button, Trayton? Let me out of here."

"No. Not until you calm your ass down and hear me out."

"Hear you out?" I shout. "You left me pregnant and alone. Abandoned us. Only to hire someone to keep an eye on me? Your sister and Jim made me think I was crazy when I told them someone was following me. Following Lexi and Me. You have no idea the paranoia I lived in daily. How could you? You were done with us! What the hell is your motive?" Glaring at him, he holds eye contact and steps in closer. "No, do not come closer to me." He stops, but he's still too close for comfort. I'm completely backed up against the wall with nowhere to move.

"You wouldn't believe me if I told you." If I didn't know better about the man in front of me, he actually looks remorseful. "Whether I believe you or not, you need to spill it before I start yelling."

His eyes lock on mine, determination filling his gaze. "All I did was for you, Maren. For you and Alexis. I know you don't see things that way, but I promise you it's the truth." I grind my teeth.

"What all did you do, Trayton?"

Letting out a defeated sigh, he mutters, "Why do you think you never ran out of money? Or when you thought you were getting a *too good to be true* deal on something you were buying. Even a job offer with an above average salary. How Jones was right there when you wrecked." My mouth gapes open. Mom's words about not catching flies pops in my head, causing me to slam my mouth shut. I'm speechless, just gawking at him. Reeling with emotions I can't even define. The silence, deafening.

"Ask me why Maren?" I shake my head no. My gut is saying I don't want to know. "Fine, you just listen." He inches closer till his body his pressed up against mine. "Because I fucking love you, Maren, I always have. But I also have always known I'm not the one you love. The one you want. That I have never been good enough for you. My naïve self never treated you right back then. I was selfish, and I refused to let you take the one thing I had left that was my own. Football. You had my headspace, my heart, and my body craved being near you. I did the only thing I could to bring myself so peace of mind at night. That was to ensure your safety and neither one of you went without."

Tears stream down my cheeks, and he wipes one away with his thumb. "I know you hate me, Maren, and I don't blame you after all this time, but know I have never stopped loving you. I just wanted you to be happy, and I knew I could not be the one to provide you the life you deserved. I also knew you both would be my utter downfall and distraction when it came to the game. Add my psychotic mother to the mix of making your life a living hell. A father too proud of his son to think he knocked some girl up and would not fulfill his destiny, and would stop at nothing to rid my life of the person I wanted most. I did what I had to do to protect you. To protect both of you."

Gasping for air, I sink to the floor, bending my knees into my chest.

CHAPTER 22
Ford

I'VE LOOKED every place I could think of in this damn hospital, and there is still no sign of Maren. It's been almost an hour since she walked off to take a phone call. Not wanting to follow her like a sad puppy, I stayed here catching up with the family, engrossed in watching the weather channel.

I feel uneasy not knowing where she is, or if she is alright. She isn't answering any of our calls or texts. Last time Dawson tried, he said his call went straight to voicemail. My computer is in Lexi's room, or I would have already hacked into the hospital's security system to check cameras.

Darcy showed up about ten minutes ago, looking unsettled and keeping quiet. Come to think of it, I haven't seen Trayton around since we left the room. There is no way she is alone with him. Just can't be. I huff, running my hand down my face in frustration.

"Still no word?" Madre asks, then she turns to the muted Darcy. "I see that look on your face, what do you know?"

Her eyes widen. "I don't know anything, Mrs. Hart. Other than that Trayton needed to talk to Maren, so maybe that is what they are doing. I honestly can't tell you if they are together or where either are." Madre rolls her eyes, and I can't help noticing the animosity that she has toward Darcy. Dad squeezes her shoulder, urging her to relax. "Here, I'll call him and see if he answers," she says quietly as she stands up and walks away. I follow. After a few rings, she waves her phone in front of my face, showing no answer.

Dr. Hunt then walks through the double doors toward us. "I've been trying to call Miss Hart but couldn't get an answer." He looks around us to realize she is not here either. "Well, I will have Dr. Leeds page her overhead, but in the meantime, Alexis is back in her room and sleeping. The procedure went well and has been sent off. I would say at least two of you can head up, so she is not alone when she does wakeup." I motion for Dad and Dawson to go, since they have not visited with her yet. I still need to find Maren.

Once the three of them walk through the double doors, I turn to Darcy. "You need to find him now!"

"Ford, I can't force him to answer his phone. If they are together, then it's probably a long overdue conversation needed to be had. Chill."

My head snaps back around to her. "Did you just tell me to chill? I am not going to fucking chill, Darcy! You hid her away for six years. I don't trust that son of a bitch or you at this moment. Never have with him. I also know that you know damn well where he is. You might have perfected your lying over the phone, but in person, your dilated pupils are a dead giveaway." She blinks, staring at me in disbelief.

"I don't know, Ford. She overheard something she wasn't supposed to hear earlier, and he chased her down the hallway. I think they got on an elevator, but there is no telling where they are now."

Right then, I hear a shout coming from the open corridor outside the waiting area. "Help, someone help?" Turning the corner, I see Trayton with my girl in his arms.

What in the actual hell? I see only red until they are closer. Then I notice Maren limp in his arms. "What the hell happened?" I grit out through clenched teeth.

"We were talking, and she was really upset, started gasping for air, then passed out." I scoop her out his arms, moving to a chair to sit, holding her. A nurse rushes over to check her vitals. Glancing over her, I notice her skin is pale and clammy. Shallow breathing.

The nurse looks up at me. "Any history of fainting or passing out?"

"She has a history of severe panic attacks." My eyes shoot to Darcy.

"When did those start and for how long?" Madre and I trade looks of concern.

"When um, right after Tray left. Quite a bit during the pregnancy and some afterwards. I haven't known her to have one for years now."

The nurse asks me to carry her back, so she can be monitored since her blood pressure is low. I begin to follow, until I hear a *SLAP!* Quickly turning around, Madre is giving Trayton hell. Darcy is in the middle, trying to separate them, only to get plummeted by her hand as well. I carefully lay Maren on the ground in order to pull my mom off of them. I catch her words as I run closer to them.

"You sorry bastard. You and your actions nearly killed her. Could have killed your daughter. And you, how can you be a mother yourself and not think to call me when she was slipping away?"

My eyes widen. *What in God's name is she talking about?*

Darcy takes a few steps back. "Maren made me promise. I was respecting her wishes, Mrs. Hart." I look over at Trayton, who looks just as confused as I am.

"She told me everything, every sordid detail. As much as I want to be thankful for you being her rock, I will never forgive you for not contacting me. Truly, what would you have done if she did die? Were you ready to make that call, knowing you did not do everything possible to keep her alive? To reach out to her own mother for support. Who she needed!" she cries out.

"I'm so sorry, Mrs. Hart. I was protecting Maren. She was my priority and was struggling fiercely. The last thing I wanted to do was cause her more problems that could possibly have sent her completely over the edge. I was only thinking about her and the baby. No one was meant to get their feelings hurt or even know. She swore me and Jim to secrecy. The last thing I wanted to do was betray her trust."

"It's more than feelings that got hurt, Darcy," Madre spits out. I have never seen this regal woman this out of sorts before. Like all her emotions over the years and weeks since the girls have been back broke through. She stills, a look with intent to kill.

"Can someone tell me what the hell is going on?" Tray asks, looking between the two women before us.

I hear a moan as I turn back around to Maren, seeing her roll over on the floor with the nurse next to her. "She is waking up."

I fall to her side. "Maren, hey. Open your eyes, baby, I got you." She rapidly blinks, trying to get her bearings. I also notice her skin getting color back from the grayish white.

"Where...where am.." Her eyes pop open. "Oh God, Lexi."

"Ssshhhh, she is okay and back in her room. Everything went well. Dad and Dawson are with her now." I rock her in my arms on the floor as her tears start to fall like the heavy rain outside. I tell the nurse, "I think she is fine, but will let you know if we need further assistance."

I'm not letting this woman go anytime soon. And I don't for a long while, rocking her, kissing her forehead over and over again as she releases her bottled up tears onto my shirt. Darcy and Trayton are off in a corner in a heated discussion. Madre sits on the floor next to us, running her hand through Maren's loose curls.

"My baby girl. The hell you have been through."

Knowing Maren is drifting in and out of sleep at this moment, I turn to Madre. "What was that about?" Her face is red and twisted from anger, and I watch as she tries to resurrect her mask.

"I'm so sorry you had to see that side of me, Ford. I just snapped."

A light laugh escapes me. "Yeah, I saw that."

"Don't get smart with me, boy. As for what it was about, that's Maren's tale to tell. I thought maybe you knew already, but with how calm you have been with Darcy and the fact that Trayton is still alive, and not even black and blue, I realized this morning you had no clue what happened." She takes a deep breath, "I'm going to splash some cold water on my face, then head up to Lexi. I know Maren is safe with you. Just be easy on her, Ford, when she does confess." I nod, and she kisses the top of my head, then Maren's.

I continue to rock her, looking over to Darcy and Trayton, now with Darcy in tears and Trayton looking murderous. I can only ponder to myself what must have happened. That alone is enough to make me want to tear them all down and destroy their lives.

CHAPTER 23
TRIANGLE
Maren

I̲n̲ a̲ n̲i̲g̲h̲t̲m̲a̲r̲e̲.
Disoriented.
Lack of control.
He loves me.
He was a puppet master all this time.
Ford...
I need to get to Lexi.

All the things swirling in my brain right now that I need to shut off. But I can't. I'm a mom. I need to get to my daughter. I need to remove myself from Ford's arms and see my daughter. I feel his lips on the top of my head as I try to sit up. "Slowly, Mar, I got you." I snuff a little, because damn it, I know he does right now. But will he, afterwards? Taking a deep breath, I stand up. Ford is right in front of me. Lifting my chin up to face him, he murmurs, "Are you okay?" Words escape me so I nod my head. "You scared the hell out of me, Maren. I have many questions, but they can wait. I'm sure you want to get to Lexi."

"I do," I whisper, my voice cracking.

"Thank God, you're awake." Trayton's voice rolls over my skin, leaving prickles. I turn to him.

"Yeah, I'm fine. Don't worry about me. I need to get to Lexi."

He quickly grabs my hand before I can get away. "I have always worried about you, Mar. Let me make this right."

Astonishment shoots through me at his audacity, and I straighten my shoulders, chin up. "Helping save your daughter is what you need to do. Afterwards, that is all you will be to her and me. A legit blood donor." Ford comes up behind me and places his hands on my shoulders in concern. I shake them off and move away, looking between the two of them. "I'm not as breakable as you both seem to believe." Ford tenses, jaw ticking.

Trayton stands defeated. "Just give me a *fucking* chance, Maren." His emotions are unhinged.

"A chance for what, Trayton? To be father? You signed over your rights to her. To be a boyfriend? You left when I was willing to make something work with you. Now you're a big ol' NFL player living the dream. How would either of us even fit in to your life? Huh?" I pause for a moment not to let him answer, but because I'm mortified by that question as if a spectacle of hope poured out of my mouth. I notice the hurt in Ford's eyes as they darken. He's trying to read the room, figure out what happened between Tray and I. Him questioning my own thoughts of how I would even fit into Trayton's life at this point.

Darcy reappears to my left. It's then I realize what I scene we are making in the middle of the waiting room. She gives me a weak smile. "Maren, I had no clue what happened after I left. Darcy never let on that anything was wrong," Trayton states, fueling my anger.

"You weren't to know, Trayton. No one was. It was my problem to bare. The last six years have been my burden of humiliation, picking up the pieces, raising a daughter alone, surviving. You were not to be part of it. Here I was thinking I was independent, keeping us level, only it turns out you have been pulling the strings all this godforsaken time."

Ford abruptly stands between us. "Someone needs to fill me in on what the fuck is going on. Right the fuck now."

Shaking my head in angst, I start to back away. "I need to see my daughter." Turning on my heel, I walk away from the three of them. My concern right now is Lexi. The three of them can duke it out for all I care. I'm so done, right now.

Ford

Fear.

Exhaustion.

Heartbreak.

Unraveling.

All in the span of a couple of hours, I feel like I have lost all control on *everything*. My hand twitches with the need to hit, spank, revolt, to do more then letting my grasp go on this whole situation. I stare over at Trayton, visibly distraught.

"She is not yours to have, Trayton, regardless of what tricks you are trying to pull," I growl out.

"Fuck you, Ford. Maybe she's not yours either."

Gritting my teeth, I force out, "Mother fucker," stepping forward, ready to kick his ass. Only to be tackled by his bodyguards once my fist hits his jaw. "Can't handle your own damn battles? Once a pussy, always a pussy," I spat at him from the ground.

"Let him go," he tells his men. They shake their heads in hesitation. "I said, let him go. This is my damn battle." I throw my arms in haste for them to release me, and this time they do but stand close. Trayton steps up, toe-to-toe.

"That girl is a better person than you and I will ever be. I have always loved her, but she has always loved you. Trust me, I live with my own guilt for how I treated her. Not talking her out of having a baby but persuading her that all would be okay, just so I would have a tie that binds us. I'm a fucking asshole. I don't need you pointing that out every five seconds, fucker." I huff in anger, clenching my fists. "Maren will never forgive me or take me back. That I know for certain. I just am looking for a chance to be part of that little girl's life, in whatever capacity she will let me. I've grown up. I have an amazing career, and my parents can fuck off when it comes to me claiming Alexis at this point."

He runs his hands down his face in frustration. "Damn it, Ford. For once, I am trying to do the right thing by them and follow through. Not that I think you deserve her either, but I won't get in the way if you are who she and Lexi want in their lives." My hands come up to grip my hair in anxiety and pity. I have despised this guy for so long. Been jealous that he had a place in Maren's heart and life while I was away. How even when he was being a jerk, he made it easy on her being around him.

I watch Darcy come up to him, place her arm around him, and leave. I'm just standing in the middle of the waiting room, speechless. Just then, the doors open and out walks Dawson and Dad. They share a look of concern as they walk toward me. Our dad, placing his arm around my shoulders, utters, "come on, son. Let's go talk this through."

We walk outside into the pouring rain, the wind blowing, becoming soaked like we are in no rush to remove ourselves from the hurricane's forces. The three of us gather in the car, then he drives us down to only the only bar that stays open regardless of a hurricane or blizzard. Lucky 12 Tavern. Only three other customers are brave enough to still get their buzz on before we wash away. Taking our seats, Dawson looks at me.

"Spill it, Merrick. We have all the time in the world." So, I do. From everything that transpired after they left for Lexi to what went down before they found me. All my thoughts and feelings along with tears come pouring from my body as if I'm no longer in control. Completely broken.

CHAPTER 24
LIGHTS OUT
Maren

When I came to her room earlier, Lexi was wide awake, chatting with Dawson and Dad about crabs, *The Little Mermaid*, and protecting the underwater and being conflicted on eating seafood. Because it tastes so good to her, but she doesn't want to upset Ariel.

Gah, I wish my life concerns were that easy.

I crawled into her bed as Dawson convinced her that mermaids eat seafood too, and we all are helping control the population of the seas. All she said was okay, then laid back against me. The guys said their goodbyes, and now Mom just walked in. I arch my eyebrow in concern of her look.

"Not now, Maren," she mutters, along with the stern look I know better than to question. Then she graces us with a huge smile, walking over to the bed and kissing Lexi on the head. "How's my little princess feeling?"

"I'm okay, Glam-ma. Just a little sore." She looks outside to the dark clouds and rain. "Mommy, is the hurricane going to hit us?"

"Um, there is a chance. But you could not be anywhere safer, okay? Right now, we are being hit by the outskirts of Ophelia. We are just praying she takes another sharp turn to the right and heads right back out to the open sea. You have enough to worry about, other than a silly hurricane, okay?" She nods, then cuddles into my body. Silence fills the room until I hear her shallow breathing as she falls asleep. Looking back over to the couch where Mom sits, I raise my brow again. "You want to talk about it?"

"No. But I know you need to know before someone else tells you." She pauses, then takes a deep breath, "I slapped Trayton and Darcy, along with yelling at them." Her face is set in stone, her voice regal as if she has no remorse.

My mouth falls open. "When did that happen?"

"When you were passed out from whatever on earth happened to you. The commotion probably is what brought you back. I snapped, but it will not happen again."

"Mom, it's okay that you did. I don't think anyone is going to blame you for losing your shit in the waiting room. I'm sure the staff has seen plenty."

"Maren, language. And whether they have or not, that is not who I am. Enough about me causing disarray. What happened with you and that Adair boy to make you pass out?"

Yay, more about my past I get to relive. "My panic attacks started while I was pregnant. When I mentioned I was in a dark place before, Mom, I didn't really care to elaborate. But I would have them frequently. Everything was too much all the time. After I had Lexi, they lessened after the first year, and then I've been doing better. Trayton had the nerve to tell me that he loved me. That he hired a bodyguard to watch over us, was the puppet master behind my car loan, my paycheck, and just about involved in every aspect of my life without me knowing. When, the whole time, I thought I had it together. I would get random bonuses and raises. Stupid deals on both my cars. Never had to pay out of pocket for my time in the hospital or any of our sick visits, always being told it was covered by insurance." I make a tsk sound, my mom looking back at me in disbelief.

"Well, can't say he didn't owe you both." I lightly shrug my shoulders, not to wake Lexi. "Then what else happened?" she asks.

"He started to apologize again and in front of Ford. Ford lost his shit. Like back in the day, next level anger, so I walked away. I refuse to get in the middle of their pissing war with each other. It didn't help that I made a comment to Tray about how we would fit into his life. I noticed the hurt Ford had after I said it. And I didn't mean to; it just flew out of my mouth before I could think about what I was saying. I don't want Trayton. I could care less if I ever see him again after this is all over, but I'm just tired and frustrated, and I wasn't in the mood to reassure Ford.

"Because, Mom, as much as I love that man, who's to stay this is going to work? The question I asked Tray is the same one I ask myself all the time when it comes to Ford. Yes, we come from the world in essence, but we live two different lives now. Ford is a tech app billionaire with Dawson, attending fancy dinners and galas, who lives in his crazy huge beach house because he wants to be home and close to you all. I know he finds comfort when he is helping Dad on the docks and fishing. But who's to say he stays? Who's to say I'm enough for him at the end of the day?"

"My sweet, Maren. You have always been enough to anyone and everyone. The fears you have is part of being in love. These are conversations you need to have with him, sweetie. He was hurt by you, but he is ready to move forward with you also."

Twirling my ring around my finger with my thumb, I mumble, "Yeah, maybe." Then we both jump at the sound of a large BOOM right when the lights go out.

A nurse pops in. "No need to panic." I'm thinking she is still trying to convince herself. "The backup generators should kick in here in a few minutes. But the lights will remain dim until the power comes back on."

"Um, okay. Anything we need to do? Are her meds still going?" Right then, we hear a surge of power being released. The lights come back on, on the machines.

The nurse looks relieved. "She should be good, but if you

notice anything unusual, just come get one of us at the station. Sometimes these machines like to restart or become finicky."

Pressing my lips together, I can't help but think what a colossal mess this all is. As much as I am worried about my own daughter, I also know there are patients here in way worse shape then she is and critical. "We should be fine. Please go take care of those that are in more need. I'll let you know if there is something we can't handle."

"Thank you for being understanding. We will check on her soon." She wasn't kidding that the lights are dim. It's only the afternoon, but one would think it's near dusk as dark as it is outside. Wind howling against the windows.

Mom stands up. "Let me see if I can get ahold of your dad." I watch as she rings him, hangs up, rings again, then hangs up. "Hmmm, I just keep getting a busy signal."

"That means either a tower is down, or everyone is cramming the signal. Surely, they are fine. Not like they would leave the hospital."

"True. We will just wait. I am sure they will make it up here shortly to check on us."

While Lexi sleeps, we wait.

Ford

THE THREE OF us are still at the bar when the power knocks off. All we can hear is the hard-hitting rain on the roof as the winds sound like they could rip right through this place.

"Maybe we should go back," Dawson states.

My dad looks fear-stricken. "Son, we are not driving back in this. That wind is liable to pick the car up and send us all flying or send an object flying into us."

"Fuck!" I let out in frustration. I try to call Maren and Madre, but there's no service. "We didn't even let them know we left, did we? We need to get back." Think Ford, think. You need to get back to Maren and Lexi before this hurricane lands right on top of us. "You two stay here, I'm going to walk back."

My dad plants his hand on my shoulder firmly. "No you're not, son."

"It's less than five miles away. I can walk behind the buildings to shield from the wind and haul ass where I can't. I need to get back, Dad." He sighs, looking back at Dawson. Dawson's look tells me he's in if I'm doing this.

"Fine, let's go," Dad states, standing up. He is as much of a stubborn man as Dawson and I are. There is no telling him to stay. We brace ourselves, pushing the door open against the winds.

It feels like bullets and knives stabbing into our flesh as the rain pelts us. We walk to the back of the building and start to make our journey. We watch as the sea surges up over the seawalls, flooding the road.

Dawson yells over the wind and rushing water, "Is this a good time to say this is one of the craziest ideas you have ever had, Ford?"

I laugh, "Fuck off, Dawson. You know you want to get back to Izzy!" Still yelling, I ask, "Does she know where we went?"

"Shit, I forgot I told her we were going to take you somewhere. She was going to the cafeteria. Maybe she made it up to the room with the girls."

"Still no signal!" my dad hollers, squinting down at his phone. "Yeah, so much for electronics and weather when all technology is wiped out."

"New app idea, Dawson. A message app tied to a weather app that does not need internet or phone service in emergencies like this."

"Best idea ever!" he says, shouting back to me. We are soaked to the bone, whiplashed from the wind, and petrified that we are three idiots about to be washed away into the ocean. We round a corner of a long commercial building where it opens up to where you can see both sides of the island.

"We need to make a run for it until we get behind that hotel over there. Dad, you good?"

"Hell, I'm in better shape than both of you."

"No time for jokes, Dad." I roll my eyes, taking a gander at the tall, beer belly man in front of me. Yes, his legs and arms are solid muscle, but he lacks endurance. "Dawson, you run in front; I'll stay behind him." He nods and takes off. Dad starts to sprint, with me trailing behind.

Running, exhausted, and skin burning from the wind and rain, we are halfway there. Dawson stops suddenly, and we catch up. He points out to the right of us.

"Holy shit!" the three of us exclaim. Two waterspouts are weaving their way in our direction.

"Keep running!" I shout. "Dad, now's not the time to record this shit!" I yell, catching him with his phone out.

"Your mom won't believe us." Rolling my eyes, I grab his other arm that is free of the phone to keep him moving. Luckily, as fast as they were moving, they dissipated into the air as if they never existed. But here's the thing, if you know, those fuckers can easily funnel back up into the clouds, then drop somewhere else. I don't plan on staying to find out.

Once we reach the hotel, Dawson pries the doors open, and we step inside for a breather. Our throats are burning from the wind, running, and all the shouting. We turn to see guests huddled in the main area. I'm sure just like us, they lost hope in Ophelia missing us completely. We never thought she would turn at the last minute toward us.

Looking back through the opposite door, I see the waves spray over the edge, the waves reaching the bottom of the fishing pier that stretches way out into the sea. Another waterspout is further off in the distance. Ophelia is enraged, and all I need her to do is keep pushing to the right to avoid havoc on the rest of the island.

"You ready, Ford?" Dawson asks, pulling me out of my thoughts.

"Yeah, let's do this." We all three shiver as the wind wraps around our drenched bodies. "Okay, so we have buildings to block us for the most part for the next mile." I can see the hospital from where we are standing. With the clouds, haze, and rain, it looks a hundred miles away, though, only two and half at this point. "Let's go!" I shout, and we sprint off behind the buildings shielding us from most of the wind.

Once we reach the large opening between us and the hospital, we lean over, hands on our knees, catching our breath. It's one thing to run for cardio, another to run against all elements and for your life. It's just us in the open from here on out.

"You good, Dad?"

"I'm good. Don't worry about your old man." At this point, the roads are flooded, sand is everywhere, blowing against us and into our eyes, causing us to squint while pushing through the wind's forces. If anyone is watching us from their homes, they indeed know we are complete idiots for being out here right now.

Halfway there, we hear hollering from a few houses down. "Mr. Hart, over here! Dawson!" We turn around to find Duncan waving his arms at us. Then he jumps in his side-by-side, wading through the water toward us. "Get in." I don't even question him; I just do with Dawson and Dad following.

"Thank you, Duncan," Dad says. "Can you get us to the hospital?"

"Sure can, sir. But can I ask? Why in the hell are you headed that way in the middle of a damn hurricane?"

"I guess the gossip mill is not churning this week," Dawson jokes.

"No, man, its churning on low, but everyone has been consumed by Ophelia." I stay mute, not caring to talk to this guy. Sure, its Neds' nephew, but he also wants Maren.

Dawson speaks up because he is more friends with him than I am. "Lexi is sick, so her, Maren, Mom, and Izzy are all there. We were there too but ducked out a while ago before the storm worsened. Thought we had time. We were fearful of driving, so we decided to make our way back on foot."

"Oh, shit, man. I had no idea. Well, you are some brave sons-a-bitches, that's for sure." We all chuckle.

"More like having a death wish," Dad jokes. I chuckle at the old man. He himself braved the angry seas, lost men along the way, survived to tell about it, and add stories to Nags fisherman folklore.

Duncan is flying through the water in his toy. If we were not already soaked and wet, we would have been by his driving through the flooded roads. He drives us to the front door, and we immediately notice the power is out here, running on generators only. I rush off the side-by-side, yelling, "Thank you."

There's no time to stop and properly say goodbye. I need to get my girls. Need to know they are okay, despite all the bullshit that has happened today.

CHAPTER 25
THE CALM
Maren

Izzy showed up about thirty minutes after the power went out. She was down at the cafeteria when it happened, and she let us know the boys had left to take Ford for a breather. *Ford.* The man who for some reason is determined to be in my life, but who I devastated earlier. The vision of his eyes, rugged and defeated, accosted me. I need to apologize; we need to talk.

All this drama and crazy shit with Tray needs to end. I knew it would be a shit show having him here, but damn, I saw none of this coming. Speaking of, I haven't seen him or Darcy since I left them downstairs. Right now, the four of us are hanging in Lexi's room, watching the storm whip through our home. Mom's out of mind with worry about where they guys could be, since we officially have no service now.

I'm blaming myself; that I pushed Ford to leave, and the others followed. They are out in this damn storm because of me. All the *what ifs* invade my thoughts of not once have I reassured him of my feelings. Yes, I have been caught up with Lexi, but every time he looks to me to give him some piece of me, I deny him. I need to prepare myself for the possibility that he doesn't show back up here when the others do. I honestly would not blame him, but I will need to find an excuse as of why when Lexi asks.

Dr. Leeds and Dr. Hunt came in a bit ago and stated that they have a direct line to what Ophelia is doing and her impending doom. She is wreaking havoc over the tip of Roanoke, hence why the winds and storm has picked up here. Word has it though; she keeps veering right. Which is what we want her to do. To head back into the Ocean with little damage and not turn back around.

Dr. Leeds also stated they were going to bring Lexi down to the infusion room to start her platelet transfusion, but with the elevators out, they are just going to complete it here in her room. That way she is comfortable if we lose all power and not stuck somewhere else in the hospital. We are expecting the nurses to roll in within the hour to begin.

Luckily, she is awake now, and Dr. Leeds was able to explain the process in *Lexi* terms. Dr. Hunt did an examination on her and noticed several more bruises coming to surface and feels it's best to not delay anymore. With Ophelia looming, he stated it could be days before we have biopsy results back.

I feel like every aspect of my life is a waiting game. Wait to see what Ophelia is going to do. Wait to see if we get swept away to sea. Wait for results. Wait for her to feel better. Wait for the guys to return. Wait for our phones to work to check on the outside world.

"Maren!" The heavy door swings open by a battered Ford. "Ford, oh my God, are you okay? I thought...I thought that you left," I stutter out, trying to find my words. Mom reaches him first for a hug, not caring that she is now soaked.

"Dad and Dawson are headed up this way." His words cause Izzy to jump to her feet in anticipation. I know she has been playing her worry down to help Mom.

"What on earth happened?" she asks in shock. He locks his eyes on me. Before me I see a disheveled, soaked to the bone mess of a man.

"Ford, you're back," Lexi squeals, happy to finally get a word in.

"Sure am, mini bar. Um, let me go dry off and put dry clothes on before I give you the world's biggest hug."

"Okay, but hurry up. I haven't seen you all day," she sasses to him. The grin stretches across his face as he locks eyes on me again, shuffling her hair before heading to the bathroom with his bag.

As soon as he disappears, Dad and Dawson show up, followed by, "Duncan? What are you doing here?"

"Well, hello to you, too, Miss Hart." He gives me a cheesy smile.

"No, but really, why are you even out in this?"

"Just performing my neighborly duties for three crazy men trying to get themselves killed." Dad shakes his head, taking Mom into his arms.

Dawson does the same with Izzy, and she chuckles. "Ew, Dawson, you are wet and you smell." He nuzzles into her neck, making her laugh as she tries to push him off of her.

Looking at the three of them, I shake my head. "I don't think I even want to know."

"You don't," Ford says as he steps out of the bathroom. "But we lived to tell the tale. Just later. I have things I need to do." First, he walks over to Lexi, carefully scooping her up in his arms as he sits on her bed, kissing the top of her head. "How's it going, mini bar?"

"Boring. Power is out, so I can't watch movies. Mommy and Izzy are playing cards with me. But Mommy is too com..competit..too competitive to lose, so she is no longer fun to play with." I gasp; they all laugh as if it's true.

"Well, I am here to save the day. What do you want to play?"

"Old Maid!" she shouts excitedly. He reaches over to the table next to the bed and grabs the deck.

"Here you shuffle these then pass them out. I'll be right back." I watch as he gently places her back down on the bed, then he struts over to me. Standing in front of me, my eyes gloss over. "Maren," he whispers softly, his eyes reminding me of sunflower fields that I could be lost in all day. Before I move or speak, his hand is in my hair at the nape of my neck, tugging me toward his body. His other arm wraps around my waist, holding me tightly against him. Ford's lips hover over mine. "I'm here." This is the end to my resolve. I shatter in his arms, no more strength to hold myself together in front of everyone. Ford picks me up bridal style, turning us to Lexi. "We will be back in a few minutes, mini bar. I need to discuss some things with your mom."

"Okay, hurry up." My parents and Izzy just stare at us in wonder while Ford carries me out of the room, sobbing like a toddler who lost her favorite toy. Using his evident charm, he gets the nurse to tell him where a vacant room is for privacy to talk. She's unsure at first but finally relents to his billionaire smile and handsome looks.

Once in the room a few down from Lexi, he places me on the patient bed. I'm a snotting, sniffling mess, trying to reign emotions back in. "Maren, we won't leave this room until you share the last six years with me in full detail." The wave of familiarness of him close to never being able to lie to him and always do as he requests rolls over me.

Wiping my eyes, I begin. Starting with learning when I was pregnant up until I got to the cause of panic attacks. He is raging. No question, he would kill Trayton if we were to see him right now. Ticking jaw and clenching fists, he grits out, "Continue," in a dark voice. One I don't recognize. He's pacing back and forth as I run through the events of Lexi being born early and her near death experience. How my own life was touch and go from the moment they admitted me for an emergency c-section to the following days of my body being too weak to fight off the Anesthesia, severe anemia, and low blood pressure on the verge of being nonexistent. Pausing again, I look up at him while I shift uncomfortably in my seat. His eyes pool with tears as he shakes his head and walks over to me, kneeling to be on my level. "Fuck, Maren. I need you to continue, but please just give me a minute to get my shit together. I don't know if I want to squeeze you tightly or punch a wall."

"I get it. Take the time you need." He begins pacing back and forth between the wall and countertop, flexing his hands this time, looking distraught. There is no clock on the wall, and I left my phone in Lexi's room. Thinking about it, it's been at least ten minutes of silence. I twirl my ring to pass the time.

Suddenly, he walks over and kisses me on the forehead. "Continue."

"You sure?" My eyebrows raise in question. I won't lie, Ford looks as if he is going to snap. Probably with the next set of information I reveal.

"Yes, I need to hear it all." I walk him through my healing process along with Lexi's. Her time in the NICU to bringing her home. How I pushed to get my life together in order to support us. How Darcy was my guardian angel along with her family during the years. How brilliant and kind Lexi was from beginning but caring less about Trayton to when he signed over his rights to her.

Standing up, I walk over to him, taking his hands in mine. "The last bit involves Tray." He nods, pulling me into his chest, before stepping back so I can continue. "The shit that has gone down today has been exhausting and overwhelming, but let me start on where I was before you found me passed out."

Slipping my hand from his, I turn around to sit on the bed again. "I found out that one of Tray's guards was the one following me around all this time. I overheard Darcy and the guy talking, then Tray walked up, solidifying my thoughts on how I knew that man. The man, Jones, was the one that helped me after I wrecked my Jeep. I was a fumbling mess, but he sat with me in the pouring rain until help came. He looked familiar then, but I could never put any of it together until today. I had mentioned to Darcy and Jim multiple times I felt I was being followed, but they swept it under the rug of paranoia of being a new mom. It turns out that not only did Tray hire someone to follow me, but he also involved himself in our life. Had a part in my paycheck, from random bonuses and raises. Helping with bills to getting a discounted rate at Lexi's school." His goes into an open mouth stare.

"It freaked me the fuck out, Ford. This guy who abandoned me was taking care of us all along. Then he confessed that he had always loved me but knew he never treated me right. That he needed to focus on football and keeping me at a distance was best. Plus, he caved to his parents' wants of not claiming Alexis. All his confessions took me back to all those times I was struggling, only for a bill to be paid, or a glitch in the system happened, to having random groceries left at our doorstep. I was working, finishing school, and raising a daughter. It was a fucking lot, so I went with it. Refused to question any of it, as if maybe I was getting a lucky break. It wasn't luck; it was always him. The man I despised with my every being for all this hell I had gone through."

Running his large hand through his already tossled hair, he murmurs, "Fuck, baby. I can't imagine your emotions through finding this out. Doesn't mean I want to murder him any less though."

A little giggle slips from my mouth. "That's the thing; I don't know how to process any of it. Part of me wants to forgive him after knowing all this, but the other part is that I had so much hatred built against him over the last several years, I don't know how. But I will say, Ford, Trayton never knew how bad off I had gotten. Darcy never shared with him the extent, so all that with my mom today was somewhat of a shock to him."

He cocks his eyebrow. "Mom told me earlier about her losing her shit and how stunned Trayton was."

"Yeah, the woman broke all the rules in the waiting room. After she left, I honestly saw the pain the news caused him and then he and Darcy left."

"I won't keep things from you either, Mar. I got a punch to his jaw before his guards took me down." I look at him in shock and fear. Fear the old Ford was making an appearance. A side of him he has learned to control. "All good, I promise. We had a few more words, and then he left. He told me he would not get in the way of us being together, that he knows it was him you never loved. Is that true?" He melts me with his somber eyes.

"Yes, that's true. I never loved Tray like that, more of a close friend with benefits. You were the only one I have ever been in love with."

"Were or are?" He saunters closer, lifting my chin up to meet his gaze.

"Both," I whisper. His sensual lips meet mine, and I know my knees would give completely out if I was not already sitting. Our tongues tangle in a seductive dance as he steals my breath away. Relentless-ness and desperation roll off on him onto me. For once, a feeling of belonging sends shock waves through my heart. A haze lifts around me, where it's just him and me. No Trayton, Lexi's not sick, no blonde Grace, no drama, and no hospital walls enclosing around us. *Just us.* All consuming us.

Ford

I
Am
Out
Of
Control.

SNAP OUT OF IT, Ford. I pull away from Maren in order to stop from fucking her on this bed. To keep from throwing her against the wall followed by the counters. When my body catches up to my brain, I release her wrists that are pinned above her head against the small bed. *When did I even crawl on top of her on this damn thing?* "Sor...Sorry, baby."

Her hand grazes my face. "Ford, please don't apologize. I would have stopped you eventually."

A dark laugh releases from my soul. "I don't think you would have been able to." Her face twists up in question. Is this really the time to tell her I need control in all areas of my life? In order to stop from beating the shit out of someone, I relent to rough, sometimes painful, sex. That BDSM gave me a sense of control when I felt I was losing the battle. "Can we save that conversation for another day?"

"Yes, of course. We have had enough of a whirlwind today.

Let's get back to Lexi." I let out a breath as if I was holding it in desperation, begging for her not push. Maren pulls herself together, running her fingers through her messy hair, straightens her clothes, and then opens the door.

I quickly close it. "I promise we will talk, but please know I will never hurt you in that way."

"It's okay, Ford, really."

"I just saw that hint of fear flash in your adoring eyes. I just want you to know; you can trust me."

"I trust you, Ford. If you saw fear, it was quickly replaced with curiosity of your statement. Now, let's go." She takes my hand, sending a zing of excitement through my nerves, and we head back to Lexi's room right when all the power goes back out. The only sound to be heard is the heavy rain and hail ricocheting off the windows, and in the far distance, the storm surge warning. It seems Ophelia is not far from making landfall.

CHAPTER 26
CALM IS OVERRATED
Maren

As much as I would love nothing more than to dwindle on the enticing sexy thoughts of Ford's tongue licking down my neck, kisses on my jawline, hands holding mine in place, and his Irish spring bourbon scent mixed with rain engulfing all my senses, *I can't*. While we were gone, Lexi was hooked up to her transfusion. Once we walked into the room, the power went extinct.

Twenty minutes later, there's still no sign of coming back on. All we hear is the wind and rain from outside, along with the little beeps coming from Lexi's own backup standalone battery to keep the transfusion from stopping. I'm sitting behind her on the bed to help her stay still and comfortable. Ford sits on the other end of the bed, his large frame hunched over, cross-legged, playing old maid with Lexi via phone flashlights.

Every so often he and I will lock eyes, then he gives me one of his *melt my inside* smirks, and I have to sigh, then look away. I may not know for certain what my future holds with Ford in it, but right now, the future looks promising. We just need to focus on getting Lexi well and back to our new normal.

Knock. Knock.

"Come in," my mom summons. Shyly, Darcy peeks her head around the door with Trayton's head leering over her shoulder.

"Hey, we just wanted to come up and check on Lexi and fill

you in on a few things from our end." I glance over to Mom and Dad with their stiff shoulders. Ford keeps all his attention on Lexi as if his mortal enemy did not just walk into the room.

"Sure, pull up a seat," I say.

Izzy stands up, motioning to her spot. "Here, Darcy, you can have my chair. I think Dawson and I are going to take the million stairs to the cafeteria for some snacks and soda."

"Thank you." Darcy sits with Trayton hovering behind her, while Izzy and Dawson step out.

"So, what's up?" I ask, playing with Lexi's hair.

"Well, we just wanted to give you the heads up since quite a bit has happened today. We spoke to our parents earlier, and they should be back in town by Friday, and well, um, they want all of us to meet up to discuss the unraveling events."

"Absolutely not," Mom spits out before I can process that the Adair's are coming home and want to meet. I see fear flit through Darcy's eyes.

"I'm just the messenger, and I whole-heartedly agree where you're coming from."

"Why now?" I question, asking for all of us.

This time, Trayton speaks up. "To say they are stunned as I am home is an understatement. Them finding out it was due to Lexi's illness has sent them into an upheaval. I've let them know my personal life is none of their concern, especially when it comes to you and Lexi, Mar, but my PR team is also my dad's legal team. They just want us to get ahead of media fallout before everyone finds out post-Ophelia."

Gritting my teeth, I force out, "What the hell is anyone going to find out about, Trayton? Everyone in this room and hospital has signed non-disclosure agreements. You promised me she would be protected from your limelight."

"What I promise and what actually happens can be two different situations, Maren. If someone leaks that I'm here, which has already happened, it's just a matter of time before someone realizes I'm here for her." I feel Lexi tense against my body, telling me she has been listening to this whole conversation while playing cards. That she is sensing the change in my own aura. This also catches Ford's attention, as I watch his head swivel in Darcy and Trayton's direction.

"You need to handle this," he growls out. "Do what you need to do. If you need assistance, ask. You need help taking care of someone or persons, you come to me and Dawson. Because I am telling you now, Alexis and Maren will not be pulled into *the Trayton spotlight*. No one outside of this room, except her doctors, will know the true relation between you all. This town can gossip all it wants, but with no confirmation, rumors are just rumors."

Ford is very demanding in his delivery. Enough for Trayton to take a step back and actually think before he speaks up again. "I agree. Let the three of us ,plus a few of my men, meet outside this room to discuss further."

Ford nods. "Just tell me when and where. I'll make sure Dawson is there."

Reading the passive aggressiveness of the room, Darcy tries to take back the reins. "In more news, due to Trayton coming home, it seems our dear parents want the town to host a welcome home parade for the all-around small-town hero turned pro."

Flabbergasted, I gape at her. "Seriously, Darcy. You know we have a hurricane on the way, let alone the aftermath could take weeks to clean up, if not months."

"I said the same. You know very well how the Adair's can turn any devastation into a flourishing event. They even have Mayor Cahoon on board. Slated for a town parade next Thursday as long as the clean-up efforts are not overly cumbersome."

Pushing my fingers against my eyebrow in annoyance, I mutter, "Whatever. Who's to say we are even out of here by then. Let alone, a lot can happen by then. I'm not adding that to my itinerary." I look over to my parents, who are just acting as bystanders to this whole conversation. My mom looks like she could strangle these two, then pay off the judge to sweep it under the rug. *Scarily, I think she could pull it off without having to pay anybody off.* My mom is no Adair, but she has this town as much in her back pocket as they do.

Looking back over to an annoyed Trayton and a stressed Darcy, Darcy shakes her head. "We just wanted to give you the heads up. On the bright side, Jim and the kids will be coming in for the festivities."

"Yay, Uncle Jim and cousins!" Lexi exclaims. She loves them all so much, and I know I will enjoy them all being here, regardless of the reason. "Um, Aunt Darcy. Are you and Trayton staying with us when we go back home?"

Darcy lets out a slight laugh. "No, honey, we will stay at our parent's house. Right now, we are just staying at the hotel across the street. But, as of right now, it seems like we are sleeping at this hospital tonight."

I hear a slight knock before the door opens again, and Dr. Leeds strolls in. "Look at all of you here." She gives a big grin in Tray's direction, and I swear you can hear the eyes roll in the room. "Just wanted to come check on Lexi and make sure she is feeling okay and hoping the nausea medicine is helping, too." Lexi nods. Right then, the power kicks back on. "Oh thank God, I was hoping they would get the back-up power on before nightfall." We can hear cheering out in the hallway and other patient rooms. Angelica walks over to check the machine supplying Lexi's platelets. "Only two more hours to go. You are doing great, Alexis."

Lexi beams. "Everyone has been playing cards with me and keeping me busy."

"Well, good. A nice distraction through a boring process is always helpful. Maren, Trayton, can I see you in the hallway real quick?"

"Sure." Ford comes over to help lift Lexi up a bit, so I can slide out behind her. Before following Trayton, he grabs my upper arm, with a look of concern. "It's fine. Just hang with Lexi until I get back." He nods, kissing me on the forehead. Forehead kisses may not mean a lot to others, but I swear it's one of the most endearing ways to be affectionate. Squeezing his hand on my arm, I slip out to see what else is going on.

"Sorry for pulling you out of there; there is just a lot going on right now and I didn't want to say a whole bunch in front of Lexi and a large crowd."

"Alright," I say skeptically.

"First thing, Ophelia is heading for us but veering to the right. It looks like the south end of the island is going to take the worst of the hit. We could definitely experience another power outage due to the winds, and we're still expecting a hefty storm surge over the seawalls and flooding. Lexi has two more hours to go; we will give her another round of nausea medicine if needed. Then we will start back up a round of steroids. Tomorrow, if all goes well through the night, we will run another set of blood work along with a blood transfusion." Turning her attention to Tray, she murmurs, "I know you mentioned you need to head out for a few days. What kind of schedule are we looking at it?" Now I'm the one lost and confused.

"I need to head back to Philly by Friday for the weekend, and then I can be back on Monday. There are several press junkets I can't miss, and I need to attend some practices." My mind wanders when he is going to announce to everyone else that he is leaving. And will he actually come back?

"Okay, that works. Let's have you donate again tomorrow afternoon and that should get us through until you're back on Monday. We still have the extra bag on hand now also."

"Just tell me when, Doc; I'll be there." That sends Angelica into a fit of giggles, patting his arm.

Clearing my throat to bring the conversation back to Lexi, I ask, "So what you're saying is, we will definitely be here through the weekend?"

"Honestly, Maren, it could go either way. We could start to see improvement to where she could go home to be more comfortable and then come back for the transfusions. The biggest thing right now is getting her platelet count back up and pushing her body to create more on its own again. It also comes down to is she safer here than at home due to storm damage, power outages, let alone cell service coming back up. I say right now, we focus on one day at a time."

"Alrighty, then." I give a sharp nod, pressing my lips together.

"Great. I will go update Nurse Nikki on the plans for the evening as well as a few more rounds I need to make. See you two later."

"I remember her being peppy in high school, but how does she maintain that level day in and day out with literal chaos surrounding her?"

I chuckle at his remark. "And that is why she is a doctor, and you are not."

Laughing with me, he says, "Yeah, I guess you're right. Hey, Maren, care to join me on a walk to talk?"

"Are you going to trap me in an elevator again?"

"Absolutely not. Learned my lesson on that one real quick."

"Sure. Let's head to the café to grab a coffee. I know I could use one right now."

Reaching the café, it seems everyone else had the same idea now that power exists, and everyone has a chance to get their caffeine fix.

"Talk," I tell Tray. He looks over at me with a quirked eyebrow. "Judging by the line, you have about fifteen minutes to speak freely, then five minutes back to the room. So, you better start talking."

"Good to know you still try to run the conversation."

"I try when I'm not being held hostage in a state of shock."

He lets out a light laugh. "Touché, Maren Hart." He pauses, then speaks, "Look, I know you and I will never be an item. And I also know I signed over all rights to Lexi as a parent, but I wanted to know if there is some way I can be in her life." There is no hiding the shock on my face. "I know, I know," he grumbles, throwing his hands up as an accused victim, "I know I have no right to ask, but I wanted to see if there's a chance. Of course, by your rules alone."

Taking a deep breath, I let it out slowly, choosing my words carefully. "Trayton, this goes back to what I asked earlier. How does she fit into your life? Let alone, no one is to know she is yours, so how do you expect to have a relationship with her? Sure, Darcy is your sister but also a friend; I can explain that regardless of if it fuels rumors. But you having direct contact with her in public will be a media nightmare for her and this town. I brought her back home to be with family and have a chance at a normal life. Granted, we haven't gotten that far down normal yet, but that's the plan."

Looking back up to him towering over me, I can see the pain in his eyes of all the regrets he's made. "I don't know the answers yet, Maren, but I would like to try."

Remorse floods over me with a touch of forgiveness. This man in front of me is trying. Isn't *that all I wanted over the years?* "No promises, Tray, but I'll talk to Lexi and Ford about this. Also, I would like to get her better and home before dealing with the *maybe*."

He grins like a kid on Christmas morning. "That's all I'm asking, Mar."

I can't decide if I feel a weight being lifted or the weight just being shifted.

CHAPTER 27
MURKY WATERS
Maren

The past twenty-four hours have been a complete nightmare. Last night alone was one for the books as the scenes replay in my head. By the time Trayton and I made it back to Lexi's room, there was a shift in the room. Ford wouldn't look at me, my mom's shifty eyes were glossed over. Izzy and Dawson were back, but he was pouting in the corner as she gave me a sympathetic smile. Darcy looked unaffected with her poker face on. I pushed through the awkwardness to love on Lexi, who was beginning to look several shades of white and green.

With a little under an hour to go, we were hoping she would have made it through vomit-free. As quick as she said, "Mommy, I feel sick," the puke shot out of her mouth and nose, all over the bed and floor.

A nurse ran in once I had pushed the button several times to assist. Dawson sped out of the room, knowing he is a sympathy puker, with Izzy hot on his heels. Ford helped the nurse and me roll up all the sheets to dispose of them as I washed Lexi's face with a cold, wet washcloth. The nurse was adamant about getting the last thirty minutes in, so we waited. *And waited*. Thirty minutes felt like three hours in the desert with the amount of animosity swirling in the air.

Once her treatment was complete, the nurse unhooked her

from the machine, as well as all her monitors, so I could bathe her. Once she was clean, back in a clean bed, and a room smelling of bleach and that all-consuming hospital smell, she passed out, curled up with Mr. Pickles. Who luckily was not in the blast zone earlier. The nurse came and re-hook her up to the monitors again and started back her IV on a nausea med and steroids.

Once she walked out of the room, I looked to the remaining people. "Can someone tell me what the hell is going on?" Darcy motioned to Tray for them to leave. My head snapped in their direction. "Darcy what happened after we left?"

She twists her hands together, avoiding eye contact. "I thought it would be okay to share them with them, but based on their reactions, they probably should have been burned or I should have least asked you."

"What did you share, Darcy?" I ask through clenched teeth. Out of the corner of my eye, I see my mom raise a folded piece of paper in her hand. "You didn't?" My eyes pooling with tears. "Those were not to be read unless something happened."

"I know; I just thought they would want to know how much you loved them and needed their forgiveness. I talked to Dawson earlier, and he filled me in on how things are going here. How he has been struggling with having you back home."

Taking a deep breath, then cracking my neck both ways, I look at her dead in the eyes when she finally glances up at me. "Let me get this straight... You gave them the letters I wrote to them during a time I was hurt, broken, and there may have been a possible horrific ending. Instead of them lathering in the love I had for them as you thought, they are wallowing in the pain I was in, remembering the last six years of being gone and telling them to move on with their lives because we all needed to find peace in the dumbest decision I have ever made."

She nods, defeated. "I'm sorry, Mar. I thought it would help them know a piece of you during that time."

"Darcy, I love you, but right now I need you to leave this room." Trying my damndest to not lose my ever loving mind right now, I try to recall what is said in all these letters. The door closes behind them, and I turn to Mom and Dad. "I'm sorry if anything in the letter hurt you. That was never my intention."

My dad comes up, pulling me into his large embrace. "We are just thankful you are home. I said before, the past is the past, and we all need to move forward."

"But Daddy," I cry out.

"No, buts, Maren. The letter was an insight into your thoughts and fears. None of that matters now."

My mom joins us. "We love you, sweet Maren."

Sniffling into Dad's chest, I ask, "Is Dawson going to be, okay?"

Rubbing her palm up and down my back, she murmurs, "He will be, sweetie, he will be." She looks over my shoulder to whom I can assume is Ford. "Your dad and I are going to head to the café and figure out where we are going to sleep tonight." Dad kisses me on top of the head, and does the same to a sleeping Lexi, before they walk out of the room.

My eyes locked on the wind and rain whipping through the outside world. Wishing I was out there being washed away with the rest of the useless scraps.

Ford

FOUR IN THE morning I lay awake with Maren crushed against my body on the rock-hard sofa bed. Pondering over the events of last night. Maren and I were in a stand-off as the silence became suffocating. Her letter shook me to the core. I'm not even sure she remembers what she wrote, but those words are now branded in my mind.

"Can I see the letter?" she asks. Unfolding the paper, I hand it over. As she scans the page, I recite the words in my head.

> Ford,
> I have written many letters to you over the past several months. Now, I find myself writing another one that I am also not sure you will ever receive. See, the previous letters were asking for forgiveness. Checking in on you to make sure you were well and succeeding. But this letter is different. I know now I don't deserve your forgiveness because I never earned your love in the first place. We were not in the best place when I left. Arguing, hurt feelings, me trying to figure out why you acted like an oven switch toward

me. Why around us was always filled with tension. Over time, I have learned, that the person I need to forgive is myself. For not acting on my own selfish feelings for you. For not trying to see if you reciprocated them. In my gut, I felt you did. But it could have been me reading many scenes we had together completely wrong.

    Right now, I'm not in a good place, and my own future is questionable at most. If rumors haven't become truths now, then let me give you the truth. I ran away with Trayton to Tennessee to live with his sister and family. Why you ask would I do such a crazy thing? Well, I'm pregnant. Not that Trayton is around to witness this, but I'm almost eight months. My health is not great, and the doctors not only fear for my precious girl's life but for mine as well during delivery. I've not been kind to my body, regardless of the fact of being an incubator for another life. My mind and heart want no part of it as I am scared and feel so alone. Disappointment runs through my veins. Regret harbors my soul. I was told to get my life in order, incase of an "event." Meaning the event of death. Though I have been trying to be better and praying to a God that knows I turned my back on him, but the damage has already been done. So, with this letter, there are a few things I wish to say and then ask.

    Firstly, I love you, Ford Merrick. I believe I have loved you since the first time Dawson and I saw you at the movies. Granted, I was young, but something inside me was drawn to you, never wanting to be untethered. Now that I'm older, I believe it was my soul.

Secondly, you were my best friend. I know you are Dawson's, but you saw me in a way no one else did. You loved my dreams and goals as if they were your own. Though none of those are coming true, having you in my life was enough.

Thirdly, if no one has told you recently, you are the man your momma would be proud of. She loved you so much, Ford. Your dad also. Not sure where you are now or what you are doing, but I know in my heart you are worthy and a son your parents are proud of.

Fourthly—that one just sounds odd—but keeping in trend. I hope you have found ways to channel your anger and emotions with me not being around. I won't lie. I loved being your anchor. Your infinite possibilities and reasons, I believe you once told me. If I make it to becoming a mom, I hope she sees me in the light you always did. But I promise myself to make sure she feels every ounce of love and pride from me daily. Knowing you and your story only proves life is short and unknown.

Fifthly, now is the ask. If I don't make it to the other side of this, and she does, my ask is that you raise her with Dawson. I have asked the same from Dawson in his letter. I know the both of you will do right by her and, of course, our parents to have huge role in her life, but they are older, and I know Dad will eventually retire and take Mom around the world as he promised. I don't want them taking on the burden of another child. Now you may ask, why give you and Dawson this very burden. Because you two are the best of me. Surely, Dawson will marry eventually, and *conversations will need to be had on custody. Who, what, when, and how will need to be answered. But I know you two will do what's best. And I also hope one day you fall madly in love and marry someone that understands every small entity of you as much as the larger ones. And will understand and love my little girl just the same.*

Sixthly—sounds even weirder. This is your out. If neither of you want to take on this ask, I understand and will not hold it against you. Nor do I want you to carry any guilt. I want you happy, Ford. Whatever that entails. Arrangements have been made for Darcy and Jim to adopt her, and of course, you can visit. At this point, I just want it all laid out on the table. And again, who's to say you even read this. That I don't miraculously survive for a second chance. Then again, if you are reading this letter, my demise has been met. And, for that, I'm sorry I never had a chance to hold you one last time.

I know this was a lot to take in. I, myself shedded some serious tears writing yours alone. I love you, Ford, always have and always will. Maybe I will have a chance to be more than a "friend" or "sister" in the next life. Until then, be happy, Ford. Live, laugh, and prosper. And love. You have so much love to give.

P.S. My darling daughter will be named Alexis Jane (like your momma) Hart.

Good-bye, Mar

I gander at her tear-stained cheeks, reliving that moment in time where she thought she would die. Where she felt alone but wanted to confess her love for me and do best by her daughter. The same daughter that lays in the hospital bed and has captivated my heart since arriving home. No doubt in my mind, if the inevitable happened, I would have taken Alexis in. To have a piece of Maren with me always. To have a piece of my mom, now knowing her middle name.

Regret fills me as I should have told her those many times, I loved her, too. Instead of giving her whiplash with my emotions. Instead of burying my cock in a nameless pussy to try and forget her. To hide my own shame and anger or being left alone and abandoned by another person who said they cared for me.

Looking over at a sleeping Lexi, I grab Maren's hand and walk us over to the sofa bed. Pushing a stand of hair behind her ear, I whisper, "Look at me, Maren."

Sobbing, she whimpers, "I can't. I just can't, Ford." Instead of pushing the topic, I pull her into my body, letting her cry into my shoulder. Palming her back in light strokes in comfort as she mumbles apologies.

Despite all the hurt she has caused me, and I know my feelings are not inept, but her soul has been shattered and needs to be slowly pieced together again before we can move forward.

"You are too good to me!" she cries out. "After all the hurt, hiding, and back and forth we have had, you are still here. Maybe as Dawson stated, I really am the problem. I should take Lexi and start over where no one knows me. Free you of all of my burdens."

Desperate fury rumbles through me, pushing her off of me, then cupping her face in my hands. "Dammit, woman, I dare you to say that again..." She blinks in confusion. "Let me make one thing clear. No one is leaving, Maren. I'm for damn sure not going nowhere."

As if our final resolve snaps in place, our lips crash together. Her desperate to salvage the pieces of me she needs to make herself whole again. For me, it's the need, the want, the lust for her to consume every fiber of my being to be only hers. For her to trust what we have is worth moving on from the past to begin a future together. For her to let me heal her and be there for her and Lexi.

"You awake?" Maren's voice whispers over me, Pulling me back from my thoughts.

"Yeah, I am. You okay?"

"Honestly, no, but for the first time in a long while, I feel like I might be with time."

Leaning over to kiss the top of her head, I quietly murmur, "You will be, baby. I promise you will be." She snuggles in closer as we lay there listening to Lexi's monitors beep and storm die down outside. Wondering if we will be able to see the sunrise this morning through the broken up dark clouds.

CHAPTER 28
SUNRISE
Maren

I AWAKE TO BRIGHTNESS. A brightness I have not seen in days as I catch Ford adjusting the blinds. "Sorry," he whispers. "I was trying to close them a little to keep from this room lighting up."

"No, just leave them. It's good to see the sun this morning. We need the reminder to push past our sorrows to ready ourselves for the day to come." He gives me a smirk, then walks off to the restroom. I glance over at Lexi, who is still sound asleep with Mr. Pickles in a death grip. Yesterday was a big day for her, and she did way better than I anticipated.

My attention quickly pulls in another direction when a slight groan, like the sound is being shielded from the bathroom fan and shower running. Silently, I tip-toe over to the door, holding my ear against it. Another guttural groan. Masking my mouth with my hand, I feel like a teenager spying on something indecent.

Hell, maybe I am.

Like is he really yanking himself in the hospital room shower. "Fuck yeah," I hear in a low, gravel tone. Grinning from ear to ear, I'm speechless but also feel the pool of wetness between my legs. *Totally not the time or place.* After yesterday, having him pinning my arms above my head, licking and sucking my neck and lips, feeling how hard he was against my stomach... *Jesus*, who couldn't be wanting more.

Taking one look back at Lexi, still sound asleep, I slowly push the bathroom door handle down, slipping quietly into the steam-filled bathroom. I see his silhouette through the shower curtain. One hand on the wall in front him as his other tugs hastily on his member. I'm not bold enough to undress myself and jump in with him, especially not here. Knowing lines would be crossed and would prefer not knowing my body spent time with him inside my sick child's shower.

Who's to say I can't at least take a glimpse?

I carefully pull back the shower curtain with my fingers, nearly gasping when I catch his rippling back muscles down to his taunt ass. His arm muscles flex with each stroke. His moans are deeper, more intense than the last. He must be close to his release.

"I know you're there," he grunts out. Turning around, locking his eyes on me, he struts toward me while fisting his cock. My eyes widen in being caught, but there is no looking away now. No apologizing for witnessing the God-like scene playing before me. "This," he slowly slides his hand down, over his cock, "this, Maren, is what you do to me. You make me so *fuck-ing hard*. I've lost count the number of times I've had to off myself over you." My breath hitches. "Your face, your smell, *fuck*, your taste, your damn laugh, everything about you turns me on. My body aches for you."

His free hand whips to the back of my head, wrapping my hair around his fist, then pulling my head back just enough to look right at him. Ford licks up my neck to my lips, then thrusts his tongue into my mouth. A moan escapes my mouth into his, and he swallows it down. I am a ball of tightly twined sexual tension needing release. Every kiss, every tightening of my hair is like an impending orgasm. "I'm going to come all over you," he pants against my lips.

"Do it," I mutter, sealing my dare with a stroke of my tongue over his naked chest and across his collar bone. I place both hands on his chest, running my nails down his indented stomach until I reach the beginning of his trail. The trail I want to follow all the way down to get a taste. So, I do, knowing he is about to explode. And I am *fucking* here for it. His breath becomes heavy as I remove his hand, while bending down to my knees on the cold, wet tile floor.

Before he can speak, my tongue licks the tip, tasting his sweet pre-cum. Only leaving me to crave more. Hooking my one arm around his muscular thigh to hold me in place, I take my other, gripping him literally by the balls. He moans out, gripping my hair tighter. Then, I make my move, first licking the under base before slipping him between my lips.

"Maren, I am about to....errr.....Jesus fuck...take me now," he grits out. Knowing I'm only going to get in a few sucks before I welcome my breakfast, I suck hard, moving my mouth up and down his hard cock. Feeling it swell in my mouth for release, my teeth bite down with just enough pressure, grinding him and breaking the dam. He shoves himself to the back of my throat as I take in the warm liquid, my eyes watering, trying not to choke but loving every damn minute of pleasing him.

When he tries to pull his semi-hard dick from my mouth, I tighten around his balls one more time and suck hard again, earning another sexy groan from his lips. Slowly pulling my mouth off, I drag my tongue along the length, then lick the tip. *Damn*, if I'm going to let any of him go to waste. Still kneeling, I look up at him, with hooded eyes. His hand wraps under my chin. "That was hot, and you are so beautiful." Ford helps me off the ground and into his wet arms. "That was incredible, baby. Let me know when we can do that again."

I smile, then reality hits me. "Pencil me in for once we are out of this joint." This earns a chuckle from him as he realizes what we just did and where. Giving me a side glance, I'm sure he's half wondering if we screwed up and I'm going to freak out and half giving into indulgence for once with no regret. "Let me walk out first and field her." He nods, walking to his bag to pull clothes out.

I slowly open the door to see her flipped over facing the

opposite wall. Walking to that side of the bed, her eyes are still closed and breathing steadily. Thank goodness! I know we tried to be quiet, but it still was not our finest moment. Rubbing her arm, I say, "Hey baby girl, you want to wake up for mommy? It's to get some breakfast." She yawns and stretches, then mumbles something incoherent.

Hearing my phone beep, I walk over to the sofa bed, and well, it looks like we have cell service finally. The text is from Mom, letting me know we have service now, and she is on her way with breakfast. I go to knock on the bathroom door right when Ford steps out. "Oh, hey, um, Mom is on her way up with breakfast and guess what?" He quirks his eyebrow. 'We have cell service."

Wrapping his arm around my waist, he pulls me into his clothed chest, kissing me softly. "That's great news. Now we can hear and view the aftermath."

We hear a knock on the door. "Come in," we say in unison.

"Isn't it just a beautiful day today!"

"Good morning to you, too, Mom. You are way too chipper."

"I have every reason to be. Your dad and Dawson went to check on the house, and no damage was done, just a few limbs and a tear in the pool liner, but nothing we can't easily fix. The dock will need a few repairs, and all the shops and restaurants of the pier were flooded, but again, nothing life ruining. Also, Ford, you guys have a few trees down, flowerbeds are wrecked, a few shingles off the roof, but standing with no flooding."

"Good to know. Thanks for the update, Madre," he says, walking over to kiss her on the cheek before grabbing a plate of food, taking a seat next to Lexi's bed.

Ford begins scarfing his food down like a savage, causing me to burst out laughing. "Hungry, Ford?"

"Not everyone had a hearty breakfast like you did this morning, baby." He winks at me, causing me to blush, head-to-toe.

"Maren, did you really already eat breakfast? How long have

you been awake?" Luckily she is busy organizing food on the table to pay me a lick of attention.

Giving him a death stare, I mutter, "It was really early this morning, Mom, like half a sausage biscuit. Ford's just mad he didn't get a taste."

"You bet I am. But it's fine, I'll get a taste later." I'm now gawking at this man to shut the hell up.

"Ford, honey, do you want me to run down and get you some sausage?" He nearly chokes on his food, making me grin. Then she looks at me. "You know better, Maren. You always share. What on earth are you teaching my grandchild?"

Laughing, Ford almost drops his plate of food. "No ma'am, I do not need anything else; this is delicious. I just like giving Maren a hard time," sending me another wink behind Mom's back.

She sighs. "Maren, how could you not share?"

"Oh my gosh, Mom, it was a small biscuit." Gritting my teeth on the last part, I watch Ford's playful eyes look discerning. "Besides he was busy, and I had to tend to Lexi. I forgot about the rest, then threw it away." Ford is now the one rolling his eyes at me. I mouth, "you started it," and catch a hint of amber spark in his eyes.

"Fine, alright then. Ford, keep her in line," she states as if I'm not standing right next to her.

"I plan on it," he says in mock-seriousness and salutes her.

"Smart-ass," I whisper.

"Language," she snaps back, walking over to the bed. "Alexis Jane, it's time to get up now."

"Let me sleep, Glam-ma," Lexi grumbles sleepily, rolling back over and pulling the sheets over her head.

"I would, but it's almost eight-thirty. Time to rise and get some breakfast. And if you open your eyes, you might get to see the sun shining."

This gets Lexi's attention, inching the sheets off her face. "Is the hurricane gone?"

"It is, baby girl, it is. A possible rain shower here and there, but the worst is over as Ophelia surfed out to sea," Mom says with heightened excitement.

"Mom, how does the south end look? I know they got hit the hardest." As we live closer to the northern end of the island, the hospital is almost center, hovering closer to the sound end of the island. Hence why we were receiving the horrendous outskirts of Ophelia.

"Several houses went down or were damaged beyond repair and flooded buildings. Rex's bait shop was completely flattened, but if you ask me, it wouldn't take much. Hopefully now he can rebuild a sturdier building. For those that did not move their boats, they are all stacked on top of each. Not sure I heard of anyone's boat coming out unscathed for the ports down there."

"Oh, wow," I say.

"The church is getting volunteers together to head down today to help through the wreckage along with taking water and supplies because power is not back on yet down there."

This is when both Ford and I glance around. "Wow, I just realized it's actual power running and not the generator."

"Seriously, what were you two doing this morning to be completely oblivious and not sharing food?"

"Just living in our own little world," Ford jokes.

Mom takes it seriously. "Whatever works; I know this hasn't been easy on anyone, especially this little girl right here." She smiles, going to tickle Lexi.

Ford moves around Mom to sit her up so she can eat. We do our best to keep her from tangling herself in all the cords she is hooked up to. Mom places her plate on her tray table, then slides it over Lexi's lap. "OOOO Pancakes! My favorite!" she exclaims. "Ford, can you please cut them up for me?"

"Sure can, mini bar." I sit down on the sofa bed and watch the scene unfold before me. For the first time in ages, I feel like a person. A wanted and loved person that has a chance to be normal and give her daughter the world.

CHAPTER 29
Ford

OTHER THAN THIS MORNING, which, *shit*, was totally unexpected but welcomed, today has been uneventful. Jerking myself off is nothing new, especially over the last six months. Using my hand to jerk off to Maren has been my go-to since my hand found my dick as a teenager. Only one time did I use one of Dawson's hidden Playboy magazines he shared with me because the tits and sleek pussy on that model was like nothing our young sexual brains could ever imagine. Maren has been my go-to. Whether wrong or right, she fulfills my thoughts and fantasies.

Now that I have had a small taste of her cunt, a taste of her sweet honey, and seen her grown-up body on my bed, I'm having to relieve myself a few times a day. I push the need aside when busy or in a crisis, but this morning, I broke. With all the high emotions, the sexual tension lying between us since the room incident, and her lying next to me all night, my balls were blue and heavy.

When she sucked me off, I wanted nothing more than to throw her body against the door to fuck her. My own restraint is weaning. My control bending when she lets me see her in a different light. When she banters with me and genuinely smiles. Parts of her that I have missed and haven't seen in over six years. Her vibrant spark is beginning to re-ignite.

I left Maren and Madre back with Lexi to step out and deal with clients since we have been unreachable for over a day. Dawson is out helping the town, so it's the least I can do to work with our secretary, Josef, to reschedule meetings and calm down clients and investors. Several thought we washed away to sea and needed to know what was going to happen to their money. I get it, but damn, if we did die, could you please mourn us for a few days before calling the office demanding a bank note?

After calming everyone down, responding to important emails I couldn't pass off to Josef, I scroll through missed texts. Grace's name catches my eye.

GRACE

> Just wanted to let you know I made it home. Daddy sent a helicopter to get me out since traffic was hellacious.
>
> Please let me know if you are okay. Watching the weather channel.
>
> Dammit, Ford. I know you don't want to talk to me, but let me know you're fine.
>
> I'm sorry, okay. I crossed a line. Don't push me out, please.
>
> I can't get a hold of Dawson either. Please be alright!!!!!
>
> Hate me, but let me know you're alive!!!
>
> Fuck it. I'm coming, even to pull your floating dead body from the ocean.

Good Lord. Running my hand down my face, I take another look at the time stamp. This was last night around ten o'clock. Surely, she really isn't coming. Maren and I are finally leveling out; Grace cannot show up. Ringing her up, *please answer*, I beg out loud.

"Hello!"

"Hey, Grace."

"You are fucking alive!. That's just peachy, Ford."

"Sorry to worry you, we just got cell service this morning."

"It's two in the afternoon, you are just now getting to me?"

"Yeah, I am. There has been a lot going on. Please tell me you are not here."

"Okay, I won't, but I would be lying."

I let out a breath of air. "Where are you, Grace?"

"I'm with Dawson and your dad. Dawson found me at the house waiting for you. We went down to the dock for them to see what materials they need, and now, I believe we are headed to the hospital. Geez, Ford, Dawson told me about Alexis. How awful. Is she doing okay?"

Is it wrong for me to not trust my best friend for several years now? I can't tell if she is being genuine right now or trying to get close to me. Dawson has no clue what happened that night when I dropped her off, but he cannot bring her here. "She is okay. Look, Grace, I'm not sure you should be coming up here. It's been a stressful few days, and I'm not looking to add it for anyone here."

"Too late." She hangs up as I hear a slamming car door. Turning around, I am met with an exuberant Grace jumping into my arms. Dawson thinks nothing of her in my arms; he knows we are close. He knows we dated, and she pulled out of the emotional slump I was in for so long after Maren left. Last thing Dawson knows is that she is pining over her long-lost ex-girlfriend, having no clue she hit on me the other night, wanting to push Maren out of the picture.

Dad pats me on the shoulder walking by with Dawson. "D, where are you going?"

"We are going to head up and see Lexi for a bit before heading back to the dock. Dad grabbed her some candy earlier."

"Nice, tell Maren I'll be up in a few."

"Why don't we just join them?" Grace asks.

"No," I say sharply.

"Seriously Ford, you can't keep us apart forever. We are both in your life."

"How exactly do you see yourself in my life, Grace?"

"How ever you will have me." She runs her hand over my forearm. "Come on Ford, we are best friends. We walk in the same circle of friends; my parents adore you and invest in your company. We are bound together, whether you like or not."

"Grace, we will never be. I need you to understand that. No funny business."

"Sure, scouts honor." She nods her head in all seriousness, giving me the signal. She is right; we are tied together. Her dad does business with Dawson and I. We did hang around the same people in New York and California, but that doesn't mean I'm tied to any of them. More of a show and tell when we are all together. Dawson and Grace have been the only two people over the years I trust with any important information or personal.

"I'm not taking you up to the room, so you can take a seat in the waiting room for Dawson and Dad to come back down."

Rolling her eyes, she mutters, "Fine, whatever." We stop short of entering the waiting room when I notice Trayton and Darcy. I do a quick glance with a head nod to move Grace past them. Not that I think she would have a clue how he was, but I don't want to take any chances because she would talk to a chicken if it clucked at her.

"Holy shit, is that *THE* Trayton Adair?" she whispers in excitement.

"How the hell do you..."

She pushes past me, heading in their direction. "Hi I'm Grace Quinnby," she says, putting her hand out to shake his. She waits for him to acknowledge her, wiggling her fingers slightly. He looks my way, and I nod, annoyed.

"Trayton, this is Grace, a long-time friend. Grace, this is, of course, Trayton and his sister, Darcy."

"Oh, my goodness, I completely forgot you came from this small island. My daddy is obsessed with your career. Doesn't hurt when you make him money in bets. Oh, but don't divulge that information, he is the governor of New York after all." Trayton smiles at me, but I can tell he is confused on who she is and why she is with me.

"Look, I need to head upstairs to check on Maren and Lexi. Care if Grace hangs with you for a bit?" I stuff my hands in my pockets, acting like this is a completely normal thing to say to my nemesis and ex. I can only pray they all keep their mouth shut on why they are here and who knows who.

"It's fine, I'm just waiting on Angelica to pull me back for more," looking over at Grace, then back to me, unsure, "um, more donating."

"Okay." With that one word, I walk away. I don't give a shit what he's doing with Dr. Leeds.

"Ford," he says, stopping me in my tracks. He comes up next to me, talking softly, "I need to fly out tonight for a few days. Can I get a meeting with you and Dawson before I leave?"

My eyes narrow because I know what this meeting entails. "Sure, come find me after your donation." We part, and I head up to the room. Extremely thankful the power is back on and for the elevators.

Excited to see the girls, *my girls*, I waltz into the room, only to be met with an ice cold glare from Maren. Choosing not to address Grace with her at the moment, I head over to Lexi's bed. Bending down, I give her a hug. "How's it going, mini bar?"

"Okay, I guess. Just *soooo* bored," she sighs dramatically, throwing her head back against her pillow, exasperated. "Oh, but wait, Dr. Hunt said I might get to go home tomorrow. But I will have to come back for more treatments and results."

"Well, wouldn't that just be amazing," I say, looking at everyone's excited faces and Maren's fake smile. I should have warned Dawson not to say anything, but not sure when I could have mentioned to him that Grace really isn't gay, she hit on me, and Maren can't stand her. Taking a seat next to Maren on the sofa bed, I whisper, "She just showed up."

"She has a way of doing that, doesn't she?" she quips back under her breath.

"Maren, there is nothing there between us."

"That's fine Ford, but she needs to be gone. She can't be in this hospital when Trayton waltzes around like he owns the damn place with his bodyguards. I don't want her near Lexi. She gives me a bad vibe, Ford."

Pushing her hair behind her ear, I cup her cheek. "I get that. But we do business together, plus we have all been friends for a while. I will talk to Dawson about how to handle this, okay? Just give me some time." She nods in understanding, leaning her forehead against mine. "Too late on the Trayton part." Maren pulls back with anger setting in her eyes, turning a forest green. "She spotted him before I could stop her. She knew exactly how he was without a word from anyone."

"Well damn," she states.

I chuckle. "Yes, damn. But I left her down there, and Trayton was waiting on Dr. Leeds to pull him back to draw more platelets. I guess he is leaving tonight?" I ask, rubbing my thumb in circles on the back side of her hand.

"He is. Maybe it will calm down here a bit with him gone for a few days. Even more so if we can go home at least."

"Has Lexi asked anymore about him or to see him?"

"No, and I honestly can't tell if that should worry me or excite me. But um, I will mention that he asked to get to know her more." My face goes stern, clenching my jaw, "Calm down there. Please. I told him I would think about it, only because he is doing this life saving act for Lexi. Let alone, Tray may be a douche-canoe at times, but he's not a bad person. He knows he signed over all his rights, so I think he is just looking to be a friend or Uncle-like person in her life."

"What about all his fame and media? As much as I despise the man, I enjoy the game and respect him as a player. And he is one of the best out there right now. His popularity is going to grow."

She looks down to our hands. "I know. It's in the back of my mind. Right now, I told him let's just get her healthy and home, then deal with that what-afters"

"Alright. I'll follow your lead," I murmur, kissing her on the forehead. She smiles, and I swear every indecent thought runs through my head at lightning speed. Clearing my throat and slightly adjusting myself, I stand up to walk over to Dawson to chat. To give my mind a break from all sexual things Maren.

Right then there is a knock, then the door opens. We all turn to see Dr. Leeds walking in, followed by Trayton and Darcy, then you guessed it, Grace. Tightly running my fingers through my already messed up hair just enough to feel some pain, I feel Maren tense behind me.

Dr. Leeds breaks the silence. "I really do love walking into this room with all the smiling faces and everyone being in here. Again, we won't mention the hospital policies." Which earns her a chuckle from the group. With tablet in hand, she says, "I do want to go over some results and the next steps."

"Ugh, before you continue, Doc, can I grab Dawson and Ford?" Trayton asks.

"Of course. There are plenty of us in here to relay the message," she says, giving him a wink. Not subtle at all.

I glance at Maren. "It's fine, but take her with you." Her finger points at Grace, also not being subtle.

"Grace, come on," I say as we follow Trayton out the door.

CHAPTER 30
BREAKING OUT
Maren

After the guys left and took the pageant queen with them, Angelica continued with her spiel. Lexi's labs were improving, but her bone marrow hasn't kicked into gear yet to create its own again. Without the biopsy results, Dr. Hunt is unsure how to address that piece of the puzzle. On the bright side, she is no longer anemic and hydrated, but this needs to be monitored as well. Dr. Hunt wants to give her body another twenty-four hours to see if it can kick back in naturally. Being that this has been a whirlwind of a few days, they offered to let us take her home, with strict stipulations.

1. No leaving the house, bed rest only.
2. No outside visitors that she has not already seen here. We do not need any new germs, and everyone is to have an extensive cleansing before going into her room.
3. Medication to give as directed.
4. Check blood pressure and heart rate every two hours.
5. Document any new bruising or new rashes of pinpoint-sized, reddish-purple spots.
6. If worsens, bring her back immediately.

7. Lexi is to return tomorrow afternoon @ 2pm for another transfusion and blood work. We keep our fingers crossed that her blood work will show more improvement to where she doesn't need to come back until Monday. In hopes, by then, we may have results for a plan.
8. For all of us to get some rest.

With those directions, Mom began to make an organizational chart and shopping list. The shopping list went to Dad who was waiting on Dawson to show back up.

Instead, we got a text from Dawson and Ford, stating they had some urgent matters to attend to and would catch up with us later. I texted Izzy to get the scoop, but she knew nothing as she was at the house cooking casseroles for those most affected and without power and that Grace had joined her. I rolled my eyes in annoyance and didn't bother reaching out to Ford. Dad slipped out on his own to shop as Mom and I worked on packing up the room to head home. Angelica stated it could take up to two hours, just get all the orders in and medicines together.

Now we are just waiting. Lexi is on Ford's tablet watching a movie, Mom is on her phone organizing her life, and I'm just here. Just here, feeling completely off balance, which is the polar opposite of how I felt this morning.

"What was Grace doing here?" Mom asks, breaking my incessant thoughts.

"No idea. Ford made it sound like she just showed up out of worry but didn't care to talk about her much to get the details."

"Understood. You know she has nothing on you."

"Is that a statement or a question, because I think she has everything on me. I don't run in those circles that Ford does or even Dawson for that matter."

"Again, you have his heart. You always have. I've heard Dawson and Ford talk about those people. It's all for smoke and mirrors. Why else do you think they decided to come back to this small-town island to settle down? They want no part of that lifestyle more than a few times a year. They know this is where they belong and call home."

"I guess. It's hard to think of them as these tech savvy billionaires because I've known them all my life. Plus, every time I see them, they are in jeans and t-shirts working on the dock or fishing boats with Dad. It's *just* weird."

"I can see how that is weird for you, especially not being here for the transition of their lives. Those two boys of mine have done nothing more than be extraordinary in the projects they take on, putting money back in the community, volunteering, and always showing up for your dad and me." The last comment takes me. Not to think my mom was being vicious of her statement, but it hurts. It hurts because I haven't been here for them. It hurts to know I have missed so much of all their lives while having my own. It hurts because I will never get that time back, and neither will they. I continue to stay silent, not knowing how to respond.

"Like I said before, Maren, you don't get to decide what's best for Ford based on your own assumptions. Besides, I thought you two were doing alright."

"We were. Maybe we still are. I was fine until Grace showed up. I don't trust her, and I am not sure how to handle her being so close to Ford and Dawson. When I texted Izzy, Grace was over there helping her bake. She is embedded in the lives of people I want to be near. Call it jealousy or whatever, but after what she said that night to me, my guard is up with her around."

"Did you tell Ford what she said?"

"No, and not like it's been up for discussion with everything else happening." Swirling my hands in the air, I hope she gets the point. "Honestly, I'm just ready to get Lexi back home and push through whatever she has going on and just take it day by day with Ford at this point."

"Well, maybe you two can have more time to chat once we are back home and on a schedule."

"Maybe." I shrug my shoulders. *Do Ford and I need to talk?*

One hundred percent, yes, but I am just so over the corkscrews of this emotional rollercoaster. I can't seem to get off, no matter how much I cry and scream.

Knock, knock.

"Come in!" I shout. Mom and I look at each other when the door never opens. I walk over, finding Tray on the other side.

"Hey, Mar, I...um," he blows out a breath, running his fingers through his hair, "I'm about to fly out, but I wanted to check and see if I could say good-bye to Alexis."

"Um, sure. Come on in." Stepping aside, Tray strolls in with a bouquet of bright, colorful Gerber Daisies. I feel the corners of my mouth lift into a grin, watching how uncomfortable Tray is in this moment. Trying to navigate some sort of a relationship between the two of them. Lexi looks up from her movie. "Hi, Trayton."

"Hello, Alexis."

"You can just call me Lexi."

"Alrighty then, Lexi. I...um, brought these for you."

"For me?" she exclaims, and I giggle as her dramatic side takes flight. "These are so pretty, thank you."

"You're very welcome. Heard you get to head home today."

"It's true, I do. Can't wait."

"Well okay then." He rubs his sweaty palms down the front of his jeans. "So, I've got to head out for a few days, but I will be back on Monday. Just wanted to stop by and say hi, and I guess goodbye."

"Mommy always says it's not goodbye. Just see you later."

"Then see you later, little Lexi."

"See you later, alligator," she says with the biggest grin, causing him to laugh as he walks out.

"Mommy, what do I do with these?" she asks as the flowers sit on her lap.

"Here let me move them. When we get home, we can put them in a vase with water, so they last, okay?"

"Sounds good." Then she goes back to her movie, flowers forgotten.

Mom lets out a giggle, and I side-eye her. "Well, if that hasn't been the most awkward thing I've had to witness recently."

"He's trying, Mom. Whatever this is going to be, he seems to be trying." She nods in acknowledgement at least.

The door opens again, revealing Dr. Leeds. "Who's ready to go home?" I swear this lady is the most chipper person I know.

"I am!" Lexi squeals.

"Awesome. And it seems I ran into your chauffeur on the way up here." In walks Duncan as she opens the door further.

"Mom, I thought Dad was coming to get us?"

"He must have had something come up, so the guys must have sent him."

"That is true, Miss Hart. Dawson asked if I could deliver you all to the house as they were finishing up business."

"This is very kind of you, but I'd hate to put you out."

"No putting me out, Maren. Just being neighborly, plus my uncle would kick my ass if I left you all here stranded. So, let's go. What can I grab?"

Placing my hand on his arm to get his attention, he stops and glances at me. "You truly are a handsome catch, Duncan. Thank you."

He blushes a little. "I know you are with Ford and all, but I would still like to be friends and try to get on Ford's good side."

"Of course, we can. And good luck with Ford. Keep being sweet to me, he might not ever come around."

A heavy laugh escapes him. "Very true. Then this will be my last act of kindness toward you because Dawson asked."

"Fair enough." I enjoy how Duncan makes everything just *easy*. I turn my attention to Dr. Leeds and the nurse unhooking Lexi from the monitors and helping her get dressed.

"Okay, Maren," she says, handing me a large canvas bag. "All her medications are in here along with a blood pressure machine and pulse ox. Keep them at home for the weekend, and we will see how the next several days go. Both mine and Dr. Hunt's contact information is the bag just incase and call us with any concerns."

I pull her into a tight hug. "Thank you so much, Angelica. You have literally been our angel since we got here."

Hugging me back, she murmurs, "Of course, Mar. I've always adored your family, and that is one precious girl you got there. But hey, we still get to see lots of each other on this journey. And hopefully we will have her results soon to plan an attack."

"An attack?" Lexi yells, sending us into a fit of laughter.

"Not an actual attack, baby doll, but a plan of attack for what is making you sick."

Her mouth forms a big "O". Then, she whines, "Can we go now?" nearly begging.

"Yes, let's go," I say, heading to her bed to help her down. Duncan seems to have all our bags, and Angelica puts Lexi in a wheelchair, while the nurse pushes her. We all follow behind, excited to leave, in hopes we don't have to spend many more nights here.

CHAPTER 31
HOME
Maren

Driving down the road in Duncan's Tahoe, we take in the sights from Ophelia's aftermath. Thankful the damage was not worse, but she put several families out of homes and without power. Fishermen were right on Nags Head not being a direct hit, but I think they underestimated the damage she would ensue during her wrath crossing over.

Luckily, the further north we drive, the less damage we see. Finally pulling on our parent's road, I'm shot with exhaustion. Like the feeling you get when you are almost home from a long trip, powering through the last hour or so, but once you hit home, all you want to do is crawl into your own bed and sleep for days. That's me right now. Firstly, I need to get Lexi in the house, bathed, then situated in her room.

Duncan whistles out, pulling my attention from my phone to him. "This town sure knows how to show up."

"Excuse me?" I ask, scrunching my eyebrows.

"Maren, look out in front of you, not my handsome face." Rolling my eyes, I look out the windshield, and sure enough, it looks as if the whole town is standing in the yard and street to welcome us home. Standing on the front porch is my dad, Dawson, Izzy, Ford, and Harper.

"Oh my god! Mom, did you know about this?"

Grinning, she chuckles. "I might have had a little clue." She turns to Lexi. "Look, babydoll, all these people are here to see you and wish you a fast recovery."

Her green emerald eyes grow larger by the second. "All for me? That's just silly." Duncan parks in front of the house and gets out, heading toward the back door to help us out Lexi is already unbuckled and about to jump out of the car, but luckily, Duncan catches her, then puts her down on the soft grass.

"No more crazy stunts right now, baby girl, Okay?"

"Okay, Mommy. Can I go say hi to everyone?"

"Well, Dr. Leeds doesn't want you getting any extra germs, so how about you go stand on the porch with the others, and you can tell everyone thank you from there." She skips off to the porch, and I cringe until she makes it safely and, in Dawson's arms.

Harper comes running off the porch to me, embracing me in a hug. "I'm so happy you are home, and she is okay enough to come home and that there is no damage here. It was driving me crazy not being able to text or call you, but then Ford reached out and let me know what was going on, and I just couldn't wait and …"

"Girl, slow your roll." Harper is speed talking, and I can barely understand all she is saying. We both laugh and settle in each other's arms. I miss the feeling of being able to lean on her regardless of the issue. I look up over her shoulder to my family on the porch, giddy as I am to be surrounded by love and support.

Turning around to the crowd, pushing back the tears, I say, "Thank you so much for this turn out to welcome Lexi home. We still are unsure of what the cause is, but we hope to know soon. As much as I know you would all love to hug her, as she wants nothing more than to say hi all to all of you herself, we were told to lessen the amount of people she has contact with to avoid weakening her immune system further."

My mom comes up next to me, grabbing my hand. "And thank you all for the casseroles, baked goods, and gift cards. With us being in the aftermath of Ophelia, none of this was expected but greatly appreciated. We love you all so much, and we know we can push through the hardships with your support to enjoy the good times."

Lexi yells from the front porch, "Thank you everybody!" then whispers something to Dawson, who then says something back to her before she shouts again, "You are all the very best, and I can't wait to get back to boating and fishing soon."

The crowd goes crazy with hollers and claps. "Come on, let's go in." Now that we are both bumbling crying messes. Mom wraps her arms around me, with Harper following. I'm more shocked when I see how much food, flowers, and cards have been delivered. Lexi is amazed and already convinced all the flowers will be going in her room to admire.

Ford

WHAT A FUCKING DAY. Once Tray pulled Dawson and I aside, I knew business needed to be taken care of quickly. His men had names of those employees of the hospital. We had to have our people track down and make them understand their silence was a necessity for their future.

Some may say we threatened those people, others will deem those threats as protecting the ones we love. Either way, hours were spent tracking them down and handling business.

In the middle of that, I called Harper to let her know the girls would be coming home today because I knew she would want to see them. I had no clue she would play telephone and have half the town show up at the house prior to their arrival. Delivering flowers, food, gift cards, hugs, and support. It took Dawson, Dad, and me back.

As much as we do for others in giving back to the community, it is a completely different feeling to be on the receiving end. Hard to explain, but I can say it's not a pride thing but more like feeling undeserving of someone's good will. Seeing Lexi's face in response to the crowd then all the surprises on the porch was well worth the chaos of the day's events.

The girls are still all in the kitchen, eating casseroles, crying, and laughing over this afternoon's events as Lexi sits on the couch with Dawson and I watching Princess Sofia. Dad is asleep in the recliner after all his shopping adventures today. Honestly, I think we are all spent emotionally and physically after the monotonous days we have had. I get up to grab another beer. "Hey, D, you want another one?"

"Yeah, thanks, bro. Hey, can you check on Izzy for me?"

'Sure." Walking around the corner, I find Izzy in the middle of Maren and Harper laughing. I walk over, pulling Maren off the stool into my arms, kissing the top of her head. "You good?"

"I am just exhausted. Thinking about heading up soon to get Lexi bathed and into bed. Dad already moved a TV in there for her, so that should keep her from doing too much wondering if I can keep a cycle of Disney movies going."

Chuckling, I mutter, "Sounds like a plan. She is in there happy as a pearl in a clam right now." This earns me a full smile from her.

"Good to know."

Reluctantly I let her go, heading to Madre for a hug before grabbing a couple of beers, then walking back to the couch. Tossing one to Dawson, I say, "Izzy seems right at home with Maren and Harper. I don't think you need to fear her not fitting in or Maren disliking her. I've seen Maren lean on her quite a bit this week."

"That's true, and I'm glad to hear it." He takes a swig, then looks back at me. "So, want to tell me what's going on with Grace?" The stress resounds in my body, causing me to crack my neck.

"Shit, is she still at the house?"

"No, Izzy took her to the hotel."

"Oh, good. Yeah, I really need to talk to Maren about it, but between us, and please don't come for me, but Grace is still hung up on me."

"What do you mean, *hung* up on you? I thought she was," he takes a look to Lexi to ensure she is not paying attention to us, "you know."

"Trust me, I thought so, too. She hit on me Sunday night when I took her back to the hotel. Practically threw herself at me. I have been very up front with Grace for years and recently about Maren. Maren can't stand her, so I'm not sure what to do. We have business with her and her family."

"Damn, man. I didn't know it was that serious. But that explains why she has been pushing us for information about Maren. Let me handle the business side, and you just avoid her for right now. But you definitely need to tell Maren because she will gut your balls if she finds out from someone else."

"Don't I know it," I grumble, tossing my beer back.

"Alexis Jane, are you ready to take a bath?"

"Coming, Mommy." I watch that little girl get up and run into Maren's arms. My heart swells at the sight of them together. Thoughts of having kids with Maren rack my brain. Will they look like her or me? Maybe both. I hope they all look like her with her green eyes and have her personality. I watch as Maren carries her upstairs, causing a ping in my chest. The young girl I was infatuated with has turned into a beautiful, strong woman that I am utterly in love with.

There are no other words to describe this profound connection with her. A connection that has always been there, I feel it in every fiber of my being. Craving her, wanting her, to just be near her. The need to be tied to her in every way is consuming.

Turning to Dawson, I ask, "D, when are you asking Izzy?" His head about snaps off when he turns to look behind him to make sure she isn't there.

"Bro, we can't talk about that now. Not here."

Glaring at him, I clench my jaw. "She is five sheets to the wind in the kitchen, we are safe."

He relaxes a bit. "Fine. I was thinking about next month at the gala in NYC. Why?"

"Can you speed up your timeline?" You would have thought I sucker-punched him.

"You better be kidding, Ford," he grits out.

"I'm not. But I am trying to be respectful. I have plans I would like to set in motion sooner than later."

Running his hand down his face, he then sits forward, placing his beer on the table, elbows on his knees leaning into me. "Fuck, you are serious. Well, um, NYC was my first choice, but second would be at the pond by her house. She loves it there."

"Well, why was that not your first option?"

"Because I know how much she loves to get glammed up and shit. But I see where you're getting at."

"Alright, so let's make it happen."

"Shit, Ford. We are supposed to be down at her parents next weekend for her nephew's birthday party. I can't make that happen."

"Sure you can. Name what you need, and I'll take care of it. You already have the ring. I know it's burning a hole in your suit pocket."

Shock washes over his face. "How the hell do you know that? I haven't told a soul."

"Because I know you, D. Besides I have the same problem."

"Motherfucker," he jokes. Checking behind him again, you can tell he's nervous for Izzy to pop around the corner. "Fine. Let's talk details tomorrow when we are not in this house, and I'll have Mom invite Izzy over."

"Good. Now, we have a plan on moving forward."

"Damn you. You're going to owe me big for the amount of stress you are causing."

"Always in your debt, D. Now, if you excuse me, I'm going to go check on my two favorite girls." I take the steps two at a time to find Maren snuggled in bed, reading Lexi a book. Leaning against the doorframe, I take a picture with my phone.

"Hey, no pictures, I look like a hot mess," Maren says.

"You are a beautiful, hot mess, baby." Lexi makes a confused face, but then smiles. "I'm going to take a shower and get ready for bed." I wait for hesitation and the ask of where I'll be sleeping, but it never comes.

"Okay, I'll see you in a bit."

I walk over to kiss Lexi on the forehead. "Goodnight mini bar."

Lexi wraps her little arms around my neck and sleepily murmurs, "Goodnight, Ford." Strolling out of her room, I feel the most at ease than I have in a long time.

CHAPTER 32
ABOUT LAST NIGHT
Maren

WALKING into my bedroom last night to a half-naked Ford was like my all-time fantasy. Granted, I have a lot of them tucked away, but seeing this one come to life had my panties soaked in seconds. Ford lay there with his arms bent, tucked underneath his head, resting on my pillow. The sheets pooled low on his waist, giving me a spectacle of his impressive chest, the contours of his muscles, and the six glorious indentions of his abdomen, which were more defined by the dim lamp on the nightstand. His dark hair a perfect tousled mess to his long lashes I can admire when his eyes are closed. I caught myself literally drooling as my eyes continued scanning over the Adonis of sculpted perfection lying there. Now, I'm in the shower, replaying last night.

"*You coming to bed anytime soon, or are you just going to keep staring?*" *he asks softly, but my body felt his voice as a shout when he first spoke. After I gave myself an internal pep talk, I slid into bed next to him. He quickly pulled my back to his chest, engulfing me in his large arms.* "*Sleep, Maren,*" *he whispers in my ear. How the hell am I supposed to sleep with his hard dick against my ass? I'm horny like a bee in pollen, and he smells delicious. I wiggle my ass a bit against him, under the guise of trying to get comfortable.* "*Maren,*" *he growls, and if that doesn't turn me on more. I wiggle again, grinding back against his hard length.* "We need to sleep," he murmurs, locking his arms tighter around my body.

"I don't think I can," I whisper back. "It's like I've reached another level of over-tiredness and being wired."

A dark laugh releases from him. "Baby, you are pushing me to do bad, bad things to you." I'm able to turn enough in his arms to face him.

"Maybe I want you to do bad things to me." He releases a groan in frustration with a hint of desperation. "Please, Ford. I need you to touch me. Make me forget all the craziness. Make me feel pleasure."

He sits up on his elbow, staring down at me. His other hand slowly glides down my chest to the hem of my shirt. His palm reaches underneath, creating light circles between the hem and my panty line. I push my hips into his hand, demanding more. "Maren, baby, you are going to be the death of me."

"You keep telling me that, but you're still here." Cupping his face, I bring his lips to mine. I can feel him caving against me, falling into the kiss, but I don't let up. I not only want him but need him. Pushing my own desperation onto him, I move my hand down his stomach and slip under his boxers. Jackpot. I wrap my fingers around his bulging thick shaft. His groan vibrates through me.

"Fuuuuk, baby." In one motion, my hand is pulled out of his boxers, and he is settled between my spread legs. "I'm not having sex with you tonight, Maren, not here and sleep deprived, but I promise I'll make you feel good." A whimper escapes me. "Now be a good girl and stay quiet for me." I moan at his words. I am very limited in sexual experience with only Trayton and my vibrator, but I'll be damned if him saying Good Girl doesn't make my toes curl and fire ignite within me to be the best girl for him.

He slips his arms behind my knees, hitching my legs around his waist and allowing his clothed hard cock to rub against my entrance. Rolling his hips into mine, he leaves me breathless for more. The friction between us is palpating and hot. Leaning over and pushing himself against me, he licks up my neck, leaving soft

nibbles along the way. Causing me to bite my lip so hard to keep quiet, the sweet iron flavor flows into my mouth. I arch up to meet his continued thrust, his fingers digging in my hips for control.
"I'm so close, Ford," I whisper out.
"Not yet, baby."
Please GOD give me more! I scream in my head.
As if he heard me, he growls, "Don't scream to God, you only say my name."
"Ford," I moan out.
"That's more like it, but remember you need to be quiet." Biting down on my lip again to stifle any noise, his thumb comes up and releases my abused flesh before his tongue invades my mouth. He groans as he pulls away. "I can taste your blood. You like a little pain with pleasure, baby?"
"Mmhhhmm" is all I can get out. Ford bites down on my lip and sucks, causing my eyes to roll in the back of my head as his mouth devours my sounds. Pulling back, he flips us over so I can straddle him. Ripping my shirt down middle in the hottest thing that's happened to me to date, and he carelessly tosses it on the floor. I'll do with the loss of my shirt another time, when I'm not chasing the best orgasm I have ever had.
His right hand glides up my stomach to my chest, palming my breast while the other hand finds its way under my panties to my clit. His thumb creates tight, fast circles in just the right spot as I continue to grind against him. "Ford, don't stop," I say breathlessly.
"I don't plan on it," he growls out. If I didn't think before that he could go faster, he surprises me when he does before inserting two fingers inside me, curling them in a come here motion that sends me over the edge. He lets me ride out my orgasm, grinding against him, coming down from my high. I watch as he removes his fingers, then places them in his mouth to suck clean. Once he's thoroughly satisfied he's gotten all of my essence off his digits, he pulls me down to twine his tongue with mine. The act has me nearly begging for more. Tasting myself on him is a new level of exhilarating. "See what I mean, pure honey drips from you, baby. I can't fucking get enough."

"Neither can I," I speak softly, diving back into his mouth for more. Then I trail kisses down his taunt body to his boxers.

"You don't need to, baby."

"But I want to," I whine, pushing out my bottom lip in a pout. Not wanting to be stopped.

"Only if you sit on my face first." My eyes go wide with shock and excitement. Cocking my head a little in question, I'm about to voice my thoughts, but before I can, my question is answered as he grips behind my knees, yanking my body up toward his face. "These need to go," he murmurs, fingering my underwear. "Hope you aren't attached." His words haven't even registered before he tears and yanks off my soaked panties. "Much better," he grunts, placing my center over face. "Relax, baby. Be a good girl."

Got it, good girl, be quiet, but holy fuck, his tongue just swiped through my folds, and it's pure bliss.

He swipes again, more slowly, leaving me breathless. Then he begins to flick his tongue deep inside while his thumb strokes my clit. Jesus Mary and Joseph, if this is sin, I am a devout sinner. "Ford," I etch out, "this is too much...I..I can't be quiet." I punctuate my words with a moan.

He groans inside my pussy, sending a vibration through my whole body. Something snaps in me, and I am now pushing myself down onto his face instead of trying to escape. "That's it baby, give me all you got." And I fucking do. My pussy is bucking and thrusting all over his goddamn mouth, needing to feel his tongue swirl deeper inside me, needing his nose up against my clit. His free hand comes up to cover my mouth, which I proceed to bite down on the inside of his palm to remain quiet. I'll be damned if he doesn't call me a good girl once we're through.

Right when I am about to hit my precipice, he withdraws, leaving me panting and aching. Aching and pulsing so hard it hurts. "I know what will keep you quiet," he grunts out, twisting my body around so I'm riding reverse cowgirl on his face. "Suck it," he demands.

I gawk at his cock which is at full attention, dripping pre-cum *onto his pristine abdomen. And I don't want a drop to waste. Leaning over, I forget all about feeling self-conscious that my ass is legit in the man's face, and I lap up his cum before licking his bulging head and kissing the base. Then I engulf his shaft until I feel him hit the back of my throat. He's literally tongue-fucking my core, sending my moans into hums over his cock which I can see the goosebumps form on his legs when I do. "You feel so good, baby. I'm about to explode. Be a good girl and mute yourself by swallowing my cum." I suck harder and push my gag reflex away to take him deeper as my core contracts, coming all over his face. I do become his good girl, when I feel his cock swell then suck every last drop of him down my throat. His fingers grip the sides of my ass as he leaves no mess behind either.*

Knock, Knock.

"Mar, you okay in there?" Ford asks. Shit, how long have I been in the shower, reminiscing about last night, fingering myself off?

"Yeah, getting out now." Turning the water off, I climb out, then wring out my hair, and wrap a towel around me to escape the steamed-up bathroom, except I hit a brick wall.

"Whoa there. In a hurry?" I look up at Ford with frustrated and embarrassed eyes. "Let me guess, thinking about last night?"

"I'm not having this conversation with you," I grit out, stomping off to the bedroom. He follows, closing the door behind him and locking it. "Ford, I need to get dressed; Lexi has an appointment in a few hours."

"In a few hours. Madre has her downstairs eating breakfast. Now, tell me why you were in the shower for so long." I look away, flustered, knowing my cheeks are bright red.

"I was just enjoying the shower. It was relaxing."

"I bet it was relaxing," he says, slowly sauntering over to me. I try to move away, but he blocks me. *Where the hell did this dominating man come from?* His eyebrow quirks up as if he's trying to read my mind. "Maren, let me tell you a truth."

"Um, okay," I whisper slowly, looking warily at him.

He cups my face. "I'm a very sexual being, and I think it's cute how shy you are, but know that I am going to break you from shielding yourself from me, mentally, physically, and emotionally when it comes to sex. Last night was just a little taste of what's to come." His palms leave my face to glide up and down my arms in an effort to relax me. "I plan on taking my time with you, indulging you."

A gasp escapes me. "Where...where is this coming from?" I ask, not because I'm scared, but intrigued, nervous.

"The more I am with you in that aspect, the more unhinged I become. Not saying that to scare you, but the want and need is getting harder to abstain from with you. To let myself completely go with you." His thumb lingers over my lower lip as he intensely stares down at me. "I know what I want and how I want things."

"What if I don't agree? What happens when I don't want your wants?" The question of him leaving me is embedded in my mind. *Was he like this with Grace? When was the last time they were together? Fuck, when was the last time he was with anyone?*

"Don't go there, Maren. Your eyes give away all your thoughts. I'm not leaving you. I'll be damned if I'm letting you go after all this time. I told you before I'm not going nowhere, and neither are you. I will tame my preferences if it means keeping you. I will continue to hold back in fear of losing you if you're not comfortable, but you can never, ever think again that you are not enough for me."

"Ford, I...I don't know what to say. I lack so much sexual experience in general. I want to please you, but not at the risk of being harmed."

"I know you do, and you will because you're my good girl." As this rolls off his tongue, I find my face leaning against his palm. His free hand slips between my legs to my center. "Jesus, you are soaking wet."

"Ford," I whimper while he caresses my wet inner thighs. It's like my brain short circuits when he says *good girl*, and I'm trying to wrap my head around who this man is in front of me. Ford has always had alpha tendencies, and I have tested several of these traits in the past, but this is a whole other level of dominance. My body aches to share this domain with him, but my brain is firing off warning signals.

"Mommy." *Knock, knock, knock, knock.* The doorknob twists.

"Mommy, no locking doors. Your rule." *Knock, knock, knock.*

"Coming, Alexis, hold on, I'm getting dressed." Pushing Ford out of my way, I rush to grab underwear and shorts from my dresser then throw on a loose fitting tee on. Ford opens the door once he sees I'm ready.

Lexi walks in the room and eyes him up and down suspiciously. "I had a feeling you were in here."

"Why do you say that?" I ask. Ford grins ear to ear like my almost six-year-old didn't just cock block him.

"I saw his truck outside, but he was nowhere to be seen. So Glam-ma had me come get you two for breakfast."

He lifts her up carefully in his arms. "Come on, mini bar, I'm hungry." He sends a wink my way before they walk downstairs chatting about anything and everything. My heart feels like bursting with the sight of them together.

Ford

CRASHING onto my bed at the house, I'm struck with a sense of wonderment from last night and this morning. I had planned to come home and take a nap while waiting for Dawson to show up to talk about proposals, house, and business, but here I am, running through events of the last several hours. Becoming hard as a rock.

Maren was fucking salacious, and I almost wish we had been here instead so I could hear her loud screams echoing off the bay windows. But I wouldn't trade last night for anything. She blew me away with her need to be pleased, her need to please, and how she reacts to being called a good girl almost made me come by the reaction of her body and flash of light in her eyes. Three orgasms left her twitching and writhing. I am positive I could have pulled more from her, but we were both exhausted and five minutes into her body relaxing against mine, she was asleep.

I won't be admitting to her for a while that I could hear her light moans from the shower and her saying my name. That was a damn ego boost this morning, not that I needed one. It's probably a good thing Lexi came to retrieve us when she did. I'm unsure if I could have held back on Maren this morning. It wasn't so bad last night as the bedroom is on the other side of the house away from the parents and Lexi, but the bedroom does sit right over the kitchen where everyone hangs out in the morning. We are grown adults, but yet we should behave in the same house as the parentals. *Or at least try to at this point.*

Guess I'm taking my second shower of the day. *Which Maren fantasy can I pick from?* I think while stripping out of my clothes, turning my waterfall shower on. One comes quickly to mind, reminding me of her fucking my face last night. Already hard, a few strokes set the tone and sensation.

Dawson and I have been sitting here for two hours, game planning his proposal and talking shop. He stated he had already made an offer and bought the beach house for sale several doors down because Izzy had fallen in love with it when they first started dating and she visited. It's a stunning cream color with a wraparound front porch and hammock ocean side. Then the front has two garage spots with bamboo doors and cascading stairs. Three stories like ours is and the ocean side is all windows, making for spectacular views.

His plan solves the dilemma of the house because I was going to be firm on not wanting to part with it. I had wanted this house forever because Maren would always talk about how she loved the pool out front with a view of the ocean, and the view from the top balcony, which is off my room, was romantic and surreal. She described it as the perfect book nook for her to read and write with the ocean air blowing on her. Granted, I paid for the majority of the house, because it was an impulse buy once my realtor told me it was on the market. I told D just to move in and split the mortgage. Everything else in this house is my name.

Still, I wasn't looking to ruffle feathers if he didn't have a game plan. So, proposal, check. House, check. Business, not great. We now have to fly to California early next week to whip in shape two techs who are behind on our deadline. Literally showcasing this new app in a month, and it is a game changer. But we need to get in front of it before someone else catches on and beats us to the production line.

We work through a few other contracts and then zoom in Josef to talk schedules. He kindly reminds us we have four different gala's coming up in the next three months. Two in NYC, one in California, and another in North Carolina. I'm sure I can get Maren to the Carolina one as it's not far, but I'm not sure about the others based on Lexi's condition and school starting back up soon. Speaking of... "Shit, what time is it?"

"Almost four, why?" Dawson asks.

"I need to go. I'm supposed to meet the girls for ice cream after Lexi's appointment."

"Yeah, go, I got it from here. Guess I'll see you in a few for dinner."

"Sounds good." I race upstairs to gather myself together, then head into town.

CHAPTER 33
DIP MY CONE
Maren

Mom went with us to Lexi's appointment, and I dropped her back off at the house to start dinner as I take Lexi to meet Ford for ice cream. We got news today. Not the best news but not the worse either. I'm still trying to wrap my head around all the what-ifs and how this could be a potential issue for the rest of her life.

"Mommy, I see Ford over there."

Looking to my right, I smile. "Yep, that's him. Hey, wait for me. You need to hold my hand since we need to cross the street. But I need to call Aunt Darcy back real quick, so just stay seated." Darcy was blowing up my phone earlier, and for whatever reason, she refused to text me when I asked her if everything was alright.

"Alright." You would have thought I told her Mr. Pickles was shredded in the wash.

Luckily she picks up, first ring. "Hey Dar, what's going on?"

"Shit, Maren, so much. First, how is Lexi doing?"

"Fair. The doctor cleared her for a few outings, so we're about to meet Ford for ice cream. I messaged you her latest update in the group chat."

"Fun, and yes. I got it, I just haven't had a minute to read over it all."

"Okay...so what is going on?"

"Don't freak out."

"Already freaking out." She should know better than to say not to do something because I automatically do.

"Oh, peachy keen. So, guess who got home this morning?"

I grimace, already knowing who it is. "I didn't think they would be back until tomorrow at the earliest."

"Well, when they heard the damage wasn't bad and had a clear flight path, they came home. And my mother is on a warpath."

"What for? Trayton is his own person, he doesn't stake a claim to her and was doing a good deed. Let alone, I have not asked for nothing."

"Maren, we all know that, but you know she is legit crazy. Just be on the lookout. She thinks the whole town knows he is the father, even though I tried to explain to her that they don't. She will be the one confirming the rumor mill."

"Damn her."

"Mommy, don't say bad words."

"Sorry, baby doll." I cringe.

"Geez, Darcy, Trayton isn't even here to be a buffer."

"I know, and I reached out and told him. He told me the soonest he could be back is Sunday night. If I were you, I would lie low this weekend."

"Sure. We will try. Thanks for the heads up."

"No problem. I love you both!"

"We love you, too, bye!"

"Alright, Lexi, let's go." She holds my hand crossing the street, then rushes into Ford's arms as soon as we enter the picket fence area of the ice cream shop. Holding her on his hip, he wraps his other arm around me, kissing me on the head.

"Rough day?" he asks.

"You could say that. Especially with the news I just got from Darcy." We take our seats on the bench.

"Oh really, what's going on there?"

"The Adairs came back early."

"Shit."

"No bad words, Ford. Jesus gonna get you."

We both chuckle. "How about we just start a swear jar for you, mini bar?"

"What's that?" she asks, looking up at him intrigued.

"Every time someone close to you says a bad word, they owe you a dollar. You take that dollar and put it in a jar or box and save up for something real nice."

"I think I get it. So that means Mommy owes me a dollar from a word in the car, and you owe me a dollar for just now. And Uncle Dawson says plenty of bad words." Her green eyes light up. "Mommy, can I save up for a dog?"

Looking dismayed, I grumble, "Good going, Ford," while rolling my eyes. "Maybe, baby doll, maybe."

"You always said we needed the space and money for one, so I'll handle the money part."

"I'm sorry, but when did my five-year-old just throw one over on me and become so smart?"

"Almost six, Mommy, and I pay attention."

"That you do. That's fine. Space problem solved, it can stay at Ford's." He is stunned into silence, causing me to laugh out loud.

"I got you, mini bar," he replies, giving her a wink and fist pump.

"Great, another set of conspirators I have to watch out for," I mutter, mostly to myself.

"All good things, Mar. All good things," he murmurs sweetly, placing a kiss on my cheek. "But right now, we are here for ice cream. What will it be, mini bar?"

Tapping her chin, she looks deep in thought, until her face breaks into a wide smile. "A banner split, please, with extra cool whip."

"Coming right up. For you, baby?"

"I'll take a chocolate dip cone." Ford's face almost goes white.

"Nope. Anything but that?"

"Why? That's my favorite ice cream. It's what I want." He pulls me up to stand next to him and turns me away from Lexi.

"I've seen what you do with those dip cones, Maren. It's where my fantasies started with you."

"Good lord, Ford," I chuckle, slapping him in the chest playfully.

"I'm not kidding. How you suck the vanilla ice cream out of the top. How your tongue flicks and takes long strokes over the ice cream before it melts down the cone. We are not in the place for me to get a hard-on. Let alone, every guy here would get one, too."

"You, Ford, are exaggerating."

He throws his hands up in defeat. "Okay, fine. If my memory serves me correctly, I will be hard as stone three licks in watching you. Then you are going to be punished."

"Punished for what?" I snap out.

"For being a bad girl and going against my wishes."

"Really!?! Bring it on." I square my shoulders and squint my eyes in a dare.

He walks off to the counter, shaking his head as I sit back down with Lexi who is watching a few kids on the playground. She breaks my heart with the longing look in her eyes. We've already had the talk about how, for now, she can't be playing on playgrounds or rough housing because it's too dangerous. Along with that, there is a good chance she will miss the first few weeks of school.

Which in turn, when I let Harper know, she was quick to tell me she would come over after school to teach Lexi and help keep up with her work. A life saver that woman is.

Lexi notices me watching her, so then she comes over to cuddle with me. "I know this is hard, sweetie, but it won't be forever, and we will find ways to still have fun." She nods her head against my chest. I'm thankful for the cooler weather settling in as I have the urge to dress her in long sleeves and pants until the bruising calms down. The last thing she needs is more stares and rumors swirling that someone has taken a baseball bat to her legs.

The town knows she is sick, but seeing the black and purple bruises in person is gruesome.

Ford comes up next to us with treats in hand. "Here we go, a banner split with extra whip for Princess Mini bar, and a *DIP* cone for you." We say thank you, grabbing our treats from his hands.

"Let me guess, double chocolate chip mint for you?"

"You guessed right. I'm surprised you remember."

"Seriously, how can I not? You eat the worst flavor of ice cream."

"Maren Rose Hart, how dare you discriminate against my ice cream flavor." Lexi laughs at our banter and the faces we're making at each other.

"Can I try a bite, Ford?"

"You sure can." He takes her spoon and dips it in his cup of ice cream. She pops it in her mouth, and her eyes light up.

"This is so yummy."

"Verdict is in, Maren, you're voted off the island."

"That's fine. I'll find someone else who enjoys me." Knowing I'm stepping right into his game, I break off the top of the chocolate of my cone, and I begin to suck the ice cream out. "Oh no, my ice cream is melting," I cry, being overly dramatic just to push him over the edge. I go to lick the dipped part from bottom to top, then swirl my tongue in the broken top. Then twirl the cone around my tongue to get all the melted vanilla from flowing over the edges of the cone. Ford's eyes are a glowing amber and bugging out.

Clearing his throat, he says hoarsely, "I think you had enough, Mar."

Taking another lick of the cone, my lips curl in a Cheshire grin. "No, I'm just getting started." Then I start to break off the chocolate pieces, popping them into my mouth so all that's left is the vanilla.

"I'll be giving you something to dip later," he says in a gravelly voice. Twirling the ice cream cone over my tongue sticking out to give it a swirl look, I lock eyes with Ford the whole time. "You're killing me."

"Again, you keep telling me that." He gives me a devilish grin that tells me I'm in for something later.

"Alright, I need a distraction from your mouth. Tell me about the appointment."

"Well, let's go from lighthearted to disheartened."

"That bad?"

"Not really, but let's save it for later. I'm sure she is done hearing about it, and she is the happiest I've seen her today."

"Sounds like a plan." Turning to focus on Lexi, he asks, "How's your banana split?"

"Yummy!"

"I can tell. You have demolished it." They laugh, and it's the best sound, warming my heart. "You know Glam-ma is going to have a fit if you don't touch any of your dinner because you're full of ice cream."

"I'll eat a few bites, I promise."

"Maren Hart!" I hear my name shouted from somewhere behind me. Turning around, I see Mrs. Adair in her running attire, sprinting toward me with her partner in crime, Mrs. Lockett. On instinct, I stand up to block Lexi from her. Ford comes to the other side of her.

"How dare you come back to this town, with all the trouble you caused!" she spits in my face.

"Excuse me, Mrs. Adair, I'm having a treat with my daughter and Ford, so I need you to leave."

SLAP!

My skin stings where her hand met my cheek. Tears pool in my eyes as Ford immediately steps in between us to thart off another attack. "Mrs. Adair, I have never laid a hand on a woman in fury, but you are about to be the first if you do not step away right now," he demands.

"Ford, how can you even be with this whore? She is only entrapping you because of all your money."

I see his fists clenching at his sides at the same time as my fingernails are creating bloody crescent moons in my palms. "Leave NOW," he says, growling out each word. She finally gets the hint and takes a few steps back. I'm back next to Ford instead of behind, both of us shielding Lexi.

"Fine, you can't say I didn't warn you. As for you, Maren, you leave my Trayton out of this. She is not his, and he doesn't need to be attached to you and your abomination."

Fuck this bitch. I'm fucking done. Stepping forward, I ball my fist and lay a punch to her jaw, knocking her off her feet. "You do NOT ever talk about my child that way. Who do you think you are talking about any kid in that manner? You might have a bone to pick with me, but you are to leave her the hell out of your mouth and thoughts. She is innocent in all of this."

Ford is having to pull me back before I go completely postal on this woman. I can feel the stares and growing audience. Mrs. Lockett bends over to help Mrs. Adair up. "I'm pressing charges."

"Be my fucking guest. Let me tell them how you are slandering a child. Let me tell your son what you said."

She comes back for me, but Mrs. Lockett holds her in place as Ford steps in front of me again. I pick Lexi up in my arms and hightail it to my car. Strapping her in, we take off back home. I'm too much of a shaken mess to even worry about the consequences and leaving Ford behind.

Ford

I TAKE OFF, running back to my truck to get to Maren and Lexi. Maren disappeared with her so damn fast while I was blocking the evil Adair from coming after her again. That woman is bat shit crazy and lucky I didn't snap her neck for attacking my girls. But fuck, I'm so damn proud of Maren for getting a swing in and putting that bitch in her place. I'm not a Trayton supporter, but I know he is going to lose his fucking mind when he finds out.

Speaking of, let me call him right now since we exchanged numbers the other day.

"Ford, man, miss me already?"

"Shut up, smartass. We got a fucking problem."

"You said they were handled."

"Believe me, those people are handled. The problem is your crazy bitch of a mother." I hear him let out a long sigh at the other end of the line.

"Darcy told me they came back early. What happened?"

"Where should I start? The part where she made a scene in the middle of town or slapped the hell out of Maren, calling her a whore?"

"She did fucking what?!?"

"Or maybe when she called Alexis an abomination." I can

hear his blood rising through the phone with steam releasing in a feral hiss.

"No she fucking didn't."

"She did, sir. She did with half the town as witnesses."

"I'm going to strangle her myself. She has no right to talk to Maren that way, let alone attack my child." My skin crawls a little with the sound of him calling my mini bar his child, but I can't erase the fact that technically she is.

"Look, man, Maren doesn't know I'm calling you. After she threw a punch, knocking your mom to the ground with a few choice words, they hightailed it out of there, and now I'm heading to the house in hopes to meet up with her."

"Fuuucck!" I hear something break. "Are they okay? Maren and Lexi I mean?"

"I think so, but I know Maren was pretty shaken up. Your mom threatened to press charges for assault."

"Jesus, Ford. That escalated quicker than I anticipated."

"Agreed."

"My mother won't be doing shit. I have an hour before the next press junket, I'll call Dad to calm her ass down. Can you just, fuck, I don't know, keep Maren and Lexi home until I get back?"

"No, but you know they are mine to protect. And if your mother starts shit again, I won't be holding back."

"Understood." The line goes quiet for a few beats when I'm about to pull in the driveway.

"Alright, I'm at the house."

"Yeah, okay. Go check on them, and thanks, man, for keeping me in the loop."

"Sure, bye." Hanging up, I can't help feeling a shift. Much to my disliking, maybe there needs to be a shift to accept each other to be in Lexi's world. Whatever the future holds for us all.

Stepping out of the truck, I see Madre on the front porch swing, swinging Lexi in her lap. She nods her head toward Maren's car. My eyes lock on her still sitting in the driver's seat, bent over shaking. I slowly approach, not to spook her, opening the door, then bending over her to unbuckle her seatbelt. She is having a panic attack, gasping for air, body wracked with an onslaught of sobs and tears. Picking her up out of the seat, we sit down on the front lawn, holding her in my arms. Rocking us back and forth.

"Breathe, baby. I got you," I murmur in her ear, calmly running my fingers through her hair." I feel useless trying to soothe her, but her breathing starts to even out after several minutes.

"Ford," she squeaks out.

"I'm here. I got you, baby. Lexi is fine. All is fine."

"How could she say things like that?"

"Because she is an evil, selfish person. Because she knows you are better in every way than she will ever be. Because you possess something she has never had."

"What would that be?"

"Her son's love and a grandchild she will never know."

Maren lets out a cautious laugh. "Trayton needs to know."

"I've already taken care of it. He knows and is handling her. And if she comes for either of you again, I'm handling her."

Wrapping her arms around my waist, she nuzzles into my chest. "Thank you."

"Never thank me. You are my everything, my oxygen. I'll fight to keep you safe and close. The same for Alexis."

A choked sob escapes her. "I love you, Ford Merrick. I keep fighting my feelings to protect myself from hurt and to protect Lexi from more loss. But more so, to protect you from me because I'm unstable and nothing. I wanted time to get my shit together, to prove to you I'm worth being in your world. Worthy of your heart, but all this has been so fast-paced I've not been able to get my bearings. Add in Lexi and all the bullshit drama with Grace, Trayton, and Dawson, and it's just been too much." Another strangled cry rocks her body. "Just too much."

Tucking my hand under her chin, I tilt her face to get her to look at me. A great tremor takes over her body, tears racing down her cheeks. "My Maren. Look at me." Once her emerald greens lock on me, I reassure her, "You are not nothing but my everything. I am no man without you. I have been a hollow shell of a human while you were gone. I spent so much time in the past, needing to become the man worthy of you. You were going to make a dent in this world, and I wanted an earned front row seat to all of it. Not because I asked to be there but because you wanted me there."

"I always wanted you there, Ford. How could you not have seen that?"

"Because I was a dumbass boy, needing to grow up. I focused on becoming the type of man I felt you deserved. Needed to control my anger without having to lean on you. To become financially stable to buy you the big house and support your dreams."

"I just needed you."

"Don't I know that now. But here we are now. Together."

She nudges back into my shoulder. "Some dent I made. Only a path of destruction in my wake."

"Not at all. Part of your dent is that beautiful, amazing child you brought into this world. And you have all the time to make many more dents in this world. Mark my words, Maren, all your dreams are going to come true. I'm going to make sure of it." She shudders before relaxing against my body. A state of tranquility washes over me, letting me know we are both right where we belong.

CHAPTER 34
NEWS IS NEWS
Maren

Dawson and Izzy arrived to find me in Ford's lap, a sobbing mess. Once we got in the house via Ford carrying me then sitting me down at the kitchen bar, Mom started handing out homemade margaritas. When she found the time to make these, I have no idea, but I am welcoming a vice to dissipate the edge. I sit there, sipping mine, while Ford retells the events at the ice cream shop. I find myself giggling with Izzy when he reenacts me punching Mrs. Adair and then flanking on the ground. Mom had settled Lexi in the living room watching Disney channel. Which is a good thing with all the words flying out of everyone's mouths. She would make bank in a ten minute period.

"That family is going to make me go crazy in public," my mom announces. We all cheer and clank our glasses.

Dawson chuckles. "That," he points at her, "I want a front seat for."

"You all behave," she mutters, giving us one of her evil glares.

"Only if you do, Mom!" Dawson spouts back, causing all to laugh.

Ford comes up behind me, rubbing my shoulders. "You good?"

"Yeah, much better." I sigh, leaning into him as we listen to the chatter.

Dad walks in thirty minutes later, looking like he has aged ten years. "The town is in an uproar," he states, shaking his head.

"What's the word on the docks, pops?" Dawson asks

"That my daughter is a bad bitch and the town is happy to see someone knock Evelyn Adair down a few pegs." I'm floored by those words flying out of my dad's mouth. "Look, I'm just repeating what the guys were saying. They were all giving me high fives and fist pumps once word got to us."

"I swear this is the most gossiping town ever," I say, downing my second drink.

"No. All small towns are, we just might have an extra evil villain," Ford states.

"Well, enough gossip of our own, who's ready to eat!?" Mom asks, causing us to shout, "Me!"

I head into the living room to grab Lexi but find her passed out on the couch snuggled with her blanket and Mr. Pickles. It's been a long day for her with another transfusion, pumped full of meds, then a sugar high and emotional drama. I sit next to her, tucking her tighter in her blanket and pushing her mess of curls out of her face.

"She asleep?" Ford comes over, whispering.

"Yeah. Let's just leave her. She can eat later if she wants." Allowing him to take my hand, he helps me off the couch.

We take our time getting back into the dining room, then we take our places at the table. Ford next to me, and Izzy and Mom across from Ford and I. With Dawson and Dad on the ends. Mom has already plated the shrimp alfredo, and it sits before us, salads with a basket of cheddar rolls in the center. Izzy says Grace, then we dig in. A slight moan escapes me when I take my first bite. One of the many meals I have missed being away. No one makes shrimp alfredo like my mother. It's like she has perfected the perfect mix of spices with the best homemade alfredo sauce that oozes parmesan and garlic flavor. Add in fresh shrimp with a kick of Cajun. Chef's kiss.

The table laughs. "You good there, Mar?" Dawson asks.

Shoveling more pasta into my mouth, I nod my head. "Just sooooo good," I mumble around a mouthful of deliciousness.

"Goodness, Maren, don't talk with your mouth full," Mom commands, making the whole table shake with laughter wholeheartedly.

We chat while stuffing our faces. Stories Dad heard about those witnessing Ophelia rolling in and cleanup needed. Dawson and Ford talk shop, telling us about their newest app that could change the trajectory of ordering cars through Share-Ride. The app can dwindle down to make and model of car, find a driver you like, down to requesting a quiet driver or one that you can socialize with to even showing you around town for an extra fee, which would be huge for tourists. Along with route planning instead of only point A to point B.

Pride transcends over me with how much those two have accomplished and continue to create.

Then Mom brings out her famous chocolate mousse pie and *Baileys*, and I know this is where the heavy talk starts. Now that we are all together and the easy chatter is out of the way.

Dad leans back in his chair, waiting for Mom to serve the pie. "So, Maren, tell me about my granddaughter's day and the results I hear that came back."

Twirling my ring on finger, my anxiety makes itself known more than my nervousness. "So, Angelica, I mean Dr. Leeds and Dr. Hunt, seem optimistic. Basically, the results showed she has ITP which is Immune Thrombocytopenic Purpura." The table looks at me with wide eyes of uncertainty and confusion of not knowing what I just said. "Meaning she either has some underlying condition or some infection that brought this on. Positive side, it's not cancer like leukemia or lymphoma so that was the good news today. The bad news is we don't know yet if this is acute or chronic, meaning she will either have to deal with this and medications with possible transfusions the rest of her life or her body is going to start fighting back with the medications and treatment, and this becomes a fluke thing that could last for several weeks or a few months. They took more blood work today for more testing and to recheck her levels as Angelica felt she was looking anemic again today."

The table is silent, absorbing the information, until Dad speaks up. "Glad we are getting answers. Seems like this is moving in a positive direction." Leave it to my dad to always try to see the plush side of things.

I shrug my shoulders. "I guess. Though they released her for limited outings and visitors, no playgrounds, no wrestling like she loves to do with Dawson. And she is going to miss the first few weeks of school. Basically, she needs to be bubble wrapped until her body can produce enough platelets again to protect her body, especially her head, because if her head gets hit with even the smallest of a quarter it could cause a head injury or internal bleeding. I just hate this for her," I say, my voice thick with emotion as I slump in my chair. Ford's hand squeezes my thigh in reassurance that I'm not alone.

"At least she has all of us now to keep her plenty entertained. And didn't you say Harper would come by to teach her, so she doesn't fall behind?" Mom asks determined we have a plan.

"That's all true. Just hate it for her."

"Well, I'll be around more now that I'm moving up this way," Izzy states.

"What!!?" We all look at her and Dawson.

"Surprise!" Dawson shouts. "I bought that cream-colored beach house a few doors down from Ford's house." Mom squeals in delight, rushing over to hug Izzy and him. "I wanted to wait to share the news, but I figure we could all use something cheerful to focus on."

"This is amazing news! Does this mean I will have another daughter soon?" Mom teases.

I see a wink being passed between Ford and Dawson. "Time will tell, Mom, time will tell."

Izzy, oblivious to Dawson's words, squeals, "I'm so excited; I've loved that house since I first visited and can't believe D remembered." I stand up and make my way around the table to hug Izzy and Dawson.

"I'm really happy for you both and excited for the future. Lexi will be ecstatic to know Princess Izzy will be just down the road daily." Izzy gleams. "When is the big move-in day?"

Dawson speaks up, "Within the month. There are minor changes we want to make, and I want Izzy to have time to pick out furniture and décor. We have the time to turn it into a home before moving in and doing stuff here and there."

"Ford, what will you do when I steal your bro from you?" Izzy jokes.

Tittering, he mutters, "I guess get a dog," giving me a wink with a Cheshire grin. "Not sure what I will do, though, being all alone in that big house, day in and day out."

"I know someone looking for a roommate."

"Who?" I snap toward Mom.

"You!"

"Not funny, Mom. Lexi and I are not invading Ford's privacy nor am I entertaining this conversation right now." Looking away annoyed, I mouth, "sorry" to Ford.

He leans over and whispers, "It's not like I haven't already thought about having you two live with me." My mouth gapes open in bewilderment.

"No catching flies, Maren," Mom vocalizes.

With a piercing stare from Ford, I ask to discuss this later. Right then, the doorbell goes off. Mom spouts off, "Who honestly could be here this late?" as she gets up from the table and heads to the door. We all gather behind her as she opens the front door. We are just as nosy as the next Nosey Nancy.

"Oh shit," flies out of Dawson's mouth when the door opens fully, showing the stunning yet annoying pageant queen on the other side of the threshold.

"Hi, Mrs. Hart and uh, family. Sorry to interrupt, but I was wondering if I could have a few minutes of Ford's time." Her voice irks me as it's so stated and polite. Ford lets out a heavy breath.

"Sorry, bro. I completely forgot to talk to her earlier," Dawson responds to Ford's frustration. Izzy and I look at each other perplexed.

Ford turns to kiss my cheek. "Let me go deal with this."

"Sure." I watch as he walks outside, shutting the door behind him. I watch their silhouettes turn left to the large swing and sit.

Mom and Dad walk over to attend to a waking Alexis. "I'll get her ready for bed, Mar. The rest of you help Dad with the kitchen."

"Thanks, Mom." I turn to head back into the kitchen when Izzy catches my arm.

"Maren, I just want to say I'm sorry if my friendship with Grace causes you distress. From what Ford and Dawson have told me, you and Ford are made for each other. I told Grace to back off, and I didn't agree with her tactics to win him back." She almost had me walking away like their friendship was no big deal to me. They have been friends for years. Until her last words have me whipping back around to face her.

"What tactics?"

"Oh dear, I thought Ford told you? Please forget I said anything." she pouts.

"That's kind of hard to do." My voice is rising. "I don't have a problem with you being friends with her, Izzy. She has been in your life way longer than I have, but I'll be damned if I'm dealing with more bullshit today."

Dawson comes running around the corner. "What the hell Maren?"

"I don't know Dawson, ask Izzy." His eyebrows sync together.

"Izzy?" Crocodile tears start streaming down her cheeks.

"I was apologizing for Grace. I thought Ford told her about Grace coming on to him the other night at the hotel."

Taken back, I let the words sync in for two-point-five seconds before I'm flying out the front door. Only to be met with Grace crying into Ford's chest, him comforting her like he was comforting me earlier. As if she felt my presence, I watch as her mouth locks on his. I see red with rage, yanking her off the porch swing, off him, and throwing her against the house. She might have a few inches on me, but growing up with Dawson, I learned how to throw a punch and use my size as a weapon.

Slapping her across the face, I scream, "You fucking bitch! How dare you come to my home to win him back. In front of my family and kid. Do you have any fucking decency in that whore brain of yours?" She goes to slap me back, but I catch her wrist.

"You must not know who I am," she grits out.

"I don't give a flying fuck who you are or who your daddy is."

"Maren!" Ford shouts, grabbing my shoulders, but I shake him off.

"You can have him, sweetheart, because honestly, I don't want your leftovers or anyone in my life that sees you as a decent person."

"Maren," Ford growls out this time.

Turning to face him, I shake my head, backing up with my hands raised. "No, Ford. Leave and take her with you because how dare you be there for me and *my* daughter like you just didn't hook up with her a few nights ago."

"It was fantastic, too," Grace remarks.

"Grace, shut the hell up!" Ford counters.

"Leave, both of you!" I scream.

Grace has the audacity to lean closer to me, venom spewing from her painted lips. "I'm glad you came to your senses about letting that dream of yours go. He would always come back to me. Only I can please him sexually. Knows his demanding tastes. You were just a teenage crush. Don't worry, I'll make sure he forgets *all* about *you*."

With her last words, I grab her hair, dragging her to steps of the porch, dragging her down them, then tossing her on the ground while she screams for help. No one dares to come near me. My mom and dad fly out of the house behind Dawson and Izzy.

"What in the cane is happening?" Dad shouts, ping-ponging his gaze to Grace and me, then to Ford. My dad shakes his head. "Fix this, Ford," he grumbles, then walks back in the house, taking Mom with him.

Izzy steps toward Grace, but I throw my hand out. "Don't or you are dead to me as much as he is," I seethe, pointing to Ford.

I'm done faltering in front of this man and need them all to leave.

Ford

"Seriously, Maren," I utter, taking a step toward her. Watching her fight against her tears. "Dawson, please take Grace back to the hotel."

"Ford Merrick," Grace cries. "Look at me."

"Grace–Get. The. Fuck. Away from me. You have caused enough damage that's why I've been avoiding you. Do you not think I know what you said to Maren that night in my driveway? Then I told you there would be no us in that hotel room when you threw your body at me. I told you again when you showed up at the hospital. There is no you and me. Don't play me for a fool, Grace, it won't bode well for you in the end."

I watch as she straightens up and pushes her shoulders back, trying to regard herself. "Fine, you're just fooling yourself, Ford. You will come begging on your hands and knees for me when she can't satisfy you. When she can't handle your pain and pleasure." I step toe-to-toe with her, looking down at her. Eyeing her through her bullshit meter ticking in the red zone.

"Really? Because I haven't touched you in years, Grace. Not because you were with someone else, but because you were not a memorable fuck. You were more like an emotional support dog that I needed, so thank you for that. Because that woman behind me has always been my fantasy, my personal pain and pleasure." Grace's cold gaze fixates on me.

"How...how dare you talk to me like this!"

"You need to leave now, Grace."

Dawson walks toward her, putting himself in between us. "Come on, Grace, Izzy and I will take you back."

She begins to walk away with them toward his truck, then turns back around. "You will pay for this, Ford."

"I already am. Trust me." Once they are in the truck and drive off, I turn back to Maren. Her face hardens in concentration, but her body is trembling. "Let's go inside, you are shivering," I murmur, placing my palm on her arm.

"Don't touch me," she spats out.

"Fuck, Maren, we can do this out here or inside, but we will be having this damn conversation. You are not fucking cutting me off again. No way in hell."

"What the hell is that supposed to mean?" she questions.

All my unresolved emotions with her rise. "What that means is that six years ago you up and left in the middle of the night. Disappeared with no contact. All you said was bye in a fucking letter. Did I not mean more than a fucking hand-written goodbye?" I see resolve and fear flicker in her eyes.

"It means you were my anchor but left me to sink. To figure out how to handle shit on my own. Maybe I needed that, but that anger I had for losing you, along with my parents, turned me into a damn sadist. I needed to feel in control because I was unraveling in every aspect of my life. Ask Dawson. If I wasn't getting in fights, I was hungover. No motivation. You destroyed me by leaving. I have this magnetic pull to you, and I was willing to push all my pain aside for a chance with you. But you find every damn reason to push me away. You know damn well Grace is nothing to me, but that gave you the perfect out, didn't it? You tell me you're not worthy to be mine, but that's your own bullshit ideologies. You sat in my lap right on that lawn today and told me you loved me. Confessed your thoughts and fears. You had me thinking for a moment we were moving forward. Then the first whiff you get of a threat, instead of fighting for me, you pass me off. Holy shit, Maren!" I'm shouting now, knowing we will all be the talk of the town in the morning.

Madre appears. "You two either bring this inside or find privacy. Quit showing your crazy to the neighbors."

"I'm going inside," Maren states.

"No you're not. You are coming with me."

"No, I'm going in to be with my daughter."

"Maren, go with Ford. Lexi is sound asleep and safe."

"Ugh, quit siding with him."

"I'm not, but you two have quite a bit of unresolved history that needs to be worked through and not dragged out like last week's trash."

"Whatever," she mutters as she stomps to my truck, jumps in, and slams the cab door.

Running my hand through my hair, I jump in, and we take off to my house. I send off a text to Dawson asking for privacy tonight. He is happy to oblige and headed to the local B&B.

CHAPTER 35
PURE HELL
Maren

THE DRIVE to Ford's house is nothing but awkward silence. How the hell did today go from okay to wonderful to a shit storm to a full cup of happiness to fucking hell? This is not the life I came back to live. Now, I'm stewing over Ford's festering confessions of how I broke him. How he became a sadist, which now puts his words in more perspective.

His words to Grace replay in my mind of how I was always his fantasy. But I'm also his pleasure and pain. Can I fix this between us? Do I fix this, is the bigger question? We have been swirling around each other for weeks now with so many events and people interfering, we haven't been able to focus on *us*. To dig beyond the surface of our heartstrings and convictions.

Ford pulls into the driveway and steps out. "Come on." I follow him into the house. We reach the kitchen, and he pours us two glasses of chilled bourbon. He walks to the opposite side of the bar from me. "Anything to say?"

"Honestly, I don't know what to say, Ford. I'm still processing your confessions. Not once have you mentioned any of that. You have only shared your need, your want, and your lust for me. Telling me you love me. Telling me tonight you've been thinking about Lexi and I moving in with you. Only to find out less than ten minutes ago that you have been harboring hate for me and that you're a sadist. So, no, still processing."

He looks at me with a strangled expression, but I am unable to read him at this moment. I know I need to be honest with him because tonight could be what breaks us to no repair. Not even as a friend, if that's the only relationship I can manage with him after tonight.

"But you're right. I push you away every chance I get. I was barely in a relationship with Tray six years ago. Always longing for you. Every time you showed up out of the blue to check on me or to order me around, I just wanted you to kiss me. To confess your feelings for me. Yet, you never did. When I left, I left with the impression you saw me as a sister, maybe a protective friend, but nothing more. Now never dated between him and you. Not saying I need that experience or want that because you are the only man I have ever wanted. This is what I have always wanted. To be accepted, loved, and understood by you. I've also been clinging to a past that doesn't let me choose."

Panic sears my chest as he stands unwavering. "Ford, I can never apologize enough for the pain and brokenness I caused you. I would sell my soul to take all of the hurt from you and bare it myself, but I can't." Tears steam-roll down my cheeks, my gut telling me this is done. Swallowing hard, I shift foot to foot. "I'll order a car and go. Just please don't walk out on Lexi. She loves you too much to handle your loss." My eyes rove over him one last time before stepping toward the steps that lead to the front door.

"What about you?" he asks.

Turning around, I find him right behind me. "Excuse me?"

"Do *you* love me? Can *you* handle the loss of me?"

Biting my bottom lip, my eyes cloud with tears. "Yes, I love you. And no, I can't handle the loss of you, but I will have to if that's what you want. If this is too hard for us to continue."

"Ask me what I want, Maren." My heart is palpating in the unknown. Do I want to ask and hear what I have feared over the last hour? Do I trust this process to get us over the hurdle? "Ask me, Maren. Ask me what I want," He says, this time sounding more like a demand than a request.

Trembling with fear, I flick my ring with my thumb. "What," I swallow hard, "What do you want, Ford?"

He forces himself in my space until I'm up against the stairwell wall. "I fucking want you. All of you. I want you to move in with me. I want you to marry me so I can own those lips of yours, so I can devour your pussy daily, and worship your body anytime I want." His thumb grazes over my lower lip. "I want to be tied to you in every physical and emotional way. I want to wake up with you in my bed every morning and be the last thing I see before I close my eyes at night. I want you to wear my mother's wedding ring, and I want to adopt Alexis Jane as my own daughter. I want to watch you succeed at teaching and find your love for writing again. I want to indulge myself inside you while reviewing your brilliant, published works. I want to travel the world with you as you planned to do all those years ago. To experience other cultures, find people's truths and worldly possessions through your eyes and words." His palm pets the side of my face, and I lean into him. "I want to be a family with you and mini bar in this house, or hell, any house of your choosing. I'm at your *fucking* mercy, baby."

My eyes take in his twinkling amber eyes hooded with dark lashes, looking at me in a way that makes me feel like the sexiest person alive. Replaying in my mind how his eyes have always found me in a crowded room, regardless of who was vying for his attention. His sharp jaw line covered by a shadow of facial hair to the curve of his lips that I swear were made to only mold to mine. I stand up on my tip toes, capturing his lips with mine.

Ford

"Fuck, my need for your lips is insatiable."

"I need you Ford," she desperately says. I tease open her mouth, then twist her tongue with mine, pulling her locked against my body where my fingers dig into her waist. Maren runs her hands to the hem of my shirt, steadily lifting up to pull over my head. Then she does the same with hers, leaving her in her pink-laced bra and denim shorts. "Touch me, Ford."

I grip her hips tighter to find control. I want all of her in this instance, but also, I want my first time with her to be slow enough to savor. Coming back to the scene in front of me, she has now shimmied out of her shorts. A deep groan releases from me, seeing her bare skin on display. Her insecurities of her body, nonexistent at this moment. She lolls her neck back, giving me the advantage to glide my tongue up to her jawline, then leave a trail of light kisses to the spot behind her ear. Knowing this is a spot that drives her over the edge. She moans softly at a whisper as her fingers scratch down my abdomen to my jeans.

"Baby, I want you so much, but I'm warning you. I'm going to drag this moment out for as long as I can stand not being inside your tight, soaked cunt." Her moan is louder this time, sending a zing through my entire body. She undoes the button and zipper of my jeans, pushing them down, and I step back from her long enough to pull my legs out of them.

Needing to be close to her body warmth, I pick her up, wrapping her legs around my waist and make my way over to the kitchen counter.

Sitting her on the cold marble top, she yelps in shock. "Don't worry, I'll warm you back up," I murmur huskily while unhooking her bra with one hand, locking my mouth on hers. My body is thrumming to be inside her, but not yet. I need to pleasure her, taste her, break her before I fuck her. I tuck my fingers in on the sides of her pink lace panties then tug, ripping them off. Her eyes go wide as saucers. "I'll buy you a million more pairs," I say, driving a finger into her wet folds. We groan together.

Slowly, I pull out, then replace one with two fingers. "Tell me your mine, Maren. Only mine," I growl out, sucking one of nipples into my mouth while slowly pumping my fingers in and out of her, teasing her clit with my thumb.

"Yes," she pants out, chest breathing heavily. "Yours." I grin against her breast before biting down on her nipple. She screams.

"You like that, don't you?"

"Mmhmm. More," she breathes out. "I need more." I pull my fingers out of her pussy, then wipe them across her lips before pushing them into her mouth.

"Suck," I demand, and she does, hard. "Good girl," I praise her, gripping her lightly around her neck before moving my hand to her chest to guide her to lie back on the counter. Then I place her feet on the counter for better access. I take a step back to admire this devastatingly gorgeous woman in front of me like an offering. Honestly, I have never been so turned on in my damn life. Never have I needed to feel another person's touch as I do her's. Her pink center glistens for me, calling me to consume.

Don't mind if I fucking do.

Bending down, I swipe my tongue down her folds. My hands reach to palm her breasts as she whimpers in pleasure. "Pure honey drips from you, baby." I flatten my tongue against her cunt to clit, then stick my tongue inside her as far as it can go and flick it over and over again. As she cries out, her hand finds my scalp, nearly ripping my hair out, but it feels erotically thrilling as I thrust my tongue in her, then nip at her clit and folds. Eating her like a starved, deprived man for his last supper. My dick is hard and tight in my briefs, so I pull them off of me, not giving her a reprieve while I do. My cock jolts in the open air as Maren grinds into my face.

That's it baby, come for me.

Moans and cries escape her, reaching her precipice on my face. I lap at her enough to contain the taste of her in my mouth but leave enough to keep her wet. Standing up, I watch her chest heave up and down. "Ford," she squeaks out, and the sound is beautiful mixed with her breaths.

"Sit up," I demand and she does quickly, her eyes pinned on me. I fist her hair in my hand, bringing her lips almost to mine. "Taste yourself off my lips and tongue." There is no hesitation when she licks her lips first, then mine, before pushing her tongue through to tangle with mine. A moan escapes her as she is desperate to find her honey. I groan, grabbing my cock and letting the head glide against her wet folds.

Maren pulls back. "Please, Ford, take me. Have all of me. You make me so wet and horny; I can't stand it. Please," she begs.

"Wrap your legs around me." She does, and I grip her ass off the counter and head to the couch where I sit, and she straddles me. "Grind against me like a good girl, but my hard cock is not to get inside you. You understand?" I ask, gripping her jaw to keep her eyes on me. She lifts herself slightly off my lap, just enough to lightly guide her cunt over my shaft, and it's torture and heaven all in one. My head slams back with a groan. "Fuuucck, baby, you're going to make me come just moving like this."

"Good," she remarks, then presses herself down against me, and holy fuck, I'm consumed with her wetness slicking my dick for her. Grinding faster, she whimpers, "I swear I'm going to come again, please be inside me."

"Not yet, baby. Not yet. Keep doing what you're doing. Show me what a good girl you are and make yourself come again." She does the unexpected when her hands glide down her stomach to her clit, and she uses two of her fingers to circle her spot as she grinds harder against me. Her other hand braces and squeezes my shoulder.

"Ford, fuck... I....I....oh...God....Ford."

"That's it, baby, come all over my lap." I bury my face in her neck and bite down, reveling in her shuddering convulsions in my lap. Maren slumps against my chest, panting for air, for reprieve.

I adjust her body to pick her up to carry her upstairs to my bedroom. My cock is leaking, and my control has snapped once I toss her on the bed. She sits up on her elbows and watches me stroke my shaft as I strut toward her with purpose. Her eyes widen in anticipation, her olive skin prickling with goosebumps.

Sliding into her sweet cunt, my cock pulses, stretching her to the hilt. "Breathe, baby, relax." Pulling out slowly, then I push back in, both of us groaning in unison. Hovering over her as I glide in and out, our eyes lock like magnets. For the first time ever, her green eyes reflect a window to her soul. I thrust deeper inside her. "Marry me." Her breath hitches. "Marry me, Maren." This is what love making is. An act that all encompasses two bodies locked and synced, tethered at the core of their souls. Overwhelming passion that explodes in connection and the urge to be one because the feeling of our bodies touching is not enough.

Slowly pulling out of her, then slamming back in, I knock the breath out of her. Picking my pace up, we groan and moan over each other. My fingers circle her clit.

Damn this feels so intense and unreal.

"Jesus, Mary and.....FORD, I'm going to come!"

"Say yes, Maren, marry me," I demand again, panting through my words.

"YES!" she hollers out when her pussy clamps down on my

cock, contracting around my length as I spill inside her. I collapse on top of her, both sweaty and breathless.

"That was incredible," she exhales out. I roll off her onto my side, pulling her back into my chest and kissing her back between her shoulder blades.

"That was ethereal, baby."

The day has been long and emotional, now physically exhausting, causing her to be asleep in minutes. I continue to hold her close to me while gleaming because I asked Maren to marry me, and she said yes. This woman is going to be my wife.

CHAPTER 36
SEASIDE
Maren

Lying awake watching Ford sleep, I'm enamored. Not only by his words but by actions, too. He has now convinced me that I'm all he wants. All of me. Maybe part of it was getting myself out of the way with all the negative thoughts and the urge to destroy a good thing I can't seem to find tangible faith in.

Tray did a number to my psyche, and where I know I'm not completely healed from the pain, I'm learning to be patient and listen to others and put faith in the unknown again. I have to. My mom tells me I deserve happiness and love as much as the next person, and Ford allows me to believe it.

Let alone, there is no saying no to Ford. This man is all I have ever wanted for so long. Plus, Lexi adores him, and I can only imagine her reaction to Ford adopting her. For her to have a person to call dad and have adventures with. For us both to feel the security of belonging.

Trailing over his collarbone and down his firm sculpted chest with just a dusting of black hair, I run my fingers through it.

"Good morning," he says as his eyes flutter open.

"Good morning," I murmur, smiling back at him.

"This is exactly what I was referring to last night."

"What's that?"

"You here in bed with me when I fall asleep and next to me when I wake." I glide my fingers gently down the side of his face.

His eyes pop open all the sudden, startling me. "Wait here" he says as he jumps out of bed, rummaging through his desk drawer.

"Close your eyes."

"Um okay," I mutter, looking at him skeptically at first.

"Are they closed? Be a good girl and don't peek."

I instantly become wet, and my brain snaps in attention to obey. Closing my eyes and then placing my hand over my eyes, I feel a dip in the bed, and my skin tingles with his closeness.

"Keeping your eyes closed and place both hands on top of your thighs." I maneuver into a cross legged position on the bed and place my hands palm down on the top of my thighs.

"Good girl," he preens, and I know I have the biggest smile on my face. He leans in, kissing my lips hastily, and I feel his smile against mine.

"You, Maren Rose Hart, are mine. Do you recall saying yes to me last night?"

I hum.... Smiling. "Words, Maren."

"I remember saying yes, Ford."

"Open your eyes, Maren."

Doing as he says, I open my eyes slowly, only to being graced with a handsome, mischievous Ford holding a vintage diamond ring. I gasp, taken back at the sheer beauty of the ring, along with how real this all just became. His sunflower eyes full of love captivate me.

"Granted, last night was not how I envisioned proposing to you, so let's try this again, shall we?" Ford states. My eyes are already wet with tears, and he hasn't even asked again.

"I love you. I have always loved you and never stopped when you left. The moment I laid eyes on you in the living room the day you returned home, all my walls started to crumble down. My heart knew there would be no letting you go this time, though, my logical brain wanted to run away. When you asked for a hug, I melted against you, proving I still wanted you. All logic went out the window that I had talked myself into on the way over with Dawson. After that night, I felt like a fumbling teenage boy trying to find his confidence. You've been home for a month now but have turned my whole life upside down in the best way. You are the missing piece to me being me. To me being whole." His thumb wipes the tears off my cheeks.

"This ring belonged to my momma who was the first woman to love me fully and the first to leave me. She always thought the world of you, Maren, and maybe she played a role in bringing you back to me, back home. But I do know for certain, she would be proud to call you a daughter and her son's wife. She told me to hold on to this ring for the special lady who will consume my heart, thoughts, and soul. Just as she stated was the type of love she and my dad had. So, with this ring and a long-winded speech, will you marry me?"

I jump into his arms, squeezing his cheeks between my hands and kissing him all over. "*Yes*, a million times yes, Ford." He slides the ring on my finger, and I'm shocked to find it's a perfect fit. "Ford, this ring is stunning, and I'm so honored to have a piece of your mom with me."

"You, Maren, are stunning and soon to be my wife."

"Wife, wow, I quite like that sound of that, husband."

With that, he flips me on to my back and ravishes me. And for another hour, I'm in pure bliss, wanting to stay in our makeshift bubble for the remainder of the day. And we do. Ford calls Mom to check on Lexi and them to find out they have her down at the docks cleaning the boats. That we plan on meeting them for dinner at Dockside.

Ford makes a few calls as I wrap my naked self in his blue satin sheet and head out on the balcony for some fresh sea air. I take a seat on the rocker he has placed out here. Closing my eyes, I listen to the waves lap the shore. I remember coming up here as a teenager because this was an extension of the McIntire's game room. I would just relax out here, thinking of my next article.

Countries I could visit and uncover corruption, help those in need.

I hear the sliding door. "Figured I would find you out here."

"Yeah," I say, sighing in relaxation.

Ford takes the chair next to me. "You know I bought this house for you."

"What did you say?" I ask in shock.

"You always loved this house and this view. You also always said you wanted a seaside house either right here on the beach or up on the hill on the tip of the north end."

"You just keep impressing me, Ford Merrick."

"Why is that?" he asks, amusement written across his face.

"Well, I was just sitting here reminiscing of the past and all the times I hung out here on this balcony. Then you come out here repeating the words in my head and remembering what I used to say and dream about."

"There is very little, if anything, I don't remember you saying or doing, Mar."

"I believe that," I say with a laugh.

"I love that sound." Tilting my head, I quirk my eyebrow in question. "I love your laugh, and I haven't heard it enough. And I love your laugh filling the space in this house."

"You make me happy."

"I promise to always try to keep you happy, baby." Standing up, he kisses me on the top of the head. "We probably should get ready for dinner. I guess I need to run you by the house to change."

"That is probably a good idea. Can I take a shower first?"

"You never need to ask. Firstly, as you say, this is our house. Do as you please." I go to object, but he stops me. "Secondly, even if this was not *our* house but my bachelor pad, you still would not need to ask."

"Got it. Care to join me?"

"Maren, as much as it pains me to tell you no, I know if I walk in the shower with you, we will not be leaving this house at all tonight. And we both have a little girl to see."

"Mmmm, very true. Give me twenty, and then we can head to the house." Ford slaps my ass when I walk away in his twisted sheet, causing me to yelp. Under the shower, I think how after all the crazy chaos over the last several weeks, I finally feel contentment. But it's almost frightening as if I need to prepare for the floor to drop, *again*.

Ford

I YEARNED to jump in the shower with Maren, but I need to do some damage control before dinner with Dawson. I did the one thing I promised I would not do before he proposed to Izzy. Propose to Maren and ask her to move in with me. *Shit!* I back out of calling him and text him instead.

> Bro, I need to tell you something.

D-MAN
> What did you do now?

> Let's just say I got carried away last night.

D-MAN
> Fuck! Did you murder her?

> What the fuck man! Murder who?

D-MAN

Grace. She was livid when we dropped her off last night. I called her father and explained the whole ordeal. He was not impressed with his little princess. But I also don't want to have to cover up a murder.

> Jesus, I did not murder her. You know the police are going to show up at the house any minute now thanks to you bringing up murder.

D-MAN

All good. You just said you didn't, so no need to arrest you.

> Speaking of murders. You might commit one.

D-MAN

You better tell me Maren is okay. Mom said she stayed over last night.

> Mar is great. Even better than great...

D-MAN

I'm waiting...

> I asked her to move in.

D-MAN

Okay...

> And I asked her to marry me last night and again this morning. Long story, but I know you don't want the details.

D-MAN

Mother fucker!

You couldn't wait one more week? ONE WEEK, ASSHOLE!

I tried, but it was in the moment.

D-MAN

I don't want to hear about moments with my sister.

Understood, wasn't sharing just telling.

D-MAN

Damn you, man. Now, we need a plan.

We do.

D-MAN

Bright side, Izzy went home this morning for work and to help with the party this weekend. Do you plan on announcing it at dinner?

Hadn't gotten that far. But she is wearing a ring and excited, so yeah, I guess we need to.

D-MAN

Not a word to Izzy.

FML

It can't be that bad.

D-MAN

She cannot find out, EVER.

Got it. I'll talk to Maren.

D-MAN

> On another note, happy for you, man. I've talked to Mom, and it seems this has been a long time coming.

> It has.

> And sorry, I didn't mean to rain on your Izzy parade.

D-MAN

> It will work out, but make sure Maren keeps it on the DL.

> On it. See you in a few.

How on earth do you tell your fiancée we have to keep our engagement quiet amongst the family for the time being and even then, lie about the engagement date to not intrude on another's celebration?

CHAPTER 37
DECISIONS
Maren

I sit at the kitchen bar, talking with Mom over this week's appointments and what I need to gather for student teaching. She still wants to take Lexi back-to-school shopping even though it could be another month before she can attend in person. Her thoughts are Lexi shouldn't have to miss out on the experience due to delays, and honestly, I can't argue with that.

About the engagement, that's being hushed like a dirty little secret between Ford and I. Poor guy, he was pitiful trying to explain the whole ordeal about Dawson and Izzy. Part of me wanted to guilt him into making him go crazy with indecision, but I could tell he already was distraught enough having to keep a promise to Dawson and hiding our exciting news. I told him to let them have their moment, and for now, we won't say a word to anyone. Just our little secret, plus Dawson. When we got to the house, I found a silver, plain necklace and looped my engagement ring through it. Now, it hangs around my neck. It helped calm Ford down a bit as well as he was not happy about me removing it from my finger. I also reassured him with the whale tale ring I never take off.

On the Adair front, it's been quiet. I reviewed a text from Tray this morning letting me know he was back in town. I've not heard a word from Darcy all weekend and haven't been in the mood to reach out after Thursday's debacle. My parents didn't even go to church yesterday, but they swore they would be attending next Sunday.

In terms of the pageant queen, Izzy confirmed she was back in NYC. According to Dawson, her father was not happy with her and promised to not pull out of business with the guys over his daughter's emotions. I'm just ecstatic she is no longer in our town, and Ford is working toward completely cutting her off. Dawson is to handle all business with her and family from here on out. I know Ford's hurt by the loss of a friend but angry over her true colors.

I'm just ready to find some normalcy in a schedule with school starting back next week and figuring out Lexi's diagnosis. On the bright side, no new bruises, and her energy levels peaked a bit over the weekend. I'm actually looking forward to her appointment today because I've seen improvement in her wellbeing.

Upon leaving the hospital this afternoon, we get stopped by Tray. "Hey Maren, Mrs. Hart, and little Lexi."

Mom internally rolls her eyes, but Lexi snarls her lip up. "You do know I'm average tall, right?" We all laugh at her words.

Trayton kneels down to her level. "I know, but you are short compared to me."

"I guess," she huffs as she shrugs her shoulders.

"Have a good weekend?"

"I did. Hung out on the docks with the fisherman."

"Sounds fun," he says.

"What did you do?"

"I was gone practicing football."

"Isn't that your job? Why do you need to practice?" she asks, sounding curious.

"Well, I need to stay in shape and workout to be better than the best. Ever watch me play?"

"Nope."

"Alright then, adding that to my list of things to fix," he chuckles. "We are going to fix that, little Lexi."

She looks up at me first, before turning back to him. "Okay then." She shrugs her tiny shoulders, then walks off with Glam-ma.

Mom turns to say, "We will be at the car." I nod my head in acknowledgement, then turn to Tray.

"Should we address the elephant in the room first?" I ask.

"I feel like there are a dozen of them."

I titter, "Can't argue with you on that." Running through the list in my head, I find right where I want to begin. "Let's start with your wonderful mother," I say, smiling like a smart-ass.

"I'm sorry, Maren. I would have bet my career she would have never reached that level of crazy. But nonetheless, you don't need to worry about her anymore. I've threatened her entire existence and to cut her off completely if she pulls shit like that again. She is never to even look at either of you if your paths cross."

"Well that makes me feel slightly better. Next on the list, Darcy. Where is she?"

"Braxton ended up getting food poisoning, so she flew back to be with them, and then, on top of the mother drama, she felt too embarrassed. But she will be back Thursday with the whole fam for the parade."

"Damn, okay. I'll reach out to her. Hope Brax is feeling better."

"He is. Um, about the parade... Are you bringing Lexi?"

"I mean it's kinda a huge town event, so yeah. Plus, we hear there is a famous NFL star on a float, so that might be cool."

"Glad you still have jokes on, Mar."

"I aim to please."

"Yeah, I see that. So, you think maybe Alexis could ride on the float with me?" My eyes must say all my thoughts in an instance. "Well, she won't be the only kid. Darcy's kids will be riding, and a few kids of some friends will be riding, too, so you and Ford can ride with her."

"Um, let me think about it."

"Understood. And can I get you all tickets to a football game and some gear?" he asks, and I just side-eye him with unsureness.

"Trayton, let's break the bottle. What kind of relationship are you looking for?"

His anxious eyes look down, then back up to me. "I should have never signed those papers; I was an idiot and was pressured. I'm not looking to fight you to undo it, and I know Ford will be adopting her, and I swear I'm honestly okay with that. I just, I mean, shit... I just want to be in her life. She is a part of me and being near her this week made me realize I don't want to miss out on her life."

"Alright, and how do you plan we do that, Trayton?" I am not amused. I can see he is struggling internally with all this, and I'm honestly not looking to make this harder on him, but shit, where was this six years ago. I also can't dismiss knowing he has been behind the scenes all through the years with her best interest in mind.

"I talked to my PR manager; we have a few choices. We, um, treat this as we are close family friends and I'm her godfather since Darcy is her godmother. Would make sense." Then he pauses.

"And the other options?" I ask, raising my eyebrows in question.

"Another option is to bite the bullet. Meaning I do a press junket, letting the world know I have a daughter but signed over my rights because I was young and stupid, but she has an amazing family taking care of her, and I'm just a lucky SOB who still gets to be part of her life." I have no poker face to hide the shock. "Think about it, Maren, please. This would put rumors to rest and keep the media from digging around and surprising all of us when the news breaks, catching all of us off guard."

Sighing, I murmur, "I hear you, Trayton, I really do. Let me think about it. Talk it over with Ford and my parents. No promises, but I will make sure we discuss the options. Darcy probably already told you Lexi was bullied and called a liar because she told a boy you were father, and he didn't believe her. So, most importantly ,I need to put her first. So, for now, just pocket those tickets and gear." I can tell he is disappointed, but this is the way of our lives right now. "All I can promise right now is you are more than a blood donor to her, like literally in more ways than one. She knows that. So, that's something."

"Yeah, I get it." His phone beeps and he looks down. "Angelica is tracking me down for more platelets. And then I'm taking her to coffee afterwards."

"Oh really? Getting on well with the doc, I see," I tease.

"She's been a breath of fresh air, also a touch of home that I have been missing."

"Look at you, Trayton, having a crush on a girl he banged back in high school."

"Again, your jokes are hilarious. But really, she's cool. She is not you, let's be honest, but I would like to see where this can go even between our both crazy schedules."

Placing my hand on his arm, I smile. "Well I'm happy for both of you. I'm sure she will bring you up to full speed on Lexi's health since I added you to the medical records list."

His eyes lit up. "You did?"

"I did, last Thursday when we were here."

"Thank you."

"You're welcome. Now don't be late to your platelet date."

Trayton pulls me into a tight hug. "You, Maren Hart, are one of a kind. Not sure anyone in this world deserves you."

Laughing, I smack his shoulder. "Don't get soft on me now, Adair. I honestly don't think my psyche can handle that."

"I'll keep that in mind, bye." He kisses me on the cheek and saunters down the hospital hallway with his bodyguards in tow. Shaking my head in disbelief, I'm not looking forward to the tough conversations and decisions to be had.

CHAPTER 38
MOVING FORWARD
Maren

THE WEEK HAS BEEN QUIET, and hell, I'll take it with no complaining. Blood work came back from Monday, showing Lexi's numbers improving, leading Dr. Hunt to hope her condition is acute. We have to wait a few more weeks for a more definitive answer.

Which allows us all some hope, but we are still keeping our heads about it just in case something changes. This time, we are pushing out her next transfusion until next Wednesday to test his theory. Of course, if we see a debilitating change, we are to take her sooner. Her bruises have started to lighten up, and her energy has definitely been kicked up a notch. All signs that she is improving.

Dawson and Ford flew out Sunday night and ended up having to be gone an extra day and are supposed to return tonight. I hear Dawson is stressing because he has his big proposal this weekend to prep for. Though Ford helped him hire staff to prepare the site. I'm sure he is also nervous, but Izzy loves him to pieces, and they really are a perfect match.

Ford and I have plans to talk with my parents tonight about Trayton and how to approach his part in her life—in all of our lives. The parade is tomorrow, and he and Darcy have both reached out, asking us to be on the float. I told him I would have an answer for him tonight. Mom has been helping the church with their float, and Dad will be trailering one of his fishing boats for promoting.

The town is crowded as word got out outside of the island that Trayton Adair, star wide receiver for the Steelers, is part of a meet and greet in town for a welcome home ceremony. Rumor has it, the mayor is going to give him a key to the city because that's the thing to do in small towns with famous people. A big part of this parade and town event is to raise money via donations to help the south-end that received the brunt of Ophelia. Should be a fun time for all, and right now, the weather is still perfect as summer begins to taper off.

Ford

THE PAST COUPLE of days have been hell. We fired two of our creators who can't seem to get their shit together and then promoted another person who hopefully can live up to our expectations or it could be possible career failure for her. Silicon Valley takes names and ruins lives. The Valley also knows Merrick's Hart Software is ruthless and unforgiving when it comes to tech trade and building.

Dawson has taken off to Izzy's parents house to set his plan in motion as I head to the house to see my girls and discuss with them, along with Dad and Madre, about the future. I'm not out to bust Dawson and Izzy's upcoming announcement, but we all need to be on the same page in terms of Trayton becoming a staple in our lives. In Lexi's life. Big changes are up ahead, and I know we all need to wade through the repercussions of all decisions. All I know for certain is that Maren will be my wife, and Alexis Jane will be my daughter.

Walking into the house, I am greeted by a high energy mini bar, jumping up in my arms. "She is becoming stir crazy," Maren says, approaching to give me a hug. Once close enough, I pull her into my arms, leaning down to kiss her forehead.

"God, I have missed you, baby." She hums into my body.

"What about me?" Mini bar exclaims.

"Well, that's just a given, right." She nods and giggles. "I brought you something."

"You did?" she squeals, shimmering down my waist and leg to get down in excitement. Reaching into my bag, I pull out a snow globe with a bear in shades and swim trunks, holding a surfboard in the center with the California sign behind him. I turn it upside down to turn the dial, and *California Dreamin'*, begins to play as the snow falls around the bear. "This is so cool. He even looks like Mr. Pickles. Look, Mommy!" Then she wraps her arms around my neck. "Thank you, Ford."

"You are so welcome. Now be very careful because if it drops to the ground, it will break. Okay?"

"Okay, I'll be extra careful. I'll put it in my room now." We watch as she walks very slowly toward the stairs, her eyes glued to the falling snow in the globe. Once it all falls, she shakes it again.

"That should keep her occupied for a bit," Maren says, laughing.

I pull her fully into my arms. "Do I get you to myself tonight at our place or we staying here?" I whisper in her ear.

"Staying here, sorry. Mom wants to leave here to head into town for the parade."

"No worries, got my bag in the car," I say as she takes my hand, leading me to the kitchen. We take our places at the table where Madre has pizza and beer served.

Dad claps his hands. "Let's get down to business. I'm hungry, and I dislike not having a plan."

We first discuss the parade float tomorrow. Honestly, I don't think it's a bad idea, and Lexi would love it, especially being with her cousins. Madre wants Maren on the route taking pictures of all the floats and people. Unbeknownst to us, she volunteered Maren to capture the parade for the local paper since the photographer would be on the Newspaper float capturing those moments.

"I'll take Lexi on Trayton's float," I say, volunteering.

"You sure?" Maren asks, her emerald green eyes sparkling with approval.

"Of course, it will be fun."

"Alright, let me text him and Darcy real quick to let them know and get the details." I watch as she does, and Trayton immediately responds with excitement and everything we need to know.

"Now that one dilemma has been resolved, we need to address the bigger one." Right then Lexi sneaks in, trying to get her own pizza undercover. We all pretend not to notice her while she giggles, thinking she just got away with a whole box of pizza. Madre follows her to the living room just to see what she is up to.

When she comes back to the kitchen, she murmurs, "She is good. She has the box of pizza, sharing with Mr. Pickles apparently, and sipping on juice, watching *Moana*."

"She really is easy to please, isn't she?" I catch Maren and Madre glance at each other and laugh out loud.

"Sure. Keep thinking that," Madre says, then takes a sip of her drink. Maren pats my arm as to be a smart-ass toward my comment.

Ignoring her, I say, "Continue, Maren, on the big one."

She pretentiously eyes me, then looks at Dad. "Trayton wants to be part of Lexi's life, which we all have known for a bit now. But now, we kind of need a game plan. He talked to his PR manager, and they came up with two options. One, Trayton becomes her godfather, like Darcy is her godmother and the media believes we are close childhood friends and family friends." I watch her expression change when she gets to the second option. "Or Trayton comes clean about having a daughter he signed rights over for, placates himself as a young, stupid boy for making a rash decision but now gets to be part of her life. Basically, we get to have more control of the narrative along with keeping the media from digging and not knowing when this could explode in our faces." I watch as the parents nod their heads, thinking through the possibilities.

"What about his mother?" Madre asks.

"Trayton told me he has taken care of her, and there is to be no more dealing with her. Whether he claims Alexis or not, she will not be in the picture."

"What about Lexi being known to the world?" Dad asks.

"Part of Trayton's statement is to let her live her life privately. He also stated that with him states away, there is no reason the press would push to stalk her or us because he is who they want the dirt on, and she is just a little kid right now. By the time she grows up, it could change, but he swore to keep her as safe as he can, along with Ford."

Dad turns to look at me. "Son, what do you have to say about all this?"

I turn to Maren to ensure she is good with me making our own announcement now. "Well sir, Maren and I have talked, and for reasons we cannot disclose at the moment, I will be adopting Lexi." Both parents look at me in bewilderment. "Please do not say anything until we say so, but I have asked Maren to marry me and move in, and she said yes. Along with agreeing for me to adopt Lexi."

Madre is out of chair, sobbing and hugging both Maren and I. "This makes me so, so happy. Oh, my goodness, so much to plan and do. And finally, for you two!"

"Mom, calm down first. There is a reason we need to keep this quiet, and I am not going to tell you, but please do not break this news to anyone until we say so."

"I don't understand."

Speaking up, I say, "I know you don't, but you will soon. I promise," holding her hand in mine. "Please, we need both of you to trust us."

"Alright then. I don't like it, but I guess we have no choice."

Letting out a light huff, I mutter, "No, you really don't. But we needed to tell you this news to help decide on a plan of action with Trayton. He knows I'm going to adopt Lexi and is fine with it. I talked to my PR team, and they agreed, Trayton coming clean now is the best option to lessen future invading. But we agreed, and Maren let me know your thoughts, but Trayton is to not make the announcement until adoption is legal and Alexis Jane Hart is Alexis Jane Merrick. Just to clear the air and no one can make assumptions that there is a chance for Trayton to fight for custody. They can view us all as one happy family unit." I watch her wheels turn.

"That makes sense, but can I be honest?"

"Of course."

"I want to be married first before you adopt her. It might be old fashioned, especially coming from me, but I would like marriage before child for you in this scenario."

"What if I say I know a judge who can make everything happen in one motion?"

"You have my attention."

"Good because you know I would have married you already if I could and have adopted Alexis, but for disclosed reasons, I can't yet. But that doesn't mean I can't set other events in motion to prepare."

She hesitates a bit, letting out a held breath. "I'm good with that, and we can work out the logistics as we go, I guess."

We both turn to nails tapping on the table. "Let me get this straight," Madre says sternly. "Ford and you are getting married, and he is adopting Lexi. Along with that, Trayton Adair is becoming part of this family to be in Lexi's life, and we are all in agreement over this. But we need to wait to announce your pending nuptials and news because?"

"Woman, come on. They are waiting on Dawson and Izzy to make their announcement." We both turn, stunned at Dad.

"What? Dawson told me, and I helped him pick out the ring. Looks like the only one in the dark right now is your mom." And she looks furious.

"Someone better start explaining right now." Her eyes turn a shade of angry storm gray.

Maren speaks up, "Mom, God, forgive me and Dawson, too.

Dawson is proposing to Izzy this weekend. Ford over here got too excited and went ahead and proposed to me last Friday morning, but he had promised Dawson that he wouldn't ask me until after he asked Izzy, and they made their announcement. We don't want to steal from their joyous time. So please do not say anything, Mother, to him or anyone beforehand, or when they come on Sunday for dinner. Let them have their moment, and Ford and I will decide on the best time to announce ours."

She shakes her head. "You all are going to be the very death of me at this rate. But I will not say a word and will take this conversation to my grave in the interest of keeping everyone happy."

We all say, "Thank you."

Madre then turns to both of us. "I'm very very happy for you both, and sweet girl, I am so proud of you. Proud of both of you really. Great things are in store for you both and for this whole family it seems."

I squeeze Maren's hand in mind, reassuring her of the promises made tonight and that the future is going to be a wonderful one.

CHAPTER 39
NUANCES
Maren

Sunday night has arrived, and we are all out at the local Mexican restaurant celebrating Dawson and Izzy's engagement with practically half the town. Even Tray and Darcy are here with her family in on the action. I did come clean to Darcy on Thursday after the parade about Ford and I, and she seemed genuinely happy. But I believe she is more excited watching her little brother flirt with our favorite doctor at the bar.

Lexi had a blast on the float, and Trayton even hooked Ford and her up with Steelers gear to rep in, which was super cool. I won't lie, it has been odd seeing Trayton and Ford getting along, but on the other hand, I couldn't ask for all this to go more smoothly and appreciate both their efforts. Right now, I think we are just fielding next steps in keeping Lexi happy and healthy.

Ten at night rolls around, and the restaurant is still hopping with drinks pouring. Mom and Dad left an hour ago to take Lexi home with them. I promised Ford I would stay with him tonight as long as he promised to get me to school on time for the teacher's workday. School starts back officially on Wednesday with students, so I'm excited to get in planning mode and embark on this next stage of life. In Dawson's drunk state, he said he was taking Izzy to the new house to do naughty things to her, and all I could do was down another drink in embarrassment for the both of them.

Ford leans over into my ear. "Just wait until all the naughty things I do to you later." His words cause the blush and alcohol to turn my whole body a shade of pink.

Playfully slapping his arm, I whisper, "Can you not in public?"

"I very much can," he growls with a predatory gleam in his eyes, then slaps my ass. I know once I blink and look back up at him, my own are full of lust. Before I can tell him to sweep me away to bed, Izzy pulls us to the tiny dance floor up by the stage. Because she is lit and I am not far behind her at this juncture, we are grinding up against each other, booty shaking to salsa music, making the guys holler before Ford comes to my aid. "You're drunk," he admonishes in his deep husky tone.

"You're drunk," I retort.

This time I receive a growl, while I shimmy my ass against his groin. "Maren, are you telling me those four margaritas plus two tequila shots have nothing on you?" His eyebrow quirks at me when he turns me to face him.

"Nope. Not at all. Just buzzed," I say back, watching him sway a little. *Or is it me that's swaying?* Ford pulls me in close to his body, and I just want to soak in his warmth and smell. His hands grip tightly on my hip bones as my head rests against his chest for two more songs. Alcohol taking over.

"Ready to go?" he asks.

"Yes, I'm drunk and tired." He laughs, wrapping his arm around my shoulders to lean on him. We say our goodbyes to the bar and walk out, getting a blast of ocean air. Which I think is the best cure for an alcohol-induced vomiting session.

Once in, before I can push a word out, his tongue is in my mouth, and I cave, welcoming every tongue lash and suck. I wore a cute dress tonight for the occasion, but I'm guessing Ford has other ideas of why I wore a dress because at dinner his hand kept rising up my inner thigh, gently teasing my core with his fingers.

Making me squirm in my seat. He told me no one was watching, but in my tipsy state, I felt all eyes were on us.

"Ford," I say breathlessly.

"Yes, baby," he says between the biting of my neck down to my chest where he already has my dress pulled down under my breasts.

"Ford, we are in a lit up parking lot, anyone can see us."

"Didn't I tell you this pussy is mine to do as I please, when I please." In an instant, I am wet with his assertiveness. I may pick a fight with him on buying the wrong pasta, but I'll be damned if I don't become more obedient than a church girl on Sunday when he demands my body like this. "I have to fuck you," he demands, pulling me onto his lap, straddling him.

In one swoop, my lace panties are ripped off before I can protest. He slides two fingers inside me; we both moan. "Fucking hell, Maren, you are already soaked and ready for me." When he pulls them out of me and sucks my juices off his fingers, a whimper escapes me. "Be a good cocktease and finger yourself as I get out of these jeans."

Again, Ford is break me out of my comfort zone, but the sensation of turning this Adonis of a man on is all the confidence I need. I slide my dress over my head, so he has a better of view of my hand sliding down to my center. With two fingers, I strum my clit and moan loudly. "Good girl," he rasps as he wrangles his jeans off, then relaxing back underneath me. "Now, slide down on me." I center him at my opening, then slowly, inch by inch, I slide down his shaft until he's at the hilt. He thrusts against me, causing my breath to wind. "That's right, baby, ride me."

A shudder rocks through me, then I pick up pace, rolling my hips over and over again as his fingertips dig into my hips, pressing me down harder on him. "I can't keep going days without you, Maren. When are you moving in?"

"I don't ... God...I don't ... *Fuck* you are so....know," are the only words I can manage to create through the moans.

"Not God, baby, only me." He begins to meet my every thrust, chasing our orgasms together.

"Please... don't...stop, Ford... Oh..." He bites his bottom lip as if wanting to hold back a little longer, and damn if it isn't one of the sexiest looks he's shown me. His magnetic eyes draw me in, tipping me to the edge of nearly coming.

"Fuuck...baby, right there... Yes... Come for me now. Come!" he demands, and my attentive little kitty listens. I pulse and constrict all around his cock, determined to milk him for every drop. His lips meet mine. "Sit next to me and rest for a few minutes. I have many more ideas once we get home." I don't even try to argue and mess with him because we both know he will get exactly what he wants, as well as I.

Ford

ONCE WE ARE HOME, I have to nudge her to wake up so we can go inside. "Head up to take a shower, I'll be up there shortly." She says okay and wobbles a little getting up the stairs, which, in turn, I find myself slowly following her until she is in the bathroom, and I hear the water running.

Heading back downstairs, I grab a glass of bourbon to relax. Tonight was a celebration for Dawson and Izzy on the road to marriage and bliss. In a few weeks, everyone will be celebrating Maren and I's vows and Lexi's adoption. Summer weather is beginning to come to an end, and there is no way in hell I am waiting until the next onset of warm weather to marry this woman. To become a family. Dawson is aware and gave me the go to move forward. Stating Izzy wants a full year to plan. I know Maren could honestly care less about the details and would be happy marrying at the courthouse, but she is too perfect, too gorgeous, too everything to not be in the limelight for once. Hence, planning has begun.

First, though, I'm going to take full advantage of her in *our* shower. Taking two steps at a time, I still hear the water running and can feel the steam coming out at the bottom of the door. I undress myself, then slowly open the door to not frighten her. I'm taken back by the view of her body on full display through the sheen glass doors. Here curls are wet and straight. The water cascades down her body as she stands there with her eyes closed, head tilted back. Stepping in behind her, I wrap my arm around her from behind, pushing her back to my front. Then shift her hair off her one shoulder to plant kisses on. I kiss and nip up her nape to behind her ear, listening to her let out soft moans of pleasure. I move my hands up her body to her breasts and begin palming them, rolling her pink budded nipples between my fingers. "Are you already clean?" I ask.

"Yes." she pants, ready to go again. "The water felt too good to leave." I let her stand there another minute while I lather up and rinse off.

"Up you go," I murmur, picking her up and carrying her out the shower to the bed. I dry her off first before drying myself, then toss the towel on the floor. "On all fours, baby, and face the window."

She attentively does, and I pat her ass gently, telling her she is a good girl. I trail my fingertips down her spine, enjoying watching quiver at my touch. "Ready for me, baby?" Not much of an ask but to prepare her as I line my cock up to her sleek wet center. I watch myself enter her, and my eyes roll back in my head. "Always so damn tight for me." I do the motion over again because I can't seem to get enough of my cock sliding into home.

She lets out a sharp moan that pushes me to slam into her the third time. Wrapping my hand around her hair, I tug her head back just enough for her to arch back, and *FUCK*, that's the spot. Her cry of pleasure tells me she is arriving with me. "That's it, baby. Take it hard and fast. Let me hear you scream." Thrusting into her, I pull her hips back to me to hold her still and tight. My groans are getting loud and shaky because hell, nothing in my life has ever felt this incredible or intimate. I rear back my right hand back and slap her ass cheek, causing her to scream my name. Her cunt constricts over my pulsing dick. "Fuck, Maren," I grit through clenched teeth.

"I don't think I have ever come so hard in my life." I see her exhausted smile on the side of her face which she turns her head, slightly in my direction. She is too spent for words. I, on the other hand, feel like I should go run a marathon as I slowly pump in and out her cream-filled pussy to revel in the pleasure just a little longer, leaving her whimpering once I pull out to lay next her.

CHAPTER 40
GETTING THERE
Maren

Three weeks into routine and I think we are all getting comfortable with the changes that have been happening. Mrs. Lambert, who I am student teaching with, is a godsend, or maybe she is enjoying the break from not having to actually teach a bunch of high schoolers all day. I basically teach the two tenth grade level literature classes, we tag team on the tenth and eleventh grade honors English class, and she lets me have input in the Seniors AP English class. She even promised to review my graduating thesis, which I have already started on.

Today, though, I'm going to be late to school because Lexi is finally heading to school by herself. Harper, the angel she is, came over every Monday through Thursday to review lesson plans and help with homework.

After multiple trips for lab work and one final platelet transfusion, Dr. Hunt and Dr. Leeds declared her healthy and recovered. Lexi's body finally kicked in gear and is now producing a sufficient number of platelets, and she hasn't been anemic for the last two weeks. Needless to say, the doctors deemed her diagnosis as acute caused by an infection, and for now, we are going to do three-month follow-ups. We are all ecstatic with the news, and she is excited to finally be in class and get to play like her classmates and make friends.

Good thing my child does not embarrass easily because she has a whole entourage following her into school this morning. Mom, Dad, Dawson and Izzy, along with myself, Ford, and even Trayton. He flew in last night just to be here.

Because you guessed it, he is officially part of the family.

News broke a little earlier than we anticipated thanks to my favorite pageant queen leaking to the press after she put all the pieces together. Honestly, I never saw it coming from her, but when we were watching her on TV, with her bold statements, I felt her actions were fitting at one last attempt for Ford to push me away. She made it sound like Trayton and I were still in a secret love affair, and I was just an awful person no one should trust and believe.

Dawson and Ford were quick to jump on a plane to deal with her, and her daddy dearest was not pleased and was tempted to let the guys press slander charges against her. But in all thing's politics and money, things were worked up behind the scenes as well as Grace being slapped with a restraining order against Ford, myself, and Lexi. Trayton was quick to hold a press junket to confirm rumors of Lexi being his and deny that we are together. Ford, Lexi and I stood on the sidelines for support and even let them get a family photo of all of us together. This is also the time Ford and mine's engagement is announced along with Ford proceeding to adopt Lexi. The press was a lot to take in.

Ford is used to a certain level of invasion and handling them, but Trayton's was a whole other level. Angelica was even introduced to the public as his girlfriend, which lucky for us, takes the heat off who we are in the small town since an NFL player's love life is more intriguing than his past.

If you asked me six plus years ago, I wouldn't be near Trayton, let alone Ford and I joining him for double date nights, sometimes even triple date nights when Dawson and Izzy join us. I would have laughed in everyone's faces and told them they were all shot out. Yet, this is our new norm when he comes home for a few days to see Lexi and Angelica. There are times, I, even now, feel like the third wheel when he and Ford get together. It truly is an odd but inspiring thing to watch unfold.

Tray is teaching Lexi all about football, and she sports his jersey around town. I know that makes him elated to see she is proud of him. Mom and Dad are tolerating him but trying. The dynamic is just odd with Darcy in Tennessee and his parents having nothing to do with Lexi, which in turn is causing a rift between them and Trayton. Not that he is angry with them about not accepting her, but they still can't believe Trayton publicly accepted Lexi as they still see her has a whore's daughter and now is tied to them forever. He deals with their wrath every time he comes home and tries to visit them.

"Oh my goodness, you all know it is not necessary for you all to escort her, right?" Harper says avidly.

My mom walks in front of our group. "Now, Mrs. Kips, you really should have known this was going to happen," she responds with a light laugh.

"That is true. I'm sure the whole class appreciates the interruption. Please come on in," she rebuts with a sincere smile on her face. We all follow behind Lexi and stand in the front of the classroom as Harper introduces her new student ,then shows Lexi where her desk and cubby are.

Immediately sitting down, the girl next to her shares her pencil and asks her to be friends. My heart wants to burst. Ford makes a growling sound behind me, so I follow his eyesight to the punk boy who bullied Lexi that day in Sunday school. Ford does the I'm watching you signal to the kid, who swallows deeply in fear. Trayton now pays attention to this scene of Ford threatening a kindergartner and walks over to the boy with Ford behind him. I see words exchanged, fear and tears in the boys eyes as Lexi's two protectors walk away. I shake my head and mouth "sorry" to Harper, who is waiting to have her class' attention back.

Knowing we have overstayed our welcome and caused a scene, we all say bye to Lexi as she talks to her friend. Mom's eyes are welling up with tears, Dawson is bummed she is ignoring us, and

I'm just trying to get out of this classroom before I have my own breakdown.

"Wait!" she shouts and scampers over to us, giving each one of us a big hug and Dawson is fist pump.

"We will see you when you get home, kiddo," Dad says, looking conflicted with emotions as Lexi opted to ride the bus to and from school and wanted to start this afternoon. And of course, we will *all* be there as her entourage to hear about her first day over ice cream sundaes. Then her new normal will be coming home to Mom's even after we move in Ford's house at the end of this month.

Almost two months back in Nags Head, this place finally resembles an actual home and life I have only ever dreamt for us. Filled with family and friends that Alexis and I so desperately needed. The road was long, jolting, holed, and rutted, but we are here now and never *going nowhere.*

CHAPTER 41
Ford

ONE WEEK LATER

"This is extraordinary, and oh my God, the view overlooks the ocean. Do you see? Please tell me you are seeing this right now?" she elates, roving by the windows that overlook the Atlantic Ocean.

Chuckling in amusement, I ask, "Anything you don't like?"

She blinks her eyes a few times. "I LOVE everything. Even down to these little spoons with sea turtles on them." Then she whispers to herself, "These are so stinking cute."

We have been at Jennette's Pier for about forty-five minutes already, letting Maren plan her wedding day. What she hasn't figured out is that the wedding is happening in six hours. Everyone is on standby right now. I wanted this day to be perfect, so as she makes comments of dislikes, things she would change, my trusty secretary, Josef, stands next to me, writing all the notes down.

Haper, Madre and I did the first pass on designing with the wedding coordinator and then let her run with it. I have to say she brought so much of "us" and Maren alone into the décor, it's uncanny.

"Honestly Ford, if we can score this place, I could think of no better place than to marry you." I'm unable to hide my Cheshire grin this go around. She has been bouncing all over the place with a million things to say and just causing me to be, *fuck*, just *happy*. There are a million words to say, but none that come to mind at this moment, on this day. "Why are you looking at me like that?"

"Like what??

"That's the look you get when you are about to get your way or close a huge contract. The same look you get when you are planning something." She squints her eyes toward me like she will be able to read my thoughts somehow, making me laugh loudly, pulling her into my arms.

"I'm just happy, Maren. Being with you here, planning our wedding. All this makes me excited and enthusiastic about the future." I grin, kissing the top of her head.

"Me too," she purrs back, wrapping her hands around my waist.

"Now, the biggest question of the day. Inside or outside?" I ask as she takes her warmth from my body to look out another window.

"Is that even a question?"she asks like I'm the biggest idiot in the room. "Outside, especially if the weather is like today. Not too hot, but just enough ocean breeze to cool you down. And the arbor they have up down there is perfect, well, almost perfect. I would like to see more of the driftwood, with loose pampas grass down the sides, accented with white, and light pink roses with hints of Baby breath." She has a dreamy look on her face.

"Yeah, that would be perfect." I turn to Josef who is scribbling as I follow Maren to another spot. "The white chairs with ivory ribbon work for you?"

"Yes, I love that elegant look. I'm totally stealing all this brides' ideas," she says, letting out a giggle. "The owner is so great letting us in here while they set up. This is making my life so much easier. Remind me to catch the bride and groom's name, so I can reference their name for planning with Josef's notes." Nodding my head, I hope she doesn't remember to ask Catherine when we see her. "Hmmm I wonder if I know them? If not, we should be friends, it seems we have so much in common." I grin at her obliviousness and admire how adorable she is at this moment. "Like look at this! Who else would think to make centerpieces out of old stacked books with a single-colored rose on top adorned with leaves and Baby's breath."

She *gasps*. "That holds the table number that looks like a page out of a book. Eeekkk, this table has *Wuthering Heights* mixed in the stack. Swoon." Now she is just being dramatic and hilarious. I also know our time is dwindling down to make changes.

Needing to get her back on track, I ask, "I take it you love this setup?"

"Yes, what gave it away?" she chuckles, grinning from ear to ear.

"Alright smart-ass, on to the next portion." She claps her hands in excitement. A waiter brings in a cart of food to taste. The cart is full of shrimp cocktails, fried shrimp, chicken, stuffed crab, three different types of potatoes, vegetables, salad, and garlic bread.

"Wow, this all looks and smells delicious. What would you choose, Ford?"

"You can have any or all you want, Maren. I've told you there is no budget." She gawks at me like she does every time I give her this tidbit of information.

"Um, well okay. Let's do shrimp cocktails for appetizers, and for those that don't like shrimp, offer the buffalo chicken feathers. Main course, fried shrimp, stuffed crab, and sirloin to choose from. Ceasar salad, of course, and um, baked potato, or fries. And can we have baskets of garlic bread for each table? Please and thank you."

"Yes, ma'am," the waiter says.

"I feel like we are marking tasks quickly off the list, what else?"

Catherine walks in with the chosen baker. "Well, we unfortunately don't have any cake to taste test, but we do have what we are setting up in here if you want to take a look?" The baker wheels in a two tiered cake and platters of gourmet cookies in all flavors, including her favorite oatmeal no bake cookies.

"Seriously, who is this person? She is like my twin picking these cookies."

"You can try one, if you'd like," the baker offers her.

Maren practically salivating, she squeaks, "Really?!?"

"Yes, ma'am. This is a sample tray; we have the rest in the kitchen and more than plenty." I watch as she takes one from the plate, and once the cookie hits her palate, she moans.

"Jesus, take me now. This is divine." Shoving the rest in her mouth, she mutters, "Why was that so good? Extra vanilla perhaps," still moaning between her words. I clear my throat to focus on her and distract myself from her lustful moans. Then she turns to look at me, "Oh shit, I should have shared with you."

"I know better than to get between you and your sweets, baby. I'll take your word and moans on how heavenly it tastes," I say with a straight face. Then she punches me in the arm, making her hand hurt more than my arm. The staff laughs over our antics.

"I'm ignoring you now," she says to me, before turning back to Catherine and the baker, "Yes to all of these. And I may need to steal your recipe for the no bakes because mine are good, but not that *goood*." Even Josef lets out a chuckle because Maren is in rare form today. Her confidence has slowly been returning, which also means less of a filter, but a plus for me, because she is less willing to shy from PDA and owning me in public. Her laugh pulls me from my thoughts. "Can I ask what flavor the cake is? I am already loving this simplistic light icing look."

The baker begins to talk, and I pray she doesn't give away the flavor because that might give us away. "This is just the bride and groom cake to share, and this flavor is a spice cake with chocolate icing in the middle between the tiers and then the light coating on the outside is a creamy vanilla." *Fuck*, I grumble to myself, running my hand through my hair, trying to play it cool.

"Huh," Maren voices. I meet the bakers' eyes, glaring for no more information to be shared

"Catherine, what time is it? I need to get back to the kitchen for a staff meeting this evening."

"Yes, please go, and I'll get the notes and add them to the file to discuss later on."

"Nice meeting you, ma'am and Mr. Merrick. Look forward to working on your special day soon."

"Thank you, both of you. This has been incredible."

"Of course. Anything else you need to look over or want to change?"

"I don't think so. Josef took notes, and I took tons of pictures. This really is going to be a stunning wedding and reception." And here it comes. "Catherine, who are the couple? I want to add the names to my notes, so we have their names to reference."

Luckily, Catherine catches my icy glare, standing behind Maren. "Stockholm," she spats out. "Groom is Jason Stockholm, and the bride is Jessica Tate."

Maren almost looks taken back. "I have no idea who those people are."

"Yes, The Tates have been vacationing in the Outer Banks since she was a child, so she wanted to be married here also."

"Awe, that's so sweet. Well please wish them the best of luck from us. I can't wait to stalk the after party pictures." We shake hands with Catherine, then I lead her toward the elevator and out the front door. We left Josef behind to start making things happen. She stops at a sign by the French doors, leading outside to the open deck. "*Two less fish in the Sea,* now that is a cute phrase."

"Come on, baby, we have lunch plans."

Maren

Exhausted.
   Feet Hurt.
   Hungry, again.
   Overwhelmed.
   Grumpy.
   Just want to fall into bed.
   Yet, I'm still running around town with my mom and Harper. "Why are we rushing? Can't we just stop at Claire's for a coffee?" I whine. I'm thankful Lexi is with the boys today because I would end up carrying her everywhere by this point.
   "No, because you took too long picking out a wedding dress," she remarks, taking me off guard.
   "You're the one who told me to try that one dress on like six times."
   She turns around toward me before getting in the car. "Do you not love it?"
   "I do."
   "Is that not the ONE?"
   "It is."
   "So why on earth, Maren, did you have to try on twenty other dresses?" Harper giggles next to me, knowing just how my mom

gets, but for the life of me, I can't figure out why she is extra amped up today.

"Just thought it would be fun." With that, I get an eye roll as she ducks inside the car, and we follow.

"Sweet baby girl, between your wedding and Dawson's and all the moving and house renovations, I'm at my wits end today. So just bear with me. We can get coffee at the next stop."

"Alright, no worries, Mom. All is good." Mom drives down the square but then takes a left into the Jennette's Pier parking lot. "Come on, ladies, we are running late."

"I know you said not to ask questions, Mom, but why are we here?"

"I forgot to tell you, Izzy and Dawson's engagement party is here tonight. She has your dress and everything you need to get ready." I turn to look at Harper who is grinning, mischievously.

"Whatever. Show me the way. Coffee STAT." Honestly, I'm too tired to care.

We walk into a huge bridal suite where Izzy welcomes me with open arms and then pulls me to the salon chair.

"Sit. Makeup and hair time," she states, and then I'm accosted by three different people. "Dean will be doing your hair; Mave is on make-up and Lin is nails. We also have Leon and Sarah to help with make-up and hair. I've got your coffee order on the way, so relax."

Making a perplexed face, I ask, "Shouldn't I be the one calming you down and you relaxing?"

"Maren, I feel like you have known me long enough that controlling the situation is keeping me calm."

"True." I plaster a smile on my face and don't argue. She and Harper take the chairs next to me, and we all relax as we get made up.

Dawson comes by with iced triple shot espresso lattes; my hero. By the time we are barbied up, minus putting on dresses, it's almost five thirty. A knock on the door startles my little slumber.

"This is for you," Lexi says, skipping in with her tight curls bouncing around. She has a tinge of make-up on just to highlight her features for pictures, I'm sure.

"Thank you, baby doll. You look beautiful." She twirls for me in her long, light pink tulle skirt that is topped off with a rose gold sequined top. Making her look older than my soon to be six year old should be, but only because I hate watching her grow up so fast.

"Mommy you need to open it."

"Okay, okay." I I slide the navy ribbon off the medium sized box and flip the top off. There is a folded note and underneath, etched in fine detail, is a glass book filled with a bunch of what looks to be more handwritten notes. I glide my hand over the top, reading the words. "Our story. Ford & Maren. Forever and a day." Not understanding, I open the folded note.

> *Maren Rose Hart, do me the honor of meeting me on the Jennette's Pier dock at 6'o clock. I promise I will make the evening better than your wildest dream.*
> *Xoxo Ford (Soon to be husband)*

I look up to see my mom, Harper, and Darcy and holy shit, Allison standing behind Lexi in shades of pink dresses. "I don't... I don't understand. What's going on?" Tears start to trickle down my face as my brain catches up to what my heart already knows. Mom walks up to me and hands me the bag with my wedding dress.

"Time to get you ready, sweet girl."

"I..um..like this happening, like right now, happening?"

She nods, holding back tears. "Stop messing up your makeup," she mutters, slapping my hand away from my face.

"I'll go get Mave to touch her up," Izzy speaks and leaves the room. As Mom removes my robe, Harper holds my dress out for me to step into. I stare at Allison.

"I need you to say something because I don't think you're

real." She laughs and walks to me, pulling me in a tight embrace. "Like I would miss your wedding day. Not even a pregnant hippo could keep me away." There is a beat of silence before we roar into laughter. "I knew you were at the African sanctuary, but is your hippo really pregnant?"

"She is, but has a few more weeks to go. We made a pact that I would stand by your side on this day and for you to stand by mine."

"Allison, I am awful. I thought I could hide behind not seeing you again, so I never reached out, even though I wanted to. I haven't lived up to our pact promises. Please tell me you're not married yet."

"Safe there, Mar. Hard do find someone that understands I will choose an animal or my own life over them if needed. I'm hopeful one will show up eventually. But hey, today is all about you and fucking FORD! Holy shit, Maren, you finally nailed him down." Laughter fills the room, and I see my mom grimace at the loudness and language.

It is 5:50 when we take the stroll down to the elevator that will lead to the doors on the deck. Lexi leads the way, throwing flower petals everywhere down the bluish-gray runner. Darcy, Harper, and Allison then follow, with Dawson leading Mom behind them. Dad takes my arm, and the moment is surreal. "This is the moment I longed for the most when you left. To walk you down the aisle to Ford."

"Dad, don't me cry again, but how did you know,?" I sniffle, trying to get my snuffling mess of a self together.

"Just always knew, baby girl. Just always knew," he says, leaning in, kissing my temple. "You ready?" I nod, and the doors open.

My eyes immediately find Ford. His sunflower eyes against the blue sky and sweeping Atlantic Ocean takes my breath away. I walk toward the love of my life. I saunter to the rest of my life, with him by my side.

EPILOGUE
Maren

OVER A YEAR LATER

Izzy had in her mind to have a winter wonderland themed wedding, which is not easy to do in the Outer Banks where the weather doesn't typically drop past fifty degrees. She spent months researching and visiting places with Dawson. Looking at logistics for family and friends to travel.

This, my friends, is how we ended up in the quaint town of Woodstock, Vermont the week before Christmas. Not that I would usually mind a destination wedding or a trip out of Nags Head, but getting around these days is brutal. Nearing nine months pregnant was not on the agenda and came to much of our surprise when we found out.

It's no secret that Ford and I never used protection. I was told the possibility of me getting pregnant was slim. The possibility of getting pregnant and carrying to term, almost zero. We had just arrived in Portugal for summer vacation, along with research for an environmental article I was writing for a traveling magazine. I'd found a few months into teaching that I missed writing—and Ford will take all the credit for pushing me to pursue writing again—but I started to dive into freelance projects and loved every piece of the process.

Now I have this one travel magazine, *Bucket List*, that

showcases articles of unique places to visit and explore for all price points. Along with updates on current culture and environmental changes. That's where I get to come in and get paid to travel to places on my own bucket list. To find the secret streets, the hidden gems, and the adventures no one knows or talks about. Interview locals. Understand what locals expect from tourism. Figuring out what tourists do to help the environment while still getting a memorable view up close.

Needless to say, we landed and ate at a local seafood restaurant on the outskirts of Libson, and at first, I was suffering from what we thought was food poisoning that lasted for three more days before Ford rushed us back home and to the hospital. Of course our favorite doc, Angelica was there to help us settle in quickly and sent Dr. Gaur in for treatment since she was now strictly pediatric medicine.

When Dr. Gaur came in with the news, I thought to God Ford was going to faint, and he might have if the nurse did not rush to his aid with a chair for him to collapse in. I laughed in the doctor's face and told him he spewed lies. At this point, I was exhausted, hangry, tired of vomiting, and just wanted to be home in my bed. Soon after my outburst, an ultrasound tech came in to prove the lab work correct as a blimp on the screen appeared, measuring me at two months pregnant.

Fast-forward to now, when I thought I would be joining in with all the week-long activities up until the big day; I'm hanging out in the lounge of the hotel by the cozy but smelting fire with a cup of honey tea. Trayton and Angelica are bringing Lexi with them on Thursday since they wanted to do Christmas with her family prior because Tray is whisking Angelica off to Italy for Christmas and the New Year. Ford and I had no qualms about them taking on Lexi for a few days, knowing they won't be around for the holidays.

Alexis Jane became a Merrick when I signed the dotted line of her adoption papers, right after I said "I do," with the judge present, making Ford her legal father. She has called him daddy ever since, and she cried when he presented her with a little single diamond necklace to wear. She still makes plenty of room in her heart for Tray and calls him Pops, which makes me laugh every time, thinking about an old man. He just goes with it.

"Hey, baby, you doing alright?" Ford takes a seat next to me in his snow gear.

"I guess. Just bored. Probably going to grab my book and read in that corner over there, in case I go missing later because I fell asleep." He chuckles into my neck, the vibration turning me on. Nothing like being married to a sexually hungry man, who is also an Adonis of sculpted greatness, but add pregnancy hormones to the mix; he just has to look at me or barely touch my skin, and I'm drenched. A slight moan escapes me.

"Do I need to tend to you before I head out to snowboard?" he teases.

I pop him in the arm. "Get out of here. I have no patience for your non-advances today. Yeah, yeah, be on your way." I wave my hand, shooing him away from me.

Dawson whips around the corner as Ford laughs. "Ready to shred, bro?"

"Yeah, bro. Let's go, bro."

"Dear lord, make it stop," Izzy whines. Just like me, she has had to hear the constant *bro* talk like they are the coolest snowboarders *eva*. Throw Trayton in the mix, and I've had to tune them when we are all together or overhear a phone conversation.

"Good luck with them today, Iz," I say with a snort.

Ford leans down to kiss my lips softly, then rubs my huge belly. "I'll see you later. Call me if there is an emergency." I give him two thumbs up and a smile, still slightly sexually irritated.

I turn back to Izzy for a distraction. "Maybe I should just stay here with you."

"Nope. This is your wedding week that you have been planning for months. I have a hot date with a book and my tea, so go have lots of fun for me." She gives me a worried look. "Go, or

I'm going to be sad. I promise you I'm fine, and I'll see you, along with everyone else that's here, tonight at dinner." We hug, and she finally leaves. I head up to our room, take a shower, throw some sweatpants and a hoodie on, and curl up on the sofa next to the window that overlooks a pristine, untouched snowy field with an adorable abandoned barn. So much for me heading back downstairs.

Hart Wedding Schedule - Tuesday: Wedding guests are to help themselves to the breakfast buffet, then have a choice of snow-shoeing, skiing, or sleigh ride. Everyone is on their own for dinner. See you around town.

Sounds like another day where my pregnant ass is staying put. Though I would love to take a walk for some fresh air. I don't make it past the pool area before I almost bust my ass, then sit on the bench for thirty minutes, calming my racing heart down and slowing my breathing. Enough adventure for me for one day.

Hart Wedding Schedule - Wednesday: Wedding guests, as usual breakfast is served in the main dining hall. Enjoy mid-day cocktails on us.
Plans for today: There is a trolley that will take you closer into town to shop. Snow-shoeing is an option for adventurous people. Of course, you can always hit the mountain up for tubing, skiing, or snowboarding. See you at The Ransom Tavern at 7pm for dinner.

Ford left with Dawson this morning to hit the slopes again. Stated they wanted to get another good day in before the weekend crowd and more wedding guests arrive. Izzy asks me to accompany her into town, so I do. She is like a ball in this town's pinball machine. And I am worn the hell out after an hour of shopping. Granted, super cute gifts have been bought, but this feels like literal hell when I'm sweating with all my layers, but as soon as I start stripping them off, I'm freezing again. My ankles are swollen, and I just want a soda. Ford leaves me to sleep at dinner time, but surprises me with a whole pizza and slice of chocolate cake just for me to devour. I knew I married him for a reason.

Hart Wedding Schedule - Thursday: Welcome, new wedding guests. Breakfast will be served in the main dining room, every morning until Sunday morning. Bon appetit! Have a day of leisure and rest.

Now, this schedule I can get behind. Even my husband is still in bed asleep. I decide to jump in the shower before I figure out what crazy thing I can do today. Sleep, read, play chess with my dad, or sleep some more.

Letting the water run over my body, I feel Ford's arms wrap under my stomach and hold my large round belly up for me. I feel like five tons have been lifted off my own body. Ford has been adamant about never skipping meals, eating all my food, extra vitamins, and protein. Therefore, this pregnancy is night and day compared to when I was pregnant with Lexi.

After a few minutes of weightlessness, he begins to trail his hands all over my body, sending tingles throughout. Without words, he walks me out of the shower to the nearest chair where he sits, and I straddle him and ride him hard until I explode. "I love you so fucking much, and you make me hard every time I look at you naked with this baby bump."

"I love you, too," I murmur, kissing him back, then trying to stand up from his lap, "but this is no bump. It's a full-on giant baby baking in here."

We both laugh as he helps me to bed. "Let's just stay in here all day. I've missed you."

"Sounds like the perfect plan," I sigh, settling into his chest for another nap.

Hart Wedding Schedule - Friday: Welcome, new wedding

guests. Breakfast will be served in the main dining room, every morning until Sunday morning. Bon appetit!
It's almost time for the BIG DAY!
This afternoon we will be taking buses up to Ben and Jerry's Ice Cream Shop for a special treat. Please be outside by 11am.
Tonight, for the wedding party - dinner will be at Worthy Kitchen at 7pm
For all other wedding guests, please help yourself to the main dining hall.

Ford and I walk out to the busses to be greeted by an excited Lexi, who I just want to gobble up because I missed her so much. Trayton and Angelica jump on our bus, so they can share all the fun things they did with Lexi.

I think I tried every flavor of ice cream while we were there. Ford stuck to his disgusting mint chocolate chip, when I couldn't even decide on one flavor. I told Ford to stop me from indulging, but he tells me he loves seeing me put on weight. I honestly think he has a death wish at this point in our relationship.

Dress rehearsal goes off without a hitch and the dinner was superb. I convince Izzy and Dawson to let me slip out early because I'm tired, uncomfortable, and now my back is aching fiercely. I need my bed.

Hart Wedding Schedule - Saturday: We made it to the BIG DAY!
Guests can start arriving on the verandah at 3pm for cocktail hour with light snacks. Wedding starts promptly at 5pm. Reception to be held over in the Woodstock Ballroom. See you all soon!

Mom and dad had Lexi most of the day to go exploring, while Ford stayed with me until noon. He went to the groom's suite to get ready as I made my way to the bridal suite to get ready with

Izzy, Angelica, and a few other friends. She made me her matron of honor as Ford is Dawson's best man. I'm thankful to sit down while I get pampered because I'm already dreading standing for the whole thirty minute ceremony.

Dear God, is it really that long? My mind reels as I slip on my heels and mentally prepare myself for the evening ahead.

"I swear, Maren, you can pull off any dress while pregnant. You are literally the cutest pregnant woman I've seen," Angelica says as I side-eye her.

"I'm just going to take the compliment, because I don't have energy to spare." Her and Izzy laugh as we head out the doors to get her married. A bit of horror flashes through my mind at the sight of the sidewalk I nearly died on earlier this week, but luckily, it looks like the groundskeeper has melted the ice, and we have a runner to walk on.

The wedding goes off without a hitch, all of us bawling because the ceremony was so sweet. Thank goodness for outside heaters or we all might have frozen to death, but it was well worth the dying to see Izzy get her winter wonderland wedding with actual fresh snow on the ground and falling during the ceremony along with lights strung up around the posts and trees.

Once inside, I was thankful to slip my heels off and have a few dances with Ford. Then I watched him dance with Lexi for several songs and danced with Mom, as Lexi proved to be the life of the party, dancing with everyone.

Midnight rings, and we all say our goodbyes with sparklers for their send off. It's going to be weird being back home with no Dawson and Izzy for two weeks as they head off on a Mediterranean Cruise.

Once their limo drives off I turn to Ford. "Take me to bed, kind sir." He raises his eyebrows.

"Did you drink tonight?" He is teasing me, I know it.

"Ha, you're so funny. But seriously, be the best husband ever and take me to bed to sleep." With one swoop, he is carrying me in his arms down the hallway to our room. Mind you, the distance was quite long. Yet, he doesn't even break a sweat, and I find that slightly annoying at the moment because I'm breaking a sweat just thinking bout *how the hell am I getting out of this dress.*

"Here let me help you," he says sweetly as if reading my mind. Once free from the damn thing, I throw on one of Ford's t-shirts and crawl into bed, in his arms.

"Holy shit!" are the words that jolt me from a dead sleep. "What on earth is going on? Are you okay?" Panic is written all over Ford's face as he is standing next to the bed. "Are you okay?" he asks, but I'm confused.

"Why wouldn't I be?"

"Because the bed is soaked. I'm pretty sure your water broke." Now is the time I panic once his words seep in my brain. I move out of the bed as quickly as I can, with water and ick dripping down my legs. My eyes go wide in fear.

"Ford, it's too early. We... We...the baby needs to stay for at least a month longer."

"Maren, baby, look at me. Do not panic. I'm calling 911 right now. I just need you to breathe."

And I do...until I blackout.

When I come too, I'm in the hospital room with Ford in the bed with me, hooked to monitors. I quickly notice a lightness to my body and look down at my not so large stomach anymore. *Oh my God, my baby. What did I do to my baby?* I begin choking on my sobs, not able to speak or breathe.

Ford wakes up to my uncontrollable sobbing. "Maren, Jesus, you had us worried. Let me grab the doctor."

"No, Ford, where is our baby?"

"I'll be right back, I promise," he states, rushing out the door.

After a minute passes, he comes back with a wheelchair. My body is drugged, and my stomach feels ripped to shreds, my mind still not catching up to everything going on as he helps me down into the chair. Ford wheels me down to the nursery, but he continues around the corner where we stop at the NICU door. He signs us in, then we head in through the double doors.

Pushing me into a room, I see a baby in what looks to be a smaller version of a crib. There's a blue blanket pulled up around the baby's waist and a blue boggin cap on the baby's head. *Oh my God. It's a boy.* "Is that...is that ours?" I ask, crying out. A nurse comes in and helps Ford get him out of his little crib with all his wires and hands the baby to me.

"Congrats, you have a baby boy. Nine pounds and six ounces, a head full of dark hair and a voice box on him," the nurse says. There is no way I'm getting a handle on my emotions right now.

"Is he okay? Why is he in here?"

"Because he was born early, we just want to monitor him more closely. You did great, Mom. Dad was right next to you the whole time through surgery and was a nervous wreck when you weren't waking up." Then it occurs to me, I had another c-section and Anesthesia is not my friend. Ford must have been frantic knowing my past with Lexi.

"I'm sorry," I tell him, and he bends down to my level in the chair with our baby boy, pushing my hair behind my ear.

"You are here with me. With us, and that is all that matters."

Our foreheads touch, and "I love you's" are whispered.

Two days later, our baby boy was discharged from the NICU, and now he is hanging out in my room until I get discharged. He is perfect in every way, and we can finally introduce him to the world. Firstly, all our family in the waiting room that have been waiting patiently. Mom and Dad enter with Lexi, followed by Izzy and Dawson.

"What are you two doing here? You should be on the other side of the world right now, sipping drinks and having fun."

"And miss the birth of my niece or nephew? Bro, tell her." Dawson says.

Ford shrugs his shoulders. "I called him as soon as the ambulance arrived in case we needed the jet. No hesitation, they turned right back around and have been here since you went into surgery. But I promise, I have not made any announcements other than a baby was born and updates on you."

"Well I bet it's been a fun few days for you all," I joke. Mom is glaring at me with that look she gets when she can't decide if she wants to reprimand me or hug me. She chooses a hug, and I'm thankful for that. Ford brings over our baby to place in my arms, then props Lexi on the bed to give me a hug and kisses the baby on the forehead.

Catching Ford's tearful eyes, I announce, "Everyone, please meet our baby boy, Theo James Merrick."

Acknowledgments

Big thank you to my family and friends and those who loved my debut novel, giving me the encouragement to push forward.

To my fans who love these characters as much if not more than I do! Who reaches out to give me play by play reactions to their readings and always excited for the next new release!

HUGE thank you to my editor, Jenni Gauntt. You are a brilliant rockstar in my eyes and can't wait to work with you on more stories! Love how we are always on this adventure together!

Huge thanks to my amazing PA team, Josefina, Jessica, Georgia, Jenny and Cass - ya'll are the most patient and understanding group of ladies ever! I know I have tortured you all with the timeline of this book, but I hope it was worth the wait 🙂

Thank you to all from the depths of my heart,
Ali Marie

If you enjoyed Going Nowhere (even if not), I would appreciate it if you left an honest review.

Connect with Ali Marie

OTHER BOOKS BY ALI MARIE

Bluebonnet Days

Caught In a Storm
Book 1 of Duet

Heart Novella Series
Heart Like A Truck
Heart Like Mine

Made in the USA
Middletown, DE
23 March 2024